The Turning

The Turning

The Forsaken Series Book 2

Phil Price

Copyright (C) 2018 Phil Price
Layout design and Copyright (C) 2020 by Next Chapter
Published 2020 by Evenfall – A Next Chapter Imprint
Cover art by Cover Mint
This book is a work of fiction. Names, characters, places, and incidents are the product of the author's imagination or are used fictitiously. Any resemblance to actual events, locales, or persons, living or dead, is purely coincidental.
All rights reserved. No part of this book may be reproduced or transmitted in any form or by any means, electronic or mechanical, including photocopying, recording, or by any information storage and retrieval system, without the author's permission.

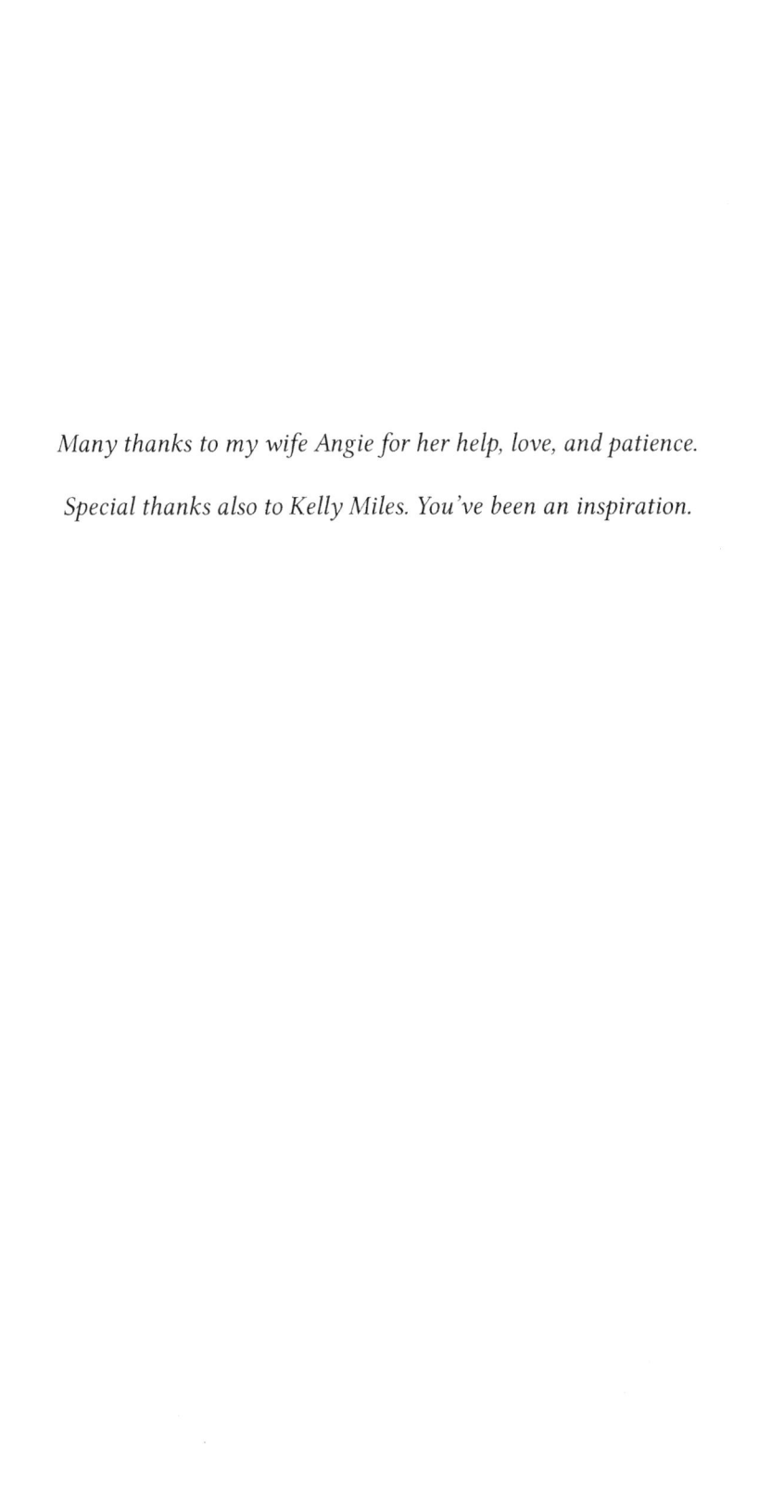

Many thanks to my wife Angie for her help, love, and patience.

Special thanks also to Kelly Miles. You've been an inspiration.

All that we see or seem is but a dream within a dream.
-Edgar Allen Poe

Prologue

The man sat at his writing desk, his laptop barely illuminating the cramped study. No writing was being done. On the desk was a heavy crystal tumbler, half filled with golden liquid. The bottle sat a few inches away. He always enjoyed a glass of whisky, opting usually for a nice bottle of single malt. However, over the last few months his drinking had increased, fuelled by the bad dreams and indecision that wracked his thoughts. The whisky had dropped in price and quality. As long as it did the job and eased him into a deep dreamless sleep, he didn't care. Another sip was taken before continuing his reading. Over the last few months he'd read more and more about vampire folklore. It appeared that every civilisation from since the dawn of time held various accounts and stories of the mysterious creatures. He was currently reading the account of an unfortunate girl in Cornwall at the turn of the seventeenth century. The web page was framed in black, twisted wraiths and skulls dotted around its perimeter. It gave the screen a macabre feel, seeming to lower the temperature in the small room. The young girl in question had been visited by a vampire before her death. The local clergy had buried her in an unmarked grave. A stone tablet had been placed in her mouth, the casket filled with Hawthorn to ward off evil. The man took off his steel rimmed glasses and pinched the top of his nose, closing his eyes as he did so. A large hand rubbed at his bearded face. A beard that was showing more silver every day it seemed. He sat for a minute in silent contemplation before nodding to himself. The fiery liquid was downed in one go, the burn spreading from his throat down into his chest. He stood and shuffled out of the study into the darkened hallway. Slipping on his sports jacket and loafers, the man opened the cupboard under the stairs. Reaching inside, he flicked the light switch, bathing the hallway in a yellowy hue. He moved garments out of his way on the hanging pole until reaching the winter coat at the back. The man reached into the large pocket, drawing out a silver cross. He weighed it in his left hand, liking the sturdy feel it gave off. His palm tingled as he slapped it with the metal object. He flexed his fingers before stowing the cross in his jacket pocket. Walking down the hallway, he scooped his keys from the side table, dropping them in his trouser pocket. A mobile phone and an old wrist watch were found next. He pressed a button on the keypad, making the display glow. Quarter past eleven. He had enough time. His watch was clipped on his wrist, the phone stashed in his inside pocket just in case he needed it. For what, he knew not. If what he may encounter was a possibility, calling the emergency services would be a waste of time. *It would certainly give the operator on the other end of the line an unusual twist to their night*, the man thought. He spotted a lighter on the window sill and put that in his pocket, purely on a whim. Walking back through the house to the front door, he stopped at a picture on the wall of his wife, Denise. She had travelled to Ipswich to tend her dying mother. She'd told him to stay behind to perform his duty. A duty that was ebbing away it seemed. She'd noticed the empty whisky bottles in the recycling, coupled with witnessing his troubled dreams. Dreams that had started several months before. On several occasions, she had woken to find him mumbling incoherently in his sleep, clearly distressed. When she'd gently questioned him at the breakfast table the following morning, he would make excuses of late night movies that had followed him into his subconscious. She'd let it go. If it needed to come out it would in the fullness of time. She also had a grieving mother, who'd recently lost her husband and was now on her last legs too. They had busy lives, full of duty to loved ones. He locked the door and walked down his front path, turning right passing a tired row of shops. What once had been a thriving community now seemed like a ghost town. The local car factory had closed a few years before, hitting the area hard. This was coupled with a world-wide recession a few years later that left its scars on the whole country. Times had been tough, and things would take time to recover. He unzipped his coat as he started sweating. Summer was struggling to give up its hold on the land. Autumn could wait.

Ten minutes later he was walking past his local pub. The Hare and Hounds had a warm glow that gave the establishment an inviting pull. It was Friday night and the revellers inside looked like they had no intention of finishing up. The man had been young once. He knew people were winding down after their week at work. As he passed by the entrance, a young couple burst through the double doors, giggling at some private joke. They spotted the man and their laughter died down.

"Hello Father Stephen," the man said. "Isn't it a bit late for a stroll?"

"Hello John, Sarah. I've had a cold over the last few days. I thought I'd take a walk before turning in for the night." He looked at the young couple. He'd known them from when they had attended the local primary school, some twenty years before. "Finishing early?"

"We thought we'd beat the rush to the chippy. It can get crowded as they all spill out of the Hounds."

"What's on the menu tonight?" he said as he suddenly smelt the aroma floating from the chip shop.

"Chicken and mushroom pie and chips for me and a kebab for greedy guts here," Sarah said as she nudged her husband in the ribs.

"Well, enjoy your midnight feast. Be seeing you."

"Goodnight Father," they said in unison, before heading off towards the chip shop. He hung back a few steps, letting them enter the brightly lit frontage before he followed. He made a right turn just before the two shops, heading up a steep dark roadway. At just shy of two metres and tipping the scales at twenty stone, Father Stephen found the ascent arduous. His breathing was ragged as he climbed further and further towards his destination. He paused and checked the display on his phone. Ten minutes until midnight. He knew he would reach the spot in time. The Vicar had only visited it once before, but it was clear in his memory. He'd caught up with Doug a few days after his friend had banged on his Vicarage door in the middle of the night to ask him for help with his son. It was the night when his whole world, his faith, his understanding had been turned on its head. A few days later the two men had made their way to the spot on a crisp winter's morning. The silent hills had seemed devoid of such fanciful tales as vampires and doorways. He had known Doug for thirty years, trusting his word implicitly. However, that word had been tested on that night. Now, as he stood at the spot he suddenly felt wary. Stephen checked his phone again. Two minutes to go. He instinctively wrapped his hand around the cross in his pocket. The coolness comforting. The night was deathly quiet, the only sound he could hear was his slowing heartbeat and breathing. He stood there looking at two stout trees, positioned three feet apart. Suddenly the wind kicked up along the hillside, sending leaves and bracken skittering across the forest floor. He felt a building pressure in his head before his ears popped. *Strange*, he thought as a low hum filled his skull. *Oh God*! In front of his eyes a faint blue glow seemed to appear between the trees. It quickly made the shape of a doorway. He walked towards it, aware that the cross in his hand was now warm. He pulled it from his pocket, letting it bounce against his thigh as he walked. He stood within reach of the doorway as it gently pulsed between the trees. He could hear sounds on the other side. Wild sounds. Shrieks and wails that seemed out of place in the Lickey Hills.

"Unbelievable. Doug was right," he muttered. Stephen was a man of Christ. All his life he'd followed the good book with unwavering commitment. Now everything that he'd once believed was being torn apart. He was staring at a doorway to another world. Another universe. Another dimension. He wasn't sure what to call it. The Vicar knew it was not part of his world. How could his God exist when this doorway did too? He made up his mind quickly, knowing he had limited time. He stepped through the void. Into the unknown.

One

September 2010

"Come on Douglas. The estate agent is waiting," Alison said through the open car door. Doug was trying to multi-task. His new mobile phone had been on charge as they'd driven down from the Midlands. Unplugging it, whilst under scrutiny from his wife was making him a bit ruffled.

"Okay. I'm done," he said as he climbed out of the car, shutting the door. He walked around the boot, coming to a stop next to his wife. She tutted. "Tuck your shirt in. Look at your jacket. It's all skew."

"Oh no! We can't have that, can we? What would the new neighbours say?"

His wife gave him a stern look as another woman approached from the house that had a sign swaying in front of it. Doug forgot Alison's expression as the other woman introduced herself.

"Mr. and Mrs. Stevenson?" They nodded. "Lynn Bustard, Atlantic Estates. How was your journey down?"

Alison shook the woman's hand, appraising her coolly. She noticed with a degree of envy that the woman was roughly her age, but wore it far better. She was slim, with short grey hair, cut stylishly. Not like the mass of red and grey curls that she fought to keep under control every day. Her face didn't look like the face of a sixty-year-old. *Maybe she'd had work done*, she thought smugly. "Mostly fine. A bit of traffic around Bristol but nothing to write home about. I'm Alison. This is Doug," she said as almost an afterthought.

Doug shook the agent's hand, a warm smile crinkling his face. "Pleased to meet you Lynn. Unusual name. Bustard?"

"Yes," she said. "Like the bird. Had a few nicknames at school as I'm sure you can imagine. Your wife told me over the phone that your house is sold and that you're looking to move as soon as possible."

Doug liked her Cornish twang. "Yes. Our buyers have had surveys done and all appears to be in order. So we're a few weeks behind them in terms of schedule. But that isn't a problem. Our son and daughter-in-law have just moved to Tintagel and we'll be able to bed down with them if needed." The agent nodded before walking up the pretty garden path towards the property. Doug watched her walk, noticing that she had dark seamed nylons on. His wife caught him looking at her legs before bustling past him, tutting as she did so. He stood for a moment, smiling. *If only all women dressed like that*, he thought before trudging up the path after them.

* * *

Jake came around the corner of the cul-de-sac, noticing his parents' car parked next to the dormer bungalow. He could see the front door was open. *At least they got here on time*, he thought. The Atlantic wind kicked up, ruffling his dark hair and clothing. The ocean was to his left. Sparse clouds on the horizon gave the vista a picture postcard look. He ran his fingers through his locks before stepping off the pavement to cross the street. He had a carefree stride, long and loping. The horrors of the last few months seemed to have been blown away on the ocean breeze. His leg was better, apart from the two scars that would forever be tattooed there. One had been a flesh wound, the other deeper. He kept his eye on them, doing what had to be done to ensure they were under control. He'd never spent so much time in church as he did now. Katherine played along, knowing it helped his leg heal. To what extent it would heal was still uncertain. He felt fine though. More than fine. He'd never felt better. Whether that was due to the sea air, or due to his love for Katherine, he knew not. He did not care. The last few months were becoming a fuzzy memory. He still had the dreams. He still woke up sometimes in a sweat, checking the bedroom for signs of danger. However, no danger could be found. All was as it should be in Jake's life. For that, he was beyond grateful. His life had risen from the depths of despair and grief from a few years previous, when he'd lost his young wife and daughter to a hit and run. They would never be forgotten. Jake knew that. Katherine knew that. He had a new focus now though. Katherine was due to give birth within the next few weeks. The last few months had been a whirl of activity, taking their minds off of the horrors beforehand. Their third bedroom had been turned into a nursery. Katherine was like the proverbial kid in a sweet shop when Jake had taken her to a retail park near Truro. They had spent most of the afternoon buying all manner of baby clothes, travel systems, bottles, sterilizers, and other items that they'd need for the arrival. Jake also bought two large cans of emulsion for the walls. Pink emulsion. The moment they discovered that Katherine was pregnant, Jake realised they had a problem. She didn't exist, certainly not on paper. She would need scans and visits to the doctors. How could she do that if there was no record of her? He'd made a call to Swanley, to ask a huge favour. Katherine needed an identity. The giant traveller and Jake had history. They had an understanding. They would help each other if needed. Swanley had put Jake in touch with an associate, who for a considerable fee had provided her with a life. He was told her identification would hold up under regular scrutiny. However, intense digging would pull holes in it. Jake knew that this was the best he could hope for. If the worst came to the worst, he knew they had an escape route. A doorway, between two trees in a far off forest.

* * *

Jake heard voices as he neared the bungalow. He looked up at the first floor window to see his mother, who was fiddling with the curtains. She noticed him and waved. He reciprocated before heading up the path, stepping through the open doorway into the hall. The voices grew louder as he made his way to the kitchen at the rear of the property.

"Hi Dad," he said, noticing an attractive older woman stood next to a breakfast bar.

"Hey Son," Doug beamed, grabbing him in a bear hug. "This is Lynn. Lynn, this is Jake."

Jake met the advancing woman halfway across the kitchen, taking her manicured hand. "Nice to meet you Lynn."

"Likewise Jake. I was just telling your father about the local pubs. I think I've won him over."

Doug nodded his agreement. "The Cornishman's Arms sounds right up my street. Jake took me to the," he hesitated, plucking the name from his memory. "King Arthur a few months back. That wasn't bad either. I think I'll enjoy life down here."

Alison entered the kitchen, making a fuss of her son as soon as she caught sight of him. "Hello Jake," she gushed, unusually so. "How is Katherine?"

"Hi Mom. She's fine. She's having a bit of a nap."

Alison looked at the estate agent. "She's expecting their first child."

"Congratulations. Sounds like you're moving at the right time."

"Well we need to find the right house first," Alison cut in, cooling the temperature in the kitchen somewhat.

Sensing a change in mood Jake decided to talk shop. "So what do you both think of the house?"

Lynn could also sense that a frosty cloak had descended over the room. She cut in before either Stevenson could answer. "I'll be outside. I need to make a few calls. Give me a shout when you're finished." She excused herself, smiling at Doug as she left the kitchen.

"What's up?" Jake said.

"Nothing Son," Doug said. "The house seems fine. It even has an en-suite."

"Your Father would buy anything from a woman who dresses like that. You can pick your jaw up off the floor now Douglas." He smiled at his wife serenely. Turning up the annoyance to gas mark hot.

"What do you think of the house Mom?" Jake said, trying to thaw the ice.

"Well, I'm not over keen on some of the decor. Bit modern for me. But it's just about the right size. I agree with your Father, the en-suite is something that I've always wanted. And I suppose the location is perfect. I just hope our furniture fits the house."

"It will love. And if it doesn't we can buy new furniture. Our sofa is looking a little tired." Alison looked at Doug and nodded sagely. The idea of some new furniture perked her spirits up. The harlot outside was forgotten momentarily.

"Well, I'll pop back home and get the kettle on. The spare room is ready for you. I'll let you talk to the estate agent. I'm sure you have things to discuss," Jake said, secretly winking at his dad.

* * *

Jake made his way along the path towards the village. The sun was on its way towards its western horizon where it would kiss the Atlantic Ocean, before disappearing for the night. Tourists and surfers walked past him as he made his way up the high street. Children sat on walls, eating ice creams while parents looked at their smart phones, glad of the few minute's peace. Jake turned right off the path into what looked like the world's oldest post office. He'd always thought it looked like a giant had been sat on its roof, bending it beyond repair. He'd been told by one of the locals that it was the most photographed post office in the world. Jake had no reason to doubt that fact. After all, who photographs post offices? He ducked inside and walked to the deserted counter.

A woman with long brown hair approached. She smiled when she saw Jake. "Hello," she said in her soft South African accent. "How's Katherine?"

"Hi Angie. She's fine. Just resting up. Not long now."

"Ah. Bless. She needs to rest now. She won't get chance once baby arrives. Tell her I said hi. I'll have to pop round and have a catch up with her." She looked at Jake expectantly.

Forgetting what he was standing there for, he hastily produced a piece of paper. "The postman left this for me," he said handing over the card.

She took it from him and excused herself to the rear store room. A moment later she returned with a small parcel. "Here you go. Must have been near a fridge. It feels cold." Jake took the small package and looked at the label. It was addressed to him. No sender's details were on the reverse side. It did feel cool to the touch, solid too. He would open it at home, away from inquisitive eyes.

"Okay. Cheers Angela. See you soon." She said her goodbyes and turned to a small elderly woman stood behind him. Jake tucked the box under his arm and made his way out into the warm summer's afternoon. He walked home, thinking about what would be a good choice for dinner as the world passed him by. The warm sea breeze blew around his bare legs and tousled his hair as he made his way along the coastal path towards his home. An imposing hotel lay far off to the left. The sun hovered behind it, slowly sinking towards the ocean. He loved the view. He would never tire of it. All his life had been spent as far away from the sea as was possible in England. Birmingham seemed a world away. Cornwall had given him a new lease of life. He'd endured hardships on his journey to this happy place. He had seen horrors and places he'd never known existed. However, the hard times had yielded Katherine. And for that, he was happy. He would never forget his wife and daughter. They were as much a part of him as Katherine was. However, it felt like their chapter had been read. This part of the book was a new journey, with each page exciting and full of hope.

* * *

He walked the last few yards back to their house, spotting his parents' car on the drive. He made his way through the carport to a side door, entering the kitchen. Katherine smiled as he entered, her sun kissed skin glowing in the late afternoon light. Her long dark locks had been recently cut, with highlights added. They seemed to catch the sun and shimmer as her hair flicked from side to side. She truly believed she belonged in this world. Salons and coffee shops were fast becoming a way of life for her, which she loved. Gone were the times when she'd wear the same garments for days on end, only to wash them in a bucket outside her family farmstead, before hanging them to dry on the porch. She now had a wardrobe filled with clothes and shoes. She had gained new girlfriends, whom she socialised with regularly. She was as happy as she could remember. The only slight downside was that she tired quickly at night. Even before she became heavily pregnant, she noticed that she started to flag before Jake. The air felt different here to her. It almost had a substance to it that she could feel as she moved around the house, or felt as she walked along the beach. She'd not mentioned it to him. They'd endured enough for now. She placed her arms on the kitchen chair, trying to heave her bulk into a standing position.

"It's okay, babe. I'll come to you," Jake said as he quickly crossed the kitchen, planting a long lingering kiss on her lips. He then bent lower and kissed her bump.

"I would say get a room. But by the looks of it you've already have," Doug said from the far side of the kitchen.

"Your Father is making sport with us," Katherine said as she smiled at the older man. "He is pulling my leg."

"As oppose to pulling on your legs?" Jake said, teasing.

"Are you teaming up on me?" she asked, a mock look of indignation appearing on her face.

Before Jake could answer his mother entered the kitchen, clearly put out by something. "I heard voices. Jake, you're home! What are you talking about? Am I missing out on something?" Alison hated it when she could hear a conversation, but couldn't quite make out the words.

"Doug and Jake were just teasing me as I'm struggling to get out of the chair," Katherine smoothly interjected. She had become accustomed to Alison's moodiness. She had quickly learned how to diffuse situations too. Katherine loved her mother-in-law to be, although she knew she was hard work. Her father-in-law was different though. He was funny and warm. Doug constantly teased her, but in a nice way.

The older man reminded her a little of her uncle. A small cloud crossed her sunny horizon. She missed Wilf. Katherine often wondered what had become of him and his villagers. She hoped they'd made it to safety. Maybe to a different land that wasn't in the grip of darkness. The cloud passed by, allowing the sunshine back in.

Alison was fussing around the sink, making a lot of noise without doing much. "Well, these men don't know the struggles us women go through. They have an easy ride in life." Doug looked to the heavens, a bewildered expression crossing his face. Katherine finally levered herself out of the chair and crossed to Alison, embracing her warmly. The tea towel fell from her grip as she was taken off guard momentarily. She quickly regained her composure, returning the hug. She loved Katherine. There was an innocence about her that the older woman felt very comfortable with. She was a real lady, never uttering a curse, unlike most of the women today with their tattoos and piercings. Alison often thought that the younger woman could have been from a classic novel, such was her way. Katherine walked over to her man, wrapping an arm around his waist, cuddling into him.

Jake kissed the top of her head, drinking in her smell. "Well, what shall we have for tea?" he asked them. "Fish and chips?"

"Well, it is Friday," Doug said. "Sounds good to me." Alison nodded before aiming a cough at her husband. Doug took the hint. "I'll get them. A bit of fresh air will do me good."

* * *

A few minutes later he was on his way out the kitchen door, armed with a piece of paper. Katherine took Alison upstairs to show her the new baby accessories in the nursery, leaving Jake alone in the kitchen. He sat down at the wooden table, his fingers clumsily unwrapping the parcel. Inside, was a cardboard box and a note. Leaving the box for a moment, he unfolded the piece of paper. Suddenly his phone chimed, informing him that he had a text. Putting the paper on the table, Jake fumbled for the phone in his pocket. He pulled it out and activated it. It was a text from a potential client, who wanted to arrange a meeting with him soon. He closed the message, backing out to the home screen. Jake sat and smiled at Katherine who smiled back at him from the screens display. It was a recent picture, taken when they'd spent the day at Woolacombe. The wind had caught her hair perfectly at the moment he'd snapped the shot. She was smiling warmly at the camera, an ice cream shack behind her with white planking, giving the shot a holiday feel. He reluctantly put the phone on the table, picking up the piece of paper once more.

> Hi Jake
>
> I hope Katherine and yourself are well. The baby must be just around the corner now by my reckoning. Exciting times ahead!
>
> Anyway, the reason for the delivery is to send you something. I wanted to mount them for you, which you might think odd. However, I think they look rather natty. Plus, Hooper really doesn't like them close by so I thought I'd pass them on to you.
>
> I will be in touch soon and may pop over once baby has settled.
> Take care both.
> Barbara
> Xx

Jake put the note down and took the box in his hands. It felt very cool to the touch. He reached for his house keys, breaking the tape on the box with his car key. He opened the box, withdrawing a wooden box frame from inside. Jake drew his breath in, holding it for several seconds. The box frame contained two small buttons that had been mounted on the backing card. The interior of the frame looked like purple faux suede, giving it a look of quality. The wood was coffee coloured and felt like oak. The buttons were about the size of a coin. Much thicker though. They looked more like toggles from a heavy coat. On each button was an eagle, its wings spread. Jake's hands were starting to tingle. He was suddenly transported back to where he'd claimed one of the buttons. He'd torn it from the coat of a young boy moments before he'd been torn to pieces by two mutated killer whales. He wasn't a regular boy though. He was a vampire. A vampire that was about to kill Katherine and himself in a dark cavern by the sea. He reflected for a moment. *How the hell we managed to get out of that place in one piece is still hard to believe,* he thought. They had escaped the cavern, only for Katherine to be snatched away by another vampire. He thought about how he and Wilf had escaped from that desolate place, chased by two monstrous pigs. He shook his head. He knew that if anyone was told that tale they'd be reaching for the phone or running for the hills. He'd sat and recounted the story to his father a few days after Doug had found Jake at the Lickey Hills, a giant fang embedded in his thigh. Doug was a believer and yet he'd found it almost too much to comprehend. Jake was at a loss. What should he do with this gift? It was harmless, yet it wasn't. The cold, dead heart of their previous owner was still imbedded in the metal. He would keep them, but not in the house.

* * *

Jake flicked the light on to his loft that sat above his carport. He climbed the ladder, the metal creaking under his weight. He stood in the gloomy space, looking around for the best place to keep them. Over by the far wall was a set of four plastic storage boxes. Each one had a lid that enabled it to sit on top of the box underneath securely. They were labelled in years. They contained Katie and Megan's things, along with some of his travel memories. He clicked off the lid from the top box. Inside was his wife's jewellery box along with handmade photo albums. His mind pondered whether to take them out and leaf through them. *Maybe another time,* Jake thought as he placed the box frame on top of them, securing the lid back in place with a satisfying click. The light was flicked off as the ladder was descended, pushing it back into the loft on its runners. The hinged door was lifted into place just as his father came around the front wall and up the driveway towards him.

"Have you got enough there?" Jake asked, eying the bulging brown paper bag that Doug was carrying.

"You know your Mom. She likes her food." He motioned towards the loft. "What you up to? Finding a place for her to sleep tonight?"

Jake laughed. "I'm sure she'd love hearing you say that." He paused. "I received a parcel from Barbara. You know, the lady from Devon."

Doug's face suddenly looked wary. "Is everything okay?"

"I think so. I'll show you when traffic inside is a little lighter. Maybe Mom will take Katherine for a cream tea tomorrow. I will show you then."

"Tomorrow it is then. Any excuse for cream tea and she's off like Usain Bolt."

Two

South of Elksberg

The lone mountain stood proud and solemn over the land. To the east, the land rose steadily towards a huge gorge that ran like a crippled spine from south to north. The north was a nondescript grassland, dotted with farms and outcrops. To the south lay swamps that carried on for miles towards the grey sea. They were crisscrossed with paths and stunted trees. To the west lay a sprawling forest that stretched as far as any eye could see. Darkened mountains lay farther off to the west, shrouded in low cloud. On the upper slopes of the lone mountain that folk called Agar a figure sat in the shadows of an enclave, brooding. He scanned the land in three directions, looking for any signs of movement. Pickings had grown slim lately. He knew why. The forest to the west lay in darkness. He could see that it was not low cloud that made it dark like before. The darkness seemed to seep from the earth, wrapping itself around the trees that had stood for countless seasons. It unsettled him. Something was wrong with that place. He knew that if he plucked up the courage a doorway could take him somewhere else. Somewhere new. Try as he might he could not bring himself to venture towards it just yet. The nights were the worst. Noises and voices carried to him from the vast forest, making him pull his knees up under his chin and shiver. The forest was actually two forests, joined together. The one, Amatoll was where Eddie had

The Turning

recently ventured. He'd entered through a doorway and had taken the soul of a young girl. That had seemed to start a chain of events that culminated with two battles. Two battles that he'd been involved in. Two battles that had taken their toll.

Eddie looked at his ruined hand. He remembered the young man whom he'd challenged to follow him and his woman. How he'd blasted three fingers from his hand with his weapon. It had all gone so wrong. Eddie was ready to be accepted into a new coven. He'd done all the hard work, travelling through two worlds to bring his new master a prize, telling his new family that a single man would be following. The trap had been set. Reggan's clan were ready for an easy fight with one man. But two men had arrived, with a strange looking creature alongside them. No sooner had the fight erupted, Eddie knew that things would turn ill. The little creature with the flaming eyes took down half of the clan while the men did the rest. He had flown at Jake, hoping to take his head clean off. The man was cunning though. He was quick and his aim was true. The hand that was aiming at Jake's head suddenly lost half of its form as the shotgun blasted it apart. Eddie had reeled back as the man fired another shot, peppering him with lead. He tried to attack, but was repelled by the older one with his cross and weapons. He fled the cave. The last thing he remembered seeing was the younger man locked in a fight with Reggan. That was when he knew all was lost. Others must have heard the fighting and were running to help. However the damage had been done. They would blame Eddie for bringing this to their door. He fled from the catacombs out into the relentless storms. He'd blindly stumbled through the landscape as stones and debris pummelled him. Eventually he found refuge in an underground lake that was devoid of life. The water fizzed and bubbled as he lay trying to gather his thoughts. He didn't feel pain like humans. Biting the remains of his damaged fingers off didn't affect him in that way. To Eddie, it looked repulsive. His grey skin was tattered and torn around the wound, exposing the yellowed flesh and stark bone underneath. Even now it had not healed. It was exposed. Only the thumb and index finger had escaped the blast. He had wrapped and old rag around it to keep it concealed. But to no avail. He needed a glove. The prey that he had encountered since were traders and wanderers. Once he'd drained their life, he'd searched them for anything of use. Nothing. He would find one though. He needed a plan.

He'd sat on this forlorn rock licking his wounds for long enough. Eddie had thought about revenge. He'd imagined twisting the head from the young man's body. Drinking his blood, before taking his woman too. However nice it played out for him, he knew that Jake was dangerous. His thoughts strayed to Elias. He had no idea what had become of Korgan's henchman. The last time he'd seen him was during the battle in the Vale. They had locked horns during the fight, reluctantly coming to an accord at the end. Elias had left the humans for him as he'd set off to hunt Jake and the woman. That seemed like a lifetime ago now. He shook his head, clearing his thoughts. He looked over the expanse of forest as the shrouded sun kissed the mountain far off to the west. He moved further into the recess, away from the wind and sounds. Curling up as tight as he could, he began to plot his course.

* * *

Far off to the east the village of Shetland was hosting a union party for two of the folk. The village had been transformed over the last few seasons. The solitary farmhouse was now accompanied by six additional homes. When Wilf and his kin had arrived in haste at Fingles, Zeebu and Zeeba the elders, had provided shelter. Over the next few days they'd held talks with Wilf and the folk from Elksberg. Although strange in appearance, with stunted bodies and giant heads, the Finglers were good allies. The next day they had proceeded to accompany the villagers out to Shetland to begin work on a new home for them. Now, as Wilf stood puffing on his pipe he thanked whatever gods were out there. His folk were safe. They had a new home, and the food was plentiful. Some of the women had even started a vegetable patch down by the ford. The ford was where Shetland joined the long rocky spit of land that led back to Fingles. Wilf remembered as he puffed his pipe how they'd just managed to pull Jake from the frigid waters before he was torn apart by two Orgas. The arrival of that young Outlander had altered the path of their lives. For the better though, as it had led them all to Shetland. One of the first jobs they'd completed when they started work was to build a bridge over the ford. The Brynn Halfsted swamps to the north had provided the wood for the bridge and homes. It was unnaturally springy, but tough as steel. The village of Fingles was built almost entirely from the special timber, as it absorbed the sea's wrath with ease. The bridge was quickly erected, giving the villagers unrestricted access to the mainland. The tides still had to be watched as the roadway to the mainland almost disappeared when the sea levels rose. Only a stout tree halfway to the mainland would offer refuge to any traveller or villager who became marooned. Wilf was content. He had almost everything he needed, with one exception. His niece Katherine was not here. She was far away, under a different sky. Wilf hoped that she was safe, happy, and that the sun warmed her skin every day. If only he could see her once more. To hold her to him and feel her warm embrace. The old man smiled at the thought. Jake would be taking care of her. He didn't hope, he knew. He walked inside the farmhouse, his stiff legs taking a moment to get going. In the snug living room, he sat himself down at the table with a thump. He reached across to the earthenware bottle and mug, pulling them towards him. He flipped the mug upright and poured a good measure of hokie. He took a swig, letting the spirit sink in. His mind was drifting back a few seasons, honing in on that night.

He was cast back to Reggan's stronghold. A dank lair that had made his brother Korgan's seem almost lavish. They had come to reclaim their loved ones. The diminutive figure that stood with them was there for his sister. Wilf played it out in his mind once more. He had spotted the bulky vampire almost immediately. Their eyes locked. Wilf remembered how they'd drawn him in, soothing his fears. The eyes wanted him to be their friend. To drop his trinkets and talk.

It had almost worked before the strange figure with them, shook him from his trance. "*Don't fall for his charms, we're here to fight,*" he said to him. The vampire called Eddie knew his hold was broken. Wilf watched frozen as Jake and Tamatan set about the hoard. Jake felled two with his shotgun, making sure with a stake to each of their dead hearts. Tamatan took down four in the blink of an eye. In a blur he sucked what life force remained inside from them, leaving withered husks on the cold stone floor. Wilf noticed the bulky one make his move. He flew at Jake, ready for the kill. Wilf watched frozen in horror, knowing that the young man was done for. Or so he thought. In a flash, Jake's shotgun had taken the hand from the beast. He fell backwards towards the tomb. Another blast had sent him crashing into the wall, beaten. That's when Wilf was spurred into action. His cross came out, shining bright in the gloom. Any foes that were still standing were pushed back by its force. The power of light over dark. He turned to see Tamatan wincing at the sign of the cross. Wilf knew instantly that it was hurting him. Although he was their companion, he too belonged to the darkness. He slipped the cross back into his bag, noticing the bulky one beating a retreat. It had been too easy. Or so he thought. Reggan was not done just yet. Jake was reloading his weapon when he was plucked into the tomb by two large hands. The outlander cried out in anger as the beast clamped its huge jaws into his thigh. Wilf watched helplessly as the monster worried Jake's leg, shaking his head from side to side. He'd come to love the strange outlander. He might have been the son that he'd never had. Now he saw him locked in a deadly battle with a giant vampire. Before Wilf could try to help, Jake raised his shotgun, firing it point blank into the beast's face. Reggan's head was blasted against the cave wall, chunks of bone and brain creating a hideous collage on the red rock. Jake fell out of the tomb, floundering on the floor before he limped back to where the now headless Reggan lay. Screaming as he did so, Jake unloaded the rest of his shotgun into the vampire's body. When the shotgun was empty, Jake pulled two stakes from his pack, stabbing the corpse over and over until he finally slumped to the floor exhausted and crying.

Tamatan had finished the rest of the fighting, leaving the floor littered with bodies. He looked at Wilf, his red eyes burning with blood lust. He then relaxed, sniffing the air. "This way," he shouted, heading off into a low corridor.

Wilf looked at Jake. "Stay here. I think he is going to lead us to his sister and Katherine." Jake nodded, sweat and blood splattered across his face. Wilf had only reached the entrance to the corridor when Tamatan emerged with a strange looking creature. Her skin was deep green that seemed to shimmer in the torch light. She moved with a grace and fluidity that seemed almost unnatural. Her eyes sparkled like vibrant emeralds, green tears running down her beautiful face.

"JAKE!" Katherine shouted from the entrance to the tunnel.

Jake looked up at the sound of her voice. "Kath," he blurted, his emotions boiling over as she broke away from Wilf, running over to him. They embraced, kissing, sobbing. Trying to find the words to convey their joy at being reunited. Jake tried to lift her into his arms but suddenly lost his footing, wincing as he put her down.

Katherine looked down at his leg as Wilf, Tamatan, and his sister joined them. "You're hurt Jake," she exclaimed as she saw a giant grey fang protruding from his leg. "We need to get you help." She looked at her uncle. "How can we help him? Do we need a healer?"

"We need a shaman," Wilf said looking worried. "And fast. Trouble is finding one. We need to get back through the doorway as quick as we can. But we may be searching for a long time in Elksberg."

"I know someone who can help us," Jake said through gritted teeth. "We need to get back to my home."

Tamatan's sister who had been silent until now walked forward and knelt in front of Jake. She looked up at him, taking his leg in her hands. "Veltan," she said in a soft voice. And bowed her head to the floor.

"Veltan is her name," said Tamatan. "She is going to delay the spread of infection. It will drain her strength. But she can take it, for she is strong."

"Infection?" Jake said as he suddenly felt the throbbing in his leg subside. It was being replaced by a tingling coolness that felt like pins and needles.

"Jake has been bitten by a vampire. And not just any vampire. By a king. A powerful vampire king," Tamatan exclaimed. "If he doesn't get help soon he may start turning. My sister is slowing down the spread. Once she has finished we must be on our way as fast as we can. Jake, who is this person who you think can help us?"

"I've known him all my life. His name is Father Stephen."

Tamatan nodded as a deep drone came rolling through the passageway. "We must move. We have won this battle but there are things deep down below us that are stirring. Things that we really do not want to become acquainted with. We must make haste, or we may never live to tell this tale."

* * *

Wilf stood there as the doorway vanished before his eyes. He shut them tight, the outline visible under the lids. "Goodbye Katherine," he muttered before turning to Tamatan and Veltan. Their eyes shimmering in the darkness. "What now? It feels like we have dark things heading our way."

"We feel it too," Tamatan nodded. Veltan looked around her, spooked by something that Wilf could not see nor hear. The forest was coming alive above them. Birds and other animals started to call and wail as wisps of mist drifted through the trees towards them. Wilf shuddered as he felt a cold wind ruffle his clothing. "Something is coming for us. We need to be gone from this place. How far to your village?"

"Not far." He pointed off into the forest as the wisps of mist were gathering around the trees, wrapping themselves around the trunks. Wilf could make out faces in the mist that almost stilled his heart. Hideous faces with blackened pits for eyes. Gaping mouths laden with fangs. The others saw this too. Veltan let out a low moan as her brother took her hand. "Follow me," Wilf said as they broke into a run towards the far off lights of Heronveld. Wilf lost his footing a few times on unseen branches and plants, almost falling over. He could not afford to stop. The forest was protesting their escape as they neared the flickering torches of his village. He called out, "FOLK. WAKE UP. WAKE

UP!" Wisps of smoke started falling from the trees, malevolent faces blocking Wilf's path to the village. He pulled out his cross and held it at arm's length as he ran. It instantly lit up, banishing the mist around him. He heard Tamatan and Veltan cry out in anguish, knowing that it was affecting them. He turned to look at them behind him. "I'm sorry. Stay with me. We are almost at Banners Gate."

"We will endure. Don't put the cross away until you reach the village," Tamatan said. Wilf could see a few of the villagers stumbling sleepily from their homes. They gathered on the village green looking anxiously at the noises they could hear in the darkness. Wilf banged into the heavy wooden gate at the edge of the forest. He half climbed, half floundered over it, landing in a heap on the other side. Two strong hands lifted him as though he was a baby, propelling him towards the group of men and women on the patch of grass.

One woman cried out in horror. "MONSTERS!"

Wilf waved his hands at them, trying to gather himself. "Folk," he began, trying to draw breath. "They are not monsters. They are our friends. They've just helped me free Katherine from the other place. The place where Reggan lies." At hearing the name, villagers started cowering and crossing themselves. "Reggan is no more. The outlander Jake put pay to him. He has taken Kath back to his land where they will be safe. Now we must flee. Whatever was lurking in that land has followed us back here and wishes us all harm." The forest was filled with noise and mist. A long tendril snaked its way through the gate and headed towards them.

"Fuckenell!" a man gasped as he pointed towards its advance. They all turned to face the oncoming mist. The women ran for their homes as children stood on the porches, crying and confused.

"WOMEN AND CHILDREN INSIDE!" Wilf shouted as the men closed into a tight circle. The long streak of mist began taking form in front of them. They all stared in silent horror as it took on a human shape. A long misty cloak constantly changed shape as it was blown by the forest. The face was a dark pit, except for two yellow eyes that shone out towards them. Wilf advanced on the misty apparition, his cross held aloft.

"NOOOOOOO," it wailed, evaporating into the grass.

Wilf looked at the group behind him, his heart racing. "I'm not sure what we've done by destroying Reggan, but something has stirred and has followed us. We need to leave as soon as it's light. Pack up everything that is vital. We leave for Shetland at dawn."

"But this is our home," a tall man called Pat challenged back.

"Look at the forest Pat," Wilf said. The men folk knew they had to flee. Any arguments were futile. "Gather up your things. We must go. We can start a new life in Shetland. Trust in me." The men made their way back to their homes leaving the threesome stood on the damp grass. Wilf suddenly felt very small, and exposed. "Come with me," he said to the couple as he made his way towards his home. Inside he quickly poured three mugs of hokie, downing his mug in one go. He lit two candles on the table before pouring another. Taking a smaller sip. The burn felt good. It felt real. Veltan sat in a wooden chair. Wilf suddenly noticed that she looked exhausted. He turned to Tamatan. "What is your plan?"

"We will head west at first light. I think that we've unearthed something that Reggan was holding under his power. Who knows what it is. Whatever it is, it is evil and we need to be as far away from it as possible. I only hope our forays were worth it." He looked at his sister, concern etched on his face.

Wilf considered his statement for a moment. "What is out west? I've never ventured too far that way. Cedric and I travelled as far as the glades at the edge of Amatoll. A pair of huge black unicorns forced us back towards home. That was long ago," he said, trying to recollect.

"We will head for Monk's Passage. It's a long road, with many foes scattered here and there. If we make it through the passage we will then cross Mantz forest." He looked at the old man, his eyes like two red orbs. "You think Amatoll is big. Mantz is huge. The trees are an impenetrable blanket which have laid waste to many a traveller over the ages. No two trees are more than this far apart," he said, spreading his arms. "It's dark as night once you're in there. That's the way they like it."

"They?" Wilf said.

"The Cravens. They are human, just. They eat anything that strays into their woods. Animal, man, monster. If they can kill it, they eat it. That will be a testing bit of sport," he said chuckling. "If we can make it through the forest I can reacquaint myself with an old friend who has a boat. He can take us to the Unseen Lands across the sea. That's where my kin hail from. I've not been there for a long time."

Wilf pondered the little demon's words. He looked across at his sister who had now curled up, lightly snoring. Her turquoise skin shimmering in the candle light. He considered his statement for a moment. "We've fought well and won through. Katherine is safe with Jake. We will build a new life at Shetland. And you," he walked over to Tamatan, holding his weathered hand out to him. "Whatever your name truly is, you now have your sister back."

Tamatan took Wilf's hand, shaking it gently. "Thank you."

"Thank you too, my friend."

At hearing Wilf's words his face lit up in a beaming smile that outshone the candles. "Tis such a strange happening that would make man and demon friends. However, we are both the better for it," he said, slapping Wilf on the back.

* * *

Wilf's thoughts were interrupted by a knock at the door. The memory blew away like sea mist on a morning's breeze. "Yes?" he croaked.

A young man entered the low slung room, a look of hesitation on his face. "Sorry to disturb you Wilf. The happy couple are about to perform their union dance. They want the Elder to oversee it."

"Of course. I will be out in a minute. Tell them to prepare." The young man excused himself as Wilf levered himself to his feet. Tamatan's words echoed in his ears. He smiled to himself. *A dark forest full of cannibals. Let's hope I'm never stupid enough to end up in that hell hole*, he thought as he made his way outside to the dance.

Three

Kerry Hardman knocked on the front door as a storm rumbled its way across the land. She stood there, kicking her feet on the stone slabs as she waited for the door to open.

"Kerry. Hi," Jake said as he moved to one side. "Come in before it pours it down."

"Thanks," she said as she shuffled past him into the hallway. "Where's Katherine?"

"She's out with my Mom. Dad has dropped them off. He will be back in a bit. He needs to see the estate agent first."

"Cool. Did they like the house?"

"Yes. Very much so. He's going to make an offer, so fingers crossed. You want a cup of tea?"

"Do you have coffee?"

"We do. I can even make you a proper one if you fancy?"

"Sounds great," she said, her smile lighting up her face. "Milk with two please." Jake walked through to the rear kitchen with Kerry following. She slouched against the counter while Jake made himself busy with the kettle and café tier.

He turned and looked over at Kerry who was nibbling her thumb. "So, how's things?"

She pinched her nose up slightly. "Good, I guess." Jake knew that he would be doing most of the talking. Unless he mentioned video games. Then he would not be able to shut Kerry up. They'd met her months before, not long after they'd moved in. Her father, a mixed race ex-hippy, was their postman. He'd recommended Kerry to Jake when he told him his that his laptop was playing up. A few hours later a mid-twenties girl with coffee coloured skin, a tangle of black hair, and square-rimmed black glasses had knocked on his door. They had both warmed to her, especially Katherine who took an instant shine to her quiet and polite manner. She started fidgeting, thinking of some small talk that would get the conversation flowing. "How's business? Still searching for lost souls?"

"You make me sound like some sort of ghost hunter," he said chuckling. "Things are surprisingly good. There has been lots of work coming my way, which I'm surprised about. I didn't think a place like this would too need too many private investigators."

"Oh but it does. Lots of people around these parts go missing. Two of my friends did a few years ago. Vanished off the face of the Earth. It's because there is not much work. People get into bad habits like drugs and theft. Then all of a sudden they're AWOL."

"Did your friends turn up okay?" Jake asked intrigued.

"Yes. One went to Ibiza with a friend but neglected to tell anyone. The other had met a man online, who was from a place called Doncaster or something. A few weeks later she was home with all her laundry."

"Well it sounds like I'll be busy for the next twenty years or so. Hopefully not too many trips to Doncaster though. It's grim up north." Kerry laughed as he handed her a thin china mug filled with coffee. The ice was well and truly melting.

* * *

The two men walked out of the estate agents' office into the late summer sun. A warm breeze blew down the high street from the Atlantic, buffeting them gently as they chatted. Storm clouds on the horizon were being blown inland towards the village.

"I'll phone you as soon as I get a response from the vendor," the estate agent said, his northern accent sounding out of place this far south.

"Thanks Jeff," Doug said happily.

"I can't see there being any problems. The house has been empty for a few months and they are keen to sell."

"I'll keep my fingers crossed. How do you like Cornwall as oppose to Manchester?"

The younger man considered the question for a second. He was a good ten years Doug's junior, dressed in a grey pinstripe suit. His greying hair was cut short and styled. The older man's hair was cut by his wife and never styled. "I'm from Salford originally. But I've not lived there for years. Before I moved here I was in Birmingham, not too far from where you live now I guess."

"So what made you give up the lights of Brum for this dive?"

Jeff laughed. "My boss didn't like me. He was my new area manager. Young, ambitious, stupid. A bit of a dick. Call it a clash of personalities. As luck would have it I got offered this job as he was sharpening the knife. Best thing we ever did. It's just me, the wife, and two dogs. The kids are all grown up now. They only come down when they want a bit of sun and sand."

Doug nodded, thinking that the younger man had fallen on his feet. "Well let's hope I'm sharing your way of life soon. I don't have any dogs, although I'd happily trade them for my wife if you want to swap?"

The two men finished their business with warm handshakes and promises to speak soon. Doug walked the few hundred yards back to his son's house with the stride of a man ten years younger. He was daring to believe that all this was within his reach. And his wife's of course. He turned right onto Jake's road as the first drops of rain started hitting the pavement around him. He looked out to sea, smiling at the thought that seeing this would be an everyday occurrence.

"Son, I'm back. Where are you?"

"Kitchen Dad. Come through." Doug walked into the kitchen to see his son sat at the table with a young woman with curly dark hair. Jake smiled. "Dad, this is Kerry. Kerry this is my Dad, Doug."

Kerry stood up clumsily, offering her hand. "Ello. Nice to meet you."

"Hello Kerry. You here to get Jake back online?"

"Something like that Dad. There is coffee in the pot. Help yourself while I show Kerry the laptop." Doug ambled around the kitchen, picking up a spoon and cup before pouring himself a coffee, enjoying the moment. He could hear seagulls. He could actually smell the air. It had a tang to it that he loved. Not the smoke riddled smog that permeated around the cities. This was crisp and vibrant. He loved it. He was actually whistling when his son came back into the kitchen.

He looked at his dad warily. "You okay? You're whistling."

"I am happy sometimes. Mainly when your Mom's out."

Jake playfully punched his father on the shoulder. "Wait here while I get the buttons. Two minutes." Doug sat sipping the strong coffee. He could hear the muted thumps his son was making up in the loft and the metallic whine of the ladder as he climbed back down. Seconds later he was sat next to him, offering him a small wooden box frame. Doug took it, has expression clouding. The small frame was cold. Considerably colder than the balmy kitchen. He inspected the buttons. Hearing the clunk as he lightly shook them in their frame. His hands were tingling. Outside the heaven's opened as dark clouds passed overhead. The kitchen suddenly felt dark and cool. "Barbara found the one in Guzman's office which was in Puerto Rico back in 1951 if I remember correctly. The other one I ripped from the boy vampire's coat in that cave I told you about."

Doug nodded. An icy dread was smothering the warm feelings he had built up over the last few days. He put them on the table, wrapping his hands around the comforting coffee cup. "What will you do with them?"

"Not sure. Instinct tells me to bin them. After all what are they? Two old buttons. But something is telling me to keep them. Not in the house of course. What do you think?"

Doug looked at the frame, sipping his coffee. "Do you not think that someone or something will one day come looking for them?"

"The boy was ripped to pieces. The rest of them were destroyed, except Elias and Guzman. Do you really think they can find them?"

"They found you on more than one occasion Son. Why risk it?" Jake let his father's words seep into his brain. He nodded and stood up, scooping the buttons up from the table. He clicked them back into the frame as he walked to the back door. He opened it, dropping them into the large black bin under the kitchen window. Doug placed a hand in his arm when he sat back down. "No more dramas. No more adventures in far off places. It's time to raise a family Son. Let's leave the last few months behind us and move on."

"Your laptop is kaput." Both men looked up startled. Kerry was stood in the doorway holding it in the crook of her arm. "You need a new hard drive."

"Sounds painful and expensive," Doug said.

Jake took the news in his stride. "How quickly can you get it up and running? I don't care how much it costs. I just really need it working."

"I can pick one up today. There's a place I use in Camelford. I can be back in an hour and have it working an hour after that. Does that sound like a good plan?"

"Kerry you're a life saver. Add the petrol to the cost and I'll give you another hundred for a job well done."

"Fifty is enough. It's best not to overcharge a private investigator. I might need your services one day."

A minute later Kerry closed the back door behind her and ran down the drive through the rain, leaving the two men in the kitchen, suddenly at a loss as what to do. Jake looked at the clock on the wall and smiled. "Pint?" Doug looked at the clock on the wall.

"Son, it's ten past twelve! I'll get my coat. Do you have a brolly?"

* * *

Kerry chewed her bottom lip as she tightened the last screw into place. Satisfied, she fired up the laptop and spent an hour configuring the machine, transferring the old hard drive into the new one. Happy with her work, she left a note on the kitchen table before heading out the back door. "Crap," she said as she'd forgotten something from inside. She scooted back into the house, appearing a few seconds later with an empty cardboard box that had contained Jake's new hard drive. The storm had blown its way east, leaving the land feeling refreshed. She lifted the bin lid and was about to discard the trash when something caught her eye. Her face took on a puzzled expression as she found herself looking into the plastic bin at what appeared to be a small wooden frame. Kerry reached inside and took it in her hands, liking the cool feel of it. "Hmm," she said as she closely inspected two metal buttons that each had an identical eagle stamped across their faces. *These are nice. I wonder why they are throwing them away?* She was suddenly unsure of what to do.

"Hi Kerry." Her head snapped up, spotting a woman at the bottom of the driveway. "You going down the beach tonight? Should be a mental party."

Kerry smiled at the woman, whose hair looked to be ten shades of red, shaved on one side. "Hi Cindy. I should be there. Have a few things to do beforehand."

"Okay. Laters," she said as her sloped off towards the high street.

"See you later," Kerry said as she headed down the drive, William's two cold buttons bouncing around in her canvas shoulder bag.

Four

Rodney Walker walked along the pavement, dodging moms with buggies and pensioners with tartan trolleys. The weather had turned, summer creeping slowly into autumn. His cargo shorts were stowed in his chest of drawers until next year. Although he knew that wearing trousers instead of shorts would relieve the ribbing that he received from his fellow postmen. He was tall and gangly, with legs that were the same thickness at the calf and thigh. His ginger hair was closely cropped and looked like it needed a good wash. He was slightly hunched at the shoulder, giving him an older appearance than his forty six years spent on Earth. He'd never been a looker. Far from it. But that didn't bother Rodney. He was constantly on heat. He would try it on with any woman, being rebutted on nearly every occasion. His philosophy was that if he asked a thousand women for a fuck, one of them would oblige. So that was his life's mission. He had been given numerous warnings at work for his lewd behaviour. Young girls avoided Old Creepy Rodney, whose hands were a little too friendly for most. His best friend was the Sorting Office Manager, which gave him the freedom to follow his life's hobby without personnel getting him on their radar. He had his own secret drawer at home that was full of fellow employee's underwear. He looked forward to nothing more once home, then getting into bed with a pair of knickers under his nose and a female sock on his prick. He would joyfully wank himself stupid until the sock was soaked. It would then go in the bin, the underwear back in his drawer. It was his special little secret and he loved it. He was not above stealing underwear from his round if the opportunity arose. He'd walk the rest of the streets with a constant hard-on at thought of what was to come. Quite literally.

This morning had been particularly successful. One of his houses had a side entrance that led to a rear courtyard. Rodney had spied a pair of black tights hanging on a washing line. He had to have them. The coast was clear and they were his. A minute later he was walking past shops and salons in the upmarket village high street with a pair of silky smooth tights tucked into his pants. He could have stopped and cracked one out right there in front of the village deli. Although that would have been a step too far. It would keep. His raging hard-on would simmer for a few more hours until he got home. He started humming his favourite tune. *Step on*, by the Happy Mondays as he turned off the high street onto a small cul-de-sac lined with pretty mews cottages. As he approached the fourth house his humming stopped as he noticed the front door open a few inches. That was not out of the ordinary. It was the painted foot he could see in the hallway that made him stop his tune.

"Ello," he said cautiously as he nudged the door open a few inches. He peered into the dark hallway, his hand tightening on the oak as he saw what was connected to the foot. A woman sat on the carpeted floor, her legs out in front of her. He'd briefly said hello to her a few times before. She had not lived there long, though she was far better looking than the boring cunt who'd lived there before. He'd reminded Rodney of a Copper. Never tipped him at Christmas neither. She must have been in her early sixties, but still was very attractive. Even slumped on the floor she looked well fuckable to Rodney. She started murmuring, making him catch his breath.

He crouched down next to her. "You okay love? 'Ave you ad a funny turn or somefink?" he said as he noticed her left breast was showing. His prick strained to burst from his trousers as his eyes took in the soft inviting flesh. She continued to mumble words that he could not hear properly. "I'm gonna get you inside. You must be freezin' if you've bin here for a while." *Maybe she'd bin 'ere all night*, he thought as he reached around her, grazing her breast with his calloused hands. She didn't seem to notice the contact as he hefted her up under the armpits and manhandled her into a cosy rear lounge. He dumped her down on the two seater sofa as he looked around for something to keep her warm. Nothing. As he scanned the room he noticed a dent in the wall high up. He looked at it puzzled. It looked like a bowling ball had been smashed into the plaster. Shaking the thought he darted upstairs to find a duvet or blanket to warm up the old girl. He'd tuck her up good, maybe getting a feel of her thighs into the bargain. *All the more for the wank bank later*, he thought, pleased with himself. On his way out of the bedroom he fished a pair of the old girl's underwear out of the laundry basket. They had been worn. Perfect, he thought. He tucked them into his cargo trousers, buttoning the flap down afterwards. Her voice drifting up the stairs made him scoot back down to the lounge. "Here we go. Let's put this around you," he said as he draped the duvet over her. He tucked it around the back of her, loving the silken material of her dressing gown. Today was just getting better and better. "Can you tell me what 'appened?"

"Huh," was her confused reply.

"I'm your postman. I've just found you on your doorstep. I fink you've been there all night maybe love. What's your name?"

She tried to shake the cobwebs. "Della. Who are you?"

"Me name's Rodney. I'm your postie. I found you lay in your hallway. I carried you in here. Are you alright?"

"I dreamed. Funny dreams." Her voice was raspy. Rodney got up and went to the kitchen, opening the fridge and pulling a carton of juice from the door.

He walked back into the lounge and sat next to her. "Ere. 'Ave some of this," he said as he held it up to her mouth. She took a few sips, the orange juice spilling down her chin. "Hang on love," he said as he went to the kitchen, coming back in with a piece of kitchen towel. She dabbed her chin. "Now what were you saying?"

"Strange dreams. Really clear though. An old friend was looking for him. Said he'd lost contact and wanted to meet up."

"Lost contact wiv' who?"

"I can't remember." She tried to piece together the jumbled thoughts in her head. "I told him I didn't have an address. I just knew it was down south somewhere. Oh where was it now? I told him the name of the place."

"Who was asking you?" Rodney said as a growing unease spread through his gut. His hard-on now deflating.

"I can't remember. An old friend he'd said. He seemed nice. Very tall. With dark glasses on." She tried to draw the memory out. "Tintagel! That's it. I told him they'd moved to Tintagel. And that they were having a baby!"

Five

He needed transport. He also needed to be careful. If the lawmen saw him it might jog their memory. He'd killed the one in charge. However, he knew that the snake would have grown a new head. A dangerous head that would have his scent on its tongue. He knew the doorway was close by. He could pass through and form a plan in the safety of Amatoll. *A baby. They are having a child.* Thoughts of revenge flooded Elias's mind. He wanted Jake to suffer. What better way than to take his baby away from him. He thought how best to do it. Images flashed in his mind. Dashing the child's brains out against a brick wall. Tearing the little body in two. Or maybe even turning it. He smiled in the darkness as the familiar forest gently creaked around him. He could take what they loved the most and turn it against them. His mind was made up. Amatoll forest could wait for now. All he needed was a mode of transportation.

In the cover of darkness Elias made his way swiftly to a nearby housing estate. He knew it was not a nice estate. He knew that he may encounter trouble. Well that was what he was looking for. The giant came across a public house that spilled music out of its doors into the night. In the corner of the car park, two cars sat in close proximity. Elias could see smoke coming out of the windows. He'd been around long enough to know that the people inside were smoking drugs. *Perfect*, he thought. *These humans will not report a stolen car to the police too quickly*, he surmised. As he made his way across the car park one

The Turning

car's lights came on as it gently edged its way forward towards the exit. Now just one remained. It was black, sleek and looked expensive. He could see the two inhabitants eyeing him. He walked closer, his hands in his pockets with his head slightly bowed. The vampire knew what he had to do as the car doors opened.

"Help you?" the driver said. Elias could see he was big and confident. The other man was much smaller and seemed to hide behind the door.

"I was just admiring your car. Nice car for a neighbourhood like this, wouldn't you agree?"

The two men looked at each other curiously. "Well it ain't for sale so fuck off and look elsewhere," the big man said.

Elias walked towards him, his hands coming out of his pockets. The men suddenly realised his height. Even the driver started to feel trepidation as the giant got to within arm's reach. "I'll make you a deal," the giant said. "Walk away now. Tomorrow you can call the police and report it stolen."

The driver laughed. "And if we say no?"

"You don't want to do that."

The man behind the passenger door walked around the bonnet, a knife in his hand. "I tell you what Granddad. You fuck off now and I won't stick this in your throat. How does that sound?" He came to within a few feet of Elias. Neither was expecting what was about to happen. The driver was frozen to the spot as the tall man back handed his friend across the face. He just about heard the clinking sound of his teeth hitting the car park's floor fifty feet away.

Before the driver could act, Elias had him by the throat. "You should have taken my offer," he said as he punched him once in the chest, shattering his sternum, ending his life. He walked to the rear of the car, holding the dead driver as if he weighed nothing. The giant popped the lid, happy to see that the saloons boot was vast. A minute later he dumped the smaller man inside too. He started murmuring as Elias was about to close the boot. He looked down at the pathetic youth who was trying to look up at him. He bent down and punched him behind the ear. A killing blow. He quickly searched them, pleased with the two wads of cash that he pulled from their pockets. The boot before he squeezed into the car. He racked the seat back a few clicks until it comfortably accommodated his massive frame. He looked at the screen in front of him, knowing that it was a guidance system. He punched in the name of his destination and put the car in gear. Five minutes later Elias was pulling onto the M5 south, heading for his quarry. Heading to meet an old friend.

* * *

A few hours later Elias saw a sign approaching for the Huntspill River. He doused his lights and pulled onto the hard shoulder, stopping a few feet away from the railings. The motorway was empty. He knew he had a few seconds before another car would light the road around him. He quickly got out of the car and opened the boot. The bodies inside were now cool to the touch as he dragged them out in the night. One by one, Elias threw them into the dark waters that ran underneath the motorway. Satisfied that they would not be discovered immediately, he got back in his car and set off once more. He'd just rejoined the carriageway and switched his beams back on as a set of headlights appeared on the opposite side of the road. *Perfect timing*, the vampire thought, smiling to himself. The two bodies would never be found. Little did Elias know, but that the river would take the corpses to the Severn Estuary which had one of the strongest tidal currents in the World. By the time the sun rose over this part of the land, the two bloated bodies would be twenty miles out to sea. The black car would be found the following morning by a man walking his dog along Treyarnon Bay. It would take two hours before it was pulled from the sea, washing away any evidence.

* * *

The sea cave was deep enough for Elias to shelter in during the day. He would not risk being seen by either the lawmen, Jake or the Bathurst girl. He would use the blanket of night as his ally. He would find them. Not yet however. First he needed to feed. He felt weakened and old, his thirst raging in the back of his throat. The following night he took a young surfer in Watergate Bay. Elias felt the strength flow back into his body as he drained the poor boy in the dunes next to the beach car park. He found another sea cave nearby, torching the lifeless husk before it could turn. By the time sun made its appearance in the east, Elias was comfortably propped between two rocks as the tide flooded the cave. Now all he had to do was find them. He had plenty of time. Time to plan.

Six

Jake sipped his coffee as he watched the early morning news. A young reporter was stood on a dark beach a few miles south of him, reporting on the discovery of a badly burnt body in a cave close to the incoming tide. The man, who was wearing a jacket similar to one Jake had hanging in the hallway said that the body was found in the early hours by a young couple who were walking along the beach on their way home from a party. The victim's identity, along with the motive, was still unclear. The reporter promised updates later before the camera cut to a softly lit studio with a man and woman seated on a long sofa. Jake turned away from the television, picking up a cup of tea before making his way upstairs to Katherine.

"Morning babe. Bought you a cup of tea." Jake placed it on her bedside table before opening the curtains. He spent a moment drinking in the view. The Atlantic was spread out in front of him. Low clouds were being blown out to sea, shafts of morning sun piercing them randomly. He never wanted to leave this magical place.

"Thanks love," Katherine said, as she carefully levered herself into a sitting position. These new words that Jake had taught her now seemed so natural to her. She loved their little pet names for each other. This strange world was fast becoming the norm for her, with its coffee shops and boutiques. Katherine felt whole. She sipped at her tea, nodding in appreciation. "You make wonderful tea Jake. Uncle Wilf would drink this all day." She paused for a moment, lost to her thoughts. "I wonder what became of him and the village?"

"Hopefully they made it out to Shetland. We have to believe that. We have to believe that Wilf is stood looking out to sea, wondering how we are." Katherine liked his logic. He sat down on the bed next to her. "I just saw on the news. A young lad was found in a cave not far from here. He'd been burnt to death."

"Oh no. How awful. Does anyone know how it happened?"

"Not yet. It will unfold in time. It's not nice to think that such bad things can happen in such a beautiful place." He put his empty coffee cup on the window sill and stroked Katherine's bump. "Hello princess," he cooed gently. "It's your daddy. I can't wait to meet you." He kissed her tummy, wrapping his arms around her back. She smiled at the sight before her. She was complete. She now felt whole. She scratched the back of Jake's head, just the way he liked it. He writhed in appreciation. He could lie like this all day. Eventually he broke the hold and kissed her warmly on the lips. She returned his kiss, pulling him towards her. He felt the stirrings of arousal as her lips melded with his, small moans escaping her lips, her fingers kneading his neck. He gently broke away, kissing the top of her head. "I need to go to work. And if you don't stop kissing me I'm going to get into bed and kiss every inch of you all day long."

"Forget work Jake. As you can see I have many extra inches that now require kissing." She looked down at her belly to make her point.

"Hmmm. I wish I could. I do have to go though. You're only a few weeks away now and I need to tie up a few loose ends. Sorry to be such a spoil sport. I tell you what. When I get in, I'll run you a nice bath and put one of those fizzy bomb things in that you like."

"I guess that will have to do. Will you be late home?" Katherine said, masking her disappointment.

"No later than five. I've got to go down to Looe to meet a client this afternoon. And I need to write up a report for the Truro job. Can you call Mom later and tell her that she left her purple cardigan here?

She will be going mental, and Dad will be getting it in the neck. What plans do you have?"

"Angie is popping round at midday for tea and cake. That's as far as my plans stretch. I'm just so tired at the moment. I may have a lie down after that."

"Yes, well a belly full of tea and cake should help you sleep babe," he teased as he bent down to kiss her. She lifted her head to meet him, their lips coming together for a moment. "I'll call you later. We seriously need to get you a mobile soon."

"I know. We can get one this week. Then you can spend a week teaching me about all that goes with it. All that *Facebook* and *What's up* stuff."

He laughed, sorely tempted to correct her mistake. He needed to make tracks though. "Bye babe. Love you," he said as he left the bedroom.

"Love you too Jake." She heard him close the door. The footsteps to his car floated up through the bedroom window. She picked up her tea as Jake's car reversed out of the driveway and headed off down the road. Katherine sat drinking her tea, suddenly thinking about the body found in the cave. She shivered at the thought as the sun was blotted out by a passing cloud, making the room feel cooler. She put the tea down and swung her legs over the side of the bed. The sun reappeared from behind the clouds as she made her way to the bathroom, readying herself for tea and cake.

* * *

As the sun vanished below the horizon, Elias made his way out of his refuge. He sniffed the air. The scent of the sea seemed to mask other smells around him. The giant vampire realised that it may make it more difficult to find Jake and the woman. He made his way along the beach, climbing the steep coastal path towards the village. He kept to the shadows as people were still milling around after a day's activities on the beach and around the high street. An imposing hotel to his left caught his eye, his long strides altering course. Elias froze as he caught a whiff of something on the wind. He tried to recall the scent. It wasn't blood. It was something else. Something that didn't belong here. He caught another hit of it, making him change his route once more. Heading for an unknown destination.

Seven

Father Stephen climbed over the heavy wooden gate, almost stumbling onto the grass on the other side. The wraiths and spirits had followed him to the edge of the forest. They kept their distance though. The silver cross in his hands kept them at bay as they twisted themselves around giant tree trunks, cursing the stranger as he fled the forest. His breathing was laboured, his pulse thumping between his ears as he made his way almost drunkenly towards a large building. He mounted the steps and crashed through the front door, landing on his knees in a low slung room. The night whinnied and whined behind him as he scrambled to his feet. He slammed the door shut, drawing a crude bar into place to keep out what wanted to get in. *Jesus Fucking Christ. What have I stumbled across?* It was all true. Doug was right. Now was not a time to question how this could be possible. It *was* possible. It was real. Father Kenneth Stephen. A middle aged Vicar from Bewdley, Worcestershire was standing in a house in another dimension. He'd watched enough sci-fi movies to realise that this dimension may be completely different from his. He'd already shared many a dream with a beast called Reggan. An unseen hooded vampire that pursued him through darkened corridors as he slept safe in his bed. The realisation that Reggan, or something similar may actually be out there made him want to dig a hole in the floor and bury himself. He looked at the window. The darkness seemed to press against the glass, threatening to break it. As he peered out he saw tendrils of mist slowly snaking from the forest towards the house. *Shit. Shit shit shit,* he cursed as he suddenly remembered the lighter in his pocket. He looked around the room, noticing several dead candles. Stephen quickly set to work, lighting the room until it was almost cosy. He felt better knowing that he could at least see his surroundings. The man suddenly felt famished. He'd neglected to bring any food or drink with him. The Vicar had not planned that far ahead. Now he stood there trying to figure out how to get through the next twenty four hours. He made his way to the rear of the house, looking for anything that he could eat. A small door in the corner of the room made him curious. He opened it and peered into the blackness. It was impossibly dark. He fetched one of the candles and gingerly ventured inside. Unsure what was waiting for him.

* * *

Eddie was awoken by shrieks and wails from the far off forest. His yellow eyes scanned the tree tops from his vantage point. Something was amiss in Amatoll. He could almost see what it was. Something was carving a path through the forest. He could just make out a point of light between the trees that was moving south. *Could it be Jake? Or Elias? Or something else?* He thought. He stood up and made his way to the edge of the bluff. The wind was behind him, no smells from the forest giving him any clues. It was gut instinct. He went with his gut as he set off down the mountain towards the ancient forest.

* * *

Kenneth Stephen set the items on the gnarled table next to the window. Whoever had lived here had left in a hurry. The house still almost felt lived in. He'd found three large strips of dried meat and two clay bottles of liquid, sealed with cork and wax. He fell on the meat, ripping off hardened chunks before chewing them greedily. It reminded him of Beef Jerky, or Biltong. Whatever animal it had come from, he didn't care. It tasted amazing. He was just finishing the first strip as he started fumbling with the waxed cork on the bottle. After a few twists and grunts the stopper came out with an audible pop. He sniffed the contents. It smelt like some kind of spirit. Stephen took a tentative sip. It tasted like whisky. Albeit like one of the discount brands from the supermarket. He didn't care though. He took two long swigs, letting it warm his throat and chest. It also seemed to steady his heart to something resembling normalcy. He set the bottle down and scanned the room. There was a large fireplace on the far wall with a small cauldron sat on the stone flags. A few shelves dotted around the room offered little insight into who had lived here. As he started on the second strip of meat he noticed that the forest seemed quieter. The thought left his mind as he continued to scan the room. Nothing of real interest caught his eye as he reached for the bottle next to the window. His eyes looked out into the night for any sign of activity. They found it immediately. A set of eyes locked onto his from the other side of the pane. Yellow, feral eyes.

* * *

Stephen tried to stand. He willed his legs to push him away from the table. His legs felt like lead though. The chair felt like it weighed a tonne. The man was paralysed. The figure on the other side of the glass smiled, revealing a pair of wickedly curved canines. They were dirty. The colour of ash. His face was grey, framed by dark hair. The thing moved closer to the window, his eyes dancing in the night, soothing the Vicar's fears. In his mind's eye he was suddenly young again. Walking through a beautiful forest with his lovely girlfriend, Denise. They were holding hands, smiling at each other. *Denise.* He suddenly remembered his wife. *What will she think if I never return home? It would destroy her.* He willed himself to stand, breaking the glare with the vampire briefly. He slowly walked backwards into the room as the monster outside moved away from the window. Stephen could hear heavy footfalls on the wooden boards outside, until they stopped in front of the door. The door flew open, the bar splintering, scattering itself across the floor. Mist flooded in, carpeting the floor knee deep. Kenneth watched as the vampire glided in, closing the gap between them to ten feet. He was much shorter than the Vicar. Stocky though. His arms hung down by his sides, his hands lost in the mist. The larger man felt his head start to swim again. A wind kicked up outside, knocking the door against its splintered jamb. Mist was blown around the room, extinguishing all but one of the candles. The room was returned to its darkened state. Kenneth could now only just about make out the features of the thing before him. The eyes now seemed to increase in power as they glowed brighter than the solitary candle.

"You're not from this land," it said. "You came through the doorway in the forest." He shuffled a few steps closer, the boards under his feet creaking. Father Stephen caught the smell of the vampire as it drew nearer. A wet, sick stench that seemed to coat the back of his throat. It suddenly stopped and sniffed the air. He recoiled a step as if slapped by an invisible hand. "You're a Shaman. I can taste it in the air."

Father Stephen finally uttered his first words. "I'm a Vicar. A man of God." His words sounded empty in the gloom.

"Then your blood is of no use to me. I'd rather drink horses piss."

"Then," he faltered. "Then leave me be! I made a mistake coming here. I will be on my way home very soon."

The vampire shook his head slowly. "I doubt that Vicar. You will never leave this forest. Not as a human anyway. Maybe you can drink from me. Maybe that will open your eyes to the truth. Not the preaching's from a book. Come. Come closer to Eddie." Stephen took a step backwards as Eddie glided closer. He lifted a ruined hand to his lips, biting his wrist, holding it out to him as an offering. "Drink." Stephen shrank back further at the sight of yellowed flesh and oozing black blood. He suddenly became aware of the warmth on his hip. Without taking his eyes off of Eddie he slipped his hand into his pocket, almost cursing as the metal cross stuck to his flesh. He pulled it from his pocket, holding it at arm's length in front of him. The room lit up, blinding Stephen. Eddie fell back, landing on his side in the mist. His screams filling the small room. Stephen's fist tightened on the hot cross. It hurt like hell. He embraced the pain though. It was his ally. It would focus his mind on staying alive. He took a step forward, noticing that even the mist seemed to shrink away from the cross. It billowed and puffed itself towards the corners of the room as he moved. Eddie was scrambling to his feet like a boxer who'd been floored. He staggered into the table.

Stephen sensed salvation. "GET THE HELL OUT OF HERE! GO ON. GET OUT!" He pressed his advantage, shepherding Eddie towards the front door His fist was now numb and tingling but never wavered. He held it steady. Eddie fell through the doorway, crashing into the wooden railing that ran the length of the porch. The creature snarled as the man approached, drawing his legs underneath him, ready to spring. Light spilled onto the porch and grass beyond as Father Stephen walked through the door. *How can this crucifix work on him?* He thought. *If there is no God then this cross should be useless. But it's not. I can feel the power flowing through it. What does this mean?* He was lost in his thoughts for a moment. Eddie sensed the cross's power diminish slightly. He braced his legs against the rail, hurling himself forward into the Vicar. Stephen was a big, powerfully built man. However, the wind was dashed from his lungs as the vampire's shoulder landed in his stomach, propelling them both backwards into the house. They skidded on the wooden floor, the mist swirling around their bodies as they came to a halt in a tangle of limbs. Stephen was dazed and winded as he looked up at Eddie above him. In his rage, Eddie had forgotten that his adversary was a man of God. He went in for the kill, his dirty mouth swooping down for Stephen's neck. Kenneth was dazed but he saw the vampire's intentions. He brought up his hands to ward off the attack. He was still holding the cross. It was now almost welded to his palm. The metal prong at the head of the crucifix entered Eddie's mouth, jabbing into the roof, almost puncturing flesh. Blinding light and the vampire's screams filled the room as the cross did its damage. Eddie flew from the house, smashing through the wooden porch before fleeing into the forest. Kenneth sat up groggily, a sharp pain in his side making him wince. His sight had not yet cleared. Light shapes danced across his vision as he rubbed at his eyes. The wails and screams of the fleeing monster died away as his vision took in the room once more. He slowly climbed to his feet, his breathing harsh and ragged as he held his ribs. The Vicar knew something was broken. He took a deep breath in until the pain was too much to bear. His breath exhaled fiercely, as he held onto the table for support. Pulling a chair out, he slumped down, arms banging on the wooden table top. He checked the time. *Almost two o'clock.* Realisation hit that he would have to spend another twenty two hours in this world before he could make it home. Twenty two hours in a land full of who knew what. He'd already met a vampire, barely surviving the encounter. What else was out there that could harm him? He felt evil all around him. The forest seemed to radiate it. His thoughts went to Jake. *How had you survived here? What horrors had you seen? How in hell did you stumble across this place?* He knew that if he made it home he would have to find Jake and Doug and tell them what had happened. His eyes found the clay bottle, grabbing it for a long swig. The spirit calmed him. He found the stick of meat he'd started and continued eating it, trying to plan his next twenty two hours in this unknown place. Trying to get home to his Denise.

Eight

Kerry sat on her bed, headset on, playing her favourite video game. She was pitted against an online buddy from California. And she was kicking his ass. Her parents were asleep on the other side of the house, their bedroom door closed. It was way past midnight but Kerry wasn't tired. She was a night owl, who'd probably sleep until the early afternoon, much to her parent's annoyance. The room was dark, save for the light from the screen. That's how she liked it. It made the game seem more real, like she was in a movie theatre. The top window was open a crack, letting in the sea air. She always slept with the window open, whatever the season. It had been a warm night with a pleasant breeze blowing in from the ocean. Now as she sat cross-legged in a pair of joggers and vest top she started to feel a chill. She pulled the duvet up over her shoulders to keep warm. The video game was in mid battle and she didn't want to pause it to put her bed socks and fleece on. She would do that later. Kerry heard a cat howl in the distance, like it was squaring up for a fight. Her cat, Gizmo was out somewhere. Probably patrolling the gardens, garages, and roadway at the back of the houses she guessed. Another howl filtered in through from outside, making her look around at the window. It had become misty. Not like normal. Really misty, cold too. She paused the game, her buddy forgotten. Taking her headphones off, Kerry slid from the bed and shuffled to the window. The mist was really thick. It seemed to stick to the glass, swirling and pulsating. The woman had never seen mist like this. She shivered involuntarily, hugging herself to keep warm. She could not even make out the garage at the bottom of the garden, such was the thickness of the fog. Her hands were placed on the sill as she tried to look at the house next door. As she did so, she knocked the frame containing Jake's buttons. They fell to the floor, landing in a muted clunk on the carpet.

"Shit," Kerry said, scooping them up. "What the," she said, holding the frame. It was freezing. She set them down on the sill, rubbing her cold hand on her joggers. A deep drone from outside made her look up suddenly. Gooseflesh broke out on her skin, Kerry hugging herself tighter. Something was wrong out there. *Was that a ship's horn?* she thought. *There it was again. What the fuck is it?* She peered left and right, trying to see into neighbouring gardens. *Nothing.* It was like pea soup. She looked towards the garage at the bottom of the garden, noticing for the first time two glowing red points of light in the air. Her face looked puzzled. "What the hell is that?" They vanished for a split second then reappeared. They looked to Kerry like far off car lights. She shuddered again, feeling increasingly cold. Something started moving on the sill. She looked down to see that the frame was gently vibrating. *What the hell is happening?* She watched it transfixed as it gently rotated on the white painted sill. She looked out the window to see that the red orbs seemed closer. Her heartbeat was now racing, her breathing constricted. Kerry turned and grabbed her inhaler from the shelf, administering a double blast as she felt a panic coming on. She sighed heavily, placing both hands on the sill once more to try and steady herself. The frame suddenly shot left, shattering against the wall making her gasp. She pulled the top window closed and dove onto her bed, pulling the duvet all around her. She lay there shivering, her breathing hoarse, teeth chattering. The woman tried not to look out of the window. She buried her face in her pillow, trying to shut everything out. Something in her head was telling her to look. Something in the back of her brain was cajoling her to take a peek. Her head shifted right, one eye opening. Nothing. The mist was still there though. She sat up in bed and looked at the window, rubbing her eyes with the palm of her hands. Kerry opened her eyes, looking at the window. Looking at two red eyes, staring in at her. She could make out the shape of a head too, floating in the mist. A scream erupted from her mouth as her back crashed into the bedroom wall.

"WHAT THE 'ELL IS GOING ON IN 'ERE?" her father said, flicking on the light switch. He found Kerry cowering on the bed, half wrapped in her duvet. He hurried across the room towards her. "You okay Kerry? You're shivering."

"A FACE. THERE'S SOMEONE OUT THERE," she screamed, her feet scrambling, trying to propel herself backwards into the wall even further. The man ran to the window, stopping short when he saw the mist.

"There's nothing there love. Just a lot of fog. I've never seen it this thick before. I can't even see the patio." He looked at the computer screen, then at his daughter. She was shaking and sobbing. He picked up a video game case, staring at the zombie on the cover. "You sure all this late night gaming isn't messing with your head? Maybe you were mistaken. There is no one outside Kerry." He sat on the bed cradling her in his arms, rocking gently for a few minutes.

She seemed to relax in his embrace, her breathing easing. "Thanks Dad. I'm okay, now."

"Your imagination got the better of you. Killing zombies before bedtime is not a good idea. Maybe some gentle music or a book might be better. Are you sure you're alright now?"

Kerry sighed, suddenly realising she felt weary. "Fine. Maybe I was too engrossed in the game. Although I swear I saw something. Go back to bed Dad. See you in the morning." He walked over and kissed his daughter's head before heading back to his bedroom. The room was plunged back into darkness. Kerry looked out the window. The mist was still swirling, although it seemed to have thinned somewhat. She walked over and looked out. No red orbs could be seen. *There was something out there. I swear there was.* Kerry suddenly remembered the buttons. She reached down and picked up the broken frame, laying it on the sill. She pulled the buttons out and inspected one of them. It was ice cold, heavy too. The woman flipped it over in her hand, rubbing her thumb over the fixing on the back. *They certainly are strange. I must tell Jake and Katherine about it. There is something very wrong with this*, she thought. A deep drone sounded in the distance, making gooseflesh pepper her arms once more. She drew the curtains before getting back into bed. The window stayed shut that night. Kerry drifted off to sleep. Her dreams were deep and clouded. *She found herself in a dense forest. No break in the trees could be seen. No sun overhead. Animals and noises were all around her as she tried to make her escape. Every turn was greeted by more trees and more noises. What she could not see in the forest was a pair of red eyes, high up in the branches. The unseen figure watched the girl walk aimlessly, trying to find a way out. In his hand, two cold buttons. Two cold buttons with eagles emblazoned across the front.*

* * *

A few hundred yards away Jake and Katherine slept. Their window was open a couple of inches, letting the cool sea air in. A deep rumble carried on the wind, drifting through their window. Jake's eyelids fluttered. He turned over, murmuring something from his dreams.

He was looking out from atop a lone mountain. To the east, he could see the massive gorge that spilt the land. Birds were flocking towards it in their droves. He looked north-west towards the huge forest. It was covered in mist. He could barely make out the lofty tree tops as they struggled to reach above the swirling fog. The mountains to the west lay in perpetual darkness, rumbles of thunder and flashes of lightning could be seen on the far horizon. Jake looked down the mountain as movement caught his eye. He moved to the ledge, peering down, catching sight of the two faces smiling up at him. Elias and Guzman had found him. Two sets of eyes burning bright in the oncoming night. Jake ran back to the cave, trying to find something to protect himself with.

"It's too late, Jake," a voice said from behind him. He spun around to see them advancing on him. Guzman's tongue poked out between his teeth, a leering grin on his grey face. Jake put his hands up to protect himself from the inevitable attack. He closed his eyes as they swooped towards him, ready for the kill.

"JAKE." He shot out of his dream, sitting up in bed, hands in front of his face to ward off the attack. Nothing happened. No attack. There had been no vampires. He'd been dreaming. A sob next to him made him look towards Katherine. She was in pain.

"Kath. What's wrong?" his brain was not yet fully in gear.

She looked at him, tears in her eyes. She managed a pained smile. "Get the bags. Our baby is coming."

* * *

Elias leaned against the stone wall of the massive hotel that was perched on the cliff top. He was trying to piece together what had just taken place. *What is that girl doing with the buttons? Does Jake know her? Does she know where the buttons came from?* A car passed by a few hundred yards away, making Elias turn his body away from the light's glare. He was at a loss regarding the buttons. He knew where the girl lived. He would keep an eye on her. A few hundred yards away a man emerged from a house, hurrying towards his car. He opened the car's boot, throwing two bags inside before slamming the lid and heading back inside. Elias saw him clearly. "Jake." The vampire quickly advanced on the house, mindful to keep out of sight. He ducked down as Jake reappeared with Katherine. She was dressed in a long red robe. She looked in pain. Jake helped her into the car before heading back into the house again. Elias almost cried out when he caught his scent. He rolled over on the grass, holding in his scream in his throat. "REGGAN," He turned over as Jake came out of the house once more, locking up and jumping into the car. Headlights lit the driveway before the car pulled out, heading left down the road at a fast pace. Elias lay there, catching his breath. *He has Reggan's scent. How?! What is going on here?* he thought. He made his way over to the house, hiding in the shadows of the carport. All the other houses on the street were in darkness. The only sound was the far off sea, crashing on the rocks below the hotel. He checked the kitchen door. Locked. Elias was sure that all doors and windows would be secure. He'd expect no less from a former police officer. Breaking into the house was not an option. He didn't want to be hasty. He needed a plan. Elias needed to think. *She is having his baby. There is no rush. They will be back soon. Then I will know more and know what to do.*

* * *

Minutes later he was lay in his refuge, trying to think. The last time he'd seen Jake was the night that his former master, Korgan, had been destroyed. Jake had been there. He was responsible for the death of the great king who was poised to retake control of his land, and his brother's land too. Elias and Jake had locked horns shortly after that, with Jake coming off the victor. Elias would forever carry the scars on his grey flesh that Jake had inflicted in the ancient forest. The vampire had fled shortly afterwards, taking a long sleep in a barn way up in the Tundra. He knew not what had transpired after that. Reggan's scent was as clear to Elias as if he'd been stood there with Jake. *Maybe Jake did to Reggan what had been done to Korgan,* Elias thought. *It is possible. Somehow. I need to get more information.* He thought for a moment. *I need to find Guzman.*

Nine

The phone in the hallway started ringing. Doug navigated packed boxes in the lounge, carefully hurdling one in the doorway before he picked up the cordless phone off the telephone table. "Hello."

"Hi Dad. It's Jake."

Doug looked at his watch. *Half eight.* "Is everything okay Son? You're calling early."

"Is Mom there?"

"Hang on." Doug peered up the stairs. "Love! Jake's on the phone?"

Alison came to the top of the stairs in her bathrobe. She had a towel wrapped around her head. She looked pink and flustered. "Is everything alright?" she said, descending the stairs. She took the phone from him. "Jake. Are you okay?"

"Hi Mom. Put me on speakerphone."

Jake could hear fumbling and a few tuts from his mother as she tried to activate the speaker. "Okay, Son. Now, is everything alright?"

"Fine Mom. I'm stood outside the hospital in Truro."

"Hospital," Alison cut in. "Is Katherine alright?"

"She is now. She went into labour in the early hours." Alison caught her breath in her throat, tears immediately welling in her eyes.

Doug gently took the phone from her. "And?" he asked, unusually impatient.

"You have a beautiful granddaughter." Alison cried out in joy, tears now rolling down her pink cheeks.

Doug put his arm around her shoulders, steadying his wife. "Congratulations Son. We're both thrilled for you," Doug said, his voice cracking with emotion. "Is Katherine okay?"

"She's fine. Only needed a bit of gas and air. She was a real trooper. It took us half an hour to get here from home. An hour later, out she popped."

"Well done Katherine," Doug said, still holding his wife steady.

"Have you thought of a name?" Alison said. Jake and Katherine had told them that they were expecting a girl, being deliberately vague about the name. They had agreed on the name as soon as they knew it was a girl. The baby was to be named after Katherine's sister and mother. Doug knew Katherine's full family history. They had spoken of it often since the night the Doug had found his son in a forest with a vampire's tooth embedded in his leg. However, a family history had to be fabricated for Alison and everyone else's benefit. Doug knew that Katherine's sister had been killed by a monster. And that her mother had died under the hooves of a horse when Katherine was a girl. That story would remain just between the three of them. What Jake's mother had been told was that Katherine's younger sister Alice had died of Leukaemia a few years before. Her mother Susan had been killed in a riding accident on their farm in the Shetlands. So far, the cover story had worked fine. Alison's love for Katherine had intensified with the knowledge that the young woman had been through so much in life.

"Alicia Susan Stevenson."

"Oh, that's lovely Jake," Alison cooed. "How heavy was she?"

"Eight pounds, dead on."

"Ouch," Doug said. "I hope Katherine's not to battered and bruised?"

"She's fine Dad. She's made of strong stuff," Jake said. "Look I've gotta get back inside. I will call you later from home."

"No rush, Son. Just call us when you can."

"Give Katherine and Alicia our love, and give them a kiss from both of us," Alison said, her emotions back under control.

"I will. Can you let Rick know that he is an uncle again?" Jake immediately regretted saying the word *again*.

"We will. I'm sure he'll be in touch soon to congratulate you himself," Doug said, knowing that Jake's younger brother would probably just send a text. They were not close. Rick had moved to Hamburg shortly after completing his university studies, working for a well-known skin care company. Doug and Alison were lucky if they heard from him once a month. He was nothing like Jake.

"Okay. Thanks Dad. I will speak to you both later. Going to go home and get a few things. Love you both."

"We love you too Son." They broke the connection and instinctively embraced.

"Congratulations Grandma," Doug said.

Alison pulled away from the embrace, wiping fresh tears from her eyes. "Alicia. What a lovely name. I can't wait to meet her and give her a munch," she said as she climbed the stairs. Doug walked back into the lounge to continue the packing. His wandering mind was not on the task at hand though. It was two hundred miles to the south-west, looking out at the Atlantic with a granddaughter on his lap.

* * *

On Katherine's insistence, Jake drove home to rest. He pulled up on the driveway and climbed out of the car. His neighbour Linda was out cutting the grass. She looked up and saw him, leaving the mower in the middle of the lawn. She was friendly, if a little flirty with Jake. Katherine teased him whenever she came up in conversation, saying that the older woman had her sights set on him. She was a good fifteen years older than Jake, although he had to admit that she had something about her that he found appealing.

Her shoulder length brown hair bouncing as walked over, her smile lighting up her face. "Hiya. Any news? We saw you both head off in the middle of the night."

"Katherine had a baby girl at about half past two. Alicia."

The woman exclaimed, clapping her hands together. "Oh, that's lovely! A baby girl. Oh fabulous! Congratulations Jake. I bet you're over the moon. And probably knackered too?"

"We're both thrilled. And just a bit tired," he laughed. "Going to try and get my head down for an hour before I head back."

Linda turned to look at her lawn. "Well I'll 'ave this done in five minutes. I won't keep you up. The bin men however might," she signalled down the street at the approaching wagon and men.

"I need to put my bin out. Thanks for reminding me Linda."

"Anytime. And well done. We'll pop round once they're both settled in." Jake nodded his thanks and headed inside. Once in the house, he flicked the kettle on. He was parched. Hospital tea and coffee were not the best. He needed a proper brew. Jake could hear the advancing bin lorry, its lifting mechanism unusually loud in the usually quiet street. He unlocked the kitchen door, stepping out into the car port. The door closed behind him as he wheeled the bin to the pavement. He walked back up the driveway, his mind a whirl of happy thoughts. His mind was thinking about how to decorate the house with balloons as he grabbed the kitchen door handle. He froze, the balloons forgotten. His grip tightened on the handle as a pair of red eyes appeared in his head. They glowered at him. He remembered the eyes. The last time he'd seen them was in Amatoll. That was many months ago. Now as he stood rooted to the spot the eyes mocked him. *You're mine. You're all mine*, a voice hissed making him stagger backwards into the far wall. Jake's vision cleared as he stood there gasping for breath. *Elias. That was Elias. Why did he suddenly appear in my head?* He looked at the door handle, a shiver of realisation hitting him like a punch in the stomach. *Has he found us? Fuck! No, no, no. I thought this was all over.* He looked down the driveway to see two men dressed in council uniforms peering up at him. They were talking about Jake, although he could quite hear the conversation. He straightened, trying to compose himself. A dull throb radiated up his leg as he walked towards the kitchen. By the time he closed the kitchen door, it felt like it was on fire. He rubbed it in a futile attempt to ease the pain. Jake needed to go to church, and soon. All thoughts of balloons, babies, and family forgotten.

As he sat at the kitchen table sipping his tea, he tried to find any reason why that had just happened. *There is no way Elias could have found us here. How could he? The owner of my old house had no forwarding address. I may have mentioned that we were moving to Cornwall but that was it.* He took another sip as the answer presented itself. *The buttons! Barbara's buttons. That must be the reason. They must have done that.* He suddenly remembered he'd thrown them in the bin. *I've just put the bin out. That must have triggered it.* He felt satisfied that they were the reason for the flashback. His mood lightened slightly as he finished his tea. *The buttons are in the back of the truck, on their way to the tip. That's the best place for them,* he thought as he put his empty cup in the dishwasher, heading upstairs for a long hot shower.

Ten

Alicia and Katherine arrived home two days later. As the car bounced up onto the drive Kath caught her breath. The front of the house was decorated in various banners and balloons, proclaiming the arrival of a baby girl.

"Oh Jake. That is so lovely," she said, leaning over and kissing him on the cheek.

"That's why I'm out of breath. Thirty six balloons takes a lot of blowing up." They got out of the black car, noticing a distinct cooling of the weather. Dark clouds littered the coastline as far as the eye could see. Jake opened the rear door and smiled down at his daughter who was asleep in her car seat. He gently unclipped it from its frame, holding it in the crook of his arm as he closed the door. Katherine was busy unlocking the front door as Jake came around the bonnet of the car as the first drops of rain started falling. Two minutes later they were sat in the front facing lounge watching the heavens open outside. Katherine stretched herself out on the sofa, kicking off her shoes. Jake looked down at her and smiled. For a woman who'd just given birth, she looked amazing. She was as stunning now as the first time he saw her, on a spit of land out at sea, next to a stone farmhouse. That seemed a million miles away from the cosy setting they found themselves in. It was another world, literally.

"Tea?" Jake said.

"Can I have one of those Milo drinks, please?" she replied. "Could I have a cuddle first, though?" He knelt next to her and buried his head in her curls. She responded by wrapping her arms around his back, pulling him into her. They didn't move for a few minutes, both enjoying the moment. "We're complete now Jake. We have everything in life."

"We do. And nothing will ever change that. We're a family."

"Are you happy with your new family? Does it feel the same as it did before?"

Jake pulled himself out of her embrace and looked at her. It had been over five years since his wife and daughter had been killed by a hit and run driver. Not a day went by that he didn't think of them. Megan would be nearly reaching double figures by now. They would always be a part of him. Nothing would ever take away the love and memories he had for them. "I guess it feels the same Kath. I can't really remember how it felt the day we came home with Megan. I know that Katie was in a bit of a state because of an horrendous birth. She was stretched out much like you are now. But she stayed in that position for a few weeks. You handled birth so well."

"Well I'm used to delivering animals in back in my land. I know it's tough but a bit of grit and you get through it. My ankles are sore though. I don't suppose you'd give them a rub, once the drinks are made of course."

"Yes Ma'am," he said getting to his feet. He looked down at his daughter, who was still fast asleep. "She's so beautiful." Katherine smiled.

"Of course she is. She takes after her mother."

* * *

An hour later Katherine and Alicia were asleep. Jake knew he had a window of time to get an important errand done. He locked the front door, heading off towards Tintagel's Methodist church. Autumn was coming on a pace as a wind whipped in from the sea. He saw a few overturned bins, whose contents were now blowing around the surrounding streets. He pulled his collar up and quickened his pace, exchanging friendly greetings with a few locals as he walked up the high street. A high street that was getting ready for the winter shutdown. He turned right onto a side street and walked the hundred yards to the church's entrance. It was a small and squat, built from grey stone. A modern glass frontage had been tacked on, that Jake thought looked out of place. He ducked inside, closing the door behind him, the wind's roar silenced instantly. He turned to the look into the church for signs of activity. Satisfied that there was no one around, he took two small glass bottles out of his jacket pocket. Jake walked over to the font and filled them with water, screwing the lids on tightly before putting one in his jacket and one in his jeans pocket, close to the old wound. His leg immediately started tingling. He felt the same feeling every time. It was almost comforting to feel his leg go numb. It was as if the small bottle was somehow pushing whatever infection was in his body out through his pores. He walked into the cool dim confines of the main building, sitting himself in the front row. The wooden bench creaked as he got comfy. Jake sat in silence for a few minutes until he heard a noise behind him. He turned and stood as he saw an elderly man approach. He was dressed in dark trousers and a grey pullover. His dog collar fitting snugly into his weathered neck. His grey hair was thick and coarse, giving him a few extra inches to his five foot seven. Jake always sensed coolness about him.

"Hello Father Adams."

"Jake, isn't it?" The younger man nodded. "What brings you here today?" Jake was suddenly at a loss. They had both been regular visitors to the church since moving to the village. No one knew the real reason. The local parishioners were friendly enough, with Katherine becoming quite popular with many of them. Jake always felt slightly removed from the crowd.

"I, err, we've had a baby. A girl. I thought I'd just pop in and say thanks for her safe delivery," he said, pointing to the ceiling.

"A baby girl you say," his soft Yorkshire accent barely echoing off the stone walls. "What a blessing to the world. What name have you given her?"

"Alicia."

"Oh, what a lovely name," the Vicar said, still emitting a coolness towards Jake. "You must bring her to church. I sincerely hope she is to be christened in the presence of our Lord."

"Of course. We'll have to make arrangements whenever you can fit us in." Jake was suddenly at a loss for words.

The Vicar sensed this, deciding to quickly conclude the conversation. "Well I'll be seeing you both very soon. Give my regards to Katherine and little Alicia." Jake went to offer his hand but decided against it as the older man started to move away.

"Goodbye Father," he said as the old man walked over to a small wooden door at the rear of the church. He sat down once more and sat in quiet contemplation, a serene expression washing over his face.

* * *

Father Adams walked over to his desk and pulled out a small silver hip flask. He unscrewed the lid and took a long pull on it. The fiery rum warmed his throat and chest. He welcomed the burn as he sat heavily in his chair. The Vicar was sweating, his breathing ragged, his heart thumping. His mind was cast back fifty years to his native Yorkshire. He'd just joined the church and had been sent to a remote farmhouse with his mentor, to visit a young boy whose parents' had claimed was possessed. Back then he didn't know much about possession, but knew that his mentor worked for the wrong branch of the church to do much about it. However, visit they did. The young Mark Adams had felt evil pouring out of the youth, who was strapped to his bed with crude ropes. Standing over him, looking at the sunken pits of his eyes had made the young Vicar's head swim. He'd vomited out of the window as the half-naked youth soiled himself in front of them. He was muttering a language that was alien to him. He'd found out later from his mentor that the language was an Eastern European dialect that he'd managed to pick up on. They never returned. The youth had chewed through a rope, managing to strangle himself in his bed. Looking back now in the sanctuary of his church, Father Adams had felt a similar evil radiating from the fair looking man sat on the front pew. He had no idea why. Jake was polite, friendly, and seemed well liked by most. However, his instinct could not be assuaged. He'd invited Jake and his family back to his church, with a possible christening in the near future. He took another swig of the rum, shivering at the thought of letting an unknown evil into his home.

* * *

Katherine flicked off the bedside light and snuggled into Jake's back. He was lightly snoring, his one leg hanging out from the side of the bed. It was close to midnight. Katherine had just fed her daughter. She'd marvelled at the little infant, suckling at her breast. A little girl, totally dependent on her and Jake. She felt so protective already. The baby had drank greedily from Katherine, the caring mother stroking the baby's palm with her free hand. She was smitten. Too far gone to ever go back. She loved her daughter with every part of her being. Katherine settled her in the crib before climbing back into bed. She smiled as she closed her eyes, letting sleep take her. Alicia lay there, her breathing steady. Her little breaths visible as she exhaled. The clothing and sleeping bag keeping her warm in the cool room. The curtains were open a few feet apart, the top window open a crack to let fresh air in. As Alicia slept her breath became more visible as the temperature dropped some more. Mist pressed and writhed against the window pane, a deep drone carrying on the wind into the room. Jake stirred, pulling his exposed leg back under the warm covers, unaware of the mist seeping into the room. Two pools of red light appeared at the glass. Elias hung there, looking into the bedroom, his eyes searching. He could make out the scent of Jake and Katherine. He knew it well and knew they were asleep in the bed. What he didn't expect was the baby's scent to hit him so strongly.

"Reggan," he murmured. *She has the blood of Reggan in her veins. How can this be? Jake must have come into contact with him, being bitten somehow. He then passed this on to his daughter.* A smile appeared on his face. His lips parted, revealing small sharp fangs. *She is perfect. Just perfect,* he thought, dropping away from the window. Alicia murmured lightly, making Kath wake from her slumber. She looked down the bed at the crib, smiled and went back to sleep. The swirling mist at the window unnoticed.

* * *

Back in his sea cave, Elias lay propped between the two large rocks. The plan he was forming in his mind would need a few adjustments. He felt confident that it could be done. He would stay close by for a while to keep an eye on his little treasure. He would drink in her scent as much as he could before traveling north to the doorway. Then the next stage of his plan would begin. He knew what he needed, and he knew whom he needed to find to help him.

Eleven

A few weeks later on a blustery Friday, a removals truck pulled up at Alison and Doug's new house. They approached the truck as it pulled half onto the pavement in front of the property. Doug's Micra pulled up behind the truck, leaving enough room for the men to get on with their job. They stiffly climbed out of the car, the sea air ruffling their clothes and hair.

"Hiya," Jake called. They looked past the truck to see Jake and Katherine were heading their way. Katherine pushed a black pram in front of her, a huge beaming smile on her face.

"Oh my Granddaughter! Let me see you," Alison said as she headed around the side of the truck, almost colliding with the driver who was also gingerly climbing out of his cab. Jake's mother embraced them both before peering into the pram. Alicia lay looking up at her, a serene expression on her little pink face. "Oh what a little smasher," she cooed.

Doug tapped Jake on the shoulder from behind, embracing his son and Katherine as they turned to him. "Hello you two. Sorry. You three." He tried to get a look at his new granddaughter; quickly realising he would not get within three feet while his wife was making stupid sounds at the poor infant.

"How was your trip?" Jake said as Katherine turned to Alison to coo in unison with her at Alicia.

"Slow. We had to follow this big lump all the way from Birmingham. Took four hours. But we're here now. I just need to pop into the village to get the keys from the estate agent. Fancy a stroll? I'm sure these two can keep themselves entertained."

Alison looked at them both before they could move. "We will go and get out of the cold. I'm sure Alicia is due a feed anytime now. We will pop back to yours and let you boys get stuck in." Katherine expertly turned the pram one hundred and eighty degrees before they both took off towards Jake's house.

"She's just had a feed," Jake said.

"Your Mom hasn't though Son. But I'm sure she will remedy that very quickly."

* * *

As the sun kissed the western horizon, the village of Tintagel once more succumbed to night. In her bedroom, Kerry sat cross-legged, controller in hand, eradicating the virtual world of zombies. In a little bar on the high street, Jeff and his wife Debbie seated themselves at a little nook in a far corner. The fire was giving of a nice glow and even nicer warmth as they clinked their respective drinks together, signalling the end of a good week. Jake walked back home from the chip shop, a large brown paper bag heaving with Cornwall's finest fayre. Ajay Desai, a local handyman, should have been unloading the tools from his van to store in his garage overnight. He had always made a habit of doing so after having his van cleaned out by thieves one night in his native Leicester. He'd been struggling more and more lately unloading the van, due to his expanded waist line and high blood pressure. He wouldn't need to worry about it tomorrow night though. Because he was dead. He lay on the floor of his garage staring up at the fluorescent strip light. A few minutes before, his heart had given out on him. He'd known for some time that he was at risk. He was mid-fifties, lived alone, and existed on a diet of ready meals and take-aways. It wasn't how he'd thought he'd go though. It had crossed his mind on numerous occasions that he would either cark it halfway up a ladder, or stood in the Cornishman's arms whilst enjoying a pint or seven. He didn't ever think he would die of fright. He would be found a few hours later by a man taking his dog for a late night stroll. No one thought to notice that his van wasn't on the driveway. When Ajay was discovered, his van was far to the north, rolling along the M5 towards the Midlands. The driver drove sedately, knowing he had a few hours before he crossed over. His red eyes masked behind dark glasses.

* * *

The blue doorway blinked out behind Elias as he stood in Amatoll. He knew it was a different forest from the one he'd been in a few months ago. It was alive. Wraiths and spirits writhed and floated around the trees above him. The giant vampire was unsettled by this. *Korgan is no more. And if Reggan met the same end, what evil now resides here?* he thought as he made his way to the village. The spirits knew he was different. They kept their distance from him as he neared Banners Gate. He vaulted the wood and headed towards the largest building. The place looked deserted. As he entered the farmhouse he noticed the porch had been smashed by something. *What has happened here?* Elias thought as he bent to look out of the window. All the other buildings were in darkness. *Maybe they all perished, but no bodies lay strewn across the village. Maybe this new evil drove them away.* The night seemed to press itself against the window. He could see mist oozing from the forest onto the grass. He sat down at the large gnarled table to think. Before he could, a noise outside snapped his head to attention. He sat frozen in the darkness, waiting. The door creaked open. A pair of yellow eyes peered in from the porch.

"Eduardo," Elias said.

"You! What are you doing here?" Eduardo Guzman said as he entered the room.

"I came back to plan. While I was away much has taken place. I had hoped to track you down so you could enlighten me. You have saved me a search."

Eduardo walked across the room, pulling a chair out from the table and sat down. "What do you want to know?"

"Everything."

"When you left, I travelled to Reggan's land. They made a pact with me to bring the girl to them. They said they would welcome me into their coven if I was successful."

"And?" Elias leaned forward, elbows on the table.

"I captured the girl and took her to them. He followed me like I knew he would. He bought the old man with him along with a strange creature?"

"Creature?" Elias breathed.

"Yes. Smaller than them. It had flaming eyes. It was formidable. It killed many of them as the battle raged."

"Tamatan," Elias said. "The demon. He can be found mostly out west, towards Monks Passage and the huge forests beyond. Where he came from is unknown. Many many moons ago Reggan's minions took Tamatan's sister prisoner. They forced him to do their work. He'd travel to Jake's world and beyond, drawing the fear from humans and beasts. He is indeed formidable. What happened at the end of the battle?"

Eddie's eyes looked at the table. "I fled. I could see all was lost," he said, ashamed. "The last thing I saw was Jake, locked in battle with their master. I took off out of there. I caused their ruin. I thought they would hunt me down. I wandered for a while, trying to feed where I could. I've kept close to the mountain to the south."

Elias nodded. "How long has the forest been like this?" He motioned with his hand towards the window.

"Since Reggan met his end. The whole forest is full of evil now. Even during the day. There is a blackness that hangs over the land. Worse than before. Do you know why?"

Elias shook his head. "No. I thought that with both brothers gone, the land would return to normal. Something else is at play here." He looked out of the window to see misty shapes circling the building. Elias almost shivered. "Whatever it is, it came from Reggan's land. When Korgan was destroyed was the forest like it is now?"

"Like I told you. Since Reggan was destroyed." Silence took over for a few minutes, both vampires lost in their own thoughts.

Finally, Elias looked Guzman in the eye. "I have a plan. The last time I saw you I offered you an accord. That accord still stands. It's time I took over this land, with you at my side."

"I'm listening," Eddie said, also seeing the gathering malevolence outside. The giant explained his plan to Eddie. The stocky vampire sat listening with interest and gathering excitement as plans were laid out to him.

"It will take time until we make our move," Elias said. "I will go back to their world soon to make sure all is well. Before then we have harvesting to do. And I know the perfect place to start." There is one more thing," Eddie said.

"Go on."

"I was here recently. In this very room. A human was here. A holy man. From Jake's world. He was dressed like him."

"What happened?"

"We fought. I knew I couldn't drain him, but I wanted to have some sport. Turns out I underestimated the human. He drove me away with his cross. I fled into the forest and left him here. I kept an eye on him from afar. He spent the next day exploring the surrounding forest. I tracked him after the sun had set. He went back through the doorway to his world. I thought at first that maybe it was by chance he turned up here. But now I think different."

"Why?" Elias asked, intrigued.

"He had a cross. He came here with a cross. It was a big one. Why would he come here randomly with such a thing?"

Elias sat pondering this news. It didn't trouble him, more so made him curious. *What would a man of God be doing wandering around Amatoll with a cross in his hand?* he thought. He looked at Eddie, his red eyes shining in the gloom. "Maybe Jake had told him about the doorway. Maybe he was curious to see this world for himself. Unless." He suddenly stood, pacing around the room. He stopped and looked through the door at the smashed porch. "I have a theory. Maybe Jake was injured during the battle with Reggan. Maybe he'd been bitten. This Holy Man may have helped him when crossed back over. I saw

Jake and his child a few days ago. They have Reggan's scent. His blood is in their veins. Maybe this man was told the story and had to see it for himself. If that is the case he may live close to Jake."

"What will you do about him?" Guzman asked. A keen expression on his face.

Elias noticed it immediately. "Nothing yet. Although if you want to reacquaint yourself with him, so be it. First though we need a new family."

"Family?"

"Yes. If I'm to fulfil my plans, we need others around us who want the same. Others who will not let the same thing happen again."

"How do we do this?"

Elias's eyes bored into Eddie's. He smiled. He had Guzman on board. "We hunt. There are scant pickings to be had in Amatoll. However, there are humans to north, south, east, and west. We bring them into our new family. They will be our guardians against the humans who will come to take back what they think is theirs. We have time Eddie. We can wait years until we have what we want. But for now, we shall stay in this village. I suggest we make ourselves at home." Outside the forest was a chorus of noise. The two were not concerned though. Eddie walked to another building and lay down in an empty bed. Elias found a similar bed in the main farmhouse. He stretched himself out, put his huge hands behind his bald pate and began to think. A smile tugging at his lips.

Twelve

The doorbell rang but no one came. The elderly woman stood on the doorstep, trying to peer through the frosted glass, to see if there was movement in the hallway or beyond. Nothing. She pressed the bell again, clearly annoyed that her persistence was not being rewarded. Finally, she gave up, turned and walked down the path to her friend who was stood on the pavement. "Something's not right," she said. "No one's seen him for over a week now. All we've seen is the sign on the church doors saying closed until further notice."

The other woman nodded. "Maybe Denise lost her mother. We know she was on her last legs, the poor thing."

"But she is nowhere to be seen. Her car's not here. She must be still down south. Father Stephen is inside, I know he is. Unless he's sick. Or drunk. You know what's been said Val. Quite a few of his flock have made comments about the smell of it on him. It's not right. A Vicar should be above that." The other woman nodded sagely. They shuffled off into the oncoming wind, heading down Edgewood Road towards the bus stop that would take them from Rednal into the city centre.

In the upstairs bedroom of the Vicarage, Father Stephen lay fast asleep on the bed. The black-out blind and heavy curtains keeping most of the grey autumn light from him. His shorts and t-shirt looked crumpled and well worn. His sleep was troubled. He'd half kicked off the duvet, his legs trying to ward off an unseen foe from his dreams.

On the bedside table were just two things. An empty bottle of Whisky. And a cross. A large, silver cross.

* * *

Doug sat in the kitchen, happily munching on a piece of buttered toast. A mug of tea was in front of him and Radio Two played quietly in the background. He'd just been listening to the morning music quiz. He normally outscored the contestants who'd rang in. Today had been no different. *Maybe I'll phone in one day*, he thought as finished off his breakfast. His happy thoughts were cut off as his wife entered the kitchen.

She looked at him disapprovingly. "Are you going to do anything today?" she said, clearly annoyed at his undressed state.

He smiled. "Not sure yet. Why?"

"Well I'm going out down to the village. We need a few things from the shop. And besides, there are things to do Douglas. Sitting around the kitchen in your pyjamas is hardly productive. And you were up late this morning."

"Half eight. That's hardly late, is it?"

"Well I was up at seven. Things won't do themselves. Someone has to do them. It falls as always to the women to make sure the housework and everything else is done." She almost looked out of breath after her mini rant.

He looked at her, trying to keep his ire locked away. "Do you remember that black plastic thing I had next to my bed in our old house? What was it called again? Oh yes, my alarm clock. It went off at ten to six every day for forty years. I'm enjoying the fact that it no longer goes off. Am I allowed to relax and enjoy my retirement in peace? Or do you have plans to ruin all that for me?"

"I'm retired too," she snapped. "And I worked, just like you. And was a mother. Do you see me sitting around the house all day listening to the bloody radio? No!"

"Well that's where we are different love. I know when to relax. When to enjoy myself. Maybe you should try it. You used to be like that."

She looked up at the ceiling, slapping her hands onto her considerable hips. "Well you sit here on your arse all day, while I make sure we have food on the table. If you feel like doing anything, maybe you could call Father Stephen. Val rang me to say he's not been seen for a week."

Doug suddenly looked up at his wife, his expression concerned. "For a week? That's not like him. I'll try and give him a call."

"Yes. You do that." She stomped out of the kitchen towards the front door. "The bins need taking down to the path. Do you think you can fit that into your busy day?" she said before slamming the front door. The house was suddenly quiet, save for the gentle music playing in the background.

"Yes, I'll take them down to the path. Shame I can't fucking stuff you into one of them," he said to himself before heading upstairs for a shower.

* * *

The bedside phone had just finished chiming when Kenneth Stephen looked up from the pillow. It had rang at least ten times, bringing him out of his deep sleep. He was just about to return to the pillow when it started ringing again. "Damn it," he said as he propped himself onto one elbow, reaching across for the cordless handset. "Yes, hello." His throat felt like gravel. He looked at the other bedside table for any kind of liquid. Nothing. *Shit*, he cursed.

"Father Stephen, its Doug Stevenson." The Vicar climbed out of bed and headed for the bathroom.

"Doug, hi. How are things?" He pulled down his shorts and sat down on the toilet, relieving himself.

"We're all fine down here. Jake and Katherine had a little girl, Alicia."

"Congratulations," Stephen said as he stood up, clumsily pulling his shorts back up with one hand. He turned on the cold tap and bent down, taking a quick slurp of water.

"Thanks. I wasn't calling to tell you about the birth. I was calling because Alison said you'd not been seen at church for a while. Is everything okay?"

The Vicar was temporarily lost for words. What could he say? *I've been to another world, fought a vampire, and have now lost my faith.* He suddenly remembered who he was talking to though. This man knew about the doorway. "Err, not really. I was going to call you soon. I may even come down to Cornwall to pay you a visit."

"Oh no. Is Denise alright?" Doug asked anxiously.

"She's fine. She's still in East Anglia. This is something else. I. I went through the doorway, Doug. I know I shouldn't have, but curiosity got the better of me." He walked over to the bed and climbed back in, pulling the covers over him. There was silence on the other end of the line for a few seconds.

"What happened? What did you see?" Doug said, his voice cautious.

"Everything. It's all true. I walked through the doorway into another dark forest full of," he paused. "Of ghosts. I know it sounds crazy but that's what I saw. I walked through the forest until I came to an abandoned village. A vampire found me and tried to kill me."

"Jesus Christ! Sorry Father," Doug said. "How did you get back alive?"

"I had my crucifix with me. That seemed to do the trick. Once I'd fought him off I stayed close to the village until the door reopened the following night. I came back home and have not left the house since really."

"Did this vampire say who he was?"

"He said his name was Eddie."

"Bloody hell! That's the one who kidnapped Katherine. He is also the one who killed the taxi driver and prostitute on the Beacon Hill last year. Jake told me all about him. He started this chain of events. I need to tell Jake all this."

"Yes, I think you should. Or maybe we both can. Church is closed. I will leave immediately. I will pop into the corner shop and tell the owner I need to visit East Anglia. News will spread like a winter's bug. Are there any good hotels where you live?"

"You can stay at ours. We have a spare room kitted out."

"Thanks for the offer. But I can't stay in your house. I have a great fondness for Alison. But we both know she would start asking questions. I will come up with a cover story on my way down. A little white lie won't do any harm."

"Okay. Head for Tintagel. Call me when you get here. Do you have my mobile?"

"Yes, I do."

"Good. There's a couple of small car parks in the village. Head for one of those." Doug checked the clock. "It's eleven now. Traffic should be okay. You may get snarled up in Bristol but if you're lucky you should be here by four."

"Okay, Doug. And thank you. I will call you when I get there." The two men broke their connection. Doug sat in the kitchen thinking of a way to get Alison out of the way for a few hours. An idea presented itself almost immediately.

Kenneth quickly showered, then packed his brown leather holdall with the essentials. The last thing he tossed in there was his cross. He wanted it close by. He locked the house and stowed the bag in his boot. Crossing the road to the corner shop he exchanged pleasantries with the proprietor, dropping in to the conversation that he would be away for a few days. The middle-aged Asian man offered to take his bins down for him, to which Kenneth expressed his thanks. He left the shop with a bottle of orange juice, a large sausage roll, and a Mars Bar. Ten minutes later his black Ford Focus was heading south. Driving towards darkening clouds.

Thirteen

Jake opened the front door to see his dad stood there in the howling wind. Dark clouds had rolled in from the Atlantic, immersing Tintagel into an almost eerie twilight. "Dad, come in," Jake said as Doug blustered past him. "Go through. The girls are in the kitchen." Katherine had Alicia snuggled into her dressing gown. The little infant was murmuring in her sleep as her mother gently stroked her hair.

"Hi Doug," she beamed. "I would get up, but as you can see I have a sleeping beauty on me." He walked over and kissed the top of Katherine's head before gently tickling his granddaughter behind the ear. The infant wriggled in her sleep, a serene expression on her face.

"Tea or coffee Dad?" Jake said, heading for the kettle.

"Coffee please Son."

"Kath?" She shook her head. The three made small talk while two coffees were prepared. Jake passed the heavy mug to his dad. Doug took a tentative sip. He nodded.

"So, where's Mom?"

"Out shopping. I've left her a note to say I'd popped over her. She'll have a hissy fit for sure, thinking she is missing out as usual. I need to ask a favour of you Kath."

She looked up at him, noticing he seemed on edge. "Of course. What do you need?"

Doug put his steaming mug on the counter top. "I need Alison to look after Alicia for a few hours this afternoon." Jake looked confused. Katherine looked at Doug, equally so.

"That should be fine. Why? Does she know she's going to be asked?" Jake said.

"No. I have an idea of how to ask her. It should work. The reason I need her out of the way is because I need you two to come with me to meet Father Stephen."

"Father Stephen? He's here?" Jake stepped away from the counter, his half-empty mug in the crook of his arm.

"He's on his way down to see us. He has some news. I don't know the full story yet, but it appears that he went on an adventure through the doorway into your world Katherine." They both drew in their breaths. Alicia stirred in her sleep before settling once more.

"Why would he do that?" Jake asked incredulously.

"Curiosity I guess," Doug said. "After all, we turned up on his doorstep in the middle of the night, claiming there's a doorway to another world just up the road. Sooner or later he may start wanting to see it for himself. While he was there, he ran into Eddie. They fought, with Father Stephen managing to somehow drive him away. So, it looks like this Eddie character is still knocking around over there." Jake and Katherine looked at each other, a coldness settling over the kitchen. They all lapsed into silence for a minute, each lost in their own thoughts.

"Oh well let's wait and see what he tells us. We can't do any more until then," Jake said. Katherine looked stricken.

"Any news on my uncle? Or the villagers?"

"Nothing," Doug said. "Although I seem to remember he said that the village was deserted. Maybe your uncle and the rest of them moved somewhere else when you came back through the doorway."

"They've probably headed out to Shetland," Jake said, trying to calm Katherine down.

She digested that information, nodding to herself in an attempt at reassurance. "Okay Doug," she said heavily. "What's your plan?"

* * *

"Hi Alison."

"Katherine? Is that you?" Alison asked, surprise edging her voice.

"Yes. Are you okay?"

"Fine, fine," said towelling her wet hair. "The heavens opened on my way back from the shops. I'm like a drowned rat."

Katherine suppressed a giggle, trying to sound concerned. "Oh dear. I thought Cornwall was supposed to be sunny?" Alison chuckled dryly. "I was wondering if you could do me and Jake a favour?"

"Go on," Alison said, throwing the damp towel on the bed.

"Our bottle steriliser has just broken," she lied. "We were going to go to the shops at the weekend to buy a mobile for Alicia but we need to get a new sterilizer today. Would you be able to look after Alicia for a few hours?"

Alison looked over at the clock on her bedside table. "What time were you thinking? It's half two now. I have to be at my first book club meeting at seven."

"Would we be able to drop her off in an hour? I will get all her stuff ready to come with her. Jake said we should be there and back in two hours. Hopefully, that will give you time to go to your book club later." Katherine's heart was beating in her chest. She hated lying. Even a small white lie grated on her morals. However, it was needed on this occasion.

"Okay. I don't see why not. Doug can help out. About time he pulled his weight around here."

"Thank you Alison. We're very grateful. Plus, Alicia will enjoy spending time with her special grandmother."

Alison smiled, the frown lines on her brow temporarily vanishing. "She's a little love. It's always a pleasure spending time with her." She immediately thought of Megan. She felt a stab of pain in her chest as she remembered the smiling face of her first granddaughter. The little upturned nose and blond bouncy locks were still ingrained in her memory. She shook the thought quickly, trying to stay composed.

"Okay, we will see you in a bit. We won't bother dropping off the pram. By the look of the weather outside it's probably best you both stay home." Katherine regretted saying that. It almost felt like a premeditated command.

However, Alison never picked up on it. "Yes, we'll stay in the warm and have some cuddles."

"See you in a bit then. Bye." Katherine hung up the phone and blew out a long breath.

Jake kissed the top of her head. "Well done. Part one of the plan is complete."

* * *

Alison went downstairs looking for Doug. She checked every room in the house, becoming more frustrated when she found no sign of him. She walked out of the kitchen door and headed over to the garage, trying to dodge the downpour. The woman opened the wooden door and stepped inside. "There you are. I've been looking for you."

"You've found me," Doug said, his back to her. He was leaning over a stretch of counter-top, fiddling with something unseen.

Alison frowned. "What are you messing around with? Katherine and Jake are dropping Alicia round in a bit. I need your help with things."

Doug straightened and turned to face his beloved wife. In his hand, he held a small white plastic box. "Sorry love, but you're on your own. The alarm sensor in the garage has packed up," he lied. "While you were out it started beeping in the hallway. I've switched the alarm off at the main fuse board to stop the noise. But I need to go and pick one of these up today."

Can't it be left until tomorrow?" Alison said, her voice raising an octave.

Doug shook his head. "Only if you want to put up with a loud beeping noise throughout the house all night. It goes off every few minutes. You can hear it everywhere. I need to go and pick one up."

"Just leave it switched off overnight. Then pick one up tomorrow." Alison's face was flushed red. She did not like being challenged back.

"That will void our buildings and contents insurance. Plus, your granddaughter will be here for a few hours. Do you want to take that risk in case anything happened?" He knew that Alison had no idea if he was telling the truth or not. She left all the bills and technical jobs to her husband.

She let out a breath, shaking her head. "Fine. Just don't dawdle or get side-tracked." She turned and left the garage, muttering something under her breath.

Doug smiled and put the redundant security light sensor back on the worktop. He checked his watch. "Right. Let's go!"

* * *

Half an hour later, Doug was sat in his car as the rain battered the roof from above. The noise was almost deafening. He just about managed to see Jake's car pull up opposite, reversing into a space in the municipal car park. He flashed his lights once. Doug reciprocated. He was enjoying himself, despite what news was to come. The clock on the dashboard told him it was quarter to four. He turned on the heater to de-mist the screen. A few minutes later a black car drove into the car park and found a space. Doug watched the cars lights extinguish as his phone lit up on the passenger seat. "Father Stephen. Is that your Ford that just pulled in?"

"Yes it is. I made good time. Bristol was fine. The weather however, is not. Where shall we go to talk?"

"There is a tea room fifty yards away. It's nice and cosy. We can hot-foot it there."

"Sounds good. See you in a minute." They both broke the connection. Doug opened his car door and was instantly bombarded by rain. He quickly got out and locked the car, pulling his raincoat hood over him. His hair was already half-soaked in the five seconds it took to get the hood over his head. He waved at Jake's car, pointing to the corner of the car park. Jake and Katherine climbed out quickly. A purple umbrella sprang up over Katherine's head in an instant. Jake mimicked what his father had done. They trudged over to the tea room, heads down, hand in pockets. Katherine's umbrella was fighting with her. It took two hands to keep it steady as wind and rain pummelled it. Father Stephen climbed out of his Ford and said a loud hello before falling in with them as they headed for the tea room. They bustled their way in, shaking themselves dry. Katherine almost caught Jake in the side of the face as she put her umbrella down.

"Whoa. Careful babe," Jake said, dodging the wet brolly.

"Sorry," she said, clipping it shut. The tea room was almost devoid of customers on that rainy afternoon. They all thought that that was a good thing. A tall blond lady approached them from behind the counter. As she approached Jake noticed that she was as tall as he. Maybe even slightly taller. She had dark rimmed glasses and a friendly expression on her face. They all turned to face her.

"Well hello there," she said, her Texan drawl out of place in a Cornish tea room. "Nice day, wouldn't you say?" She stood with one hand on her hip, the other holding a small pad.

Doug smiled back at her. "Hi. You're not a local girl. Texas right?"

She smiled. "You know your accents sir." Jake and Katherine looked at each other. Jake rolled his eyes in semi-embarrassment.

"One of my former colleagues was from Texas. What brings you to Cornwall? It can't be the weather." She laughed, and despite the situation the four of them found themselves in, managed to laugh with her.

"I married a Brit. He snared me and dragged me to these isles. My name's Dana. Pleased to meet y'all. Table for four is it?"

Doug nodded. "Yes please. Thanks Dana."

She turned and sashayed across the cosy room, showing them a small table next to a large fireplace. "Okay. What'll it be?" They all exchanged looks for a brief moment.

Doug decided to play *Mom*. "Can we have four cream teas please?" Dana looked at the others who collectively nodded in agreement.

"Good choice," she said, slipping her pad into her tabard. "Coming right up."

* * *

She knocked on the door as the rain continued to beat down, the canopy overhead offering little protection to the onslaught. She peered in through the frosted glass, hoping to see some sign of activity. No one was there. Kerry puffed out a breath, noticing how it clouded in front of her face. The winter was on its way.

"They've gone out," a voice called. "About twenty minutes ago. Headed off in the car somewhere." She turned to see a woman peering out through her front door.

"Oh okay, thanks. I will come back later." She headed off towards the village, hands in pockets. Her one fist ice cold.

* * *

The plates were empty, save for a few crumbs and splodges of cream and jam. Eight miniature pots sat next to the plates, their contents decimated. Four small chrome tea pots sat next to the empty pots. They sat next to four china mugs. There was hardly room on the table for anything else. Dana sat in the corner of the tea room, a cross-word book on the counter in front of her. She was deep in concentration, tapping her pen between her teeth. The four sat huddled close together, their elbows struggling to find a place amongst the crockery and pots.

"And you managed to fight him off?" Jake said in a hushed tone.

"Yes. Well, the cross did most of the work," Father Stephen said. "I just held it. He eventually fled into the forest. I stayed in the house until the sun came up. Well if you can call it that. It felt like perpetual dusk. Does the sun never shine through?"

"No," Katherine said quietly. "Even before I was born, the land was in darkness. Korgan, who was taking the long sleep, held the clouds low over Heronveld and the surrounding forests. While the clouds held, his minions gathered folk to feed to him. They crossed over into other

The Turning

lands, like yours, to bring back a select few. The folk who lived there endured a hard living, trying to survive off crops and livestock."

"Doug filled me in on Korgan. And I've dreamt of his brother, Reggan, ever since that night with the tooth. That's what compelled me to go and see it for myself." He looked at the other three, their expressions solemn. "When someone tells you that all your beliefs are fake, that all you stand for is not true, then you need to see evidence. I now know that we have at least one parallel dimension connected to us. It could be more. It could be infinite. What still puzzles me, is the cross. If Jesus is not the Son of God then why does a cross ward off these monsters?"

He looked at Katherine, who shook her head. "I don't know. I'd never heard of Jesus until I met Jake. He told me the story. We have similar stories in our lands. Good against evil. The cross in our land is a sign of light against the darkness. Maybe that's where our lands and folk have crossed over during the ages. We have animals in our land that my uncle Wilf said were from this land. In this land, you have vampires that cross over from mine. I never would have thought such things a few seasons ago. We just lived a simple life in our little village. It was only after my sister, Alice was taken by one of them that all this started happening. Not long after I met this fine young man," she said, placing her hand over his.

"So, what do we do?" Doug said, finishing his tea.

"I'm not sure we can do anything," Jake said. "It looks like Wilf and the other villagers moved to Shetland. If they did so, they should be out of harm's way. Korgan and Reggan are both gone. The forests are deserted, save for a few ghosts. Elias and Eddie are out there somewhere. Will they find us here? I doubt it. But if they do, we'll have to deal with it."

Doug suddenly had a thought. "Jake. What did you do with those buttons?"

Jake turned to his father as he gulped down lukewarm tea. "I threw them in the bin. Best place for them I think."

Katherine looked at Jake, a look of surprise on her face. "Buttons? Do you mean the ones that Barbara had?"

"Yes. She sent them to me in a frame last week, along with a letter. She had no need for them. I put them in the loft but then decided to get rid of them." He paused as a realisation struck. "I had a flashback a few days ago. When I was taking the bins out. A flashback of Elias. The buttons were in the bin when it happened. I thought at the time that that's what triggered it."

"You never said anything," Katherine exclaimed, a hint of annoyance in her voice.

"You've got enough on your plate at the moment babe. I didn't think it important."

"What are these buttons?" Father Stephen felt like he was the only one in the dark.

"When I first met Barbara at her home in Devon, she showed me one of the buttons." Jake paused, checking to see that Dana was engrossed in her puzzle book. Satisfied, he continued. "She told me that when her boss vanished from his office in 1951, she found a metal button the floor. She kept it, and it remained a secret until she showed it to me last year. They are so big," Jake a circle with his thumb and index finger to show the Vicar. "The button was unnaturally cold. Like it had just come from a deep freeze. When I went to get Katherine from Shetland, we encountered a boy vampire called William. I ripped an identical button from his coat just before he was destroyed. I took the button back to Barbara. She's kept them ever since, well, until she sent them back to me." Outside the window the rain continued to beat down. A figure in a dark rain coat passed by, stopping to look inside while the four were in discussion. The door chime rang as the person entered the tea room. Kerry shook herself dry, pulling her hood back, before walking over to them.

"Hi Kerry. You-" His voice died in his throat when he saw her face. She seemed drawn and pale. Deep purple smudges sat beneath her brown eyes.

She pulled a chair up and sat down. "I need to talk to you Jake. I'm really sorry. I never meant to take them. But I thought you were throwing them away."

"What are you talking about Kerry?" Katherine said, a concerned tone edging her voice. "Throwing what away?"

"These," she said as she placed William's buttons on an empty saucer.

"Fucking hell," Father Stephen exclaimed as gooseflesh broke out over his body.

* * *

Outside the rain gradually stopped until just a few spots fell from the heavens. Miles inland the rivers and tributaries struggled to cope with the incessant downpour as the clouds unleashed themselves over the green moorland. In a house overlooking the sea a middle-aged woman sat contented on a comfy sofa, cradling a smiling infant in the crook of her arm. There were no stresses or strains on her face. She was at peace. At long last.

* * *

Dana walked over to the tables, a concerned look etched on her face. "Y'all okay?" The buttons were in Jake's fist. Slowly turning it numb.

"Fine. Sorry for my outburst," Father Stephen said. "I got a bit of a shock. Err, could we have some more tea please?" They all nodded. He looked at Kerry.

"Could I have a latte please?" she said, timidly.

Dana looked at the group, raised her eyebrows and nodded. "Four teas and a latte coming right up." She cleared the contents of the table onto a nearby tray and walked off towards the rear kitchen, clinking as she went. They all sat in silence as they heard the activity out back.

Finally, Jake spoke. "Kerry, this is Father Stephen. He's an old family friend. You've met my Dad, before. Father, this is Kerry. A friend of ours. It looks like she has stumbled across something that she was not meant to."

Stephen extended his hand across the table. "Nice to meet you Kerry." She shook his meaty paw, her hand almost disappearing in his grip.

Jake took a deep breath. "Kerry. You can walk out of here now and we'll never speak about this again. Or you can stay. Your call."

Kerry looked at all four of them, weighing things up in her head. She started drumming the table with her fingers. She seemed to make up her mind, nodding to the group. "I want to stay. Things have been happening since I took the buttons home. I think someone was outside my window a few nights ago." Katherine gasped.

Jake closed his eyes and bowed his head. "Tell us everything," he said to her. She was about to begin when they heard cups being placed onto a wooden tray. Dana opened the swing door with her hip and walked over to the group, carefully placing their drinks on the table. She turned the handles to face her customers with a flourish. They thanked her before she got comfy once more with her cross-word.

They all looked at Kerry, who suddenly felt very small. "A few nights ago, the night we had real thick fog I saw something at my window."

"Something?" Jake asked slowly.

"I was gaming. It was very late. I noticed it was really cold in my room. I looked out over to the window to see thick mist spilling in through the opening. So, I walked over to look outside. I couldn't even see the patio. It was crazy thick. It was then that I noticed a faint pair of red lights in the sky. They looked like car brake lights on a foggy night. As I was looking I knocked the buttons from the shelf and bent down to pick them up. When I looked back out of the window, the lights were right there. They looked like eyes. I could almost see a face. I swear that's what I saw. I screamed my head off. Dad burst into my room wondering what the hell was going on. When I told him what I saw he blamed it on late night zombie games." The four others around the table looked at her, grim expressions on their faces. "Since then I've been having really strange dreams. Really vivid. It's always the same dream. I'm floating over a land. A land I've never seen before. There are no towns or cities. It's like the Highlands or something. There is a huge cliff that runs as far as I can see. I float over the cliff and head downhill towards a far-off coastline. There is a rock out at sea with buildings on it. People are dancing outside. Like they're having a party."

The Turning

Katherine gasps, tears peppering her eyes. "Jake. That sounds like Shetland. If she is seeing it, they made it out there." Jake placed his hand on hers.

"Let's hope so. Carry on, Kerry."

"I float back inland. I can see swamps and little villages as I head back over the cliff. As I float on I can see a huge mountain off to my left. Lighting is flashing all around it."

"Mount Agar," Katherine said to Jake. He nodded.

Kerry continues, her voice steady. "There is a huge forest in front of me. It has dark clouds above it. I always swoop down at the same moment, between the trees. There are ghosts floating around the forest. Hundreds of them. I see a village in a clearing. No one is there. It's like something out of a teen slasher movie. I can feel something watching me as I float past. But I can't see. It's like the dream is only letting me what it wants to." Kerry's eyes seem to glaze over. Her subconscious talking for her. "Then the forest goes dark and I find myself in front of a doorway with a blue glow. I walk through into another forest. This one is different. Only a few ghosts are here. And then it happens."

"What happens?" Doug said urgently.

"I hear a hiss. Then a pair of eyes flies through the darkness. Yellow eyes. Then I wake up in bed, in a cold sweat. What does all this mean?" Father Stephen looked across at Jake and Katherine.

Jake addressed him. "This looks very much like Katherine's land. How Kerry described it leaves little doubt about that."

The Vicar rubbed his bearded chin. "Can I see the buttons please Jake?" He handed them across the table to the Vicar. Stephen opened his large palm to inspect them. He picked one up, turning it over like a thick coin between his fingers. Perspiration appeared on his brow. He placed them both in his palm once more, closing his hand into a fist, squeezing them. "These buttons are evil. I can feel it." He looked at each of them. "I can feel evil seeping out of them into my hand. Incredible. How can an inanimate object be like this?" He said the last words to himself.

"William could have worn that coat for hundreds of years," Jake said. "His evil. His coldness could have infected his clothing, making them cold. I suppose that is possible. After all we're talking about vampires in another dimension. Anything is possible."

Kerry's jaw fell open. "Vampires!" she gasped. Katherine put her hand on her arm and gently shushed her. Dana looked up briefly, shook her head and carried on with her puzzles.

"Kerry," Jake said. "Like I said. You could have walked away, no questions asked. Now the cat is out of the bag. I may be wrong. I really hope so. But the thing you saw at the window could be someone we know. They may have been drawn to you through the buttons. If that's the case, then we have a problem." They all looked at each other.

"Is this Elias or Eddie?" Doug asked.

"Elias, I think. He has red eyes. Eddie has yellow. If he has found us then we have to deal with this. Or get the hell out of here."

"We've run far enough Jake," Katherine said. "It looks like he will follow us to the ends of this world, or any world. I'm scared. Not for me. We have a little girl now. We need to think about her."

Jake placed his hand on hers. "So, what do we do Kath?" He looked into her eyes.

He could see she was close to tears. She spoke, her voice shaky with emotion. "Be ready for them. We've done it before. We can do it again. No one is going to hurt my family."

"But how do you get ready? And when will it happen?" Stephen said. "Kerry saw this thing at the window a few days ago. If it was going to hurt you would it have done it by now?"

"I don't know Father," Jake said. They're not bothered by time like we are. Elias has been around for probably a thousand years or so. He's patient and cunning. He may be close by, waiting for his opportunity to either kill us, or do something that hurts us."

"But it could be nothing," Doug said. They all looked at him. "Look. I do believe that Kerry saw something. What it was, who knows? It could be this Elias. It could be something else. I just don't think we should overreact. But as you say, we can prepare ourselves. How do we do that?"

"Crosses would be a start," Katherine said. "Adorn our houses with them. Would Alison notice?" She aimed the question at Doug.

He pulled a non-committal face. "Probably not. I could buy a couple and say I saw them on offer. She'd not object to them. She is a churchgoer after all."

"Okay," Jake said. "That's a start. What else? Weapons. It's fairly easy to make stakes. I've still got mine above the car port. I can also lay my hands on a shotgun if needed. I have a few contacts that could help." Outside the wind and rain seemed to die away in the blink of an eye. They all turned as a ray of sunlight pierced the gloom, shining in through the window. It glinted off the cutlery on the tables, lighting the cosy tea room a little more.

Doug looked at his watch. "I will need to get back soon. Alison's probably got the timer running and it's her first session at book club. Best not rile her." He looked at Jake. "What's the best bed and breakfast in the village?"

"Gordon House. It's only a few hundred yards away. We've stayed there a few times. There should be rooms. Shall I give them a bell?"

Father Stephen shook his head. "No, It's okay, Jake. Just point me in the right direction. I will get a bite to eat and have an early night. We'll carry this on tomorrow if we need to." He looked at Kerry. "Will you be okay?"

"Sure. I guess, I think so. After all, I play games filled with zombies and aliens. A few vampires thrown into the mix isn't the end of the world." They all smiled at her twisted logic.

"I've got your number Kerry. I think we should talk some more soon. But if anything else strange happens. I mean anything. Call me. Straight away."

"What about the buttons?" she said.

Jake stared down at them on the table top and pondered for a moment. He scooped them up, pushing them into his jacket pocket. "I'll get rid of them later. I'll throw them off the cliffs next to the hotel.

Hopefully the sea will carry them away, or bury them." Kerry nodded, before fishing her mobile out of her pocket, checking the screen for activity.

Doug stood up and walked over to the counter to pay for the drinks. Dana looked up from her book and smiled. "What's the damage?" Dana rang up what they had on the till as Doug fished a bill out of his pocket.

She handed him the change with a warm expression on her face. "There you go. Hope to see you again. Next time try and come when it's quieter. I've been rushed off my tootsies all afternoon."

Doug laughed, dropping the change into a small wicker basket marked *tips*. "We'll be back. Next time I may bring the wife. Make sure you have cake. Lots of it."

* * *

A few minutes later they were all heading off in opposite directions. Kerry hurried home as the wind kicked up once more off the Atlantic. She suddenly felt exposed. She needed the sanctuary of her room. She would give the zombies a miss tonight.

Doug drove the short distance back home, pulling onto the drive as a bin lid skittered in front of the car. He could see his wife stood in the window, arms folded.

"Hi love. I'm home," he muttered as he climbed out of the car. He headed for the garage, aware that his wife would be too. He pulled a small plastic bag from a drawer under the counter and removed a small alarm sensor. The door opened, sending leaves blowing around the stone floor.

"Did you get what you wanted?" she said, a touch of softness in her voice.

"Think so. I will fit it in a minute. How's Alicia?"

Alison smiled, her face transformed. She stepped away from the door jamb and walked deeper into the garage. "Fine. She's having a

The Turning

nap. Although I'm sure Jake and Katherine will be back soon. It's almost tea time. I need to get ready too. How long will you be?" The softness in her voice now gone.

"Ten minutes."

"Okay." She left him alone, heading back through the garage door. Doug walked over to the far wall. He knew what he was looking for. He reached up to the overhead rack and pulled a length of wood out. It was an old piece of railing that he'd brought with him from the old house. It was planed and smooth, cylindrical in shape. He felt the weight, liking the solidity of it. *Four-foot long. I can cut this in half and make two stakes from it,* he thought. He carried it over to the workbench, setting it down. Picking up his saw Doug placed the wood on the edge of the worktop. A few strokes later and one piece clonked onto the stone floor. He put them together on the counter as the wind rattled the metal door in its frame. He made a mental note to make the stakes tomorrow. It would not take more than an hour, he thought. He'd fit it in somehow. Closing the garage door behind him, he made his way out into the carport. The wind assaulted him as he picked up the bin lid, buffeting his clothing as he scurried back towards the kitchen door. Doug walked back into the house, making sure the fuse board cover was back in place. *Job done,* he thought, satisfied.

* * *

Father Stephen found the guest house. He pulled into a parking space and climbed out of the car. Gordon's House did indeed look inviting with mellow lighting that spilled out through the windows into the grey afternoon. He made his way to the reception with his bag slung over his shoulder. He stepped out of the windy Cornish afternoon into a warmly-lit hallway. Ahead was a small counter, covered in flyers, advertising local attractions. More tourist information could be found on a small table that led through to another room. To the right was a staircase and another room that Stephen guessed was some kind of guest lounge. The Vicar set his bag on the floor by the counter, pulling a hankie out of his jacket pocket. He pulled his glasses off, carefully cleaning them as a female voice made him look up.

"Well good afternoon. You looking for a room?" Stephen quickly digested the fact that the voice was American. He looked up to see a woman descending the stairs.

"Hello. Yes, you'd be correct. Are there rooms available?"

The woman walked past him, skirting the counter before addressing him. "Sure are. I'm Kelly," she said, extending a tanned hand.

Stephen took it, liking the smooth, yet firm grip. "American right?" he said. "Mid-west?" She smiled. It was only then that he was aware of just how attractive she was. He put her at mid-thirties. Her brown hair was full of bounce and life, cascading around her face. Her skin flawless, tanned lightly.

"Correct. Y'all know your accents right?"

He smiled at her. "Well, I've seen many movies. It was just a guess. What brings you to these isles? I've already met one American today. At the tea room."

"Dana," she said. "We're buddies. There are a few Americans in the village. And a few Australians, South Africans, and Kiwis too. Maybe Tintagel is a bit of a magnet for such folk. Although looking at the weather today, I'd much rather be back in Tennessee." She chuckled to herself, her hair bouncing some more.

He was suddenly curious. "Did you marry a British guy like Dana?"

"Fraid not. I wasn't that lucky. My husband is from the States. We came over a few years ago. Thought we'd try something different. We'd ran a cattle ranch near Nashville. I'm sure you've seen City Slickers right? That kind of thing. Getting rich dentists to round up cattle, so they can forget the troubles in their city lives. Anyways, it all got a bit much. I had a few health problems that made us re-evaluate things. And here we are. From Tennessee to Tintagel."

"I like the how that sounds. Would make an interesting name for a novel," Stephen said, enjoying how the recent turn of events, however strange, had led him to this point.

The Turning

"Funny you should say that but I am a writer. Well kinda. Call it a guilty pleasure. I do what I can, in between looking after this place, two boys, and a husband who makes more mess than the guests." She laughed again. It was soft and melodious.

It made Stephen laugh too. He knew that he'd made a good choice coming to this guest house. "What do you write?"

"Fiction. I'm a cowgirl at heart. My two books would probably be classed as romantic novels. Romance with a bit of bite. Not slushy trashy stuff. A love story, mixed up with bad guys and action. Is that your kind of thing?"

Stephen put his handkerchief back into his pocket as he considered the question. "Well, I read a lot. I'm a Vicar. So aside from the good book, I generally read anything and everything. It's good to have broad horizons, don't you think?"

"A Vicar? You're not dressed like one?"

"I'm off duty. Batman doesn't wear his suit all the time does he?"

Kelly settled onto a high stool behind the counter, firing up her computer. She chuckled. "You have a point there. So, how many nights will you be staying with us Mr Wayne?"

Stephen guffawed, his meaty hand slapping his thigh. "Ha ha. I wish! My names Kenneth. Kenneth Stephen. Some call me Father Stephen." He paused as he thought about her question. "I'm not sure. At least three days I think. Can I let you know as we go along?"

"Well, we're not exactly bulging at the seams. That sounds fine to me Kenneth. Have you driven far?"

"From Birmingham. I'm down visiting a few friends and colleagues." Kelly passed a piece of paper across the counter. Rummaging around her desk, she found a biro, placing it on the counter. Stephen took the pen and started filling in the form. A few droplets of rain water fell from his hair, wetting the paper. He grunted, trying not to smudge.

"Well, I can rustle you up a bite to eat. It won't be much I'm afraid. The kitchen's closed for the night."

Kenneth looked up and smiled. "No that's fine. I really fancy fish and chips. This is Cornwall after all. I can't leave without having a portion." He slid the pen and paper back to the proprietor, running his hand through his damp hair.

"True. There is a real good chippy just around the corner. I'd always heard about English food when I lived in the States. Y'know, fish and chips, Cadbury's chocolate. It's one reason that I'd never go back home. Your food is so much better than the food in the States. Oh, and don't get me started on pasties and pork pies. Although they do tend to stick around longer than I'd like," she slapped her hips to indicate what she meant.

"Nonsense. You look fine to me." Kenneth suddenly realised that he may be flirting with the young lady. He blushed, looking for an escape route.

Kelly smiled at him, her already attractive face radiating warmth and a touch of mirth. "Why thank you. If only my husband could be so complimentary. Are you married?"

"Yes," Kenneth said.

Kelly slapped her thighs in resignation. "Oh well. I guess I gotta stick with him for a while longer then as you're taken." She winked at him, his face reddening some more. All talk of vampires, parallel universes, and crucifixes, forgotten. He looked around the reception to find something to help him change the subject. He noticed a pallet on the far wall. It was painted turquoise with sea shells etched across the front. *Wherever you go, go with all your heart. Confucius*, was painted in a deep mauve across the front. Kenneth walked closer, admiring the artwork. A little sticker at the bottom showed him the price. Twenty pounds.

He smiled as he noticed a few more positioned about the reception. "Are these yours? They're very nice. And very nicely finished."

Kelly smiled. This time a beaming smile that gave the Vicar a warm feeling inside. He knew they were hers. "Well, thank you for the compliment. Yes, they are mine, Dana's too. We're business partners as well as buddies. Those there pallets are kinda big in the States. Lots of folk decorate their homes with them. So, we put the feelers out here last year. It seems you Brits like your arts and crafts too. We sell a modest amount. Dana has a dozen or so at the tea room. It all adds to the mix, wouldn't you agree?" Kenneth made a mental note to purchase one. His Vicarage could do with a bit of colour.

"Right then. I suppose I better get myself fed. Could I leave my bag here while I nip down to the chip shop?"

"Sure. I will set a place for you in the dining room. I need to do a few chores afterward. Just leave your finished plate on the table. I will clear up later. If you go out the front door, turn left. Fifty yards, turn left, hundred yards and you're there. Their cod and chips are delish. Do you want a few slices of bread and butter to go with that?"

"That would be most kind of you Kelly. Thank you for your hospitality."

She handed over his key, before heading through a door to another room. She turned to him and smiled. "Enjoy your stay, Father Stephen," before disappearing, the door swinging shut after her.

* * *

Thirty minutes later, he was stretched out on his bed. His shoes had been kicked into a corner of the room. His luggage thrown on the floor next to the bathroom. Outside the wind assaulted the land and everything on it. Kenneth could hear his window frame rattling gently. It lulled him. As did the food and pot of tea he'd just consumed. The day was taking its toll. The dimly lit room suddenly felt very cosy and safe. He drifted off to sleep. His last thoughts were of a cattle ranch in Tennessee. Wild horses running through long grass. Rocky peaks on the far-off horizon that reached up to the endless blue sky of the American Mid-West.

Fourteen

Eddie sat in the shadows, looking out across the open expanse of grass that separated the forest from the lake. The inn was clumsily sat at the edge of the water, a misshapen collection of wooden structures. Lanterns hung on front porches that meandered around the inn's perimeter. Many windows glowed in the darkness, hundreds of candles trying to fight the oncoming night. Eddie's yellow eyes shone in the forest. His grey skin sallow and lifeless. He could smell a cacophony of aromas drifting across the grass. They twisted around the trees before assailing Eddie's senses. Many of the smells were sour, making his nose twitch. However, a few made him almost drool. His keen eyes could see movement and activity through the windows of the main rooms. He guessed that maybe a hundred humans were in there. Of that hundred, a handful would be promising. Guzman would wait. He had all the time in the world. Or worlds. Elias was elsewhere. He'd told Eddie what to do before he left. To Guzman, this was sport. This was fun. The chase, the hunt that would result in a good feed. That would bring more of his kind into their family. A flock of birds flew across the surface of the lake, their calls carrying on the wind to Eddie's hideout. The sun was about to set. Its milky appearance almost hidden by the low clouds and mists. The doors to the inn suddenly burst outwards. Men spilled out onto a patch of dried grass that faced the forest. Eddie watched with interest as two men squared up to each other. A dozen men circled them, jostling for position as the fight sparked. The bigger man landed a stout punch to his opponent's face. Eddie could hear the snap of bone as the smaller man crumpled to the ground. He could barely make out what ensued next as the bigger man was lost from view. The crowd closed ranks around the two men. The vampire could hear the sound of flesh being pounded before another sense hit him. Blood. Sweet blood. Eddie knew that the smaller man was now bleeding, the aroma leaving little doubt that he should stick around the Tacklebox Inn tonight. The crowd dispersed, leaving the prone figure sprawled out on the grass. The last man spat loudly on the wooden porch before slamming the inn door. The evening had grown darker. Eddie could still make out the fallen man. He was not moving, although Eddie sensed he was still alive. He moved from his hideout to the edge of the forest. Guzman scanned his surroundings until he was satisfied the coast was clear. In the blur of an eye, Eddie had covered the open ground, dragging the man back to his hideout. He laid him on the forest floor as the young man started to come around. Eddie looked down at him as he groggily opened his eyes. He could see he was a fair-looking lad, with a mass of blond hair. His nose had a nasty split across the bridge that was oozing blood. The blood was starting to drip down into the man's eyes, forcing him to turn over and clumsily wipe at them.

He sat up, facing away from Eddie as he tried to come around. He touched his split nose and winced. "Fuckenhell. That hurts like a bitch."

"Do not fear. You will soon feel no pain my friend."

The man tried to look around to see who was addressing him. He could make out Eddie's form stood in the shadows. "Who are ya?"

"Just a friend. A friend who saw you take a beating. I moved you away before they killed you. You're safe now. Safe with Eddie."

The man rose to his feet, shakily walking over to the figure in the shadows. The figure's head was bowed, as if in prayer. "Well, thank you for your concern, friend. My name's Hagen. Did you say your name was?" His voice died in his throat as Eddie raised his head, locking eyes with the young man. Hagan's mouth tried to mouth the words that he wanted to say. Words that would never come out. He'd spoken his last words as a human. He stood there swaying on his feet as Eddie approached, his canines appearing from beneath his full lips. His yellow eyes shining bright in the darkness.

* * *

"I'm not missing my first meeting Doug. You can drop me up there. I'm sure the rain will have eased off by the time I leave."

Doug looked out of the window. "Love, it's pelting down. And windy. You really want to go out in this?"

"I'm not going to be sat outside. I'll be fine. And anyway, you've been out today, gallivanting around while I looked after Alicia."

"But you enjoyed it." Doug could sense a row coming on.

"That's not the point Douglas. I did enjoy it. But you left me little choice in the matter. I had to see to Alicia. You were not here. It's always the woman who has to take care of things. Well you've had your fun. It's time I had some 'me' time. I'll get my coat. It starts in ten minutes." She trudged off upstairs as Doug walked to the cupboard in the hall. He slipped on his coat and grabbed his keys off the shelf.

"I'll be in the car," he shouted upstairs. A grunted reply was all he heard. He pulled the front door shut and quickly walked around the corner of the house to his Micra. By the time he slammed the driver's door shut, his hair was already wet. The car started first time as the wind and rain rocked it violently. He backed up a few feet to make it easier for Alison to get in. Doug sat waiting, the heater on full, the wipers on intermittent. He contemplated his evening as his wife came out of the house, slamming the front door. Her red jacket in stark contrast to the grey sky behind her. She too, was wet by the time she blustered into the car. Alison clicked her seat belt into place, settling her ample rump into a comfy position.

"So, what will you do while I'm gone?"

"I was thinking about watching an episode of Phil and Kirsty that I'd recorded."

"I was thinking that you could hang those pictures that have been under the stairs for weeks. They won't hang themselves. Phil and Kirsty can wait."

"Of course. My night is now complete," he said as he put the car in reverse and backed out of the driveway. Five minutes later he pulled up at the entrance to the visitors' centre. "If you need a lift, just call."

"I'm sure I can walk back. It's only ten minutes or so." She left the car, struggling to slam the door shut as the wind took hold of it. Doug watched as she made her way to the entrance of the hexagonal wooden building. He hit a button on the dashboard, filling the car with his favourite talk radio station. Pulling out of the car park he slowly made his way back home, his tyres splashing through puddles that would soon become much larger. High above the village the persistent rain started to collect and gain momentum as gravity forced it downhill towards the sea.

* * *

She said a few polite farewells before heading back towards the main street, the wind propelling her across the car park towards a stone wall. Alison almost banged into it, her hand halting her progress. "Bloody hell," she cursed as she looked at her dirty palm. She pushed her paperback into her coat pocket before rubbing her hands together in a vain attempt to clean them. The rain had died down to just a drizzle, but the wind had increased. It seemed to be blowing itself out to sea. Her hood was pulled up as she set off down the main street. As she stepped into the road her foot landed in what felt like a river. "Oh my God!" Alison exclaimed as she saw that the main street was more like a fast-moving tributary. Her feet were now submerged in icy water, making her shudder. She was lucky that she had her sturdy shoes on, with rubber grips. *Shall I call Doug?* she thought. *No point. I'll be home by the time he drags himself off the sofa.* Hunkering her head down, she set off home as the wind whipped around her. It was pitch dark. No street lamps lit the village. *Must be a power cut*, she thought as the water splashed around her ankles. The woman could just about make out the fork in the main street. Left would take her down towards King Arthur's Rocks, the world-famous heritage site. Right would take her home. She plodded forward with renewed determination, sensing she was almost there. A noise behind her made her stop and turn as the wind momentarily dropped. She thought she heard a whooshing sound from the direction of the visitors centre. Peering back up the main street, she tried to see where the noise was coming from. Nothing but blackness peered back at her. Alison turned around to continue as a swell of storm water struck her legs from behind, sending her floundering in the road. The force of the surge was enough to send her rolling down the left fork, towards the dark violent Atlantic. Her mouth filled with black water as she was swept further down the slope. She came to a stop next to a wrought iron railing as the surge lessened slightly. Alison expelled a jet of water from her mouth and nose, crying out in anguish. She struggled to get to her feet, slipping and sliding as the water flowed around her. Slipping again, she started to slide towards the sea when a hand grabbed her arm. A vice-like grip encircled her limb. However, she also felt it was a gentle hold, not threatening. Strong hands helped to her feet, moving her towards a hedge, away from the torrent.

"Are you hurt? You seem to have taken quite the tumble. Lucky I was passing."

Alison pulled her haphazard hood from her head to get a look at her helper. It was so dark. The rain had started again. She could make out a shape in front of her. A dark shape in a dark coat. She suddenly realised how tall her helper was. Alison craned her neck to get a look at his face. *He's huge*, she thought. *Where did he come from?* His dark glasses shielded his eyes. On any other occasion, she'd have thought it odd to be wearing such things at night. But she was disorientated. "Err, no I'm fine, I think. A little bruised and soaked, but I'll be okay. Thank you so much for saving me."

"Think nothing of it. I was stood next to the hedge, waiting for the water to slow down." His voice was soft, yet firm. It carried over the wind and rain to Alison, who would never admit that she was normally hard of hearing.

    She started to feel calm. Her breathing soothed as the man let go of her arm. "What's your name?" she said as the wind kicked up again. He shielded her from the brunt of it.

    "I have many names in many lands. But you can call me by my real name. The name that fits the land where we are heading," he said softly as he removed his glasses. His red eyes penetrated the night as he breathed, "Elias."

Fifteen

"Jake. Have you heard from your Mother?" Doug said down the phone line, his voice unusually tense.

"No Dad. I thought she was at the book club?"

"That finished an hour ago. She's not home yet. I've tried her mobile but she left it in the bedroom. The weather's awful. I just hope she's not had a fall or something."

"Give me five minutes Dad, and I'll be round."

"Thanks Son."

Jake hung up the phone as Katherine came to the lounge door, resting on the jamb. She looked sleepy, dressed in her favourite dressing gown and pyjamas. "Is something wrong Jake?" The concern in her voice was evident as she looked at his expression.

"Not sure. Mom's not back from book club. It finished an hour ago. Dad's worried that she may have had a fall on the way home. The weather is pretty bad. I'm heading over to their house now."

"Be careful my love," Katherine said. Jake walked over and kissed the top of her head before leaving the room. She heard the front door click shut a few seconds later. Walking over to the lounge window, she peered out at the blackness beyond. Something didn't feel right to her. Something was amiss. She shivered involuntarily, pulling her dressing gown around herself to ward off the icy feeling that seemed to invade the room. "Take care Jake," Katherine said to herself as she switched the light off, heading upstairs.

The Turning

* * *

The two men walked down the main street from the visitors centre, dodging puddles, sticking close to buildings to escape the rain. There was a steady flow of water that ran from the nearby hills. It had reduced enough in volume to barely wet their shoes. Jake's torch beam lit the street ahead, panning left to right as they made progress towards the fork in the road. The beam settled left, downhill towards the sea.

"What do you think Dad? She shouldn't have taken this route?"

"No. But we can take a walk down to the cliffs. Should only take five minutes." Jake nodded, heading left past an old stone building. Doug followed, scanning the areas where the torch didn't reach. A hundred yards down the hill Jake suddenly stopped. He bent down and picked something up off of the ground. He showed it to Doug. It was a soggy paperback book, *Captain Corelli's Mandolin.*

Doug looked at his son, his face showing concern. "That's your Mother's. She took it to book club with her." Both men looked down towards the sea as the wind and rain abated. The only sound they could now hear was the Atlantic, smashing itself onto the rocks far below.

* * *

Thirty-six hours later Doug and Jake sat in a small police waiting room, slumped in plastic chairs looking at the floor. On the counter was a plastic bag containing a red jacket. Alison's red jacket. It had been found washed up on a nearby beach by a man walking his dog. Once Alison's description had been given to the police and coast guard, the jacket was a big indication as to what may have happened. No body had been found, but both men knew that the chances of finding her alive were dwindling to a point beyond hope.

Doug sat back, looking up at the ceiling. He looked at his son, whose tears had splattered the linoleum flooring. He rubbed his shoulder, causing a few stuck tears to fall from his nose. "Come on Son. Let's go home. There is nothing else we can do now."

* * *

The foursome sat in Doug's lounge, the sombre mood as grey as the clouds that rolled across the horizon. Mugs of tea and coffee sat steaming on the small wooden coffee table that Alison had purchased from a craft fair a few weeks before. Doug smiled, remembering the expression on her face when she'd seen it. It was seldom that she had smiled over the last few years, choosing to frown and bicker with him. But when she smiled she was suddenly the girl he'd met all those years ago. The one he had fallen for. That seemed like a fuzzy distant memory now. In his heart of hearts he was more upset for Jake and Katherine. Yes, he was sad that his wife had died. And part of him had died too. The part that was once happy with her. The part that raised two boys with her. Doug had lost that now. Although she'd constantly moaned at him, bossed him about, and showed no affection, truth is, he would miss her.

Katherine took a sip of tea before looking at Doug. "What happens now?"

Doug was at a loss for a moment. The last funeral he had to arrange was thirty years previous. "I suppose I need to find a funeral director and start making arrangements. I need to call Rick in Hamburg to give him the news. How he'll take it is anyone's guess. I hope he can find time to come over." Jake stayed silent. He knew that if his younger brother were to turn up, it would be a miracle. He decided to keep that to himself. "I'm not even sure if we have a coffin."

He looked at Father Stephen, who nodded. "It's rare, but it does happen. I've presided over many funerals where the coffin has been filled with mementos and flowers. I wouldn't think too much on that Doug. It will all come together. The directors will explain everything."

Doug nodded absently before picking up his tea. Taking a sip, a thought popped into his head. A thought that was troubling. "Do you think what happened to Alison is connected to what we were all talking about?" They all suddenly looked wary. Shifting glances were exchanged by all of them.

"Okay. How would it be connected?" Stephen said.

"If something was close by that wanted to do us harm, it could be possible that they attacked Alison," Doug said.

Jake leaned forward. "Dad has a point. It's not that far-fetched. I guess nothing is far-fetched anymore. But why attack Mom? Why not me, or Katherine?"

Stephen could sense that the conversation was about to head south. "Look. Let's not get too far into this. Yes, it is a possibility. But it's far more reasonable to assume that Alison got caught up the storm." He looked at Doug, who nodded, a tight smile appearing on his face. "Let's believe that that is what happened. We agreed at the tea room that we're all going to take precautions. That should still happen. I suppose I need to make them too. After all, I've had my own encounter with one of them. It could happen again. As we said, nothing is too far-fetched anymore." They all nodded, becoming lost in their own thoughts.

"What are your plans now Father?" Doug said.

"I spoke to Denise this morning. I told her about Alison. Kinda spun it to say that I'm down here giving my support. She is still in East Anglia. She sends her condolences. Her mother is liable to go any day now. But Denise has told me to either stick around here, or head home. There will be a trip to Ipswich over the next few weeks I'm sure." He took a swig of his drink, wiping his lips with the back of his hand. "I will stay here a few more days. If you need me here Doug, I'm happy to oblige. Or if you need some space I can visit an old friend from the church who lives a few miles south. Truth is, I'm enjoying the sea air. It's helping me sleep. The lady who owns the guest house is a very welcoming too. Considering she is American, she makes a mean Full English." They all smiled, except Katherine, who had no idea what that meant. She made a mental note to ask Jake later. A flicker on the monitor told Katherine that Alicia was waking from her nap. She left the lounge, heading upstairs, leaving the three men sat pondering.

Doug looked at Stephen. "Kenneth, you go explore. See your friend. I will be okay. I'm going to be pretty busy over the next few days, so you make the most of your trip. We could grab a bite to eat later if you're around?"

"Sounds good to me." He looked at Jake. Will you be okay, Jake?"

"It's a case of having to be Father. We'll get through this. I can't believe she's gone though. I don't think it has truly hit me yet. Katherine and Alicia will keep me busy. And I'll help with the funeral arrangements."

Doug placed his hand on his son's leg, giving it a squeeze. "Thanks Son. You were always your Mom's favourite. Yes, she loved Rick too and would never say a bad word against him. But you were her number one. You were the one who picked her up from the shops, helped her with anything and everything. I know she could be difficult. But she loved you." Jake's eyes filled with tears as he embraced his father. Stephen sat in silence, watching the two men grieve together. Hoping that this was the last of their grief, he said a short prayer. To a god that he no longer believed in. *Keep them safe.*

Sixteen

As the sun dropped away from the land for another night, Mantz forest was plunged into darkness. Its tall evergreen trees jostled for position, barely able to stand alone in the blanket of the forest. At its eastern fringe a small huddle of people gathered. Torches hung from the branches, lighting the group as they stood in a tight circle. Away from the trees a large fire crackled away, set inside a stone circle. A stout wooden frame stood over the flames, its blackened surface as dark as the night surrounding it. In the centre of the group a man was tied between two trees. His arms and legs spread wide apart. He was naked, terrified, and sobbing. His eyes almost bulged out of their sockets as he looked at the group around him. They were quietly chanting. A low murmur that he could barely hear. At the centre of the group stood a woman. She was a few inches taller than the rest of her clan. She was dressed in brown leggings, crudely stitched. Her upper body was also covered in crudely woven fabric. Her arms were bare, showing off muscles that stood proud in the fire light. Her blond hair was tied into a solid plait that ran down her back. Her face was angular and handsome. The blue eyes that sat under a serious brow looked at her people. She was their leader. Her name, Karaa.

She clapped her hands, stopping the chant in mid-flow. "We give thanks to the spirits of Mantz for bringing us an offering. He was foolish enough to trespass on our lands. He will pay the price." She looked at the man. "Any last words?" He was babbling incoherently as his bowels voided. The sour, acrid stench not affecting the clan. A short, heavily-built woman threw two buckets of water on the ground beneath him, washing the mess into a shallow gulley that ran between his legs. She walked behind him, tossing the remains of the water against his backside. The clan laughed as she slapped his flesh, drawing a scream from his mouth.

Karaa smiled thinly as he sought out the boy in the semi-darkness. She spotted him, stood next to a tree. "Coop. Come here. It is time for you to take the next step. You are ready."

The tall boy walked through the circle until he stood facing Karaa. They were matched in height. He was slender, with brown hair and a kind face. He almost looked out of place with the rest of the clan. His skin was flawless, whereas the others were mottled and scarred. His teeth white and straight as compared with theirs crooked and blackened. His voice rang true as he addressed her. "I am ready, Karaa. What must I do?"

She pulled a dagger from her boot, the finely-honed steel glinting as she handed it to him. "You've seen this done countless times. Do it right. Do it true. Become a man."

He stepped forward until he was stood in front of the man. His arm shook gently as he gripped the handle as tight as he could, his knuckles white. "I call upon the spirits of the forest to take this man's soul. We offer it in exchange for your blessings. We will make sure he goes quickly into the darkness." Karaa nodded and clapped her hands. Coop stepped forward, plunging the blade into the man's sternum. The victim's eyes widened even further, looking into the eyes of the angelic boy who had just ended his life. In one quick movement Coop drew the blade down, slicing through skin and organs, continuing down until the blade reached the man's crotch. He withdrew the dagger, blood and chunks of flesh dripping from the tip, splattering the brown grass underfoot. The man's head lolled forward, his last breath escaping into the night. His organs slithering out of the gaping wound, landing in a steaming heap in the gulley. Coop stepped forward and opened the wound, thrusting his hand inside. He pulled out the man's liver, a sucking sound carrying into the forest. His hands were covered in dark blood as he gripped the organ, careful not to drop it. Looking at Karaa he took a bite, tearing a chunk of it off before swallowing it down greedily.

His leader walked over and kissed him full on the lips, the blood smearing over both their faces. "You are now a man," She said as she led him away from the group. She sat him down on a tree stump, squatting next to him by the fire-side. Karaa looked over at the group as the stout woman began dismembering the body with an axe. The rest of the group helped, readying the meat for the fire. She looked back at Coop, his beautiful face stained with blood. "At the next moon we will head west, down to the sea. We will visit my brother and I will tell him that Coop is now a man. They will shout your name and honour you. I will leave you with him for four seasons. You will learn their ways. Hunt with them, fight with them. My brother will take you to the most northern and southern tips of our land. Your eyes will see much. It will make you stronger, more cunning, more of a warrior. Then you will return here to be with us once more. We have plans to head east. You've seen Amatoll from the slopes of Monks Passage. You've seen the darkness that hangs over the land. We will go there. To take. To plunder. To feast. By the time you return to us, you will be ready. You will lead that party, with Karaa by your side." She placed her hand on his thigh. "But on this night, you will lie with me. You're a man now Coop. You must do what men do. But first we eat." She kissed him full on the lips again, her tongue invading his mouth. Wrapping itself around his. He immediately felt arousal as he let himself be kissed. He could taste her scent, mixed with the metallic taste of blood. He closed his eyes and fell in love with being a man.

He watched them kiss. He was sat immobile in the darkness of the forest. His yellow eyes hooded. The kiss ended with the woman standing up, stretching her arms up into the air. The boy stood up and walked over to the group who were tying arms and legs to a frame over the fire. To Eddie, their scent was unusual. Not sour, but odd. Almost like the beasts from Reggan's land, he surmised. However, the woman with the yellow hair had captivated him since he'd first set eyes on her. She was magnificent. A warrior. Eddie had to have her. And he would have her. Before the sun came up, she would be his.

* * *

Later in the night the fire had died down to a carpet of embers, gently crackling away between the stones. The clan had retired to the forest, Eddie following from the darkness. After a short distance the impenetrable trees opened out into a clearing. Heavy logs had been secured into the existing trees to make small buildings. Windows were cut into the sides of the structures, giving Eddie a view inside. He counted the cabins. Twelve in total. This would make it difficult. He needed to remain unseen until he found his quarry. If they saw him he would either fight or flee. And he'd seen how they dealt with intruders. He kept out of sight in the trees, waiting for a sign. The camp was settling down for the night. Torches and candles were being extinguished in the cabins until only one remained. Eddie circled the camp, coming around the side of the largest structure. The two windows still spilling light out into the forest. He heard low moans and grunts as he stood next to the window, almost moulding himself into the logs. He peered inside through slitted eyes. The boy was lay on a carpet of dark furs, his long legs pointing towards the window. The woman was sat on top of him, grinding herself into him, her breathing heavy. Eddie shrank back as she uttered a cry. A brief, stark exclamation that carried out through the window, into the trees. Eddie heard the rustle of limbs and furs as the woman collapsed on top of the boy. He could hear low voices. The youth was out of breath. He couldn't quite make out the words that were being exchanged. The boy suddenly got up, leaving the cabin. Eddie watched as he stood naked in the darkness, relieving himself against a tree. His one arm propped against the trunk as he held himself with his other hand. Eddie came up behind him silently as he continued to spray the bark. He had no wish to kill the boy. He was here for the woman. In a lightning move he rapped the boys head against the trunk. Coop fell almost silently to the ground. Eddie shrank back into the shadows, waiting for the woman to come looking for him.

Sure enough, she came out of the cabin, naked. She spotted Coop's prone figure on the ground and moved quickly to his side. "Coop. What is wrong?" She turned him over to see an angry red welt on his forehead. "Did you fall?" She shook him. He was out cold, but breathing. Karaa suddenly came on guard, aware that someone was nearby. She let go of Coop, coming up on the balls of her feet, ready for an attack. Nothing. No one was there. She looked around the forest for signs of danger. It was quiet. She relaxed slightly, suddenly aware that she should get Coop back into the cabin. She lifted him easily, throwing him over her shoulder. She carried him back to the cabin, laying him out on the furs. He was still out cold. Karaa covered him in furs, putting a rolled one under his head to keep him comfortable. She stood up, remembering that she too needed to relieve herself. She heard a noise behind her. Then nothing but blackness.

* * *

Karaa woke three days later in Wilf's old house. She was lay on a double bed in a back room of the house. Eddie sat in the corner, waiting for her to wake. Her yellow eyes looked at the ceiling, red veins running across them. She screamed in pain, her throat feeling like it was on fire.

Eddie was next to her, holding her down. "Be calm. Everything will be alright."

She looked at him, hissing. Her lips pulled back to reveal fangs that had burst through her gums. They were wickedly curved, grey in colour. "Who are you?" she demanded. "Where am I?"

"Your name is Karaa. I found you in the forest. You'd been attacked by beasts. I brought you here and made sure you were safe. You're like me now. You'll never grow old. You'll never die. You are Eddie's." She calmed down, looking at his face. His skin was grey but she could see he was handsome. She smiled at him. He was about to smile back when she screamed again. *She's thirsty*, he thought. *I need to bring him to her.* "Wait here. I have something that will take away the pain. He left the room for a moment, returning quickly with a bundle over his shoulder. He dropped the boy in the bed next to her. He was semi-conscious, moaning as he landed in a heap. Eddie reached down to the boy, snapping his neck, his life blinked out in a sickening crunch.

"Who is he?" Karaa asked, suddenly aware how good he smelt.

"He's nobody. I took him from another land. We will talk about that soon enough. But for now, enjoy him." Karaa lifted the youth into her arms, wrapping her legs around his back. Eddie left the room, walking out of the house to sit with Hagen on the stoop. On the bed Karaa held the boy tight, savouring the smell that was making her drool. She sank her fangs just below his ear, her eyes rolling back in ecstasy as she drained the blood from the kill.

Seventeen

December, 2010

Jake opened the front door, smiling at his father on the door step. Doug was holding a large red sack with white fluffy trim.

"Merry Christmas Dad," Jake said, hugging his father. "Where's Alicia's presents?"

"Oh shit, I forgot them," Doug said handing Jake the sack. They made their way into the lounge, where Alicia and Katherine were sat by a huge fir tree, decorated in white lights and tinsel. A wicker angel sat on top, almost touching the ceiling. Alicia cooed at Doug from her bouncer. Her little white stockinged feet bouncing up and down at the sight of him. He got on all fours, planting a kiss on her forehead. She giggled in ecstasy, grabbing his nose with her dainty hand. "Hello princess," he said.

"Err. What about me?" Doug climbed to his feet, gasping in awe at his daughter-in-law to be. Katherine was dressed in a mauve velvet dress that finished just above the knee. Below the knee, she wore dark nylons that seemed to sparkle. Her hair was down, cascading around her face in bangs. She had minimal make up on. Just a hint of eye shadow.

Doug gave her a bear hug, kissing her on the cheek. "Merry Christmas you."

She pulled back, planting a kiss on his lips. "Merry Christmas you," she beamed.

"Kath, you look beautiful. Far too good for that scruff bag in the corner." Jake rolled his eyes, walking out to the kitchen.

"Shall I trade him in for the older model?" Doug laughed. In the short time he'd known Katherine, he'd grown to love her dearly. She was like his first daughter-in-law Katie, only cheekier. He loved their banter. It made him feel younger. It helped him get over the loss of his wife. This his first Christmas in over forty years without her. For all her moaning and complaining she would have loved to have seen Alicia and Katherine on Christmas Day.

Doug smelt the aroma wafting into the lounge. He suddenly remembered that he'd skipped breakfast. He sauntered in to find Jake putting on his oven gloves. "How's the dinner coming along?"

"Not bad. Just need to baste the turkey then put the veg on. Do you want a drink Dad?" Doug checked his watch. Just after midday.

"Okay. Have you got anything to nibble on? I missed breakfast. My belly thinks my throat's been cut." Jake smiled at his father's turn of phrase.

"Got some boiled bacon in the fridge. We had it for breakfast with toast and mustard. Help yourself." Doug walked over to the fridge. He opened the door to see stocked shelves full of alcohol and food. He spotted the bacon, on a plate underneath some foil. Pulling it out he walked over to the counter, the fridge door slamming shut. He popped a piece in his mouth, his eyes closing in ecstasy as he savoured the salty meat. Five minutes later he had two pieces of toast, smeared in English mustard, laden with bacon. He stood eating it as Jake brought him over a glass of ale in a pint pot. "Get that down ya Dad," he said, taking a slurp of his own beer.

"Cheers Son. Merry Christmas," Doug said as they clinked glasses.

"Merry Christmas Dad. Here's to Mom." Both men fell silent as they thought of Alison.

A silence descended over the kitchen until Katherine walked in with Alicia on her hip. "Princess is due a nap. Don't you two get into any

The Turning

mischief while I put her down." She walked over to Jake, who kissed her and Alicia in turn.

"Sweet dreams button," Jake said, on account of her cute button nose. Doug placed his own kiss on the top of her head before Katherine headed out of the kitchen.

She paused at the doorway. "Can you fix me one of those fruity ciders please babe? I don't want two thinking you can have all the fun." She stuck her tongue at both of them, drawing smiles from Jake and Doug.

"No problem babes. I will have one ready." She left them stood in the kitchen, absently sipping at their drinks.

Doug suddenly remembered something, putting his glass on the counter top. "Father Stephen called me last night. Bad news. His wife died a few days ago."

"Oh no!" Jake said. He knew that they'd just returned from East Anglia, attending the funeral of Denise's mother. "What happened?"

"It looks like a heart attack. He found her out the back of the Vicarage. She must have been putting something in the recycling. Kenneth was in the shower. He came down to find the back door open. She was in the yard. He phoned an ambulance but she must have been dead before they arrived. Poor guy. He's had a rough couple of months."

"She can't have been that old though," Jake said, still reeling from the news.

"Sixty-four. Which is no age. Kenneth said she'd struggled with her blood pressure and cholesterol over the years. I suppose as shocking as it sounds, it's not uncommon."

"When's the funeral?" Jake said it instinctively, half knowing the answer.

"Well everything shuts down over the Christmas period. He'll probably start the arrangements after the New Year." Both men stood in silence, each with their own thoughts.

"You don't think that something else happened to Denise?" Jake said tentatively.

"I had thought of that. But it just looks like it was natural causes. I still can't believe sometimes that all that stuff happened. Doorways, vampires. It's still keeps me awake some nights, wondering how it's all possible."

Jake slapped his dad on the shoulder. "Join the club. I've had my fair share too. Let's just hope that all the drama and adventures are far behind us."

Doug raised his glass. "I'll drink to that. To Denise." They clinked glasses once more, Jake draining his pint, heading for the fridge. He heard footsteps coming down the stairs as he cracked open Katherine's favourite Swedish cider.

She walked into the kitchen, noticing the coolness that had descended. "Is everything alright?" she said, heading over towards the fridge.

Jake handed her a fancy pint glass, filled to the brim with a purple liquid. "Father Stephen's wife died a few days ago. Heart attack."

Katherine's eyes widened in shock. "Oh no! That's terrible. Poor man. How is he?"

"As well as can be expected."

"Does he have any children?"

"No. They couldn't have kids. His only family is a brother in Portugal. He's up there on his own by the look of it?"

Katherine looked close to tears. She put her drink down and walked over to Jake who put his arm around her, squeezing her. "You should call him Doug. Invite him down." She looked at Jake. "How do you say it? The roads should be quiet. He could be down here in a few hours. He shouldn't be alone, especially during this special time." Doug nodded, heading out to the hallway to make the call. Katherine turned to Jake, her eyes misty. He lifted her chin gently, kissing her. She let him kiss her, pushing her body into his, needing to feel close to him. Jake snaked his hand into the back of her hair, drawing a gasp from Katherine in between kisses. They parted, both sets of eyes fuzzy and out of focus.

The Turning

"I love you Kath. You're an amazing woman. You're beautiful. Sexy. I mean really sexy." She smiled at him, her eyes closing ever so slightly. A warm sensual smile that only he had seen. "And you're an amazing mom. I'm so lucky to have met you."

She kissed him on the cheek, raising gooseflesh along his arms. "You're not so bad yourself, Jake Stevenson. I think I may keep you on for a while longer." He laughed, loving her dry sense of humour. "My sister would have loved you. She'd have mooned over you like the soppy wench that she was. I miss her. She was scatty, always up to mischief. But she had a good heart. You'd have gotten on with her like a house fire." Jake laughed. An uncontrollable laugh that made him almost double over.

"I've done it again haven't I?" Katherine said, laughing with him. He regained his composure, hugging her tight.

"Sorry babe. I couldn't help that. It's get on like a house on fire, not a house fire. Two very different things."

She pulled away from him, smiling. "Don't tell Doug. I know how you two like to team up on me. You both make sport at my account."

He handed her the cider, taking his own drink in his hand. "Deal," he said as the two clinked glasses before taking swigs.

Doug walked back into the kitchen, grabbing his own pint. They both looked at him expectantly. "He'll be here in a few hours. I thought he would politely decline the offer. But no. He won't make dinner, I'm sure there will be plenty on offer tonight. He can stay at my place for as long as he wants. He'll be on the road in a few minutes." He took a pull on his ale, wiping his lips with the back of his hand. "He'd not even thought about a Christmas dinner, poor guy. Oh well, hopefully this will take his mind of things, if only for a few days." He took the rest of his boiled bacon on toast and sat at the kitchen table, munching away contentedly.

"Right," Jake said. "Let's get the rest of the dinner on the go."

* * *

They waited for the sun to set before they left their refuge below the monastery. Eddie had used the same storeroom a few times. He knew that it was safe. They made their way through dense trees and shrubs, vaulting a high fence before walking out to the crest of the hill.

Karaa looked out at the far-off lights of Birmingham. Her eyes had never taken in such a sight. "It's beautiful," she said, standing close to him. Her muscled arms now the colour of ash.

"This is the world that I came from. It may look beautiful to your eyes, but it is a dangerous place. Even for us. We must be quick. The doorway will open soon. Come." They made their way down the forested slopes until they were faced with a high brick wall that backed onto houses. They silently made their way through the deserted streets of Rednal, shrinking behind hedges when cars rumbled by. A few minutes later, they were stood at the back of the Vicarage, hidden in a row of conifers. Two sets of yellow eyes looked across the frosty lawn to the dark house.

Eddie sniffed, not liking what his senses were telling him. "He's not here. Merde!"

Karaa looked at him. "What does this mean?"

"It means there is no prize here tonight. I wanted to finish what I'd started. His woman was just a taster. She was dead before I had chance to do anything. Where can he be? Wait here while I check something." She nodded as Eddie moved away, across the lawn to a side gate. It opened with a squeak as he shouldered his way through. *His metal beast is not here. He's away,* he thought as car headlights lit the road. It was growing misty as the night gathered pace. The beams of light meandered by, heading off down the road away from the Vicarage. Eddie made his way back to Karaa, checking the windows and doors as he went. She was stood where he had left her, unmoved, waiting. "He's gone. And I don't know where he could be. We have to leave this tonight. The doorway will open soon. We need to get back to Elias. Maybe we can find someone else as our prize."

"I'm thirsty. I do not care who it is. Let us hunt."

The Turning

* * *

They made their way around the outskirts of the Lickey Hills, searching for signs of life. They were not to know that it was Christmas night and that most people were home with families and loved ones. Eddie was about to give up hope when he spotted a car leave the road nearby. They watched as it bumped its way over the uneven ground of the car park before stopping next to a low wall. The lights extinguished, leaving the car park in darkness.

"We may be in luck. Let's get a closer look," Eddie said eagerly.

* * *

Beth sat in the passenger seat as the man killed the ignition. He turned to her, a waft of expensive aftershave assailing her senses. His arm made its way behind her neck, pulling her gently towards him. She let herself be led. He kissed her with little care or skill. She could taste booze on his breath. She didn't care though. This was better than being sat at home with her dull parents, watching re-runs of old TV shows. This was exciting. She had told them that she was heading over to Claire's for a few hours. Her parents were not impressed. Christmas was for families, not friends. But she didn't care. As soon as Jay had called, only one thing was on her mind. Escaping. Jay was her boss at a local estate agent. The owner of three branches in the Birmingham area. He was over twice her nineteen years. His head was clean-shaven. His eyes piercing grey. She was drawn to the power and confidence he exuded. She loved how he looked in a business suit. It made her weak at the knees. Knees that his hand was caressing. She looked into his grey eyes. He smiled, knowing that she was putty in his hands. He kissed her again. She'd not been kissed by many boys at school, having no benchmark as to what was good or bad. She just accepted the fact that he was experienced and knew what he was doing. She sat back in the car seat, lost in the moment. His hand squeezed each of her large breasts, a little gasp escaping her lips.

"You have great tits bab," he said as he started to kiss her neck roughly. Beth closed her eyes, her hand pulling his bald pate into her dark curls. A warm feeling was seeping through her stomach, settling between her legs. She knew this feeling, albeit not very well.

His hand trailed down her dress, along her legs to her knees. She felt his hands part her legs. His touch was urgent and impatient. She opened them, allowing his hand to travel north, along her thighs until his fingers were between her legs. They probed, no finesse or care. They were trying to find a way in. "What are these?" he said, breathless.

"They're me tights!"

"What are you wearing tights for bab?" He sounded annoyed.

"It's cold out there. I want to keep my legs warm."

"Do you not own any stockings?"

"No. Why are you going to buy me a pair?" she asked keenly.

"Bab. I'll buy you a hundred pairs. As long as you always wear them for me. It makes it easier." She knew what he meant.

"Does your wife wear them for you?"

He looked at her, a sour expression on his face. "We don't do that kind of thing anymore bab. I've told you what she's like. She'll be sprawled out on the sofa now pissed out of her head with a bottle of Prosecco next to her. She doesn't love me, she just loves my money. I've had it with her. As soon as the New Year is over I'm going to divorce her."

"What about the children?" she asked.

"I'll sort that out. Anyway. Let's not talk about her. I am here with you. I want to be with you Beth." He was about to kiss her when he noticed the mist outside. His window was open slightly, the cool night air seeping in.

"What?" she said, noticing his frown.

"Look at the fog. There was none of it a minute ago. Now I can't see shit." He looked about the car, baffled by the occurrence. "Hmm. It's gone colder too," he said as he buzzed his window closed. The few tendrils of mist that made it through the window cooled the back of his neck. He cast it from his mind as his thoughts floated back to the girl sat next to him. He kissed her again, his hand moving back between her legs. He was breathing heavily as he nuzzled her neck. He found the spot he was looking for.

"Oh Jay. Oh, that's nice. Right there. Oh my God!" She was flushed. Her head pressed into the seat rest. Her eyes opened as she heard the fabric of her tights rip. Hungry fingers finding their target. "Oh God. Oh yeah. Jay. Yeah baby, that's nice."

"You like that bab? Shall I keep going?"

"Please Jay. Don't stop," she said, her breathing ragged. His finger slid inside her, making her open her eyes. She looked through the windscreen at a pair of yellow eyes staring back. She screamed, the noise deafening in the confines of the car.

Jay shot back, hitting his head on the driver's window. "Fuck! What's up? Did I hurt you?" Her eyes were wide and feverish.

"There's something out there? I just saw it." She was breathing rapidly, almost hyperventilating. Jay looked outside at the dark misty night.

He could see nothing. "Probably just kids. Do you want me to take a look?" she nodded dumbly, her face stricken. He looked at the digital clock on his dash. Ten o'clock. *Bit late for kids*, he thought as he opened the door. Climbing out, he walked around his BMW, scanning the nearby bushes for anyone. They were alone. He could hear Beth's breathing slowing from inside the car. He suddenly realised how cold it was. It had dropped several degrees since he'd jumped in his car twenty minutes before. A far-off sound echoed across the hills. He looked about himself as the sound drifted by.

"You hear that Jay?" Beth said from inside the car. He could see her fidgeting in her seat.

"Yes, I heard it. It sounded like a whale call. Like the ones you hear on those relaxation tapes. Strange? There's no one out here though Bab." He made his way back inside, slamming the door shut with a meaty thunk. "You okay? I think we're alone. I tell you what. I'll lock the doors. That will stop the whales from getting us." She laughed at his quip, feeling better that he had gone outside to check. *He's so brave*, she thought as she leaned over, kissing him passionately. Their teeth clashed and tongues entwined as their mouths came together. She broke away, panting. He smiled at her. "Wow. Where did that come from?" He was fully aroused by her kiss. His eyes flicked down to his lap, flicking back to lock eyes with her. Beth's hand slid clumsily up his thigh until she was rubbing his hardness through the material of his expensive trousers. She wasn't adept at this art, but he didn't seem to care. He positioned himself against the car door, facing her as she stroked and cajoled him. "Oh, now that's nice, bab. Don't stop."

"Do you like that Jay?" she asked, fishing for a compliment. He nodded slowly, hoping for more. He got his wish as his trousers were unzipped. She reached inside, fiddling momentarily with the button on his underwear. He exhaled. Closing his eyes when she drew him out of his trousers, gripping him firmly. Her hand started moving up and down, gradually speeding up until Jay was writhing in pleasure in his seat. His one hand was pushed against the ceiling, the other around the headrest as Beth continued to pleasure him.

"Oh bab. Wank me faster. Do you wanna suck it?" Jay said breathlessly. He felt her shift position as she continued to cajole him until something else was gripping him. His eyes opened wide as she took him deep into her mouth. He looked down at the top of her head as it gently bobbed in his lap. "Fuckin hell Beth! Oh that's nice." He heard her mutter something unintelligible as she continued. She began using her mouth and hand at the same time, looking up at him, her eyes almost smouldering.

"Am I doing it right Jay? I've only ever seen it done in porn movies."

"Oh God Yes. But careful bab. I don't want to cum just yet. I want to feel your body on top of mine." She smiled, reaching down between her legs. Jay heard the tear of nylon as she made a hole in her underwear big enough for what they needed.

A sound outside made her look passed his gaze. "You hear that? Sounded like something hit your car."

He wasn't paying attention to anything but her. "What! My car's fine. No one's out there. Relax." Beth moved over, climbing on top of Jay as he quickly tugged his trousers down to his ankles. She grabbed hold of his hardness, guiding it inside her. Slowly sinking down on top of him she let out a small gasp as he filled her warm body.

"Oh God!" She exclaimed, her body tensing.

Jay thought he'd hurt her as she cried out. "Are you alright?" he said in a genuinely concerned tone.

Her breathing was loud in his ear. "Fine. It's my first time Jay. I've only ever used my fingers before this. I'm good though, I think," she said as she tentatively started to move back and forth. Beth gradually increased the tempo as the pain dissipated. Her breathing became urgent as the pleasure inside her built. Her breasts were pushed into his face, her head bouncing off the ceiling as she started to ride him more urgently. He reached down, pulling her thighs in rhythm with her movements. They were too lost to hear the bump from outside. The tentative pull on the door handle went unnoticed. The car was rocking now as Beth's gyrations were becoming more and more forceful.

"Oh Beth," Jay breathed. "You're gonna make me cum in a minute. Do you want me to?" Another bump on the car from outside caught Jay's attention, making him look to his left.

"Please Jay. I'm close too. Why don't we both cum together. That would be so romantic," she said, her voice scratchy and hoarse. She started bouncing in his lap, getting herself ready for the home straight. His hands pulled and pushed her thighs as her tempo and the friction intensified, her moans becoming louder and louder in the confines of the car.

A loud thump on the bonnet caused Jay to look past Beth's shoulder. He froze in his seat. A pair of eyes were looking back at him through the windscreen. Yellow, feral eyes. Even in the mist, Jay could make out the features clearly. The face was grey with dirty stained teeth poking out from under the lips. Jay's eye's opened wider as the figure smiled at him. "NOOOOOOOO!" he screamed as the window next to him shattered into a thousand pieces. Beth's orgasm was cut short as two hands pulled her roughly through the window. She hit the ground, the wind expelled from her lungs. She lay motionless, looking up at a set of smiling yellow eyes peering down at her.

Jay sat in his seat, frozen with fear. His hard-on rapidly deflating as his brain tried to take in what was happening. Before he could move, the passenger door was ripped from its hinges. He looked across the car, his eyes wide with terror as a pair of hands grabbed his arm, dragging him out into the night. Karaa threw him across the car park, tearing his clothing. He floundered on the wet gravel, unable to see much in the thick fog. Jay climbed to his feet, tugging his trousers up as she approached. His mouth hung open in astonishment as he saw her striding towards him. Her long blond hair framed a white face. Her fangs were wickedly curved, almost dripping in anticipation of his blood. Her eyes yellow, tinged with red.

"Oh my God," Jay said, before taking flight towards the golf course, a long wail piercing the darkness. He was in good shape. He played squash twice a week and ran when he found the time. He would give anyone a run for their money in a race, except Karaa. As Jay reached the fence that divided the car park from the golf course she was on him. Pinning him against a large tree she ripped his shirt open to expose the flesh underneath. She was primed for the kill when she stopped, sniffing him. Her nose wrinkled in disgust as something in his scent repelled her. He smelt sour. She didn't know that it was a combination of cologne and a sexually transmitted disease that made him unappealing. He sensed an opportunity, lashing out with a punch to her jaw. Two of his knuckles shattered as he connected with her greyish skin. He screamed again as she grabbed the back of his neck, smashing his face into the tree trunk. His scream died in the night as it echoed across the golf course. Karaa pulled him back from the bark before slamming his face into it once more. His head shattered, sending chunks of brain, blood, and flesh flying into the grass all around her. She let go of the back of his neck, his lifeless body slumping to the floor. Karaa, former chieftain of the Eastern Cravens, stood magnificent in the moonlight. She looked down at the pitiful human and smiled. Holding her head to the stars she shrieked the war cry that was still locked in her subconscious. Her turning had not eradicated all of her former self. She walked back to Eddie and the girl as her cry echoed around the Lickey Hills.

"Tranquillo," Eddie said as he lifted Beth to her feet. Her breathing was shallow, her pulse racing as the vampire pushed her against the bonnet of the car. He locked eyes with her, smiling as he saw he visibly relax. He could smell her. It was a heady mix of perfume, blood, and sex. Eddie was almost dribbling as his hands lifted her dress up over her waist. Beth let it happen, lost in his eyes. She felt like she was floating on the wind as she started to sway on her heels. Guzman gently laid her across the bonnet, taking care to make her comfortable. She looked up at the clear sky, seeing far off stars shimmering down at her. She felt at peace, a gasp escaping her lips as Eddie sunk his teeth into her thigh. Beth was almost euphoric as Karaa licked her face before turning her head to one side. She gasped again as the vampire bit into her neck, helping Eddie drain her of her human life. No thoughts of Jay or her parents clouded Beth's mind as she slipped from the world. Her last thought was of a large forest, covered in mist, welcoming her like an old friend.

Eighteen

Jake's phone started playing a tune at nine o'clock Boxing Day morning. He fumbled around the bedside table, unplugging the phone from its charger. "Yeah," he croaked.

"Jake Stevenson?" a familiar voice said.

Jake opened is bleary eyes. "Yeah," he said pulling himself into a sitting position.

"It's Tony Oakes. Merry Christmas."

Jake grabbed the sports bottle next to the bed, taking a long suck of cool orange squash. His fuzzy brain coming online immediately. "Tony. It's nine a.m. on Boxing Day. What's up?"

"What do you know about Eduardo Guzman?"

Jake almost jumped out of bed. Katherine stirred next to him, turning over, murmuring in her sleep. "Why do you ask?" Jake said, thinking rapidly.

"The murder up the Beacon Hill last year. The hooker and the taxi driver. Forensics pulled the print of one Eduardo Guzman from one of the deceased. Ring any bells?"

"Yeah. Daz ran it through the database, then through Interpol if my memory serves me right." He paused, remembering his best friend and brother-in-law. He felt a pang of sadness, remembering finding him dead on his lounge floor. He'd been beaten to death, his skull caved in by Elias. He thought about Daz often, still trying to come to terms with his death. He wished he was still around. He'd have loved Katherine and Alicia. "The print came back a dead end. The results said it came from this Guzman character, who'd disappeared in the Caribbean sixty-odd years ago. As soon as the Chief heard that he discounted it as an error. Why?"

There was a pause on the line. It felt like Oakes was weighing something up. "I don't like you Stevenson. I thought you were involved with the goings on in Rednal and up the Lickeys. I thought you were hiding something. Looking back, I was wrong. I know that now. I'm still not your biggest fan, but I need some information. What happened after the lead went cold?"

Jake made a snap decision. Lying would not be an option. So, he decided not to lie. He also decided not to give Oakes the whole truth either. "Daz did a bit of digging, with me going off on a wild goose chase for him. That ended with Daz being killed. The guy got away remember. I take it he was never seen again?"

"Mr Smeets vanished into thin air. It's almost as if he'd hopped into a parallel dimension."

Jake's fist gripped the phone, wondering just where the conversation was heading. "Why are you asking me this now?"

"We've had another attack. Up the Lickeys, by the duck pond. One man dead at the scene. And a young woman missing."

"Jesus!" Jake said, waking Katherine up. She sat up looking at him, mouthing if he was okay. He nodded. A concerned look etched on his face. She got out of bed, shuffling out onto the landing.

The silence was broken by Oakes. "Looks like a local guy was having a bit of fun with one of his office juniors. Her bag was in his car. A Beth Ruston. Nineteen years old. The guy is a Jay Miles. Forty-four years old, married with two kids. The door to his BMW was half ripped off, similar to the taxi drivers up the Beacon Hill. He was found a hundred yards from the car. His head had been repeatedly smashed into a tree. Not much left of it. Pretty grizzly, even for me. We found Guzman's prints on the car door, which now begs the question, who is this guy. You say he vanished sixty years ago?"

"Yes. Just after his twenty-first birthday. So why is an eighty-year old man killing random people half a world away from where he grew up?"

"Good question. The print must be correct. The first attack, yes, I'd have agreed with the Chief. But two attacks, with similar outcomes and locations makes me believe that it's all linked. We need to find this Guzman, whoever he is, and however old he might be. Do you have any information that might help me Jake?" He used his name, trying to coax him into helping.

Jake knew how it worked. What could he tell him? That Guzman is a vampire, living in a parallel universe. Jake knew that he had to play dumb in order to make this go away. "I can't help you Tony. Nothing ever came back on this guy. Whether or not Guzman knows Smeets is anyone's guess. And Smeets vanished as you put it. I'm not sure what can be done, unless you can find Smeets." There was silence on the line. Just a faint crackle could be heard by both men as thoughts ran through their respective minds.

"Okay, Stevenson. I know it was a long shot. Where are you living now by the way?" The question was direct. Oakes was exploring all avenues.

"Tintagel. North Cornwall. Do you know it?"

"Never been to Cornwall. What are you doing down there for work?"

"I'm still doing the same thing. There is a steady flow of work down here, more than I thought. I can choose the jobs I want. No stress. It's almost the perfect life."

"Are you with anyone?" Another direct question. Jake imagined Oakes on the other end of the phone with a pen and pad, scrawling the information down as he received it.

"Yes I'm with someone. We've just had a little girl." *Shit,* Jake thought. *That was too much information.*

"A little girl you say." Oakes did the maths. "That means you would have been with her last year?" Jake's brain was in overdrive, trying hard not to raise any suspicion. Sweat started to pepper his brow.

"Yeah. We met online. We were kinda getting serious back then but lived apart. We made the decision to give it a go. So we moved down to Cornwall."

"Online huh. Well it's all the rage these days I guess. So where is the lucky lady from?"

Jake had a cold feeling of dread collecting in his gut. His next step was tentative. "Scotland."

"A northern lass. Congratulations with the baby by the way."

"Thanks. We're delighted."

"What's your good lady's name?" Jake's stomach plunged once more.

"Err Katherine. Why?"

"Katherine…?" Oakes asked, pressing for information.

"I think Katherine is enough for you Tony. My private life is just that. Private. Don't take that the wrong way. I had a tough few years up in Brum. I'm down here to make a fresh start."

"No offence taken. I may be in touch again soon. Talking of vanishing into thin air. I'm still not sure if it was you who tussled with one of my officers up the Lickey's last year. The mystery man gave him the slip. The officer said the guy just disappeared. That wasn't you was it Jake?"

"No." Jake said cautiously. "I don't know anything about that Tony." The line went dead. Jake sat back against the wooden headboard, blowing out a long breath. He vividly remembered the tussle in question. An officer had rugby tackled him through the doorway into Amatoll forest. They'd wrestled on the forest floor before Jake sent his adversary reeling back through the doorway as it closed. It was the first time since then that he'd actually thought about what the police officer would have seen. One minute he'd seen Jake. The next, nothing. Just a dark forest. He looked out of the window to see grey skies reaching down to kiss the Atlantic. This was his fresh start. Their fresh start. This news was very troubling.

Katherine walked in with two mugs of tea, noticing the concern on Jake's face. "What's wrong?"

***

Tony put his phone down once he'd checked his Facebook feed. He looked at the pad in front of him. *He was defensive. He knows more than he's letting on. And who's the mystery woman that he wants to keep secret?* A plan started to form in his mind.

***

"What do you think?" Jake asked as he took his first swig of tea.
"It's not good news. But maybe Eddie just came through to feed. I'm still trying to take all this in Jake. What threat is this to us?"
"Not sure. Maybe nothing. It was just the way Tony questioned me. It felt like he was digging for something. I have a feeling he's going to be in touch again very soon. He asked about you too. Wanted to know your name. I don't want him trying to dig up information on you babe. That would drop us in the shit." Katherine took a swig of her tea.
"What would make him go away?"
Jake thought about it for a moment. "Honestly. I'm not sure. We can't tell him any more than he already knows. We'd be chased by the men in white coats."
Katherine knew what this meant. She sighed. Then suddenly a thought hit her. "What about Father Stephen? Do you think Eddie would be a danger to him? After all they fought back in Amatoll. Eddie may remember that and try to seek him out."
Jake suddenly got a sinking feeling. He reached for the phone, hitting a speed dial. "Dad. Hi. Are you both okay?" A pause. "Good. I'm coming round. There has been some developments."

***

"Well that changes things," Doug said, rubbing his chin.
"And the police are now certain that the print belongs to Eddie?" Father Stephen sat on Doug's settee in his stripy pyjamas. A pair of tartan slippers completing his morning attire. Jake sat opposite, on the edge of the other smaller settee.

The Turning

"The first print belonged to him too. But they discounted it because they found out how old he was. Not many octogenarians can snap someone's head off. So, it looks like he's lurking about up north. We have to now consider that he, or Elias, or both could head this way."

"So what do we do?" Doug stood next to the fire, on arm resting on the surround. He too was still in his pyjamas, but with a burgundy house coat thrown on to keep him warm. Jake thought about his father's comment. He had no idea what they could do.

"I don't know Dad. Part of me feels that I should go and see what's going on up there." Doug tried to answer his son, with Jake raising his hand to stop him. "But the other part knows that it would be suicidal. I'd be leaving Katherine and Alicia vulnerable here. I could also get myself killed. But if one more thing happens I will go. We've had too many things occur recently. The buttons. Kerry's episode in her bedroom." Jake looked at the Vicar. "You fighting with Eddie." He paused. "And Mom dying too. Anything else happens. I'm going back Dad. And if I do, you must stay here with Katherine and Alicia."

Doug shook his head. "No Son. If you're going through that doorway then I'm coming with you."

"No you're not Doug." They both looked at Kenneth Stephen. "If you need to go back through Jake, I'll come with you."

Nineteen

Heronveld lay still in the murky daylight. No animals strayed close to the village anymore. They had given up their warm refuges, never to return. Certainly not until it was safe. The new residents seemed to give off a toxic aroma that kept all away. Even the spirits in the forest kept their distance, aware of the evil that now resided in the clearing. In the former Bathurst's home, Elias lay stretched out on a lumpy bed. His arms behind his head. Eyes closed, his breathing light. Across the clearing in another home, Eddie lay next to Karaa, their hands touching as they slept. A smaller cabin sat at the far end of the village. The forest seemed to be reaching over the fence to claim it. In the back bedroom, Hagen and Beth lay entwined. Beth muttered in her sleep, her lips caked in dried blood. Hagen was unmoving, his breathing steady. Outside on the porch a body lay on its side. The head lay in the forest hundreds of yards away. Worms and small insects had already taken up home in the mouth and other orifices. Blank, glazed eyes staring up into the ancient forest. There was movement in the tree line as two figures emerged into the clearing. They were dressed in crudely stitched clothing and fur boots. The female was old and stout. Her width almost matching her height. Her arms were thicker than the male's thighs.

Coop held a spear in his hand as his eyes surveyed the village. He could feel a coldness emanating from it. He absently rubbed the fading

The Turning

red lump on his brow, trying to listen for danger. He turned to the woman. "What do you think Sharla?"

The woman looked at Coop, her ruddy features once pretty, before time and a diet of human flesh had taken their toll. "I sense a coldness here." She held an axe in her meaty hand, its head swishing in the long grass. "Stay close." They moved towards the smaller cabin, the mist on the grass almost reaching their knees. They took a step onto the porch, treading carefully. It groaned under Sharla's bulk. They found themselves looking down at a corpse. They looked, their eyes taking in the sight. This was not new to them. Sharla actually felt hungry. She pushed her finger into the stump of the neck, feeling for warmth. It felt like the back end of a dead cow to her. Cold and lifeless. "He's been drained. A vampire did this." Coop immediately came on guard, his spear quivering in front of him. They both peered inside, looking for what could have done this. "I'll go first," Sharla said as she raised her axe. Coop edged forward behind the squat woman, his eyes almost feverish. They came to a door at the back of the building, both seeing the sleeping figures lay on the bed.

"Vampires," Coop whispered, almost in awe. He'd heard about the creatures that were lay sleeping in front of them.

"Don't move, Coop! They may be asleep, but we would be foolish to attack." To Sharla they looked like a young couple in love, entwined in each other's arms.

"What do we do?"

"Check out the other buildings. That way we know what we're dealing with." They edged out of the creaky house as quietly as possible, Coop almost tripping over the corpse on the porch. They made their way across the clearing, heading into the largest home. There they witnessed Elias sleeping in the back bedroom. They both sucked in their breath when they saw the size of him. As they came back out into the clearing they both sensed that the sun had started its lazy descent across the sky towards the western sea. They made haste to the next home, creeping inside to see who they would find. Sharla's axe led the way through the living area towards the rear. Her meaty arms holding the weapon as if it weighed no more than a feather. Peering around the door frame, Coop saw her flinch.

"What is it?" he whispered.

"This cannot be so," she said. Tears appearing at the corners of her eyes. Coop peered around the doorway to see Eddie lay sleeping. He was holding someone's hand. Another vampire. With a long blonde braid and grey skin. She lay there peacefully. *Karaa!* Coop almost cried out, Sharla's hand managing to clamp the noise inside his mouth. "Shhh. The sun is setting. They may wake at any moment. We need to go. Now. She is not Karaa anymore Coop. She is a monster. If she wakes you will see that. And we will die here. Come." Coop took one last look at his former chieftain. Tears rolling down the flawless skin of his face. She still looked magnificent to him. Her grey skin looked lifeless compared to the vibrant colour it was when she was alive. When they lay together. When she made him a man. Now she would kill him if she woke. Or he would kill her. He made his way silently out onto the village green. Sharla was waiting for him. He looked passed her, seeing tendrils of mist spilling from the dark forest into the clearing. It looked to Coop like the mist was alive. It unnerved him, sending a shiver running through his body. "We need to go now, and swiftly. When they wake they may pick up on our scent. We need to put some distance between us and them." They took off into the forest and the glades beyond, running side by side. They followed the setting sun as it kissed the top of Monks Passage, heading towards the forest beyond. The shadows lengthened as they kept pace with each other, neither slowing. They would only stop to rest when the forest thinned, merging with the glades beyond. By that time, they should be out of the vampire's range. They hoped. A deep drone came from the forest, stopping them in their tracks. The duo turned, looking back the tree line.

"What was that?" Coop said, his ears trying to pick out any more sounds. It came again. A low, far-off sound that made the hairs on the back of their necks prickle.

"They are waking," Sharla said, her breathing laboured. Coop looked into the forest, suddenly captivated by it. The dark shadows seemed to call his name as they crept towards him through the grass. The trees seemed to meld into one dark blanket that spread across the glade, inviting him to come closer. His eyes glazed over, his shoulders relaxing. Sharla stood next to him, her axe poised. A hiss floated through the trees, out into the long grass to where they stood. It broke Coop's trance. "We must go. I can feel their eyes upon us." Coop took one last look at the tree line. To the forest that looked so intriguing. A stinging blow on his shoulder broke the spell. "They're calling to you. With their magic. Turn and run with me now." He did as Sharla asked, heading west towards the high walls of the passage.

* * *

They came to the familiar cabin in Monks Passage as the moon tried in vain to penetrate the blanket of cloud. Sharla quickly set to work, starting a fire outside the main door as Coop used his skills with the spear to bag them two fish for supper. They were as long as his forearm, black and slippery. He handed them to Sharla who deftly gutted them with a knife from her boot. They sat in silence as the fish cooked on skewers. Both were lost to their thoughts as a gentle crackling sound carried to their ears, telling them the fish were browning nicely.

"What shall we do when we get back?" Coop said as he turned the fish over.

"We will talk with the clan. Then I think it is worth talking with Karaa's brother. It will take time to send a messenger and have the arrangements made. Maybe half a month's cycle."

Coop nodded. "What do you think her brother will say?"

Sharla considered this as she too turned her fish over. "Lars will seek revenge. The messenger we sent when Karaa went missing will be there by now. They may already be on their way to us." She turned to him. "There will be fighting ahead," her eyes flickering in the firelight. "Are you ready?" Coop nodded. She leaned across and ruffled his dark hair. "No longer the boy. You're now a man Coop. If there is to be a fight, you will be at the front with Lars and me. You've earned the right." Coop smiled, holding her free hand. They returned to silence, watching their dinner slowly cook above the flames.

* * *

Later, as the fish bones crackled on the embers, Coop and Sharla lay together in the cabin. She was different to Karaa. She was huge, Karaa slender. She sat on top, her breasts bouncing off his flat stomach as he rode him. Her eyes never left his as she grinded him into the straw mattress. Her long dark hair, flicking across her round face as the pleasure began to increase. Coop reached up, grabbing both her nipples between his fingers. She reacted immediately to his touch, her eyes rolling back in her skull as her head was flung back. The orgasm was loud, her cry echoing through the misty passage.

"Fill me Coop. Give me your seed," she said as she was tipped over the edge of the chasm, tumbling ever downwards. He felt her tighten around him, sending him tumbling too. A short time later they slept soundlessly under furs that would protect them from the nights' chill. Their bodies entwined, keeping them warm.

Twenty

The four figures sat on the porch that once belonged to Cedric Bathurst. Elias stood before them, pacing the grass. "We can all smell it. Humans were here. I know the scent too." He looked at Karaa. "Your former kin have been close by," his red eyes shining in the night. "I don't know why, unless they know that Eddie brought you here."

Karaa's yellow eyes blinked, her lips twitching. "I'm thirsty. And you are my kin now. If they come back it will be the last thing they do."

"Do you remember any of your kin?"

Karaa's brow knitted as she tried to think. She could see a young man's face in her mind's eye. However, she could not quite make out his features His hair and eyes were dark. His face appealing, yet blurry. She shook her head. "No. I do not. But no matter. If they come, they are enemies." She smiled, her grey teeth filling her mouth.

Elias looked at them all. He was happy with his new family. The giant knew more would come into their fold. He did feel a stirring of unease about the scent they had all tasted. "It's time to move out of here. We will be safer in the Vale."

"What's the Vale?" Beth said.

Elias recounted the story of his former master. How Korgan and his brother Reggan had feuded over the ages. How they had been injured during a great battle. They sat listening, their yellow eyes shining in the darkness. He told them how he had scoured various lands, looking for humans with a certain kind of blood. A rare blood. Then he would take them to Korgan, bleeding them dry to feed him. Elais recounted to them the story of George. "The young man from a far-off land would have been the difference. Korgan would have woken much quicker with George's blood. Unfortunately, he was snatched by the villagers who'd once lived here. That started off a chain of events that brought Eddie to us many years later. Eddie, was special too. His blood just like George's. Unfortunately, Eddie was more cunning than we gave him credit for. Isn't that true Eddie?" The three vampires looked at Guzman, who sat looking at the floor.

He looked up at Elias. "Si," was all he said, before looking back at the floor.

Elias continued, drawing their attention away from Guzman. "Eddie went through one of the doorways, killing two humans. Then a man called Jake came to this land, looking for answers. It all ended with Korgan and his brother being destroyed. Our coven was also deminated. But we now have you. And one more also, who is at the Vale now, waiting for us to return."

"Who is this other?" Karaa asked.

"All in good time. She is very important to our future plans, as will become clear soon. The sands of time do not fall for us like they do for humans. We have time. When the moment is right we will make our move. But for now, let us leave this place before more enemies come. We are exposed here. We will be safer in the Vale. We can use it as our base. While I wait for the right moment to strike, you all can go with Eddie. He will take you to far-off places to feed. Can you do that Eddie?" Guzman looked up, holding the gaze of the red eyes staring back at him.

"Si," he said as a smile appeared on his face. "There are many places to show you. And many people to meet." Elias beckoned them to follow him. They made their way from the village into Amatoll forest, heading east towards the Vale. Their new home. Wraiths and spirits followed them in the darkness. They too wanted a new home. They wanted to be close to this new evil.

***

Far to the west the two figures reached the settlement on the edge of the forest as the sun began to rise. Coop and Sharla walked between the trees, calling out to the clan to rise from their sleep. Figures emerged from the wooden cabins, alert and poised.

"Everyone must come to Karaa's cabin. We will tell you all we know then." Minutes later the cabin was full. Coop and Sharla sat on two wooden stools against the far wall, taking drinks offered by a huge bear of a man. They drank the sweet golden liquid greedily, thirsty from their travels.

Coop stood to address the clan. A hush falling over them. "Hear me now Cravens. Karaa is gone. She's a vampire. We saw it with our own eyes." Gasps and cries rang out through the hut and beyond as the clan tried to digest the news. "We saw her in a village far to the east. It sits in a huge forest like this. Many of you know of this place. A lone mountain is close by." Many of the men had visited Amatoll. They knew the lands well.

The huge man who had offered them drinks spoke from the back of the cabin. His voice booming. "Who was she with?"

"Vampires. They must have taken her from us, the night I was attacked. We counted four others. They were sleeping. We just about made it out of there before the sun set. Otherwise we'd be like them now." Sharla looked up at Coop, proud that he was taking charge. He really was becoming the man they thought he would be. *Karaa would have been proud too*, she thought, a sad feeling washing over her.

"So, what is the plan?" the huge man called Borax asked impatiently.

"We must go down to the sea. We need to speak with Lars." A low muttering filled the room. Sharla sensed dissention rising. She was about to rise to quell the feelings of the clan. Before she could, Coop placed his hand on her shoulder. She looked up at him, seeing the look of determination in his young eyes. Her legs relaxed as she looked out at the sea of faces.

"What are you thinking? Coop asked.

"Why do we need Lars?" Borax demanded. "It will take at least half a moons cycle before any agreement can be made. I say we go and kill em!" A few shouts rang out across the room.

Coop looked at Borax, his lips tightening. "Where is your sister, Ashka?"

Borax's face clouded as he sought her out in the room. Spotting her he pointed her out to Coop. "There she is. Why?"

Coop pressed his advantage on the man mountain. "If someone killed her, would you want to take your own revenge, or would you be happy for someone else to do it for you?" Borax thought about the question for a moment, realising that Coop knew the answer before he'd asked it. He nodded, heading out of the cabin into the forest. Coop addressed the room once more. "I will leave at first light. Sharla will come with me. I need a few more volunteers. Think on it until sunrise. We will meet back here. Go back to your beds."

* * *

Later it was just Coop and Sharla left in the main cabin. Coop stripped off his clothing, standing before her. She looked at his nakedness, her skin flushing red as a warm feeling coursed through her body. He noticed her expression and smiled before walking over to the corner of the room, slipping under the furs. He spoke, his voice gruff. "We have a long journey ahead. We'll be sleeping in the forest with none of these comforts. Come. Keep me warm." She advanced on him, her clothes landing in a pile on the floor as she slipped under the furs next to him.

Twenty-One

Jake's new 4x4 pulled up outside the white semi-detached house. The New Year had come and gone, bringing milder, sunny weather. Katherine was unclipping the baby seat from the back of the car when the front door of the house opened. Jake waved at Barbara, who stood ramrod straight on the front step.

A middle-aged woman with a mass of red hair walked past the house. "Mornin', Barb. You okay?" she said as she slowed her pace.

"Hi Marion. I'm good thanks. Got some friends from that Cornwall here to see me."

The other woman smiled. "Not locals then?" she smiled at Katherine, who held the car seat in the crook of her arm. Katherine smiled back, liking the woman's friendly face. Marion looked down at Alicia who was just waking up. "Oh, she's a little cracker. What's her name?" she asked. Her Devonshire twang as light as the weather.

"Alicia," Katherine said proudly as Jake came around the car to stand next to her.

"What a lovely name. Oh, just look at her face," Marion said. "Proper little princess that one." She looked over at Barbara. "I envy you Barb. While you're 'avin cuddles with this little beauty I'll be in Newton Abbot doin' the bloody grocery shop."

Barbara smiled. "Oh well. You get plenty of cuddles with little Henry just down the road."

Marion smiled, instantly thinking about her grandson. "You're right Barb. I'm a selfish whatsit. You enjoy it. Be seein' ya." Jake and Katherine nodded as the woman made her past them along the path.

"Are you coming in or shall we have a tea party in the street?" Barbara said with a mirthful expression on her face. They both smiled as they made their way up the path to the house.

Jake made the introductions. "Katherine, this is Barbara. Barbara, this is Katherine." The older woman kissed Katherine on the cheek, pulling her towards her for a hug. The younger woman returned the embrace with one arm as she held the car seat in the other.

Letting Katherine go, she planted a kiss on Jake's cheek, squeezing him with a strength that shocked Jake. "And who do we have here?" she said peering down at Alicia. The baby gurgled at her, drawing smiles from them. "Come on in. The kettle's just boiled and I have cake."

"Sounds good to me," said Katherine as she walked into the cosy hallway, with Jake bringing up the rear. Placing the car seat on the floor, Katherine removed her ankle boots and coat, standing in a brown full-length knitted dress.

Barbara appraised her as Jake kicked off his pumps and hung his burgundy body warmer over the banister. "Love the dress. Really snazzy."

"Thank you Barbara. Where did we get it from Jake? I'm still getting used to all the place names."

"Totnes." Katherine nodded in recognition, mentally saying the name in her head.

"Nice town Totnes. Lots of nice boutiques and craft shops. Anyway, go on through and get comfy. I'll bring in the refreshments." They made their way into the lounge. It was as Jake remembered. Two small sofas with a square coffee table between them sat one end of the room facing an old boxy television set. A giant bookshelf took up half of the one wall, with an old music centre on the other. At the other end of the room sat a sturdy looking dining table with a laptop on a place-mat. Jake smiled. *She's still surfing the net*, he thought as the sound

The Turning

of tea being poured filtered through the house. Katherine had Alicia out of her seat, sitting her on her lap. She wore a pink outfit that was full of frills. White woolly leggings and pink booties completed her ensemble. Jake loved how Katherine dressed their daughter. She was like the proverbial kid in a sweet shop when they were looking for clothes for Alicia.

Katherine pulled out a small black bottle holder. She deftly unzipped it, removing a pink plastic bottle inside. Flipping off the lid, the younger woman tested it. "Perfect. She can have this now babe," she said as he got comfy.

Barbara came in clutching the tray of goodies, smiling at Katherine and Alicia. "Looks like we're all having treats," she said setting the tray down. A few minutes later they were all enjoying tea and homemade carrot cake. Katherine was multitasking, impressing the older woman with her dexterity and calmness.

"So, Katherine," Barbara began. "How does Earth compare to your world?" Jake smiled at her directness. She had lost none of her faculties after being attacked by Elias the year before. Jake remembered how he'd felt when Daz had told him she'd been hurt. That was right before his friend was murdered. It all seemed like a distant memory now, although he still bore both mental and physical scars.

Katherine put down her china cup, washing down the last crumbs of the cake. "Everything is so fast here. So modern and civilised. So normal. It's nice to see the sun most days. Where I grew up was so different. I suppose you could say it was a world away from this." Barbara chuckled as Katherine paused for thought. "I'd never want to return, except to see my kin. My uncle Wilf is still out there, somewhere. We're hoping he made it to safety with the rest of the folk."

Jake placed a hand on her knee. "I'm sure he did. He's a tough old crow. Believe me, I know. I've seen him take down vampires. Not bad for someone of his age."

"How old is he?" Barbara asked. Jake considered the question.

"In this world, he'd probably be in his sixties. Why? Are you after a toy boy?"

She burst out laughing, needing to put her tea on the table for fear of spilling it. "That might not be a bad idea. I'm a bit out of practice though." Katherine looked puzzled by the exchange.

"What's a boy toy?"

Jake chuckled. "Toy boy. It means when a woman goes with a much younger man. Barbara might be interested in getting together with Wilf."

Katherine laughed too. "Oh my. That sounds like a great idea. He has never had himself a wife." They all smiled, enjoying the warm feeling spreading between them.

Barbara's face dropped slightly as something came to her. "Any news on Eddie?" Jake and Katherine exchanged glances.

"Well yes," Jake began. "There has been another murder, in roughly the same place. Eddie's print was found at the scene."

Barbara gasped. "Never!" She sat back in her chair.

"Afraid so. By the way, where's your dog?"

Barbara was at a loss for words for a moment. The news shocking her. "He's out in the utility room. Didn't want him in here with the baby. Not that he'd do anything." Barbara changed tack again. "How do you know about the murder?"

"A former colleague called me and gave me the information. Because it was linked to the other murder. The one that brought me here to you. They wanted to try and get all the information out of me that they could."

"And did they?" she asked as a white van rumbled passed the front window.

"No. I mean what could I tell them? That Eddie was a vampire. That there is a doorway to another world up the Lickey Hills. The men in white coats would come running." Jake finished his tea, preparing himself for the next update. "There is more. A family friend of mine, a Vicar called Father Stephen went through the doorway a few months ago and came across Eddie." Barbara's jaw fell open. "Father Stephen was there the night I was bitten. He fixed my leg, so to speak. I still make trips to church every week to somehow keep whatever it is at bay. There have also been some bad things happening in Tintagel."

"Go on," Barbara said, fearing the worst.

"Mom died. Just before Christmas. Did you hear on the news about the storms?" Barbara nodded, her face stricken. "Well, Mom was on her way home from book club and was caught up in it. The police think she was swept out to sea by the floods."

"Oh Jake. I'm truly sorry to hear that." She reached across and squeezed his hand.

He smiled, the tears in his eyes held back for the moment. "Thanks Barbara. But there's more. When you sent me the buttons in the post, they somehow gave me a flashback. I saw the thing that attacked you. He was right there by my kitchen door. Then he vanished." The sounds of sucking air told them that Alicia had finished her bottle. Katherine placed her on her lap and gently rubbed her back, bringing her wind up after a few seconds. Jake needed to get the rest off his chest so Barbara could take it all in. "A friend of ours, Kerry found the buttons in my recycle bin. I'd thrown them away because I thought it best. Anyway, Kerry took them home with her. She came to us a few days later, telling us that she had seen red eyes at her window. The man who attacked you, who went by the name of Smeets had red eyes, remember. Although his real name is Elias. You said that when you knew him he was called Doctor Brogan. Is that right?"

"That's right. Brogan. Strange chap. Apparently very strange from what you're telling me." She sat back on the sofa, trying to take it all in. She remembered the tall reedy doctor, with his black coat and hat, who'd visited their office in Puerto Rico way back when. He'd given her the creeps. She could still recall his deep voice. Could picture how he almost floated through the office, bending to enter Eddie's before the door closed slowly.

She sat in silence recounting the past while Jake turned to Katherine. "Is she okay?"

Katherine nodded. "All the windy pops are out," she said, standing up with the baby in her arms. She walked her daughter around the lounge, her stockinged feet barely making a sound. Alicia too, was quiet and content.

"So, what does all this mean Jake?" Barbara said as she snapped back to attention.

"Honestly. I don't know. We've all gone over it, time and time again. My gut feeling is that something else will happen."

"You don't know that babe," Katherine said as she stood at the end of the dining room, looking over the small garden with a tinkling brook at the bottom of it.

"No, I don't. It's my gut feeling. I can't explain it. Too many things have happened over the last few months that make me think that this isn't done yet." He looked at Barbara who had a shell-shocked expression on her face. "I'm sorry to dump all this on you. Part of the reason I've told you everything is because I wanted to know if you've seen anything unusual?"

"No. Nothing at all. Everything has been just fine. You don't think that-?"

"No," Jake interjected swiftly, not wanted to scare the old lady. "I don't think that anyone is coming to pay you a visit Barbara. I think you're off the radar."

She put her hands on the arm of the chair, levering herself upright. She suddenly felt very old. And very small. She absently rubbed any crumbs from her slacks before walking over to the front window. The sunlight spilled in through the net curtains, warming her skin. She turned to Jake. "What do I need to do Jake?"

He stood and walked over to her, glad of the warmth on his skin after the coolness of the conversation. "If I'm being totally honest with you Barbara. The only thing I'd suggest is to buy a few crucifixes. You don't wear any jewellery. So maybe one around your neck too. They do work," he said tapping his own cross. It was black, onyx. It seemed stuck to his chest. "Which is twisted logic if you think about it." She knew what he meant instantly. *How could a cross ward off a monster? The symbol of a false god!* "If anything happens, call me. Immediately. Day or night."

"I suppose I've always got my killer guard dog to keep me safe." Her attempt at humour felt flat and hollow. "Look, Jake. I'm sure I'll be fine. I'm an old bugger now, north of eighty. Almost all my life I've tried to find the answers to what happened back in fifty-one. And now I have the answers. So, if a vampire decides to turn up again and do me in, so be it. At least I'll go to my grave satisfied that I've found out the truth." She looked through the net curtains at her front garden. "You've made a huge difference to my life. Without meeting you I'd still be surfing the net, looking for missing persons and so on. I've not done that for months. Even the other guy I was looking into, Owen, I think his name was. I gave up on that. There is a good chance that he was taken like Eddie was."

"There is every chance." Jake said. "When we went to their hideout there were empty cells. Cells that probably contained humans whom they'd fed off. And you remember I told you that George was destined for that place, before being rescued by Katherine's ancestors?"

"Yes I remember. I'm so glad he was. Otherwise you'd not have your new beautiful family." Jake looked at Katherine holding Alicia and smiled.

"You're right there. Funny how life throws curve balls at you from time to time." Barbara smiled, looking back out through the net curtains.

"Nice car by the way. What's it called?"

"It's a Pathfinder. I never knew that having a baby took up so much room. If we have another one I may need a bus."

Barbara smiled, clapping him on the shoulder. "Right! I don't know about you, but all this talk of other worlds has made me hungry."

Twenty-Two

Tony Oakes placed the phone back in the cradle and sat pondering in his dimly lit cubby hole that was supposed to be an office. The small window looked out onto the grey police station's car park. Trees could be seen in the distance, providing some colour to the drab facade. He picked up his mobile phone, finding the number he needed. He placed the phone to his ear, waiting impatiently. "Chris. It's Tony." The other man responded. "Not bad thanks. You?" He listened to the reply, drumming his fingers on his pad. "I need some info. Last year when you tackled Jake Stevenson up the Lickey Hills. Could you tell me the exact spot where you lost him?" He drummed his fingers some more as the other man gave him a location. "Okay. Cheers for that. You can go back to sleep now. Speak soon." He stood up, grabbing his jacket from the back of his chair. He awkwardly slipped it over his bulky shoulders, telling himself he needed a larger coat soon. He took one look at the pad on his desk, shaking his head before leaving the office. The pad sat on the desk. A few phone numbers were scrawled across the top of the page. Further down there was a sketch in the centre of the page. A simple sketch, done in black biro. A ghost.

* * *

Twenty minutes later he killed the ignition, climbing out of his BMW into a dull, dreary January morning. He looked across the road to Ben's Fish & Chip shop that backed onto the Lickey Hills. A few old timers were stood outside the newsagents next door, their dogs sniffing each other's backsides. He checked left and right before crossing the road as a few snowflakes started to fall. Tony zipped his jacket up over his muscular chest, the zip straining over his bulk. He was sweating by the time he'd climbed the private driveway that led to the forest beyond. He was a tad less than six feet, with closely cropped hair. Steel rimmed glasses sat in front of dark piggy eyes that regarded the world with cynicism. His heavy frame was now muscular instead of flabby. He'd spent the last two years losing the fat that he'd carried for years. Other officers called him Juggernaut behind his back. He didn't care. Tony kind of liked it. The snow was getting heavier now as the man approached the location that he was looking for. His zip strained once more as he pulled it down to his waist band, exposing the grey shirt underneath. He reached the spot that Chris had told him about as a wind kicked up, sending flakes swirling around the trees. Tony rested against a trunk, his breathing ragged. He could bench-press more than his own bodyweight, but he needed to work on his cardio. As his breathing slowed he looked at the two trees in front of him. He stepped away from the tree, his brow furrowing. The ground around the trees seemed scorched. It looked like someone had started a fire. The tree trunks had a grey residue on them that came off when he rubbed it with his palm. He sniffed his hand, expecting to get a waft of smoke. *Nothing.* No odour was given off, making his brow crease even more. He tried again, this time sniffing much harder. A few grains of the residue were sucked into his nose, becoming tendrils of smoke. He staggered backwards a few steps, blowing his nose, rubbing his face to try and somehow swat it away from him. *What the fuck was that?* he thought as his head cleared. *Something is not right here. It feels... spooky.* Tony walked back to the two trees, ignoring the trunks. He looked down at the ground to see a faint line that ran between them, across the forest floor. He bent down, his trousers protesting against his meaty thighs as he did so. He ran his finger along the line, wondering why it was completely straight. His pink palm rubbed against his stubbly chin as thoughts ran through his head. *What the hell am I looking at? A line on the ground.*

A noise invaded his thoughts. A deep drone that sounded far away, but clear. He stood up, circling the trees as the blood flowed back into his legs. Walking back to the tree he'd rested on, he pulled out his smart phone. Selecting camera, he proceeded to take a dozen shots of the things he'd looked at. For what reason, he didn't rightly know. He was a detective. And his senses were telling him that something strange was happening here. There had been four murders and one person was missing. This had all happened very close by. Jake Stevenson had chased Sergeant Harris' killer along this stretch of forest. And a man believed to have been Stevenson had fought with one of his colleagues, before somehow vanishing into the night. Something occurred to Tony as he stood watching snowflakes fall around him. The time. Midnight. All the activity relating to this had happened around midnight. *Could it be coincidence?* he thought. His instincts were telling him no. He would head back to the station to double check the information. Then he would decide his next steps.

* * *

Half a mile to the south, Kenneth Stephen was tidying his back garden. The snow was now falling steadily, starting to cover his lawn in a white blanket. He carried a large black bin liner in one hand, picking up pieces of litter that had collected over the winter. His wife used to take care of the garden, keeping it immaculate. Now Kenneth had to take over the reins with far less enthusiasm than Denise had. He moved over to the row of conifers, picking up crisp packets and empty bottles that the local kids had no doubt thrown over the fence. As he bent down to grab an empty can of lager something caught his eye. He reached into the tree line and pulled out a dagger. His brow creased in confusion as he turned it over in his hands. He walked back through the garden, kicking his shoes off onto the mat as he stepped into the kitchen. Kenneth flicked on the hot tap on and rinsed the knife under the water, cleaning off the dirt with his thumb. Grabbing a tea towel,

The Turning

he patted it dry, heading over to the kitchen table to take a closer look. Donning his glasses, The Vicar turned the weapon over, looking at the handle first. It was wooden, wrapped in leather or something similar. He tested the blade with his thumb, surprised when the slightest pressure split his skin. He put his thumb in his mouth, sucking the wound as he looked at the blade. Apart from being razor sharp it was also a strange colour, almost green in its appearance. He studied it under the overhead lights, trying to find a company logo or identification marks. Nothing. It was not mass produced. It was a one off. Hand made by someone who had attention to detail and skill. He became aware that the hand holding the hilt was starting to feel cool. Not cold, but cool. The whole thing was gently radiating an unnatural coolness. The thunderbolt of realisation almost knocked him off the chair.

"The buttons," he blurted. "It's like the buttons." Stephen sat there for a few seconds, trying to digest what his brain was telling him. *Something has been in my back garden. Something has been watching me. Something or someone not from this world.* Another thunderbolt hit him. He almost felt his heart break with the pain. *Denise. What if she didn't die by natural causes? What if someone killed her? Or scared her to death?* The chair flew back across the tiled floor, crashing into the cupboards behind. He started pacing the kitchen, his mind a maelstrom of thoughts and ideas. *Eddie. He could have done this. He could have come here looking for me, but ended up killing Denise instead.* The man walked over to the table and picked up the knife, holding it in his palm. He gripped the handle as he thought what he should do. More pacing around the kitchen, his hand gradually turning numb. The Vicar in him was slowly evaporating, being replaced by a grieving husband. A man. Flesh and blood, becoming consumed by guilt, rage, and revenge. His hand was now tingling with cold. He looked down at it, before plunging the knife into the kitchen table. It quivered, the handle pointing to the ceiling as he left the kitchen. He returned a few minutes later with a tool box. He dropped it on the table, flipping the lid open before rummaging around inside. He found what he was looking for. A chisel. Kenneth tested the blade, annoyed that it appeared blunt. He had time though. It was still morning. He had twelve hours before he needed to leave. His large hand pulled a small sharpening stone out of the tool box, along with some lubricant spray. He doused the stone in a fine mist before working the blade back and forth to hone it. Five minutes later it was razor sharp. He put the stone and spray on the counter top, aware that he may need it again before he was finished. Picking up a kitchen chair, the Vicar flipped it upside-down on the table. The four legs were thick at the one end, gradually becoming thinner at the other. Four small plastic leg ends stopped the wood from being damaged on the floor. He set to work, gradually shaving wood from the leg until the one end had a sharp point. His brow was peppered with perspiration as he tested the point. "Perfect," he said to himself.

* * *

Later that on that Friday night, Kenneth sat at the kitchen table and took stock of his plan. *Find Eddie and destroy him. Hide out in the village until the next night. Come back home.* He knew that was the perfect scenario. There was a good chance that he may never come back. *But what is there to come home for?* he thought. *I have nothing here now. Even my parishioners have deserted me. It's only a matter of time before the church comes calling, too.* He looked at the clock on the wall. Almost nine. Stephen needed to eat something and get the house in order before he left. A brown haversack sat on the kitchen table next to him. He hoped he had everything he needed in there. He hoped he wasn't stopped by the police on his way to the doorway. A thought occurred to him as he shrugged on his jacket. *I need to tell them where I'm going.* He picked up his mobile phone, dialling a number as he headed off through the front door towards the chip shop down the road.

* * *

Doug walked through his front door, into his hallway. He kicked off his loafers next to the telephone table, hanging his coat on the bottom of the banister rail. He was stuffed. He'd spent the night with Katherine, Jake, and Alicia. Jake had cooked a lamb curry that was making his belt buckle strain somewhat. The man decided to finish the night off with a beer in front of the television. The house was quiet. Over the last few months it started to feel cold to Doug. He missed his wife. He'd give anything to have her stood leaning against the door jamb, remonstrating with him for drinking too much beer, or not putting the toilet roll on the correct way. He would always wonder what had exactly happened. No body had been found. There was always a chance she could come walking back through the door. He was no fool though. Those chances were slim to non-existent. As he slammed the fridge door shut he noticed his mobile phone on the worktop. A small blue light was flashing in the corner. He unlocked the phone, noticing he'd had a missed call. There was also an answer phone message. Strange, he thought as he dialled his voicemail service. His phone told him he had one new message. Received almost an hour ago.

"Hi Doug. It's Kenneth. I was hoping to catch you before I set off. Things have happened here. I won't go into all the details but it looks like one of those things has been at my house. They may also have killed Denise." Doug stood there, mouth slowly opening as he gripped the phone tighter. "I'm going through the doorway. I want to find this Eddie character and make him pay. I've got enough with me to get it done. If you don't hear from me in the next week, you know that I didn't make it. In which case I just wanted to say farewell. You're a good man Doug. Take good care of yourself and your family. Bye." It took him a few seconds to shake himself from his daze. He redialled the number, listening impatiently as it rang out. No answer. Doug cursed, dialling Jake's number instead. After a few rings the phone was answered.

"Hi Dad. Did you forget something?"

"It's Father Stephen. He's going back through the doorway, looking for Eddie. It looks like Denise may have been killed by one of them. I don't have all the details. I just know he's on his way there."

"Shit," Jake said on the other end of the line. "It's gone ten. There is no way I can get there in time. Have you called him back?"

"It's just ringing out. What can we do?"

Doug could hear his son's breath on the other end of the phone. "Nothing tonight Dad. Tomorrow is the earliest I can get there. I've got to go up there. You need to stay here with Katherine and Alicia. And by stay, I mean stay here with them while I've gone."

"It's too dangerous Son. Think of your family. What happens if you get killed?" A pause on the line. Doug could hear Katherine in the background, asking what was going on.

"I know we're probably not going to get any sleep tonight Dad. But I will call you first thing in the morning. We can go over it then. Tonight, we will just go round in circles."

Doug could hear Alicia crying in the background. He knew this would have to wait. "Okay. I will be round first thing. I only hope we're not too late to help him."

"Me too Dad. Me too."

Twenty-Three

Tony checked the display on his luminous dial. Ten minutes till midnight. His breath clouded as he exhaled. He was impatient. He always had been. He was dressed in dark clothing, although he was not sure why. His mind had been a whirlwind as it tried to get a handle on what was happening here. The detective was still none the wiser, but knew that midnight was a pivotal time with all the recent activity that had taken place here. His mind almost started to wander again when he heard a sound. He held his breath, trying to locate it. The sound of shuffling footsteps told him he was no longer alone. He shrank back, away from the two trees, crouching down behind a fern several feet back. A large man appeared in the darkness, quickening his heartbeat. He looked familiar to Tony. He'd seen him before somewhere. The man turned to face the trees as he started rummaging around in a pack on his hip. Tony caught his breath in his throat when the stranger pulled out a large piece of wood, sharpened at one end. *What the fuck is he doing?* he thought as the man stood waiting for something. Tony checked his watch. Two minutes to midnight. His theory about midnight now looked to be correct. But what it all meant, was still out of his reach. He was at a loss as to what to do. *Shall I challenge him?* he thought as a wind kicked up in the trees around him. Tony felt a building pressure in his ears before they popped loudly in his head. He looked up at the man who was clearly agitated. Something caught Tony's eye near the two trees. He could just make out a blue glow between the trunks, gently pulsing in the dark forest. Tony squinted through his glasses, trying to make out what he was looking at. *It looks like a doorway!* he thought as he made out the shape of the glow. *What the fucking hell is going on here?* He was about to move forward when the large man walked forward towards the trees. Tony's mouth fell open as he vanished into the night. All he could see was the glowing shape between the trees. He stood up, his thighs tingling. He moved slowly towards the spot as the doorway started blinking. He made a snap decision, running towards it. As he passed through he was aware that his progress slowed, almost halting his steps before he was on the other side. He turned around to see the doorway vanish behind him. *Where am I?* He thought as a large fist connected with his jaw. Then blackness.

* * *

Strong hands pulled him upright, sitting him against a tree trunk. He groggily came around to see a dark figure stood before him. He could make out his clothing and face. He had a large shaggy beard and dark hair. In his hands, he held a large piece of wood and a silver cross. Tony shook his head, feeling a dull throb in his jaw.

"Who are you?" the man asked. "Are you following me?"

Tony dragged himself to his feet, feeling his jaw. "My name's Tony. Tony Oakes. I'm a Police Officer. Who are you? And why did you punch me? I could have you arrested."

"My name is Kenneth Stephen. Father Kenneth Stephen. I'm a Vicar, from Rednal. Sorry I punched you. I thought you were one of them."

"One of who?" The question immediately posed a decision for Stephen. The man would not believe his explanation. However, he was now here. He would soon see that he was telling the truth.

"One of the vampires. I know this will sound preposterous to you Tony. But you've stumbled into something that you shouldn't have. I think for our own safety we should head to the village."

"Vampires! What the fuck are you talking about? There are no such things as vampires." As Tony finished his sentence he could make out swirling mists in the forest around them. They seemed to take shape. His throbbing jaw slowly made its way south as the apparitions suddenly resembled humans. They had blurry faces that he could clearly see. Great yawning mouths and black pits for eyes that advanced on him. He pissed his pants as he staggered back towards a tree.

"HOLY SHIT! WHAT THE FUCK IS GOING ON!" he screamed.

Kenneth grabbed his arm, his strong fingers wrapping around Tony's considerable bicep. "Be quiet," he hissed. "You need to listen. We need to move. And now." He slapped something into Tony's palm. It was a wooden stake, wickedly pointed at one end. "Follow me to the village. It's not far. We can talk there, I hope." They made their way through the thick forest, floundering over unseen tree roots.

Tony went down hard as a wraith flew past his face. His glasses flew from his face, landing in the darkness. "Shit. I've lost me specs," he said, his face a mask of dirt and bracken. Stephen pulled his cross out of his pocket, its glow lighting the forest floor. Tony stared agape as the Vicar picked up his dirty glasses, wiping them on his coat before handing them back.

"Let's hurry. The cross is glowing. That's not a good sign. Come on." He pulled Tony to his feet before they continued their way toward a clearing in the forest. A minute later they were crashing through a rough-hewn door into an old wooden house. Tony sat down heavily on a chair, his breathing and heart rate sky high. He looked at the stake in his hand and shook his head. Kenneth pulled a lighter out of his bag, lighting candles around the room to ward off the blackness outside. Blackness that seemed to press against the window panes.

"Where am I?" Tony said, his words ragged.

Kenneth looked down at the confused man, his heart going out to him. "There is no easy way to say this, so I'll just say it. You're in another world. Maybe even another dimension or universe. If you listen to what I say, you may just live to make it home. Do you understand?" Tony nodded dumbly. "I've only recently found out about this place. A friend has already been here several times."

"Jake Stevenson?"

Kenneth was taken aback. "Yes. How did you know that?"

"I'm a Detective. The murders last year at the Lickey Hills. Stevenson was somehow involved in all of it. He's not a killer, but he knew something. Now I can see just how much he knew."

"I've known Jake all of his life. He is a good man. A man who stumbled across this by chance. It has led to much death and chaos. It all started when a vampire murdered the two people on Beacon Hill. I know all about it Tony. The prints were from a man well into his eighties. Correct?"

Tony nodded. "Yes. It was thought to be a dud lead. But the same prints appeared recently at the other murder too."

"Eddie Guzman. A man from the Caribbean who was abducted in the early fifties. He was turned into a vampire and has spent the last sixty years wandering who knows where. I met him recently in this very cabin. He tried to kill me. I only hope he does not appear tonight. He's not the only one either. Let me see if I can fill in a few blanks for you. After all, you're here now Tony. You're too far gone to turn back." Tony nodded dumbly.

"The man who killed Jake's friend in his house. I believe he was known as Mr Smeets. Am I correct?"

"You are." Tony's breathing and blood pressure were under control. "He is the prime suspect of another murder in the city."

"His real name is Elias. He's the one in charge. The vampire boss, I suppose you could say. Jake has had quite a few run-ins with him over the last year."

"This is fucking unbelievable! I only came up the Lickey Hills because I thought that somehow midnight might be the link to the crazy goings on. I never expected this."

Kenneth walked over and placed a hand on Tony's shoulder. "Believe me. It will take some getting used to. When I first found out I was all over the place for days on end." He pulled up a chair, resting his elbows on the gnarled table. Tony looked at his face for the first time. Flames flickered in the reflection of his glasses. Tony saw that he had a kind face. Rugged but kind. His shaggy black hair and beard

The Turning

were shot through with silver. Tony guessed him to be in his early sixties. He was big too. He guessed almost two metres tall. A bear of a man. He was glad to be with him.

"When did you first find out?" Tony asked, curious.

Kenneth rubbed his beard as he pondered for a moment. "About a year ago. A friend of mine, Doug Stevenson, turned up on my door in the dead of night. He had a strange woman with him. Jake was there too. He'd been bitten by a vampire. I thought it was absurd. There are no such things as vampires. Well I was wrong. I pulled a tooth as long as my finger out of his leg. When I held the tooth, I was transported here. I saw the monster that bit him. I almost soiled myself I can tell you. It was hideous. Like your worst nightmare. Only worse. Since that night, I have kept in touch with them after they all moved down south. My wife recently passed away. That's why I'm here. I think someone killed her. Eddie to be precise. I'm here to set the record straight."

"Are you mad? You're here to fight vampires with a stake and a cross? I cannot believe this shit!" Tony stood up, pacing the room. He walked to the door, looking out across the clearing towards the darkened forest. Mist was spilling out of the tree line, creeping slowly towards the house. He shuddered, slamming the door quickly. "What are they?"

"No idea. They look like ghosts. They seem to live in the forest. There is no sun here. The whole land lies under a blanket of thick cloud. There is so much to tell you Tony. Jake knows far more than I."

Something occurred to Tony. "One of my officers said he fought with Jake in the Lickey Hills. He said that Jake vanished into the night. Now I can see just how he did that. He was coming through the doorway." It was a statement, not a question.

"Yes. To bring Katherine back. She'd been taken by one of them. He came back here, and with the help of others, he rescued her and took her home with him."

"I spoke to him a few days ago. He said he'd met someone, but was very cagey. Now I can see why."

"I know you're a Detective. But leave her be. They've had a little baby. She cannot live here, as you can imagine. Jake has a new start in life. I take it you know about his first wife and daughter?" Tony nodded silently. Kenneth also stood, leaning against the table. "Well, I'm sure this is the strangest night you've had for a while."

Tony half smiled, his face softening. "Yeah you could say that. It's not often that I stumble across another world, get punched by a Vicar, and then find out that vampires are roaming around out there. I wish I'd have stayed in and watched X-Factor now."

Kenneth smiled. "My plans have changed tonight. I was to come here to find Eddie. I cannot do that now. Not with you here. I cannot put you in danger. We must stay here out of sight."

"Do we have to wait until tomorrow night before we can get back?"

"Yes. The door only-" Kenneth's words ended abruptly as he heard a noise outside. He looked at Tony who stared back at him. A creak of wood told the two men that someone or something was outside on the porch. Tony backed up next to Kenneth who stood with the cross in front of him. It started to glow in his hand, drawing a gasp from the Policeman. They watched in frozen horror as the front door slowly swung inwards, its hinges protesting. A figure entered the room from outside. Just a step. The cross did its job by keeping it at bay.

"Two of you," Hagen said. Tony could make out the vampire's face. The skin was dirty grey. The eyes yellow, feral, and cunning. They were smiling. Two curved fangs protruded beneath thin lips that were also smiling at the two men. He shuffled forward a step, but was driven back by the power of the crucifix in Kenneth's hand.

"There is nothing for you here. Only trouble. Go find another meal. We're not on your menu," Kenneth commanded. Tony heard a creak to the rear of the cabin that made him look over his shoulder. A hallway leading into darkness offered no clue as to what was back there. He turned back to the vampire near the front door.

"You smell so good. Look into my eyes. Throw away your amulet and let us all become friends." Tony was shaking. He could feel his legs almost buckling underneath him. He was ready to collapse. A hiss from behind made him spin around, coming face to face with the missing girl from the Lickey Hills. He remembered her name was Beth. He'd seen her picture a hundred times. He'd thought she was pretty, if a little young for his taste. What stood before him was the same person – but not a person. A vampire. She was still wearing the same dress she'd worn on the night of her disappearance. However, it looked dirty to Tony. Her skin was grey, like putty. Her eyes yellow and hungry. Fangs popped out from under her lips as she smiled. Tony tried to call out to the Vicar but the words jammed in his throat. Her eyes locked onto his, his body suddenly relaxing.

Kenneth looked behind him to see what was going on. "Oh no!" he said, spinning around to bring the cross to bear on the other vampire. Beth staggered backwards, her tongue sticking out through her teeth as she hissed at the Vicar. He sensed movement behind him, but it was too late. As he went to turn around Hagen smashed into the pair of them, sending a tangle of bodies and limbs skidding across the wooden planks. Beth was on Tony in a flash. Swooping in, fangs aimed at his throat. Instinctively he brought his free arm up, jamming his forearm under her chin to save himself. She pressed his arm down, trying to get within range of his flesh. He had never felt strength like it as he cried out in anguish, knowing what was about to happen. Tony could smell her fetid breath as it poured from her mouth, spittle landing on his face almost making him retch. He could feel her thighs pinned against his exposed midriff. Her flesh was cold. It felt damp and lifeless. He squirmed underneath her, trying somehow to escape. Tony knew it was futile. She was too strong. He could feel the tip of her teeth touch his flesh, as he started to feel the strength fade from his body. Behind him, Kenneth was in a similar battle with Hagen. Although Hagen could sense that this human was different. He did not smell good. He was repulsive to the vampire. Hagen didn't want to feed. He wanted to kill the man underneath him. Kenneth had a hold of the vampire's hair, bringing his cross up into his face. He swiped it across his cheek, drawing a scream from Hagen. Beth recoiled from the cross, rising up over Tony who had now closed his eyes, ready for the end. He looked up to see her shielding her face with her hands. He reacted without thought, as he thumped the stake into her chest.

"NOOOOOO!" she yelled as she felt it penetrate her skin. To him it felt like striking a brick wall. The shock of the impact shook his arm all the way to the shoulder as the vampire fell backwards. She pulled him with her, his grip on the stake lifting him upright until their positions were reversed. The Policeman threw all his weight onto her, driving the stake into her further. Beth was screaming underneath him, trying in vain to claw him away from her. Her strength was also leaving her as the sharpened chair leg was pushed deeper into her chest, puncturing her blackened heart.

"GET OFF HER, HUMAN!" Hagen yelled, momentarily forgetting about the foul-smelling man underneath him. Before Hagen could utter another word, Stephen's stake also found its mark. The vampire fell into the wooden wall next to him, vanishing in the darkness. The stake clattered to the floor, along with the vampire's dirty clothing. Beth cried out in anguish as she too crumpled under her attacker, turning to mist on the floorboards. Tony fell forward, striking his head on the rough planks as the vampire vanished from sight. Both men lay panting on the floor, neither having the strength to utter a word for a few minutes. Eventually, Tony moved round to see where the Vicar was.

He was relieved when he saw the older man looking at him, his ruddy face bathed in sweat and grime. He looked at the Policeman and smiled. "That was fun. I cannot believe what has just happened. That was like something out of a movie. Oh my." His head lay back on the floor as he stared panting at the ceiling.

Tony's breathing was also laboured. "Do you think there are more of them?"

Kenneth struggled into a sitting position. "Most definitely. Whether or not they are close by is anyone's guess. Let's just hope they are far enough away that they didn't hear the commotion. The two we've just met I've not heard of. I know of two vampires. Jake told me about Eddie and Elias. This could mean that there are lots more."

The Turning

"Great," Tony said as he too sat up, leaning against the wall. "I can't believe what I've just seen. Vampires. Parallel worlds. This is so fucked up. I just don't know what to think anymore."

"Believe me, I was the same. I've spent my whole life following the good book, only to find out that it's a pack of lies. My God does not exist. How can he when this exists alongside our world? I don't remember reading about this place in the Bible. I've drawn the conclusion that good and evil exist, in whatever world you're in. It's almost too big for the human mind to take in."

Tony nodded his agreement, his breathing slowing. "So, what's the plan?" He looked at his digital watch, tapping the screen. The display was frozen, showing a screen full of eights. He shook his wrist absently. "We've got about twenty-three hours before we need to be back at the doorway. Do we stay here?"

"I think we should stay here until morning. I think we're safer in this house than out in the forest. When the sun comes up, we'll head out and do some exploring. I've got some food in my pack, which should keep up going. I'm pretty sure there are no McDonalds around here."

Tony laughed. "God, what I wouldn't give for a Big Mac right now." They moved back into the main part of the house, sitting down at the big table next to the window. Both men were lost in their thoughts. Stephen looked calm. Tony was chewing his thumbs, trying to make sense of the last few hours.

Stephen broke the silence. "What will you do when you get home?" Tony thought about the question for a moment.

"I've no idea. What can I do? Tell my superiors? Tell them there is a doorway to another world. A world full of monsters. I'd be queuing at the dole office by the end of the week. I think I need to sit on this. Mull it over. Being hasty is not an option for something like this. How about you?"

"I will go back to Rednal with you. Then plan to come back. My wife's dead. My faith is shot to pieces. I have nothing in our world. If I die here trying to destroy Eddie, so be it. I will go to wherever

I'm going, knowing that I tried to do something. Tried to avenge the death of my wife somehow."

"What about Jake and his family? Will you tell them what has happened here?"

"Of course. I will tell them everything. Things have been happening in Cornwall too. Any information that I can give to Jake, may just alert them of any danger."

Tony nodded. "I gave Jake a hard time when Darren died. I thought he was up to no good. I need to apologise. I can now see what he'd gotten himself into. You say that Elias is the boss? Well he killed Sergeant Harris. I liked Darren. He was a great copper. A great bloke too. If this Elias gets his comeuppance I'd be fucking thrilled. Pardon my French."

"No need for pardons. I think we're past that now. Part of me thinks that all of them need to be wiped out just to make us safe. They're not going away. But how we go about that is an answer I don't have. The only person who can answer that is in Cornwall."

Twenty-Four

Elias looked out at the city below. The woman fed next to him, greedily draining a young girl who was dressed in combats and a parka. Dried blood had splattered the yellow jacket when her throat had been slashed by Elias's nails. The blood now looked black in the moonlight. Another body lay a few feet away. The man's neck had been snapped before Elias had fed from him. He stood, suddenly feeling uneasy. Something felt wrong to him. Like a far-off scream had reached his ears. He'd felt that before, knowing what could have happened. His red eyes glazed over, not focused on the majesty of Lhasa, the capital of Tibet high up in the Himalayas. He knew that he was powerless to do anything. The doorway in the chasm behind them would not open until the following night. He would not tell her. He'd keep it to himself. After all, he may be wrong. His instincts though, told him otherwise.

* * *

Daylight crept across the sky, lightening the forest until both men could make out the tree line clearly. The mist had subsided back into the forest, making the village seem almost normal.

Kenneth checked his watch, glad that it still worked. "We have seventeen hours before the doorway opens. We may as well explore a little. Pointless staying here. We may learn something."

"Sounds good to me. The station will be wondering where the hell I am. Not sure how to explain this one away."

"Tell them you have flu. And that you've been in bed all day and night."

"Which way shall we go?" Tony said as he cleaned his glasses on his shirt.

"I travelled east before. Out of the forest. There is a huge mountain out that way, but nothing else. Just grassland as far as the eye can see. West looks to be more forest. So, we could either try north or south?"

"North," Tony said without hesitation. "Let's head north."

* * *

They headed eastwards first, until the forest gave way to the grasslands. Tony looked on in awe at Agar to the south. It sat there, silently brooding. Thunder rolled across the land from the south, bringing the hairs up on the Policeman's neck.

"This way," Kenneth said, making Tony turn around to look north. They set off, keeping close to the tree line. After an hour, the forest jutted out eastwards, making the two men wonder if this was such a good idea.

"What do you think?" Tony said as he took his jacket off, wrapping it round his waist.

"Let's go a little further. Around the next bend. If it's no good, we can head into the forest."

They rounded the next bend, coming across a break in the forest. A crude roadway split the trees, meandering away into the distance. They looked at each other and nodded in unison. Kenneth pulled two bottles of Lucozade out of his haversack, passing one to Tony.

"Cheers," he said, cracking the seal. In three quick glugs, he'd polished off the bottle, burping loudly. "Boy, I needed that. How many do you have left?"

"Two more bottles," Kenneth said before draining his own. "And some chocolate bars. We'll have them later. We should keep the bottles too. In case we get stuck here longer than planned."

Tony nodded, handing him the empty bottle back. "Let's hope you're just being over cautious. I need to be back home tonight."

"Let's hope we both get back to our beds then. But we need to be realistic. We're in another world. Who know what will come running around the bend at any moment. Monster, vampire, unicorn. We need to keep the openest of open minds." They fell into silence as they pressed on. Both men noticed how the forest to their right seemed to fall away into the ground. They stopped by a huge lone tree that stood in the middle of the track.

"Strange," Tony said. "The ground really falls away sharply. Like a depression."

"Hmm," Kenneth said as he walked a few paces into the Vale. He instantly felt cold. Not chilly. A deep cold that quickly settled into his bones. He shivered. He became aware that the cross in his jacket pocket was warm. Pulling it out, he motioned to Tony. "It's almost hot. Whatever is in this forest is not friendly. Shall we carry on, or take a look?"

Tony pondered for a moment before deciding. "We've got plenty of time. Plus, it's daytime. What could go wrong? Let's take a look."

* * *

Eddie woke with a start. He looked around the dark cell in which he lay. Karaa lay next to him. On her back, hands laced on her chest. She was breathing steadily, her eyelids fluttering. Eddie sat up, looking at the heavy cell door that was hanging ajar. He'd been destined for a cell like this one, countless years before. Only a combination of street smarts and good fortune had spared him a slow death. Now he sat in the cell that could have been his prison and inhaled. Two smells hit him. One made him droll. One made him smile.

"He's come back for me." He looked at Karaa next to him. He thought about whether to wake her, opting to let her sleep. He knew they would find a way to him. Gravity would lead them. He walked out of the cell, his ears listening for any sounds. He formed a plan in his head, wanting some fun with whoever was heading his way.

* * *

"Do you think this is a bad idea?" Tony said as the trees closed around them. They had only been walking a few minutes, the forest plunging away into the ground before them.

"Only time will tell. I'm not looking forward to the climb back up," he said as he noticed mist starting to form around the trees. The temperature seemed to drop several degrees as his face disturbed an apparition in his path. He waved his hand in front of his face, an uneasy feeling creeping into his gut.

Tony walked ten feet to his left, clumsily trying to navigate the steep forest floor that seemed to lead ever downwards. "Is it me, or has the temperature dropped?"

"It's not you. It's freezing down here. Let's hope we make it back to the top. Back to relative warmth and daylight." They both stopped in their tracks, Tony walking towards the Vicar as their eyes took in the site before them. The forest fell away steeper, a black pit signalling the bottom of the crater. They could make out an entrance that led further downwards.

"That looks inviting," Tony said as a distant rumble of thunder echoed through the trees. A strong breeze ruffled their clothing as the first drops of rain fell from the sky.

"Let's head down and take a look. If it's about to pour down, maybe we can find shelter."

* * *

Coop and Sharla hunkered down behind their respective trees after spotting movement in the forest.

"How many?" Coop whispered.

"Many. More than all my fingers and toes." Coop calculated the information, his spear held firmly in his grip.

A man appeared from the murky forest in front of them. "Show yourselves now. You may live to see the sun once more if you do as I say."

Sharla smiled at Coop, standing up. "Lars. It's Sharla and Coop from the east. You got our message?" Lars approached them, his long stride fluid and easy. Coop had not seen him since he was a boy. He stared in awe as he approached. He was dressed in animal skins like them. His muscular arms bare and rippling. He held an axe over one shoulder, it gently bounced on his muscles as he moved. His head was sparse of any hair, showing a crisscross of scars, tattooed across his skull. Green eyes shone out of a grizzled face that was covered in a thick grey beard. A wicked scar ran from his one eyebrow down to his jaw, giving his face a lopsided look. Coop could see that the approaching man was a warrior. His legs were almost quivering as he clapped Sharla on the shoulder.

"Hail Sharla. You are even more beautiful than I remember." Coop looked at Sharla, who was now blushing, a toothy grin etched on her face. He'd never seen her like that before. He was almost jealous of this mountain of a man who towered over him. "And who is this whelp?"

"This is Coop. You remember him? It's been many seasons."

Lars placed a weathered hand on Coop's shoulder. "Hail Coop. I do remember. I know that my sister thought highly of you. I can see that the pup has grown some teeth. We will need you for the fight that is to come."

"I have more news. And it's not good Lars. We found Karaa. She'd been turned. She's a vampire."

Lars sucked in his breath. A pained expression appeared on his face. He leant against a tree, his axe falling to the ground with a thud. "Who did this? Whose neck is destined for my steel?"

Coop cleared his throat. "We don't know who they are. But we saw where they were holed up. A small village the east, in another forest like this one. There were many of them."

Lars whistled, the sound almost too loud for Coop's ears. Men appeared from the tree line, slowly moving towards the threesome. "Good. Because there are many of us. Lead us to them Coop. It's time to take our revenge."

Twenty-Five

Jake pulled his Pathfinder into a quiet street and killed the ignition. He checked the time on the centre console. He had thirty minutes before the doorway opened. He'd left Katherine, Alicia, and Doug a few hours before, heading north towards Birmingham. Jake's eyes swelled with tears, remembering the look on both Katherine and his father's faces. He promised he would be back as soon as possible, leaving instructions with Doug in case anything happened to him. He'd also showed his father the weapons that he may need if anyone showed up there while he was gone. They'd done all they could to ensure that this plan worked. He switched his phone off, locking in the glove box for when he got back. If he got back. He checked the street. It was quiet, devoid of anyone. He knew the place well. When he'd been a boy his best friend had lived in a house further down to road. It was the perfect place to leave his car. It was a leafy cul-de-sac that saw limited traffic. He climbed out of the car, heading round to the boot. Opening the tailgate, he carefully pulled out his motorbike. He'd purchased a new one when they moved to Tintagel. His mind took him back to when his old bike had been torn to pieces by two mutant whales. He'd barely made it to safety, remembering that it was the first time he'd met Katherine. Jake remembered how magnificent she had looked. He smiled to himself in the darkness as the memory faded. He spent a few minutes preparing the bike. Two panniers were strapped to the rear, containing fuel cans. He wasn't sure how far he'd be travelling.

The Turning

Better to be safe than sorry. Once his bike was ready, Jake put his backpack on, securing it with a buckle around his waist. His black chinless helmet was next. It clipped snugly into place as he started his bike, heading up the road at a gentle pace. He didn't want to attract any attention before he got to the doorway. Five minutes later he was at an all-night petrol station. He filled his bike to the brim and both fuel cans too. He paid the cashier, grabbing a chocolate bar and a bottle of fizzy drink for the journey. He checked his watch. Ten minutes to go. He was on schedule. He set off towards the doorway, stopping at a set of traffic lights at a busy junction. He sat there waiting as a car pulled up behind him. He looked in his wing mirrors.

"Fuck. That's all I need," he said as he looked at the Policemen in his mirror. They were eying him with interest. The lights changed to green with Jake setting off at a steady pace, turning right towards Rubery. The police car followed closely. Jake could see that the officers were interested in what he was up to. And why wouldn't they be? He was dressed in black, with a backpack on, riding along at midnight. He'd be suspicious if he were still an officer. A small island was approaching. Jake indicated left, slowing slightly. Another car was heading in the opposite direction, turning right. *This could be my chance*, he thought as he steered into Leach Green Lane, gunning the throttle. The police car had to give way to the other car, giving Jake a few seconds to gain a lead on them. The bike levelled out at sixty miles per hour as he navigated the windy road. Blue lights flashed behind him as he neared a junction in the road. The officers were now giving chase. Jake only hoped they had not taken his bike's registration before he'd given them the slip. He turned sharply left, flying down the last stretch of road before he came to the Lickey Road. He knew that once he was there he was almost home and dry. The main road was quiet, letting Jake cross the dual carriageway, turning right towards the Hare and Hounds pub. The blue lights were flashing behind him as he neared the turn he needed. The private roadway that led into the forest. He quickly checked over his shoulder, seeing the car advancing on him at break-neck speed. He expertly guided the bike off the road and up the hill towards the dark forest above him. The car was giving chase behind him.

"They've got balls following me up here," Jake said to himself. He was enjoying the thrill of the chase. He knew that the car would be no match for his bike over this terrain. The roadway was made up of mud and grass. Deep trenches had been made by the park rangers 4x4, making it very difficult for the police car to navigate. Jake turned left, twisting the throttle, sending his bike up towards his destination. The car was now several hundred yards behind him. He knew that they would probably get stuck and have to proceed on foot. He'd be long gone by then. The bike coasted the last few hundred yards, turning right into the tree line. He stopped in front of the two familiar trees, checking his watch. One minute to go. He could hear the shouts of the police officers further down the hill. They'd never reach the doorway in time to see its blue glow. The familiar wind kicked up across the forest, accompanied by a building pressure in Jake's ears. They popped as the doorway took shape in front of him. He sat for a full minute, watching to see if anything was coming the other way. Mist spilled out between the trees, twisting around his bike. He shivered involuntarily, noticing that the mist seemed to take on strange shapes. Almost wraith-like. He pulled the cross from his jacket pocket, it instantly glowing in his hand, dissipating the swirling mist around him. Torch light a few hundred yards away told Jake that his friends were close by. He needed to go. The doorway started blinking in the darkness as he coaxed the bike forward, across the void. He seemed to get stuck, an invisible resistance slowing him almost to a stop. He revved gently, sending the bike through the doorway into the other forest. Into another world.

Twenty-Six

Tony and Kenneth sat on a straw mattress, locked inside a small cell. Tony sported a large red lump on his head that had started to swell. Kenneth was unscathed, save for a few bruises here and there. They both lay there in silence, lost in their own thoughts. It had all happened so fast. They had entered the catacombs under the forest, gingerly making their way into a stone passageway. Then it had all kicked off. They had both stood fixated as a vampire had appeared in front of them. She stood there at the entrance to an ante-chamber, hands on hips, her eyes glowing in the darkness. The two men were rooted to the spot, unsure of what to do. Just as Kenneth started to raise his cross towards her, Guzman had crashed into them from behind, sending them flying into the walls. Tony had hit his head on the wet black rock, losing consciousness. Stephen had the wind driven from his lungs by the impact of hitting the cave wall. He'd gone down hard, groggily aware that he was being dragged along the floor. Karaa and Guzman deposited the pair in a small dank cell, locking the iron door behind them. When they came to they had inspected the door, amazed at the padlock and wrought iron bars that held them captive. Now as they lay there, both men pondered their fate.

"What time is it?" Tony asked, for the umpteenth time.

Kenneth looked at his watch. "Just after midnight," was his short reply. Sounds filtered through the darkness towards them, making the men stand up. The torches that adorned the walls offered scant light to them. The four figures were almost on top of them before they saw them.

Both men stood, mouths agape as Elias walked up to the bars. "Welcome. It seems that you've already met Eduardo and Karaa. Allow me to introduce you to another member of our family." He stood aside as a figure shuffled forward. Her eyes shining brightly in the gloom.

"Oh, holy fuck!" Kenneth said, as Alison approached them.

She smiled at him, a brief flicker of recognition in her eyes. "AAAAAAAAHHHHHH," she screamed as she hurled herself at the bars. She shook them, the noise deafening in the confines. Both men fell backwards, landing on the mattress. Another scream sent shivers through them as they watched frozen in horror.

"Easy now Alison. All in good time." Elias cooed.

Kenneth rose to his feet, walking towards the bars. "What have you done to her, you fucking monster?"

Elias stepped forward. "Watch your tongue, Priest. You're far from home. It's not wise to upset me."

"Do you really think I give a shit?" Kenneth was getting more and more angry. He pointed at Eddie. "That piece of filth killed my wife. I've got nothing to live for. Do you really think I care what happens to me?"

"What about your friend? Do you care what happens to him?"

Tony tried to look defiant. "I chose to be here. Whatever happens, happens."

Elias appraised Tony, suddenly curious. "Why are you here? I've not seen you before?"

Tony looked up at the giant before him. "I'm a Police Officer. I've been investigating murders back home. I know now by looking at you, that you're Mr Smeets. The same Mr Smeets that killed a defenceless woman last year in Birmingham. Am I correct?"

"Guilty as charged. Although I am far from your justice now, lawman. It looks like you've discovered something that you shouldn't have."

The Turning

"You killed Darren too." Tony's words carried venom as he spat them out.

"Yes, I did. He got in the way of my work. A worthy adversary I might add. Killing him gave me no pleasure. If that is any consolation to you?"

"Yes it is. It means that when I kill you, I'll not enjoy it either."

Elias laughed. "I give you credit for having fight in you, human. However, I think you're in no position to be issuing threats. We will leave you now. We have things to do." Elias threw Kenneth's pack through the bars. "You have some food in there to keep your strength up. You may need it." Suddenly Eddie drew in a sharp breath, causing everyone to look at him.

Elias looked at the stocky vampire, whose eyes had rolled back into his skull. "What is it Eddie? Guzman was lost somewhere beyond sound. "EDDIE!" Elias barked.

He snapped back to attention. "He's back. Jake is back. I can smell him. He's close by."

Elias smiled, turning to the two men in the cell. "It looks like your friend is here to save you. This is an unexpected turn of events. If he is here, then his family is mine to take." Elias turned to the three vampires. "Alison. Keep a watch over these two. You should get no trouble from them. But if you do, you can have some fun." Alison hissed through her teeth at Kenneth, bringing gooseflesh across his arms. "Eddie, Karaa. Don't kill Jake. Either capture him and bring him here. Or make sure that he does not pass through the doorway to his world. Because that is where I am heading once it opens. To bring some new family members back with me."

Kenneth exploded, grabbing the bars, shaking them. "YOU LEAVE THEM BE, YOU FUCKING MONSTER. IF YOU HURT THEM SO HELP ME GOD I'LL KILL YOU!"

Elias reached through the bars, grabbing Stephen by the throat, pulling him close. "I will personally take great pleasure in turning both of them. And I will let you watch." A rage filled Kenneth as he reached through the bars, grabbing Elias by the throat. To everyone else in the chamber, Elias was a giant. To Kenneth he wasn't. He was only a few inches taller than the Vicar, who was a giant of a man in his own right. He suddenly realised that for some unknown reason, he felt stronger than before. Like a new-found power had flooded his body. His fingers dug into the cold flesh of Elias's neck, the tips buried deep. The giant vampire looked into the Vicar's eyes. It was at that moment that Kenneth saw a hint of uncertainty in the red glare. Like the vampire was suddenly unsure of his strength. He let out a roar, shoving him backwards across the cell. Kenneth bounced off the rock, staying on his feet.

Elias, clearly flustered by the exchange, turned to his kin. "Watch them Alison. Eddie, Karaa. You know what to do. I have a long journey ahead of me." He turned and walked out of the chamber, leaving the five of them stood in silence.

* * *

Jake lifted his bike up the two steps, rolling it into Wilf's old house. He wheeled it into the main living area, leaning it against the wooden wall. He wanted to keep it close by just in case he needed to make a quick escape. Pulling his lighter from his pocket, he lit the candles that were positioned around the room, bathing it in a warm glow. He opened his pack on the table, taking out two large wooden crosses and a pack of black cable ties. Jake quickly made four loops from the ties before walking out onto the porch with his hands full. The man secured the crosses to the wooden uprights in front of the door. He was satisfied with his warning system. He went back inside and went through his pack again. His sawn-off shotgun was placed on the table with a dull clunk. He then pulled out his cartridge belt, laying it next to the shotgun. Next out of his pack was his new Glock-17 9mm handgun. He'd acquired it from one of his former police colleagues in return for a favour. He chose it because of its reliability. It would never jam or misfire. It would even work underwater. Plus, it was compact. It had a magazine in the stock, along with four spares. He had enough firepower to start a mini war if needed. He laid it on the table, along with the black leather belt holster. Four stakes, two large bottles of holy water, and two metal crucifixes completed his arsenal. Jake unscrewed one of the bottles, taking a few large gulps. He would apply some water to his leg too, before setting off. A few yawns told Jake that he was tired. It felt fairly safe in the house. He closed the front door, placing a chair in front of it. He did the same with the rear door. As he walked through the house he noticed some smashed furniture, along with a piece of paper on the floor. He picked it up, walking over to the table where he sat down. The small piece of paper was scrunched up. Jake carefully opened it to reveal a receipt. A receipt from a supermarket, in Birmingham.

"What the hell is this doing here?" Jake said out loud. *Is this Father Stephen's?* he thought. He read through the contents of the receipt, a growing unease settling in his stomach. Donuts and cream cakes were listed, along with lager and shave gel. *This is not Father Stephens. But who else would has been here?* He put the piece of paper into his back pocket, his mind wandering to realms beyond practicality. His brain felt woolly, his head heavy. He crossed his arms on the table, resting his head in the crook of his elbow. Within ten deep breaths he was asleep, as the forest came alive all around him.

* * *

Eddie and Karaa stood in the tree line next to the clearing. They could see a warm glow shining out from one of the windows in the main house. They moved right until they could make out a figure on the other side of the glass.

Eddie smiled, his teeth popping out from under his lips. He hissed. "There is not a sweeter smell in any land than Jake. But we cannot take him. Elias wants him alive."

Karaa looked as the human's head disappeared from view. "I'm so thirsty. He smells so good."

"All in good time. We will have him eventually. But first we must have sport. We are playing a game. Elias's game. Come." They slowly made their way through the tree line until they were ready to scoot across the grass to the house. Eddie caught Karaa's arm, pulling her back into the forest.

"What is it?" She looked at Eddie.

He looked pensive. "Someone else is coming. Many of them. Come with me." She watched as he jumped high into a tree, landing lightly on a thick branch. She followed suit, landing with barely a sound. They watched as several figures appeared from the west. Mostly men. One huge woman was with them. Karaa tried to pluck a thought from the back of her memory. It eluded her though, just out of her reach. Eddie sniffed the air. "They were your kin. I know the smell. They must be back looking for revenge. They are looking for us. But they will find him instead."

"What shall we do?" Karaa asked.

"We watch from the shadows. The darkness is our friend. Whatever happens, we will report back to Elias as soon as we can." They sat in silence as the throng of people below circled the main house.

Lars and Coop stood near the window, peering in at the sleeping form at the table. They moved back a few steps to speak. "Is it another one?" Coop said. He was excited, his heart pounding in his chest.

"I don't think he is. The skin is too healthy. I think he could be a wanderer, resting up for the night."

"So, what do we do about him?"

Lars looked down at Coop and smiled. "We enjoy a late feast is what we do."

* * *

Jake woke with a start, a noise close by bringing him out of his sleep. He looked up, his face red, eyes bleary. The front door was still closed. Everything seemed normal. He looked around the room then out of the window. Nothing seemed out of the ordinary. His head started to sink back to the table when he heard another sound. Creaking of wood beyond the front door. Jake stood up slowly and quietly. He clipped the holster onto his trousers, slipping the handgun inside. He checked

The Turning

through the window again. He saw movement in the shadows, confirming that someone or something was out there. He quickly buckled the cartridge belt around his waist, pumping the shotgun ready for action. The door creaked open, pushing the chair into the front wall. Jake stood, shotgun aimed at the door as a tall man entered the room. He reminded Jake of a Viking warrior. He barely made it under the door. His shaven head and grey beard gave him a commanding presence. He was dressed in animal skins, his boots scuffing on the floor boards as he entered. In his hand, he held an axe. It was double headed and looked to Jake like it was well-used. A cold seeping dread descended over him as he looked at the man in front of him.

He addressed Jake. "Who are you? Why are you here?" It was direct. No punches pulled.

"My name is Jake. I'm from another place. I'm here to save my friend. Who are you?"

"Lars. Of the Cravens. I'm here for the monsters that took my sister from me."

A boy entered the room and stood next to Lars. He was an adolescent, probably fifteen or sixteen Jake thought. He was a fair looking boy, who seemed out of place in Amatoll. In his hand, he held a long spear. He turned to Lars. "I've not seen him before."

Lars smiled, his teeth showing through his whiskers. "Don't worry Coop. No one will ever see him again."

Jake's grip on the shotgun tightened at hearing the words. "I have no fight with you guys. So just leave me be."

Lars shook his bald pate. "We're hungry. We need food."

"I have some food in my pack if you want it?"

Lars shook his head again. "You will be our food," he said, twirling the axe in his hand.

Jake stood for a moment, trying to make sense of the statement. His head seemed to empty of all thoughts and words as he stood looking at the duo. "Y-you want to eat me?" Jake stammered.

They both nodded their heads in agreement. "We are the Cravens. We eat anything," Lars boomed. "We have many mouths to feed out there. You will give us strength. Your death will not be in vain."

Jake moved two steps to his right, his shotgun aimed at the two strangers. "Well I have no plans to be eaten by anyone. I'm here for my friend and to kill vampires if I can. We are not enemies. Let's not start a fight here."

"There will be no fight. My axe will cleave you in two. Then we will eat you. You are not our enemy, nor our kin. Therefore, you are food." Lars took two paces forward. Coop matched his steps.

Jake lifted the shotgun higher. "Step the fuck back. Now! I will only ask once." He waved the barrel of the shotgun. "You do not want to argue with this."

Lars looked curiously at the weapon. "What does it do?"

"This," Jake said, firing at the door next to Coop. The man and boy fell backwards as a hole appeared in the wood the size of a plate. The noise was deafening in the confines of the house. Jake's ears were ringing for a full minute as he kept his eye on the two strangers. They looked at him, eyes and mouths wide open. "There is nothing but trouble for you here. Leave me be." The back door burst open, sending the chair smashing into the wall. Jake instinctively turned in one fluid motion as a man appeared behind him. He was large, dressed in dark fur. He held a small axe in his hand that was beginning its arc towards his head. He was less than six feet away from him as Jake squeezed the trigger. Lars and Coop watched in frozen amazement as their kin member's head vanished from his shoulders. Jake moved to one side as the momentum took his attacker past him, landing flat on his back on the wooden floor. Within the blink of an eye his shotgun was levelled back at the two intruders. He pumped the barrel, ejecting a red shell casing onto the floor as Lars and Coop looked at the body on the ground. A pool of red blood was spilling from the neck, coating the floor in red. Bits of skull and hair were still attached to the neck, making Coop feel nauseous.

The Turning

Lars was unmoved. He knew however that the man in front of him was dangerous. And he was full of tricks. He looked him in the eye. "He was one of my kin. I knew him all my life."

"He was going to kill me," Jake said bluntly.

"Yes he was."

Jake needed to resolve the situation quickly. If he used the shotgun again he would need to reload. His handgun was loaded and would get him out of a tight spot, but he didn't know how many were outside waiting for him. "I mean you no harm," Jake said. "But it's your call. You can either walk away now, or I will kill all of you if you want to fight. You've seen what I can do with this." He motioned with his shotgun.

Lars and Coop stood staring, contemplating Jake's offer. Lars nodded. "We will leave this place. I only hope we never meet again outlander. For your sake or mine." The man and boy walked backwards out of the doorway into the night. Jake kept his shotgun levelled, not trusting their word. He moved over to the wall where his bike was, standing against the wood, giving himself a good field of vision in case of another attack. He heard Lars issuing instructions to unseen people. Jake relaxed slightly, his pulse and breathing coming back under control. He'd just killed a man. He'd never done that before. He'd killed vampires, but never a man. He looked down at the corpse, trying to get a handle on how he felt. *It was either him or me. I don't feel guilty about it,* he thought. The sound of activity outside gradually dwindled to nothing as Jake pushed himself from the wall. He skirted the corpse, setting his shotgun down on the table. He began placing his things into his pack, trying not to stare at the brain and blood that had littered the room. As he packed his shotgun away, Jake noticed a smell. It took him a few seconds to realise what it was.

"Smoke!" He clipped his pack shut and looked out of the window. It was a dark blanket out there. Nothing could be seen. Jake pondered taking a look around the house when he noticed smoke creeping across the floor from the back door. He walked over to the rear hallway, alarmed when he saw smoke spilling in through the back door. He was about to turn around when a pair of strong hands slammed him into the wall. His vision exploded into a thousand stars as his face crashed into the wood. He could smell the attacker's fetid stench. It was more overpowering than the smoke. A sharp blow to his kidneys made Jake wince as he tried to turn around and face the unseen foe. He slumped slightly, making his attacker think he was finished. A guttural laugh behind him told Jake he was right. Rough hands grabbed at his collar, trying to pull him into the main room. Jake span around, taking the man by surprise. He used his arms as leverage to send the man into the wall. The grip on his collar loosened as the man's face connected with wooden planks. Jake heard him grunt in pain. He looked at his face. The man wasn't either of the two he'd just encountered, but he was dressed the same. *They are not done with me*, he thought as he punched the man square in the face. He went down hard, landing on his back. Even in the smoky darkness, Jake could see the man's eyes roll back in his skull. Jake quickly headed back into the lounge. He was greeted by two men with axes, smiling at him. Both were big, with blackened teeth and beards that ran down their chests. They advanced on him, axes poised to cleave him into chunks. He reacted without thinking, pulling the Glock from its holster. The men's expressions changed from smug to uncertain as Jake levelled the barrel at them. He had no time to think. He fired off two double taps, hitting both men in their chests. They fell sideways away from the door as the window next to the table shattered inwards, a ball of flame crashing into the room.

"JESUS," Jake shouted as the flaming mass landed on the headless corpse, quickly igniting the furs. Jake pulled his pack onto his back, clipping it in place. He put his helmet on quickly as Coop barged his way into the room, his spear held out in front of him. Jake didn't want to kill the boy. Aside from his spear he looked harmless. Like any regular teenager.

"YOU'RE MINE," screamed Coop, advancing on Jake, his spear tip slashing the air menacingly. *Shit*, Jake thought as he pulled his handgun from its holster. He fired at Coop, the bullet grazing his flank. He fell backwards into the door, clutching his ribs as more flaming balls crashed through the window and doorways.

"I've got to get away from here," Jake said as the former Bathurst residence quickly became a raging pyre.

* * *

Eddie and Karaa watched the action unfold from high up in the forest. They saw the two men enter and then leave a few minutes later. Their keen eyes watched, fascinated as the group of humans gathered in the forest and started to light fires. One headed around the rear of the big house, dropping a flaming torch near the back door. The shadowy figure lurked close by before entering the back door in a rush. Eddie and Karaa could make out the noises of a struggle somewhere inside.

"They are going to kill him," Eddie said. "It looks like we won't have to worry about Jake anymore." She looked at Eddie before turning her eyes down towards the village as more humans started to hurl flaming balls at the house. Two men ran carrying axes ran into the house. Something stirred in Karaa's memory. Something just out of reach. Four loud pops could be heard as a boy holding a spear entered the house. Again, her memory tried to make itself known to Karaa. They boy looked familiar to her, but she could not say from where. Another shot rang out in the night that made Karaa flinch. The house was burning on all sides now as more fire was thrown by the humans that surrounded it. Eddie turned to Karaa. "He's done for. Let us get back to the Vale to wait for Elias to return." Karaa nodded as Eddie jumped down from the tree, landing silently in the forest. She followed suit, barely a rustle was made as her feet hit the floor. They scooted off east, hand in hand as the flames from the house continued to light up the forest.

* * *

Lars could feel the heat from the flames. He started to sweat as he stood poised to enter the burning building. A loud bang told him that Coop may have been hurt. He was about to storm the front door when he heard a noise. It sounded like a roar as he strained to listen. He could wait no longer as he strode towards the flames. As he reached the front porch he dived for cover, Jake flying past him on his steel beast. Lars rolled on the grass, coming up to see him disappear into the darkness to the east, a loud roar following him. Coop staggered out after him, holding his side.

Lars went to him. "You're hurt. Show me."

Coop pulled his top off to reveal a small wound on his flank. "It's not bad. I think I was lucky. The two who went in before me are dead. What was that thing that he fled on?"

Lars looked to the east. "No idea. Some kind of magic I've not seen before. At least we know one thing."

"What's that?"

"That the outlander might be better as an ally than as an enemy."

* * *

Jake gunned the throttle as the tyres squealed on the boards beneath him. He shot out of the flaming house, the bike landing smoothly on the grass. His vision was focused ahead. Towards the roadway that wound its way out of the forest towards the east. He paid no attention to any of his attackers. He was hoping that the element of surprise would be enough. He was lucky. His attackers stared, mouths wide open as the strange contraption sped away from them. As he found the dirt track he let the bike roll along at a steady thirty miles per hour. He had no clue as to where he was going. Just away from the forest would be a start. Ten minutes later he spotted the lonely mountain, standing proud in the darkness. He coasted to a stop, weighing up his options. He checked his watch. It was still several hours before the sun made an appearance over the eastern ridge. He felt exposed out here in the open. *Culnae*, he thought. *I can head there and stay with Mungo.* He remembered the direction. It was not difficult. *East towards the far-off ridge.* The land was scant of features. Even in the dark, the tiny collection of buildings that made up Culnae should be easy enough for him to spot. He pointed his bike away from the mountain and began the second part of his escape.

The Turning

* * *

Far to the east, Culnae lay quiet. A few torches adorned the haphazard collection of wooden structures. At the centre, Mungo's Lodge was situated. Lanterns hung around the porch, giving the lodge a warm, inviting feel. A few late revellers still propped up the bar in the main saloon. Mungo, the proprietor, sat in the corner of the room. A large metal tankard was at his left hand. A leather-bound book lay splayed in the centre of the desk. In his meaty yellowed right hand he held his quill. A small ink pot was set into the desk, although the quill was dry now. He'd filled in his ledger. And he was happy. He was fully booked for the next season. After that, the elk hunt would begin. His safe would be filling up with silver and gold coins at a steady rate. Life was treating Mungo well. The last few months had settled down after all the action of the previous seasons. Vampires and outlanders had come knocking at Mungo's door. He'd seen plenty of action when the young man Jake had arrived. He smiled fondly, remembering the first time he'd met him out in the long grass. Mungo's barb had been aimed at his chest until he'd taken his steel hat off. He remembered what a good looking young man Jake was. There was no evil in him. That was the truth. Over the next few weeks, Mungo had been thrust into action he'd never thought possible. He'd killed vampires, travelled for the far-off forests past the mountain. Seen doorways to other worlds. His head had span for a few nights after Wilf had bid him farewell. He'd lay in his corner bed, thinking about all the worlds out there. He tried to imagine Jake's world. With its fast beasts and magic. He'd give anything to be able to see it for himself one day. Maybe he would. Maybe he'd take some time off after the hunt and take a trip into the endless forest to the west. His thoughts were interrupted by a small elderly man who approached. He was wearing a brown leather smock. His grey hair was wispy and wild, like his eyes. His gummy mouth was wrinkled like an old drawstring purse.

Mungo smiled. "What's up Bertie?"

"A light approaching from the west. Coming fast."

The man's smile faded at the news. He stood up and followed the aged man out of the saloon into the crisp night air. A light could be seen heading their way. "What do you think Bertie?" Mungo asked, curiously watching the approaching light. A noise could now be heard as the light drew closer. It got louder and louder as the light grew.

"Not sure. Be ready though." Both men slipped their slingshots into place, fishing pointed barbs from their pockets as they walked to the sturdy gates. The compound consisted of a circular wall, five times the height of a man. The wooden beams were adorned with spikes and brambles that warned off any potential attackers. In all the years since it was constructed it had never been breached.

"Bertie. The bolt," Mungo said as the bike came within range of their sling shots. The little man pushed a wooden beam as thick as his leg across the gates until it clicked into place in the wall. He opened the one gate far enough for them to slip through, out into the grasslands that surrounded Culnae. Both men walked loose, their limbs swinging freely in case they needed to move quickly. They saw the oncoming light and noise.

Mungo smiled as the bike slowed to a standstill. "Jake. Is that you?" he said, walking towards the light.

Jake removed helmet. "Hello again Mungo. Hi Bertie," Jake said as he stood the bike on its stand.

"Hail Jake!" Mungo shouted, rushing over and embracing the younger man.

"Good to see you Mungo. But I need your help."

Mungo's smile waned slightly. "What's wrong? Are you in trouble? Are Wilf and Katherine safe?"

"Katherine is fine. Not seen Wilf for a long while. I have a feeling he is okay though."

"They are out by the sea. I helped them move out a few seasons back. Not seen them for a while either."

Jake exhaled, smiling as he did so. "That's good to hear. I hope they are safe and well." A far off rumble of thunder made the three men look towards the lone mountain to the south.

The Turning

Jake turned to Mungo. "Can we talk inside?"

The man with the Asiatic features nodded readily. "Come. Bertie. Put Jake's steel horse somewhere safe." Bertie walked over to the bike as Jake and Mungo made their way into the saloon. The few stragglers paid them no attention as they headed over to a table in the corner of the room. They sat down on wooden chairs as a man approached. Mungo looked up at the weathered waiter. "Bring over a few jugs of beer. What food is left Bart?"

The waiter pondered for a moment. "We 'ave some cold cuts of meat and some bread. I'll slather some elk gland sauce on the bread to make it more interestin' for you. Sound good?"

"Perfect. Thank you, old man."

"Less of the old," Bart said as he walked off picking his ear with his pencil.

"So, what news?" Jake relayed the last few months to Mungo. From the moment when he and Katherine escaped Elias, through the doorway to his world. Tears rolled down the round yellow face of Mungo when he heard about the birth of Alicia. Bart had brought over the drinks, filling two mugs with a pale, heady ale. They clinked glasses as Jake told of his daughter's birth. "Good health to your family Jake. Great news!" Jake raised his mug and took a swig of ale. He was starting to feel relaxed. Bart appeared once more and placed a large wooden platter on the table, heading back to the kitchen with his pencil tucked behind his ear. The two men fell on the platter, a series of hearty grunts of appreciation were issued back and forth.

"God. This is good," Jake said in between mouthfuls.

Mungo nodded, wiping a hand across his mouth, looking at the younger man. "So, what else has been happening? It can't be all good news, or you'd not be sat at my table."

Jake took another swig of ale, thanking Mungo with a nod when he refilled his mug. "Things have started happening recently. A friend sent me two buttons. Buttons that belonged to one of Korgan's vampires. As soon as I took them into my home, bad things started happening. We think that Elias has found us. My mother vanished. We never found her. We think she was swept out to sea. We've accepted that she is dead."

"I give you my sorrow Jake. That is troubling news."

"There is more. A family friend, a shaman who helped me at the time I was bitten. Well, he was also visited. Before that he went to Amatoll out of curiosity. He met one of the vampires there, Eddie. They fought. Father Stephen managed to fight him off. But a few weeks later, Father Stephen found his wife dead at his home. He thinks that Eddie murdered her. He came back through the doorway two nights ago, looking for revenge."

"Fuckenell," Mungo said, clearly alarmed. "Did you find him?"

"No. I went straight to Heronveld, hoping that he was staying there. He wasn't. I did however meet a group of strange people who wanted to kill and eat me."

Mungo spat his ale across the table, drawing a few glances from the other patrons. "They wanted to eat you?" Jake nodded. "Fuckenell. That sounds like the Cravens of Mantz."

"They mentioned that name. The Cravens. What is Mantz?"

Mungo put his mug down on the table, a sweaty sheen appearing on his head. "It's a forest way off towards the western sea. It's twice the size of Amatoll, maybe even larger. A clan called the Cravens rule there. They eat anything that crosses their path. I've never been that far west. But I've heard stories from travellers and traders who have. The forest is so dense, no sun can get in. It's a dark evil place. A place only a fool would dare to explore. I don't know why they would be in Amatoll though. Jake, this is also troubling news. I only hope they don't head this way. I don't think we could keep them out of Culnae. Where do you think your friend is?"

Jake shrugged, a sudden tiredness seeping into his bones. "Not totally sure. If I had to place a bet, I'd say he's in the Vale. I just hope I'm wrong. Elias and other vampires may be there. Stephen would not stand a chance. I need to get there. Tomorrow."

"I can see your mind is made up. We will go with you Jake. Bertie and I. We will leave at dawn. You can bed down in one of our rooms. I'll tell Bertie to have a wagon ready at first light."

"Are you sure about this Mungo? There may be danger."

The older man took a swig of his ale, a tight smile creasing his face. "I could do with a bit of hunting. Plus, you're a friend of Wilf. I owe you my service."

Jake reached across, taking the man's meaty hand in his. "Thank you Mungo. I am very grateful."

The larger man sat back on his chair, resting his meaty hands on his ample stomach. "We'll finish up here, then Bertie will show you to your room." He reached for his mug, taking a swig. "Hmm. This is good stuff. What's say we partake in another jug?"

"Fine with me," Jake said, the horrors of the night gently ebbing away.

Twenty-Seven

Eddie and Karaa dropped down through the forest as wraiths and ghosts writhed around the stout trunks around them. They came to the steps that led to the catacombs underneath the forest. Karaa dropped through the air, landing on the stone floor. Eddie looked down and smiled, preferring to take the stairs, two at a time. They met at the bottom, heading through one of the tunnels. They came to a series of cells, looking through the bars at the two sleeping forms on the straw mattress. They both instantly felt hungry.

"The one tastes good," Karaa said. Her yellow eyes almost feverish.

"He does. But we need to be patient. We can hunt later, once we've spoken to the others. I know a place where you can get your fill." She smiled as Eddie took her hand, leading her into the larger anteroom. On the floor lay two dead humans. One was headless, the other bent into an unnatural shape. No blood had soaked the stone floor. They had been bled dry. Elias and Alison sat in a far corner, eyes closed, breathing steadily.

The giant's eyes opened as he heard them approach. He stood silently, rousing Alison with a gentle nudge. "What news on Jake?"

"He's dead," was Eddie's flat reply.

Elias looked shocked, his red eyes burning bright in the dimly lit cavern. "How?"

"We found him, in the village. He was resting in one of the cabins. Before long, humans came. I think the same humans who visited us at the forest killed him. There was a fight. They set fire to the house with Jake inside it. That was the last thing we saw."

Elias walked over to his former master's stone coffin, resting his hand on the cool surface. "That is a shame. I was hoping to personally take care of him, maybe even turning him myself. But no matter. He is gone now. I will still go through the doorway tomorrow night to bring back his kin. It just means that now we can fulfil our plans without Jake's interference. It will make it easier for us."

"What about the two who are sleeping in the cell?"

Elias pondered the question for a moment. "Leave them be for now. The shaman and I have unfinished business. I would very much like to see him suffer. And I know exactly how to do that." Eddie and Karaa nodded.

"We're hungry," Karaa said. "Eddie and I need to hunt."

"Go then. Take these bodies with you. You'll find a head over in the far corner. Take them and dump them in the forest. Something will eventually find them and feast on their rotten flesh." They excused themselves, leaving Elias alone with Alison. She slumped against the rocky wall, her eyes closing. Elias sat next to her, his mind a whirlwind of thoughts. *I did not expect Jake to go that way. But things happen. Shame. Under different circumstances, he would have been a strong ally.* He let his head rest against the cold wall, his eyes also closing as the torches flickered gently around him.

* * *

They made their way back into the forest, quickly climbing the steep incline until they were out on a dirt track. They could smell the smoke on the air as it was blown gently from Heronveld towards them. Karaa looked around herself, wondering which way to go. "We will head to the inn next to the lake. There will be food for us there. Remember. Kill them first, before feeding. We do not need any more kin just yet. Let's go and have some sport." He looked at her once beautiful face as it changed from a frown to a smile. The smile reached her feral eyes, closing slightly as her fangs appeared from under her lips. She readily took his outstretched hand as they made their way along the roadway. Away from the smell of smoke. Towards the smell of human blood.

* * *

Father Stephen sat up on the mattress and stretched his arms towards the low ceiling. He climbed to his feet noisily as Tony continued to sleep next to him. Shuffling over to the far side of the cell, he relieved himself in against the wall. He walked back to his pack, dismayed that they were almost out of supplies. He took a quick drink, leaving the rest for his companion. It was dark in the passageway. Flickering torches barely lifted the gloom that pressed down upon them. He heard noise to his right as two vampires walked into the passageway. He said nothing as they approached. The female had a face plastered in blood. It made Stephen feel nauseous just to look at her.

Eddie walked over to the cell, smiling at the Vicar. "Hello, shaman. Did you rest well?"

Stephen could smell the fetid stench that came from him. It was cloying, coating the back of his throat, almost making him wretch. "We are holding up. Did you kill my wife?"

Eddie looked at him and smiled. "Yes, I did. Although I never even touched her. She fell to the ground as soon as she saw me. I wanted to feed but I was disturbed, so I left her untouched."

Stephen grabbed the bars, his knuckles turning white. "Then very soon, I will kill you. I give you my word."

Eddie smiled. "Good. We will see who is the stronger. I look forward to that, shaman." The two vampires walked off, leaving Stephen gripping the bars. He fell to his knees, loud sobs echoing through the cavern. *I'm so sorry love. I did this to you*, he thought as tears fell from his face onto the wet stone floor.

Tony woke behind him, groggily looking over at the Vicar. "Are you okay?" he said, his voice dry and raspy.

Stephen looked over at the Policeman, wiping his face with his hand. "He killed my wife. He just told me. That bastard killed Denise.

I will not leave this hell-hole until I've settled the score." He climbed to his feet, leaning against the iron bars of the cell.

Tony also climbed to his feet, touching the lump on his head. "Hmm. Strange. The bump on my head has almost gone."

Stephen walked over, placing his hand on Tony's head where he'd banged it the day before. No lump or bruising could be easily seen. He remembered that he'd also received a few bumps and bruises as his hands felt around his own body. "I'm not totally sure why, but it seems that things are different here. It looks like we've healed overnight. I don't know about you, but I feel stronger here than I do at home. Have you noticed that?"

Tony frowned, looking at the Vicar. "Not really, to be honest." He looked at Stephen as an idea presented itself. "How much do you weigh?"

"Not sure. Twenty stone roughly."

Tony placed his hands under Stephen's armpits and lifted him up the wall. He pressed him until his head gently bumped the ceiling. Impressed, Tony dropped him back down the floor. "You're right. I lifted you quite easily. I work out at home, but I'd never be able to press that much weight over my head. So, what are you thinking in that big old head of yours?"

"Did you watch Superman as a child?"

"Yeah. Why?"

"Maybe that's what's happening here to us. The atmosphere could be different, making us a bit stronger. It could also help us heal quicker."

Tony shook his head. "This is just bonkers! You'll be telling me I can fly next?" The Policeman jumped in the air, his one arm aloft. He landed back down with a thump. Stephen laughed, glad of the release it gave him. He felt better, despite their dire predicament. Tony looked through the bars. "So, what is the plan?"

"Not sure. Elias said he is leaving tonight. He's going to head to Cornwall to bring back Katherine and the baby. I'm sure Jake's father will be with them. So, he's in danger too. I've known Doug half my life. He's a good man who may be in harm's way. He would die trying to protect them. But we cannot let that happen. We need to get to them first."

"How do we do that? We're kinda stuck here. Unless we can rip these bars from the walls and do a runner?"

Stephen looked at the iron bars, wondering if the two men had what it took to do that. "Maybe we could. But not now. If they've just come back, it may be morning out there. Let's leave it a few hours until we know for sure. They may all be asleep by then too. If we can, we need to plan what we will do. There's no point escaping this place, only to die in the forest before we can get home."

Tony nodded and walked over to the mattress. He sat down heavily, drawing his knees up to his chest. "What day is it?"

"Sunday, I think." He tried to turn the clock back in his head, recounting the last few days. "Yes, it's Sunday morning."

Tony shook his head. "The Villa are playing in a few hours. I was going to watch that in the pub with the guys."

"Oh well. I'm sure that being here over the next few hours will hold more entertainment than what Aston Villa can provide. If we make it home alive you can watch a re-run."

* * *

To the east, Culnae was slowly coming to life as the sun began its daily journey across the sky. Bertie was loading up the cart, placing weapons, food, drink, and blankets under the cover. Satisfied, he pulled the hessian cover tight across the cart, securing it in place to keep their provisions dry. Mungo walked out of the saloon, a steaming mug of tea in his hand. He was dressed in brown boots and trousers, with a white singlet on top. Bertie handed him a leather coat that he shrugged on to ward off the early morning chill.

"Thanks Bertie. Do we have everything that we need?"

"We do. There is enough food to feed us for a week. Ale too. I've put some spears and axes left over from the last elk hunt. We've got more than enough Mungo."

The Turning

The big man smiled, turning to see Jake walk out of the saloon towards them. "Did you sleep Jake?"

He looked at Mungo and nodded. "I did. The bed was very comfortable. I even managed a bath this morning. Your room was very nice."

Mungo turned to Bertie, who was about to climb onto the front of the cart. "Bertie, could you bring Jake some tea and a bit of food before we leave?" The diminutive older man jumped down from the bench seat, heading off towards the saloon with a stride of someone years younger. Jake walked over to his bike, checking it over while Mungo finished his tea.

"Is this how you travel in your world?" Mungo asked inquisitively.

"One of the ways. We tend to use something called a car. It's much bigger. You sit inside it and drive. They are fast. I'd have brought mine but it would not fit through the doorway."

"Your world sounds fascinating. One day I will visit. If only to breathe your air."

"I don't see why you couldn't one day. After all, it's not that far really. You just need to watch out for vampires and cannibals."

"Maybe I'll take Bertie with me for backup. He's like a demon once he gets going. Talk of the demon, here he is." Bertie walked over, his hands full of food and drink. The aroma made Jake's mouth water before he'd even taken them from the older man.

"Here you go, young Jake. Tea, and two bison burgers. That should keep you going all day."

"Thank you Bertie. It smells great," he said as he took them from him.

Mungo put his hand on Jake's shoulder as the outlander tried to balance his breakfast in his own hands. "Go and eat in the saloon Jake. It's a bit cold out here. We'll just be readying the horses for a few minutes." Jake nodded, walking off through the cold morning air towards the main door into the saloon.

"You feeling good Bertie? Ready for some action?"

"You know me boss. I always like a bit of a ruckus. The more vampires the better."

"Just save a few for me and Jake," Mungo said as he headed over to check the horses.

* * *

Coop and Lars stood in the clearing, looking at the remains of the house. Only a few posts that were once part of the porch remained upright. The rest of the structure was a pile of glowing embers. The rest of the Craven's sat close by, enjoying the warmth as they cooked ravens over the dying flames.

Lars turned to Coop. "Are you sure you're strong enough for the day ahead?"

"I'm fine. It's just a nick in my skin. Sharla has bound it tight. It will not give me any trouble. I'm eager to hunt. Both vampires and outlanders. Next time I see him, I'll skewer his backside with my spear."

Lars smiled thinly. He knew that the young man next to him would one day take his place. And for that he was glad. He was getting older and time seemed to be weighing heavy on his bones. "Good. We need to move out soon. The outlander was here for a friend. And to hunt vampires. That tells me they are close by. We should follow the track to see where it leads. Have you noticed the spirits in the forest?"

Coop had. The swirling mists made his flesh creep. "Yes. There are ghosts here. It's an evil place."

"I agree. We cannot be far from them. It's as if the forest is alive with spirits. We are a long way from home Coop. Not all of us will return. We must accept that. If I don't make it back, you will take my place."

"But you will-"

"We are dealing with monsters," Lars said, cutting him off. "Monsters are dangerous. We will lose some of our kin this day."

Sharla walked over to the two of them, wiping the remnants of her breakfast from her red face. "What is the plan?" she asked expectantly.

"We follow the track, then see where it leads. We are many. We can fan out, which will give us greater chance to spot their hideout, because they will not be out in the open during the day." He looked down at Sharla, his eyes lingering on her cleavage. She noticed his eyes on her, flushing at the neck.

"We move out as soon as we've eaten. It could be a long day. We need to be heading back to Mantz before the sun is too low. We cannot stay here another night." Sharla nodded, walking back over to the clan to give them the news.

Lars turned to Coop, clapping him on the shoulder. "Stay close to me. All the time. Let's hunt some monsters."

* * *

The cart rolled to a halt, veering off the track into the long grass. Jake coasted to a stop behind them. He switched of the engine, pulling the bike up onto its stand. He walked over to Mungo and Bertie who were stretching their backs out, the grass up over their knees.

"My backside is numb," said Mungo, rubbing it vigorously.

Bertie smiled. "I'll wager that the seat is numb too, having that slab of rump bouncing up and down on it!"

Mungo smiled at the smaller man. He had known Bertie half of his own life. The older man kept his cards close to his chest, but Mungo knew he'd seen many battles over the seasons. He looked at his face, marvelling that he was about to do battle with unseen monsters, yet still had time to laugh and joke. He looked at Jake. "What's the plan?"

Jake took off his pack, emptying the contents on the cart cover. The two men looked on in silent expectancy as Jake readied his weapons. He handed each of them a stake. Bertie tested it in his hands, liking the feel of it. Jake gave Mungo one of the crosses. "I've only got two of these. You need to stay close together. The cross will ward them off. I'll use the guns as much as I can. Will you be okay with your slingshots and stakes?"

"Aye," Bertie said. "We'll be just fine with these. The slingshots may not be of much use in close quarters. These will be better," he said, slapping it in his palm.

"How far to this place?" Mungo asked.

"It's not too far. Half-an-hour's walk?" Bertie and Mungo looked at each other.

"What's harf an hour?" Bertie asked.

Jake was suddenly at a loss. "Err, not long," he said. "The time it would take you to drink five jugs of ale." Bertie and Mungo both laughed as they looked at the trees on towards the west.

"We'd have sunk five jugs by the time we reach those there trees."

Jake looked up at the sky. "Well, you can show me that one day. I will hold you both to that promise."

* * *

A few minutes later they were heading towards the fringes of Amatoll forest. Jake knew the way well enough by now. He saw the track that led from Heronveld to his left. He pointed at the track to the right that seemed to bisect the forest. "To the left is Amatoll. The forest on the right is where we need to be. The Vale. Korgan's Vale." All three men fell silent, lost in their own thoughts as the low clouds seemed to press down on top of them. The track meandered between the trees, slowly climbing until Jake motioned them to stop. "This is roughly where we enter the forest. As you can see, the trees are much denser in this forest than in Amatoll over there." Both men could see the difference. The forest they were about to enter seemed too congested. Like the trees were fighting for space. It seemed dark too as they peered in from the track.

"It looks like the forest falls away into the earth," Bertie said, his mouth feeling dry.

"It does," Jake agreed. "The whole forest is like a sink hole. We need to get down into the centre of it. That's where we need to be. Do you remember Mungo?"

"Yes. It's coming back to me now. Lead on Jake."

* * *

A few minutes later, two figures emerged from Amatoll. They stood on the track, looking straight ahead at another forest. Other figures emerged behind them, gradually converging in one big group. Lars turned to them all. "I can feel something. A coldness in the air. Can you feel it?" His clan nodded, eager to follow him. "We will look in there," he said pointing into the opposite forest.

"Be ready for anything," Coop said to the clan as they started across the track. Into the Vale.

* * *

The three men stood at the bottom of the forest. It was deathly quiet. Bertie felt like the trees were looking at him. They'd all noticed tendrils of mist that were floated through the trees. No animals could be seen or heard as they had made their way ever downwards. Jake checked his weapons, his leg throbbing. He'd forgotten to douse his wounds in holy water. He quickly took off his pack, sitting against a tree as he searched for the bottles.

"What are you doing?" Mungo asked.

"I was bitten by one of them. Now I must clean the wound every so often. It keeps my leg healthy. When I don't do this, it hurts," he said as he unscrewed the bottle. He knew where the wounds were under his trousers, generously soaking the fabric. As a few drops hit the forest floor they sizzled, as if landing in a hot pan. Jake looked at the two men. "They are close by. Are we set?" Both men nodded, their slingshots and stakes ready. Mungo had the cross tucked into his waistband, Jake knew he would need it. They headed down the rough stone steps as quietly as they could. It grew darker and darker until they were stood in a dark passageway. Jake motioned for the men to come closer. "I've never been down the left-hand passage. The right leads to the main ante chamber. The cells are that way too. If Father Stephen is here, that's where we should find him. Okay. Stay close." They walked into the low-slung corridor that seemed hewn from the black rock. A few torches further down offered a brief respite to the cloying darkness. Jake took the lead, his shotgun aimed ahead. He stopped suddenly. Bertie and Mungo bumped into him in the darkness.

"What is it?" Mungo whispered.

"I thought I heard voices. Be ready. It may get very ugly, very quickly." They edged forward, their backs against the damp rock. The first cell came into view. Jake's eyes widened in shock when he saw not one, but two men sat on straw mattress. *Tony Oakes. What the fuck!* Jake thought as the two men looked up. Jake put his finger to his lips as he made his way over. Mungo and Bertie followed until the five men were only separated by iron bars. Jake smiled in relief as he looked up at the Vicar. "Father Stephen. God, I'm so glad I found you," he whispered. He looked at the Police Officer. "Tony. What the hell are you doing here?"

"Long story. I'll explain once we're away from this dive. Room service is a bitch!"

"This is Mungo and Bertie. They're friends of mine. Mungo, Bertie, this is Father Stephen and Tony." The four men nodded as one. "Who else is here?" Jake asked.

"Elias and Eddie are here. Along with two others." Father Stephen suddenly had a huge decision to make. How would Jake react to the news? He needed to know. "Jake. Prepare yourself. One of the vampires is your mother."

Jake stood there, his face a blank mask. It took a few seconds for the words to sink in. "Oh Christ. No!" Stephen reached through the bars, putting his paw on Jake's shoulder.

"Sorry Jake. I had to tell you now. At least you are prepared in case she walks around the corner." Jake walked over to the black rock, sliding down until was sat on the floor. He covered his face and silently wept. The four men stood watching for a few minutes, letting him grieve. He raised his head, his eyes impossible to see in the gloom. Jake climbed to his feet, walking over to them. Each man could see the rage in his eyes.

"He's fucking dead. Elias is mine." They all nodded, neither man thinking they should add anything. The look on Jake's face was enough.

* * *

Coop and Lars came to the bottom of the slope, waiting for the rest of the Cravens to catch up. When they were all there, Lars addressed them. "My kin. Listen up," he said, his voice gentle. "This looks like a place where monsters could be hiding." They all looked at the stone steps that led down into the darkness. A few uneasy murmurings floated to Lar's ears. He pointed at a man and a woman who were stood at the back of the group. They both held axes in their hands. "Helen, Toben, you stay here and watch for anyone who tries to escape. Anyone who is not our kin, dies. Understood?"

"We understand," Helen said, her voice much louder than her leaders. Her dirty blonde hair stuck to her face. Her teeth were blackened stumps. Toben nodded with her. His grey hair and beard almost running down to his belly. He was topless, his skinny arms mottled with dark bruises. A scar ran from his hair line, diagonally across his face. His one eye was a cloudy white orb. His nose sat a deformed ball of gristle on his face. His black mouth was devoid of teeth. They stood, axes ready for action.

Coop looked at the rest of his clan. "Be ready. Be a Craven," he said. It seemed to give the clan a moral boost as a few chanted their name.

"Craven, Craven!"

"Quiet," Lars hissed. "We need the element of surprise. No more talking from now. The clan fell silent, feeling admonished by their leader. One by one they headed down. Into the darkness below.

* * *

"Oh no," Jake said. They all had heard the voices drifting down from the forest. Jake clearly heard a word that made his stomach turn to ice.

"What is it Jake? Father Stephen said.

"I was attacked last night by some right nutcases. They wanted to eat me. It looks like they've followed me here."

The four other men looked toward the entrance to the tunnel, their expressions grave. Father Stephen broke their trance. "What do we do?"

Jake took off his pack, pulling out the shotgun. He clipped the ammunition belt around his waist and checked the weapon was ready for use. He handed the pistol to Tony. "Take this. You've fired a gun before right?"

"Yes. But not for a while." Jake gave him the spare clips hastily, dropping two on the floor. The noise echoed through the corridor as the five men collectively drew their breaths in. That was the last thing they needed.

* * *

Lars put his hand on Coop's arm. "Did you hear that?"

"Yes. Someone is down there."

"This may be a trap. Be ready, Coop. Kill anything you see." Coop nodded, his face set like stone.

* * *

Eddie's eyes open as the noise reverberated around the walls. He looked over at Elias whose eyes were also open. They looked at each other, exchanging the briefest of nods. Both vampires sat up, rousing the two others lying next to them. Eddie smiled. He could taste the sweetest aroma flowing through the cavern.

* * *

"We've got to get you out of this cell," Jake said urgently. He looked at the lock, sorely tempted to blast it off with his shotgun. Before he could ponder his options, he heard a noise coming from the entrance. He froze as two figures appeared, silhouetted against the light. They spotted the men, their weapons coming to bear.

"Fuckenhell," Mungo said as he readied his slingshot. Bertie did the same. The two figures advanced slowly, coming to a halt ten feet away from the group of men.

"We meet again, outlander. I see you have found your friend. More food for us."

Mungo pulled his slingshot taut, his arm quivering. "One more step and I'll skewer you through the throat. You and your boy." Lars looked at Coop. He suddenly realised their predicament. The rest of the Cravens were now gathered behind them. They were poised for a melee.

"I see you have brought more guests for us Jake," Elias said from behind them. Jake spun around, bringing the shotgun level. He looked at the giant vampire with the red glaring eyes, wanting nothing more than to pull the trigger. He knew though that if he did all hell would break loose. He had friends here with him. He needed to think. His eyes drifted from Elias to the figure stood next to him. What was once his beloved mother now looked at him inquisitively. Her mouth opened, revealing a black pit lined with grey teeth. Her canines almost reached her bottom lip, her tongue poking between them. She was hungry. She hissed at Jake, bringing goosebumps to his skin.

"Oh Mom. What has he done to you?" Jake said, the shotgun dropping a few inches. Tony watched behind the bars, trying to keep his eyes on both enemies. He could see the boy with the spear whispering to the group in the darkness. Tony could see they were getting ready to attack. He pulled back the slider on the gun, readying himself.

Stephen stood next to him, a large stake in his hand. He put his head close to Tony's ear. "At the first sign of movement, shoot the padlock off. We're bloody helpless in here." Tony nodded, placing the barrel of the gun against the lock.

Karaa looked through steely eyes at the young man with the dark hair. She too, could smell him. Her fetid mouth slowly filled with spit as she gently rocked on her feet. "I want him, Eddie."

"There will be enough to go around," Eddie said, wondering who would make the first move.

"You're mine Jake," Elias said, taking a step forward.

Jake pulled the cross out from his waist band, holding it outstretched. It instantly came alive in his hand, a bright glow bathing the corridor in light. The four vampires recoiled in pain, the two women screaming curses.

"CRAVENS," A voice boomed behind Jake as the inevitable happened.

* * *

Mungo and Bertie let their barbs fly, impaling two attackers. They went down hard as two more took their place. The tall man and boy had shrunk back, letting the foot soldiers start the melee. Four more barbs flew in rapid succession, three fatally wounding their prey. The forth attacker suffered a flesh wound that dropped him to his knees as others pushed past. A loud shot rang out, slowing the attack momentarily. The old padlock hit the floor in two pieces, the cell door flung open as Father Stephen and Tony charged out.

"Help them. I'll help Jake," Stephen yelled as he pulled the cross from Mungo's trousers. He turned, holding it aloft in the confines as he advanced on the vampires. They shrank back, even Elias giving ground on Jake and the Vicar as they moved in on them.

Tony unloaded the gun into the oncoming masses, trying to hit as many as he could. He roared in defiance as several went down in the darkness. The magazine emptied, Tony swearing in anger as he tried to eject it to reload. He clicked the new magazine into place as Lars grabbed him by the throat, pushing him into the cell bars.

"You will taste so good after I cook you on my spit," Lars spat into the Policeman's face.

"Fuck you!" Tony replied, grabbing the taller man by his clothing, throwing him into the cell. Lars hit the wall and fell to the ground hard. His eyes tried to focus on the figure coming towards him, scrambling to his feet to meet the attack. Lars had never been outmatched. He was taller than most men, full of wiry muscle that had been garnered from a lifetime of toil. He was shocked when the unknown foe had manhandled him so easily.

"Come on then, outlander," he said as Tony crashed into him. The two men grappled for supremacy as the battle continued outside the cell. Lars fired a punch that hit Tony in the chest, bouncing off the rubbery muscle. The Policeman never even registered the blow, firing

The Turning

his own punch into the taller man's ribcage. The sound of breaking bones carried to their ears as Lars crumpled to the floor. He'd never been hit like that before. He knew at that moment he was a beaten man. A strong hand grabbed his beard, dragging him to his feet. He was ready for another crushing blow when the Tony's hand let go of him. Lars looked into his foe's eyes as a look of incomprehension appeared. He was about to speak when Coop's spear shot out the front of his throat, coating Lars in a fine red mist. Tony tried a gargled curse before falling to his knees, the spear still embedded in his flesh. A foot on his shoulder and a sharp pull freed the spear, letting Tony fall to the cell floor, a dark puddle spreading underneath him. Coop was about to strike once more, Lars staying his hand.

"Let him die well. He fought like a beast who had the better of me. Leave him."

Coop nodded, looking at his master. "You're hurt," he said as Lars held his side.

"I am. But I will not let that stop me." They turned their attention back to the corridor as the fight ensued.

Jake and Father Stephen walked forward, herding the four vampires into a far corner of the crypt. The noises behind them made Jake turn around, alarmed to see the battle raging in the corridor. "I need to go help. Can you hold them here?" he said to the Vicar.

"I can. Give me your cross. I don't know how long I can keep them subdued. Do what has to be done."

Jake handed him the cross and turned to face the cells. He walked forward purposefully, readying his shotgun. He looked into the cell, his face dropping. "Tony?" he said as he saw the Policeman lying on his back in a puddle of blood. The wound in his neck told Jake that it was too late to help him. He brought his shotgun level, trying to find a target. He saw the two cannibals that he saw in the forest. The tall man and boy. The man seemed to be injured, the boy helping him out of the cells. Jake fired, the full force of the discharge taking them down, blowing the bodies back into the cell. "Oh no. Mungo!" Jake said as he rounded the bend into the main corridor. The big man with the Asiatic features was down, spears and axes chopping him to pieces. Bertie was further down the corridor, stabbing at anything within range. Many of the Cravens were lay sprawled on the wet stone floor, their blood pooling on the uneven ground. Bertie's left arm fell to the floor, severed by a single axe blow. He fell against the wall as another blow cleaved his head in two. Jake screamed, unloading his shotgun into the throng of bodies. He cut a woman in two as she charged him. The blast deafening in the confines. Her innards slid out of her body as Jake fired again, hitting Bertie's killer side on. Jake racked the barrel of the shotgun, the spent cartridge landing in a sea of bodies. Two more shots rang out, clearing a pathway for their escape. He quickly reloaded the shotgun as a voice rang out to him.

"Jake. I can't hold on much longer. My hands are almost on fire."

Jake checked the corridor, satisfied that no threat remained. "Hang on Father," he said as he caught sight of Bertie. The old man was sat against the wall, his ruined head lay on his slender shoulders. Jake wanted to retch but knew he was out of time. They had to get out of there. He spotted Mungo as he made his way back. He'd been decapitated. His body bore terrible wounds that Jake tried not to look at. "I'm so sorry Mungo."

"Hurry Jake. The crosses are losing their power," Stephen called, making Jake run back to the main cavern. He took the one cross off the Vicar, noticing the older man looked weary, almost spent.

"Let's go," he said as they backed away.

Elias stood, hissing at the retreating men. "You will not leave here alive. I promise you that."

Jake fired the shotgun, hitting Elias in the chest, propelling him into the others. The two men backed away quicker until they were running back through the corridor towards the forest, Jake clicking his backpack on as he navigated the fallen bodies.

Eddie made to give chase, Elias's hand holding him back. "Let them get into the forest. You and Karaa then can go after them. Lead them away from the doorway if you can. I want Jake somewhere else when

The Turning

it opens." Eddie smiled, knowing what the giant was thinking. He motioned for Karaa to follow him, leaving Elias and Alison in the cavern.

* * *

Jake and Father Stephen got to the bottom of the stairs as the younger man checked his shotgun. "Fuck. The handgun. Tony had it."

"You cannot go back for it now. We need to get out while we can."

Jake nodded reluctantly as the two men started to climb the steps into the forest.

Helen and Toben crouched behind two trees, the loud bangs and cries of pain filtering up into the forest. Mist had started swirling around their feet making them more on edge. Helen looked over at her mate. "What should we do?"

"We wait here. Lars told us to stay." They heard a noise as two heads appeared from below. They both looked at the men who were coming up the steps close by where they were stood. Helen decided to make her move, her axe ready.

* * *

"Which way Jake?" Stephen asked as they stood on the forest floor looking around. Jake tried to figure out which way the bike and cart would be when a noise pierced the forest.

"WAAAAAAA," the woman screamed as she broke from her hiding place. Kenneth tried to duck her blow but he was too late. The axe's flat head caught him square on the forehead, crumpling him to the floor. Jake was about to cry out when a man appeared before him. He too was swinging an axe, aimed at his head. Jake brought up the shotgun, firing off his last shot. It caught Toben in the chest, smashing him into a tree. He was dead before he hit the soft ferns on the forest floor.

"TOBEN," the woman screamed, throwing herself at Jake. She barrelled into him, sending them sprawling on the forest floor. Before Jake could think she was on him, gouging at his face with her sharp, jagged nails. He grunted in pain as her thumb broke the skin on his cheek, raking his flesh. Her other hand was trying to take his eyeball out.

Jake tried to wriggle from under her, stretching his neck as far away from her sharp nails as he could.

"AAAAAGH!" Jake screamed in pain as her nail dug into his eyelid, drawing blood. He threw a punch, connecting with the woman's mouth, splitting her lip and snapping off two teeth. He felt the pressure on his cheek and eye lessen as the woman screamed in defiance. Shoving her off, he rolled to one side to escape. She was on him again, trying to bite his ear off from behind. Her blackened stumps tore a chunk of Jake's hair off, making him scream again as he tried to get her off his back. Her legs were wrapped around him, bony arms holding him in a headlock. He felt a sharp pain on his ear as she nipped the edge of his flesh. In desperation he grabbed her thighs, running backwards into a stout tree trunk. The back of his head caught her in the face, knocking her out cold. She slipped to the forest floor, blood seeping from the black pit of her mouth.

"Fucking bitch!" Jake's blood lust took over as he picked her up by her clothing, punching her square in the face. He cocked his arm again, driving his knuckles into her flesh. He cried out in anger as his fist broke tooth and bone. The noise, a sickening thwack, echoed through the misty forest. Breathless, Jake threw her aside, her neck snapping on a tree trunk, ending her pitiful existence. He stood there panting, crying, on the brink of madness. He suddenly remembered Father Stephen, running to the fallen Vicar, fearing the worst. He checked his pulse. He was alive, but unconscious. Jake would never be able to carry him the half mile to the bike.

His thoughts were disturbed by Eddie's voice. "Amigo. Come to Eddie. Let us finish this." Jake grabbed the shotgun from the ground, firing a blast in the direction of the steps. Eddie ducked down, laughing at Jake. Goading him. "You cannot keep that up for too long. Come. Come to Eddie. Join us."

"Fuck you Guzman," Jake spat as he reloaded. He realised that he would run out of shells soon enough. Kenneth was out cold and could not be moved. *What do I do?* he thought. Firing off two more shots that

The Turning

made Eddie and Karaa dive for cover, Jake made the hardest decision of his life. He fled.

Eddie looked at Karaa and smiled. "We'll give him a head start. We won't be able to leave the forest in the daylight but we can make it fun." She smiled at him, her fingers lacing into his.

"Which way?" Jake said as he climbed the steep incline. He came to a level part of the forest, slowing slightly as his eyes took in the stone monument in front of him. Even in his haste, he slowed to a jog, marvelling at the size of it. A raised section at one end reminded Jake of an old band stand. A stone circle led from it, several small carved doorways stood empty between stone pillars. He jogged across it, his feet slapping the smooth flag stones. *Wow*, he thought. *I wonder if the doorways work like the one in Amatoll.*

"Jake. I can taste you on the wind," Eddie said from behind him. Jake turned and fired the shotgun, shredding bark as the vampire dived for cover. He looked across the clearing as another vampire stood smiling at him. The barrel lowered slightly as he stared at her. Karaa's blonde hair was tied in a braid that curled around her shoulder. Her grey face still showed signs of her former beauty. Jake started to drift into a daydream as their eyes locked. She sensed it, smiling wider, her canines dripping saliva onto her clothing. He tore himself free of her glare, firing another shot. She ducked, a few pieces of buckshot snagging her pale flesh. Karaa hissed as she watched the fair-looking man turn and run.

Eddie walked over, touching her arm where she'd been hit. "That won't do you harm. It takes a lot more than that to destroy us. Come. Let's go."

Jake climbed the last few feet until he'd reached the edge of the Vale. He broke into the relative sunlight, feeling better that he was out in the open. He looked right, spotting the cart and bike further along the tree line. In the distance, he could see the lone mountain, its summit covered in low-slung cloud. He took off with renewed vigour, hoping to put some distance between him and the evil in the forest. A few minutes later he was kick-starting the bike, letting it tick over on its stand while he checked the back of the cart. He pulled a clay bottle from underneath, pulling the cork from the stopper. He drank greedily, enjoying the heady ale. It ran down his neck, soaking his jacket as he continued to drink. The bottle landed in the long grass as he burped loudly. The tree line was less than fifty feet from the cart. Eddie's voice carried on the wind towards him.

"You're safe now, human! Run and hide. We've got the forest covered. You come back this way, we'll be waiting."

Fuck, Jake thought. He needed to get back through the doorway. Back home to Katherine and Alicia. *Father Stephen*! He could not leave him here with these monsters. He needed a plan. He needed help. He needed Wilf.

Twenty-Eight

Elias stood up as they entered the catacomb. They walked over to Elias, noticing his expectant expression. Alison stayed on the floor, her eyes closed. "Well," he said. What happened?"

"Jake got away as you wanted. We watched him ride off towards the east."

"And the shaman?"

Eddie smiled. "He's in the corridor," he said pointing. "He is sleeping."

The giant vampire smiled. "That's good news. Put him in the cells, for I have unfinished business with him. Jake will ride east, looking for help, but it will be of no use for him. I will be in his land, taking his kin. They will be brought here, to join us."

"And Jake?" Karaa asked.

Elias pondered the question for a moment. "I would like to turn him too. Although part of me thinks he'll die trying to protect his kin. Time will tell."

Eddie and Karaa turned, walking back to the corridor. Stephen was still out cold. They left him for the moment, concentrating on the heaped bodies on the floor. Many gave off the rank wet stench of death. They lifted each carcass, walking them up the stone steps, dumping them in the forest for whatever beast was passing. Two bodies lay side by side in the soft ferns. Their hands touching. They had travelled far together. Now Mungo and Bertie lay together, letting nature take its course.

Eddie sniffed a body on the floor. "This one's still alive," he said as Karaa walked over to him. She looked down at Sharla, her eyes showing no recognition to her former clan member. Her face was covered in blood, her body bearing terrible wounds. There was still a brief flicker of life in her eyes. A defiance that refused to let go. Eddie knelt down beside her, his ruined hand stroking her matted hair. "Shall we share?" he said.

Karaa shook her head. "You have her. I will see if there is anyone else." Eddie reached down, his hands taking hold of her head. Sharla of Mantz looked up at the stone ceiling. She felt at peace. Her last thoughts were of her homeland and the face of the boy she had grown to love. A smile tugged at her lips as Eddie snapped her neck, ready to feed.

Father Stephen was placed carefully on the straw mattress. He stirred slightly. The one side of his face bore an angry red bruise that was growing darker. Karaa looked at the two bodies on the floor. A large man lay on top of another body. His lifeless eyes staring up at the ceiling. His chest was a bloody mess of flesh. White bone could be seen, stark against the drying blood. The vampire yanked him out into the corridor, dumping her former brother on the stone floor. She walked over to Coop, lifting his arm as she started to pull his body out too. She jumped as he made a noise, a low moan that echoed through the corridor. She knelt down, looking at the boy. The flesh on his arm was tattered from the shotgun blast, half of his face bore scars too. Karaa inhaled. *He smells good.* Something in her memory, tried to recall the smell. She knew it, but it was just out of reach.

"Karaa," Coop whispered. "It's me. Coop. Do you not remember me?"

The name sent a flashback through her memory. *She could see a forest. A boy. Naked underneath her.* The memory faded into the ether, lost forever. She looked into his eyes, noticing how he relaxed underneath her stare. "I do not know you. But we can now become kin."

She lowered her mouth to his neck, her teeth puncturing the skin easily. Sucking sounds could be heard through the catacombs as Karaa drained the life out of the boy. Coop floated on the breeze as his life ebbed away. He had not a care. He was where he wanted to be. With his Karaa.

* * *

Doug put the kettle on, peering through the kitchen window for the umpteenth time that morning. It was a little after ten. The sky was dark with foreboding clouds that seemed to weigh heavy on the land. Katherine and Alicia were in the lounge. He could hear faint gurgles and cooing. He smiled for a brief moment, forgetting that his son was out there somewhere, far from home. Very possibly still in that other place. That other world. A world filled with monsters that he'd only witnessed in late night movies, with Alison sat snoring next to him on the sofa. Jake had been gone less than a day, but already Doug was fearing the worst. He knew though that his son could not return through the doorway until midnight. He would have to be patient. It was going to be a very long twenty-four hours.
"Are you okay in there Doug?" Katherine asked from the lounge.
"Err, yeah. I'm fine. Just waiting on the kettle." He finished his sentence as the kettle clicked off, its steam coating the kitchen window in condensation. He poured two mugs of tea, his mind wandering back to a far-off forest. He hoped his son had found Father Stephen. He hoped they were holed up somewhere safe, swapping stories of their adventures. He sensed that he was being optimistic. Doug needed to close his mind to the 'what ifs' and concentrate on his family that sat in the next room. He also needed to expect the unexpected. He added milk and sugar to both cups, walking into the lounge, his slippered feet barely making a noise on the carpet.
"I thought you'd fallen asleep," Katherine said. Doug could see the look in her eyes. She was trying to put a brave face on things. He loved her for that. She was strong and resilient. He would need that if the worst came to the worst.

"Sorry love. I'm getting old." His attempt at humour fell flat. He placed the mug on a coaster on an oak side table. He looked at his granddaughter and smiled. She was fast asleep in the crook of her mother's arms. "She's a real smasher," Doug said.

Katherine looked up at him and smiled. "She sure is. And she loves her grandad."

Doug fought the tears that were threatening to spill from his eyes, pushing them back as hard as he could. "Thanks love. That cheered me up." He paused for a moment before carrying on. "Are you okay in here for a bit? I need to go out to the garage and sort a few things out."

The woman nodded. "Of course. Just pass me the remote thingy so I can keep myself entertained while she sleeps." Doug walked over to the mantelpiece, picking up the black remote control before handing it to Katherine. He bent down and kissed the top of her head, stroking Alicia's cheek before he straightened up. The infant stirred slightly, moving her dainty arm across her eyes to block out the light. Doug chuckled before leaving them to their daytime television. He picked up his tea and made his way out into the garage.

"Bloody hell," he exclaimed as a cold wind greeting his exit from the kitchen. He shuffled as quickly as his slippers would carry him, through the side door into his garage. The light switch was flicked, bathing the small space in artificial light. Doug put his tea on the workbench before reaching a shelf above his head. As heavy box slid from its dusty resting place, he caught the other side with his free hand, such was the weight inside. He laid the contents out on the Formica surface, putting them in some kind of order. Six wooden stakes, two heavy silver crosses, and two large bottles of holy water completed his arsenal. He was as satisfied that this would be enough if the worst happened. He put them back in the box, leaning against the work surface as he drank his tea. *Come back safe, Jake,* he thought. *I could not take losing you too.*

* * *

The Turning

He resisted the urge to stop at Culnae. In truth, Jake had no idea who he would speak to, now that Mungo and Bertie were gone. His bike made steady progress, climbing ever upwards towards the massif that now filled his vision. As he drew nearer the sun was lost behind the cliff face, the temperature dropping noticeably on the dim grassland. Jake eased off the throttle as he entered Wooten Drift Gorge, navigating dry scrub plants and rocks. The firm ground gave way to a sandy pathway, making Jake give the road ahead his full attention. He was barely using his throttle, letting the bike putter along at crawling pace. A few minutes passed before the narrow corridor opened out into a large clearing. Jake remembered the last time he passed by this route. He smiled, recollecting the makeshift cart that the Finglers had built for Wilf and himself. It had done its job well. They had stolen ahead of Elias, snatching Katherine back from his clutches before he could carry out his plans for her. He also remembered the giants that he'd met in the gorge. The huge men from the north had helped them, all perishing at the hands of the vampires. A high price had been paid for her freedom. He looked to his left, seeing the abandoned mining station that looked like a derelict saloon from a wild-west movie. The red rock that surrounded it seemed to be slowly dragging the saloon into its embrace. *Not the place I'd want to spend the night*, he thought as he gradually increased his speed. He looked up, seeing yellow eyes looking down on him from the dark recesses in the rock. He kept his pace steady, eager to be back out in the sunlight. The gorge gave Jake the creeps. It was deathly silent. Only the sound of his bike broke the solitude. A few minutes later, after navigating a huge fallen boulder, Jake welcomed the semi warm sun on his face. He stopped the bike, climbing off to stretch. He remembered the holy water in his pack. He drank greedily from one bottle, the liquid seeming to cleanse the recent events from his body and mind. Feeling refreshed, he clipped his pack back in place and climbed back on the motorbike, kick-starting it. He twisted the throttle for a brief second, giving him a burst of speed, before clicking the bike into neutral. He was aware that he need to save fuel, preferring to coast his way down to the sea. Jake tried to figure out how many miles it was. He concluded anywhere between fifteen and twenty, which would only take him an hour or so to complete. He let the stress of the last few hours blow away on the tangy breeze, his arms and shoulders relaxing. He inhaled the sweet air, his brown hair ruffling as he headed downwards, towards his old friend.

* * *

Father Stephen sat up groggily, gingerly touching his forehead. *What happened?* he thought, his finger dabbing the inflamed skin. The Vicar tried to lever himself up off the straw mattress but his legs didn't want to comply. He sat back down heavily, noticing smeared blood on his palms. It was then that his eyes took in his surroundings. In the cell and corridor, he could see chunks of flesh and body parts littering the stone floor. A hand, severed at the wrist, rested on the black iron bars that held him captive. He felt bile rise in his throat as he noticed other body parts beyond the bars. Half a head lay on the wet stone floor. It had been cleaved in two. One eye stared lifelessly at him from the floor. Stephen closed his eyes, grinding his knuckles into them to try to shut out the image.

"Quite the party, wouldn't you agree?" a voice said in the darkness. Elias moved into the corridor, accompanied by his kin.

Stephen dragged himself to his feet, walking stiffly to the cell door. "Where is Jake?"

"He fled. Leaving you here all alone, shaman. What kind of a friend would do that?" Eddie sniggered behind Elias, his eyes glowing in the gloom.

"I don't blame him for leaving. I only hope he's home soon with his family."

Elias shook his head slowly. "I'm afraid that will not be the case. We shepherded him in the opposite direction. Eddie and Karaa last saw him heading towards the gorge to the east. If he is heading where I think he's heading, he will not be back in time to pass through the doorway. That will allow me to travel to his home and bring back his family."

Stephen's knuckles tightened on the bars. "You monster! What do you hope to achieve by doing this? You're going to rip that man's life apart. Again. He's already lost one family. And now you're going to do that to him again?"

"Yes, I am. He destroyed my master. Do you think that can go unpunished?"

"He did what he had to do to survive. You had his woman. The woman he loves. Do you think he would not fight for her?"

Elias laughed. The noise echoing through the corridor and beyond. "Of course. I have a lot of respect for Jake. He is very courageous. He has done what no other human could do. That's why when I turn him and his kin, I know I will be adding valuable members to our family."

"You bastard!" Stephen spat. "I cannot believe you'd do this to them."

"Not just me. You're going to help me do it, Father Stephen."

Stephen's eyes widened in horror. "What! Never! You think I'm going to be part of that? You're even stupider than I thought!"

Elias chuckled again. It was deep and melodious. Like the laugh of a happy old uncle. He stepped towards the bars, smiling. "You say that now. But when you're a vampire like us, you'll change your mind." He took a key out of his pocket, unlocking the new padlock on the cell door.

Stephen stepped backwards, heading towards the far wall of the small cell. The four vampires entered, barring his only exit. "Keep away from me," he said, his voice quivering.

"Eddie, Karaa. Hold the shaman down on the straw mattress. Pin his arms." Eddie walked forward first, smiling at Stephen. Without thinking, the Vicar threw a punch that caught Eddie on the cheek. He took a step back, a look of shock on his face. They stared at each other as the vampire's face creased into a smile.

"I want you to fight. Man of God," Eddie hissed as he launched himself at Kenneth. Karaa followed suit, grabbing Stephen's other arm. Before he could think, he was flat on his back, looking up a pair of red eyes. Eddie and Karaa easily held his arms in a crucifix pose. His renewed strength seemed to ebb from his body. The fight simply went out of him. He felt cold hands on his legs, sliding down his trousers until they were gripping his ankles. He looked down to see Alison looking back at him. Her mottled grey tongue poking out through her teeth. *Of all the times we spoke. In my church. In my house. In your house. When you needed my help. When I needed yours. To think that the last time I'll look at you will be in a dark cave in another world. You a vampire, me about to become one. You simply couldn't make this up.*

Stephen closed his eyes and thought of his beloved wife. "I love you, Denise. I'm coming to find you," he whispered. The words offering little comfort. A rough slap across the face made his eyes open in shock.

"Are you still with us Father?" Elias asked.

"Fuck you!" Stephen spat back.

"Defiant to the end. I'll shall give you that. Now I shall give you this." Stephen looked on in horror as the vampire bit into the back of his wrist. The grey flesh broke, spewing a black, tar like ooze from the wound. Elias straddled the Vicar, pressing the wound to Stephen's lips. He tried to fight it by turning his head away, coating his whiskers in blood. The first few drops entered his mouth, hitting his tongue like acid. He could actually feel pain as the blood trickled through his lips. Kenneth tried to cry out in frustration and anger but it just made more blood slip through his defences. He swallowed involuntarily, almost hear the sizzle of the liquid as it coated the back of his throat. Somewhere in the back on his mind he could hear Eddie sniggering. He tried to block it out, focussing on his wife. He wanted his last thoughts to be of something pure and good. Another swallow made him feel woozy. Father Stephen started to slip away. Away from the world that he knew. Away from this world that he didn't. Into an unknown place from where there could be no return.

* * *

Jake coasted to a stop, placing his feet on the stunted grass. He looked left at the small gathering of buildings called Fingles. It looked like a miniature wild-west town. He almost expected to see mini cowboys come riding along the street on tiny ponies. The small buildings were all made from wood. Rough brown planking covered all edifices as a constant wet breeze blew in from the grey sea, buffeting them. He felt like he was on the very edge of the world. That the grey horizon would spill into the black void of space. He was planning on heading towards that horizon too. Along a narrow roadway, towards his destination. Shetland. He gunned the throttle, rolling a few hundred yards to the totem-pole type marker at the start of the roadway. Intricate carving of weird creatures adorned the face of the pole. He knew first-hand what kind of beasts lurked under the forbidding grey sea. Jake was hoping that he would not have a similar encounter this time. The sea marker told him that he was in luck. The tide was low, giving him a clear run towards the spit of land out at sea. He set off, heading into a fierce wind, laced with sea spray.

Twenty-Nine

The cell door clanked shut, the padlock clicking into place. The four vampires walked back into the main chamber, gathering around the stone sarcophagus. They looked at the sleeping form within. Coop lay motionless, his arms across his chest. His once vibrant skin now had a waxy grey sheen to it. Elias pulled back his lips, exposing the fresh fang beneath. "He will wake soon. Eddie. Take Karaa and find some food for us once the sun has set. We must all rest, for it has been a busy day so far. And we have busier days ahead of us. They moved away from the sleeping boy, each finding a place to lie. Elias looked at Alison. "Do you remember anything from your past life?"

She shook her head. "No. Nothing," was her brief reply.

Elias needed to explain things to her. "The man who came this morning. The young man with the dark hair. He is your son."

Alison looked at him, her feral eyes not registering the news. "What is Son?"

"He was your boy. You gave birth to him. You raised him. Now he wants to destroy us. We cannot allow that to happen. I am going to his land to bring his kin here. Once I've done that, Jake will come once more. He will come to fight. We must make them all like us. Only then will be able to live in peace. We can then roam the lands, feeding on whoever we choose. We can go far Alison. Beyond our world. With Jake and his kin, we will be many, and we will be strong. Do you understand?"

She nodded tentatively. "I think so."

"Good. Let's rest." They all lay down. Eddie and Karaa were already asleep, their bodies entwined. Alison rested her head on her outstretched arm and closed her eyes. Elias laced his hands behind his head, looking up at the ceiling. *She doesn't understand. She is either totally bereft of memory, or stupid. However, she is loyal. Eddie and Karaa are the cunning ones. Maybe Coop too. Let's see what the Vicar brings. Either he become one of us, or he will be destroyed. I've never tried to turn a holy man before. Time will tell.* He closed his eyes and drifted into unconsciousness, as plans and possibilities drifted with him.

* * *

He made good progress, his bike navigating the rutted track with little difficulty. Jake passed by the lone tree that had recently been his refuge for the night, marking the highest part of the track. He could now see Shetland ahead of him. It was partially obscured by the sea mist, but Jake could clearly see that more buildings had been built. He felt a swell of hope radiate through his chest as he rolled down towards the end of the track. "You have been busy," he said as he came to a stout wooden bridge that stretched from the track, across the ford to the island of Shetland. The wooden beams and planks protested lightly as his bike rolled across them. As his bike hit the other side he twisted the throttle, propelling himself towards the main building.

"Jake!" Wilf exclaimed as he walked around the front of the main house with arms full of logs. They fell to the ground as he strode quickly to the younger man, who was propping his bike on the stand.

"Hi Wilf," Jake said as the two men came together. They embraced fiercely. "It's so good to see you. We never knew if you made it to safety."

"It'll take more than a few ghosts in old Amatoll to get rid of us." The older man suddenly looked wary. "Katherine?"

"She's at home, along with our daughter."

Tears peppered Wilf's eyes at the news. "You had a daughter! That's the best news I've heard since I've been here." He clapped Jake on the shoulder. "Come inside We'll get wet through if we stand here gassing all day." He turned and picked up the fallen logs, leading the younger man into what was once Wilf's great grandfather's house. Jake walked through the porch, his mind flashing back to the last time he was stood here. It was the first time he'd met Katherine. On that night, Elias and his cohorts had tried to kill them all. The giant vampire succeeded in snatching Katherine away from them which in turn lead to a cat and mouse chase across the strange land. As Jake walked into the main living area he remembered Wilf and Cedric's sister, Mo, who'd was ripped to pieces by two of her own pigs out on the porch. Elias had turned them into monstrous beasts that had chased Wilf and himself off the island. Jake often thought that it was the single craziest twenty-four hours of his life so far.

"What happened to Mo's body?" Jake asked it without thinking, realising it was a bit blunt.

The older man didn't flinch. "When we came back, Mo's bones were still on the porch. Most of 'em anyways. We gathered them up and buried her at the far end of the island, next to her animal pens. It's what she would have wanted. This was her home. Now it's ours."

"I'm glad you all made it out here safely."

"So are we," Wilf said as he placed the logs into the dying embers of last night's fire. He stirred them with a metal poker, sending flaming motes billowing out across the room. "But enough talk of such things. You're not here to ask me about my herb garden. What has happened, Jake?"

"I think we may need to sit down. Because I have much to tell you."

Wilf sat at the table next to the window and poured two large mugs of nettle tea, adding a good helping of honey and cream to each one. "Then let's get to it."

* * *

Sometime later both men sat looking out of the window at the grey sea scape. Jake had told Wilf about how after leaving him at the doorway, they had sought out Father Stephen. The family friend and Vicar had removed the fang from Jakes' leg, dousing the wound with holy water. He recounted how they had moved far from the doorway, to a house by the sea. How little Alicia had come into their lives and filled it with joy. Jake's face had turned serious when he filled Wilf in on the strange happenings in Rednal and Cornwall. Wilf reached across the table and squeezed the younger man's hand when he learnt how Jake's mother had vanished from their home, only to turn up in the Vale as a monster. He also uttered gasps and curses when Jake described his meeting with the cannibals. How they had tried to kill him, ending with Wilf's former home being burnt to the ground. Jake described the battle in the Vale. How a man from his world, along with dear Mungo and Bertie had died trying to free Father Stephen from the vampire's stronghold. The older man had accepted the news stoically, showing little emotion on the outside. On the inside he died a little, hearing the news that his old friend from Culnae was no more. Bathurst now knew that Jake was here to help his friend. A friend who was worthy of helping. The older man's story was far simpler. He told Jake how after the doorway had closed, he and the two strange demons had headed for their village. He explained how the forest had come alive with spirits, shivering when Jake told him that they still roamed there. He told him how most of the villagers had followed Wilf out to Shetland. How the Finglers had helped build a new home for them by the sea. All in all, it was a happy recollection. The older man seemed at peace with his lot. Jake knew that he was now deflating that big happy bubble.

"So, what is your plan Jake?"

"I need to go back as soon as I can and try and break him out of there. Then I need to return home. Katherine and Alicia are safe with Dad. But I won't be happy until I am back there with them."

"And you're here to ask for my help?" It was a statement rather than a question.

"Err, I'm not sure. I guess so. When I left the forest, I headed here to find you. I'm not really sure what should happen next." Jake sat looking down at the table, lost in his thoughts.

"I'll help you Jake. You're kin. I'd do anything to help you, without question or condition. However, I would like you to do a favour for me in return."

"Of course. Anything. What do you need?"

"To see Katherine. To hold your child. Is that possible?"

Jake thought about it for a split second before smiling at the grizzled older man. "Sure. They would love that."

"Good. So now we need to make preparations. When do you want to go?"

"As soon as possible. Today. Can we make it back?"

Wilf pondered the question, standing up from the table. "I think so. Follow me."

Jake walked behind Wilf to the white door that lay at the rear of the building. Jake remembered what lay beyond. A sea cave, where Katherine and he had tried to hide from William. He remembered seeing the child vampire being pulled to pieces by the two Orgas that had burst from the dark waters. He felt slight trepidation at the thought of heading down that dark stairwell. Wilf drew the bolt, grabbing a lantern from the ledge next to the door. The door opened with a squeal as tangy sea air filled the rear hallway.

"Hold on to the rail as we go down. It's a bit on the slippery side." Jake heeded the warning, grabbling the newly erected wooden rail. They headed into the dark cavern, the volume of the sea increasing with every step. They came to the bottom step, the flame in the lantern fighting against the darkness. Wilf took two torches from the wall, lighting them from the lantern's flame. He shielded them from the breeze as the flames took hold of them. Satisfied, he placed them back on the wall, bathing the shelving in front of them in a flickering light.

Jake looked at the items on the shelves, curiosity outweighing the nervousness he felt in the cavern. "You've been busy. Are you expecting trouble?"

"Always. You just never know in this land. I've made more crosses and stakes just in case." He picked one of the wooden stakes up, handing it to Jake. "Don't touch the tip. It is smeared with Orga blood.

The Turning

The Finglers tell me the blood burns when you touch it. I figured it wouldn't hurt to try it out one day."

A noise from above made both men look towards the stairs. "Wilf. Are you down there?" It was a female voice that carried down into the semi darkness.

"Aye. Come down Jessie." The noise of footsteps echoed through the sea cave until a middle-aged woman appeared. Jake remembered seeing her before. She looked at him with a face of concern.

"Jessie, you remember Jake?"

"Err yeah. Good day," she said, half smiling.

Jake returned the smile. "Hi."

She looked at Wilf. "We've got some new arrivals. Haggie gave birth to six piglets. They're in the big pen."

Wilf smiled. "Great news. Six you say? Good old Haggie." Wilf looked at the woman. In the flickering light, she looked younger than her years. Her chestnut hair was now shot through with silver. She looked at Wilf expectantly, her attractive face always pleasing to his eye. "Could you do something for me Jessie?"

She nodded eagerly. "If I can."

"Rouse the folk. I need to speak to them. And can someone make food for two hungry men. Enough food for a journey."

Her face dropped slightly. "You going away Wilf?" Her voice sounded unsteady.

"Yes. Not for long though. Jake needs my help. We will come to the big pen once we're finished here." Jessie nodded, before heading back upstairs. Wilf turned, carefully packing items into a rough hessian sack. "Be ready for a few hostilities. Folk are just getting used to a normal life. They will not like this. But I am the Elder. They will have to accept it."

"Okay. I'll stand behind you though. Just in case someone throws a rock at me," Jake said as he followed Wilf back into the world above.

* * *

Father Stephen woke. His red rimmed eyes looked up at the ceiling, trying to focus. Trying to remember where he was. He turned onto his side, vomiting a black mess across the mattress. He got on his hands and knees as more sour liquid shot from his mouth. It hit the straw, a faint hiss rising into the dank air. Kenneth dry-retched until he collapsed back onto the straw. He wiped his hand across his mouth, trying to remove the stench on his lips. He looked up at the ceiling once more, his mind trying to focus. *What happened?* Every movement was painful to him. Even blinking his eyes seemed to sting him. It came back to him. Elias, feeding him his blood while the others held him down. *Am I becoming a vampire? Is this what it feels like?* He turned on his side tears falling from his eyes. "Please find me Jake. Find me and kill me, before it's too late."

* * *

Jake and Wilf walked across Shetland towards the pens that lay at the far tip. Jake counted six new houses. They looked sturdy and fresh. He was impressed with the work that had gone on here. He could see people gathered by the pig pens, talking between themselves. Jake noted that even the pens had been given a makeover. A new enclosure had been erected with a wooden shack in the middle of it. He could hear the squeal of piglets inside, making him smile. Seeing the faces of the villagers looking at him made it a short-lived smile. They almost looked hostile.

Wilf sensed it too, placing his hand on Jake's shoulder as they stood before them. "Folk. I have news. Gather around so my words are not lost on the breeze." A tight circle formed around the two men, making Jake feel penned in. "You all remember this young man. You all know how he came to us. It was through no fault of his own. Sometimes things just happen. Well he is here now. And he needs my help. One of his friends is being held by Elias and his new kin. They are in the Vale." A few mutterings filtered through the group. "Jake needs my help to break him out of there. We will leave when our food is ready."

"How long will you be gone?" a voice said behind Jake.

"A few days if fortune favours us." He looked at a middle-aged woman who stood in the throng of villagers. "Mima, would you take over while I'm gone?"

She nodded simply. She looked at Jake, her weather-beaten face impassive. He held her gaze for a moment before she looked away.

"Good. Well I'll be back soon. Carry on with your day. And do not fret. I shall return." The villagers dispersed, leaving the two men stood next to the pens. Wilf looked at the younger man. "They are just worried. Whenever you turn up things happen. Do not let that weigh heavy."

"Okay," was all Jake could say.

"Right. Let's see what Jessie has prepared. We must eat too. The tide is back in. The roadway is cut off for a while. By the time it drops again the sun will be far towards the western sky. Let's eat, plan, and see if we can get through this adventure in one piece."

* * *

Elias woke. His red eyes taking focus in the gloom. He thought he'd heard a noise. Sitting up, he glanced at the others. They were all sleeping soundly. He climbed to his feet, walking over to the stone coffin. The boy was still asleep, although Elias knew that he was nearing the point of waking. His skin had turned an ash grey. *He'll rise tonight*, he thought as he walked over to the corridor that led to the forest. He froze mid-step as he saw the cell door hanging open. His eyes scanned his surroundings. Stephen was nowhere to be seen. He caught his foot on something, bending down to pick it up. The new padlock had been twisted open, half of the shackle snapped off. The giant stepped into the cell, noticing the dried black vomit on the straw mattress. *What happened?* he thought. *He must have escaped into the forest. If that's the case, he is lost to us for now.* Elias stood there as a nagging doubt tugged at his thoughts. He hurried down the corridor, up the steps into the forest beyond. He looked about himself for signs of life. Happy that he was alone he ran up the hill towards the track. Seconds later he was stood looking out at the break in the two forests. "The sun is well passed its zenith," he said as more thoughts flooded his mind. He turned and hurried back down to his kin. As he came around the corner into the main ante chamber he jumped. Alison was stood in front of him, her eyes searching him out.

"Where did you go?"

"Into the forest," Elias said as he strode over towards the two sleeping vampires. "Wake up," he commanded. Alison stood next to him as Eddie and Karaa roused themselves. They stood, looking expectant. Elias walked over to the coffin, three sets of eyes following him. "Stephen is gone. He broke himself out of his cell. I've checked the forest. There is not sign of him." The three stood, not moving or reacting in any way. "We need to leave this place, forever. It's not safe here for us. Jake has proved that on more than one occasion. You all saw how he kept us pinned against the wall with his cross. He will be back tonight, of that I'm sure. He will bring allies, who will try and destroy us. We need a new home."

"Where?" Eddie said.

"Mantz," was his reply.

"What is Mantz?" Alison asked.

Elias placed his hands on the cool stone. "Mantz is a vast forest to the west. Eddie found Karaa there. This young boy is also from there. It dwarfs the forests here. The clan that attacked us are also from Mantz. Most of them are now dead. I know the forest. It has buildings and places to shelter. It's not as closed in as the Vale. We could go there and use it as our new home."

Eddie nodded. "We will be able to see humans approach. Not like here. I agree."

Elias looked at the three of them. "Eddie, go and bring a human for the boy. He will wake very soon and he will be hungry. Be as quick as you can."

"What about Karaa?" Guzman asked.

"I have work to do here. Karaa and Alison will be busy while you're gone."

Thirty

Wilf tied the bag with some string, putting it next to the bike. He looked at the track that led to Fingles. The tide was dropping. They were ready to go. "We must make tracks," he said to Jessie and Mima. The two women hugged Wilf briefly, before heading over to one of the other houses.

Jake walked out of the main building, clicking his backpack into place. "Is it time to go?"

"Yes. It's time. How long will it take to get there on this thing?" Wilf sat, slapping the saddle.

Jake checked his analogue divers watch. It was almost seven. He could see that the sky was growing dim. "Two hours or so, which doesn't mean much I know. It will be dark by the time we get there, which means they will be awake. You sure about this?"

"I am. Let's go," Wilf said with authority.

They made their way down to the bridge, Wilf going across on foot. The frigid waters roiled beneath his feet. He could hear the drone of the Orgas under the dark surface. He knew they could sense him and Jake. He cast the thought from his mind as Jake headed across behind him.

"Climb on," Jake said as a fierce wind blew in from the sea. Wilf did as he was asked, holding the sack between tight. He wrapped his free hand around Jake's waist as the bike set off.

* * *

A little while later they came off the track, passing Fingles on their right-hand side. "I'm going to speed up now Wilf. It's a clear run all the way up to the gorge. If you need me to slow down, just shout."

"You'll hear no shouts from me. I'm looking forward to this." Jake smiled as he gunned the throttle, taking the bike beyond forty miles an hour. The track was flat and easy to navigate, even with the added weight. They climbed quickly, passing farmhouses that were dotted sporadically across the land. The two men spotted a few animals, wandering aimlessly. Bison and horses nibbled at the stunted grass as they passed by at speed. The gorge started to loom over them as they drew nearer. Wilf looked behind him, barely able to see Fingles. He knew they were making good time. And he was having the time of his life, sat precariously on the back of a steel horse as it sped towards the split in the massif ahead.

"Gonna slow it down through the gorge. The track is a bit dodgy here and there," Jake said as he navigated the fallen boulder.

"You do what you think is best," Wilf said as the wind suddenly died. The bike sounded loud in the confines of the gorge, the echo of the engine bouncing off the red walls. They passed through without incident, coming out of the gorge as the sun was about to kiss the mountains to the west. Jake looked past Culnae, towards the forests beyond. Something looked odd. He pulled the bike to a stop, signalling for Wilf to climb off. The old man obliged, dropping the sack on the grass.

"Look!" Jake said. "The forest."

Wilf strained his eyes to see what Jake was looking at. Even he could see it. The Vale was blanketed in smoke. Both men could tell it wasn't mist. It was a mixture of black and grey, billowing out through the trees. "The forest is on fire."

"It is," Jake said, feeling uneasy. "Why would it be on fire?"

"I've no answer to that. Let's get down there and find out. I need to take care of something first," Wilf said as he walked away, unbuckling his trousers. Jake followed suit, relieving himself as he watched his possible escape route go up in flames.

* * *

"What do you want for tea?" Doug called from the kitchen.

Katherine was getting Alicia ready to for her bath, gathering up her toys from the carpet. "I'm easy. Whatever you fancy. I've got to bath missy first though."

Doug walked to the doorway and smiled. Katherine was tidying up, Alicia sat in her bouncer, her feet in the air. Doug had gotten used to children's television. He knew that the program being shown was the last one before it turned off for the night. Strange fluffy characters danced through a green forest. It looked safe and inviting as a blue figure with a red blanket danced through the trees. He thought of his son, who would be in a very different forest. One full of ghosts and vampires. He tried to banish the thoughts, concentrating on the girls. "Does steak and chips sound good?"

"Sounds wonderful. I'll be down in a bit." She reached down, unclipping her daughter from the bouncer, lifting her into her arms. Alicia cooed, nuzzling her mother's neck, making Katherine giggle. She walked over to Doug, turning so the baby could see her granddad. "Give grandpapa a kiss," Katherine said. The baby smiled at Doug, melting his heart once again. He took her head in his hands and planted a kiss on her curls. She looked at him, her deep brown eyes blinking, her eyelashes fluttering.

Doug smiled, kissing Katherine on the head too. "I'll get things ready. Don't rush yourself love." He walked back into the kitchen, opening the fridge. He pulled a can of Old Speckled Hen out of the door compartment, cracking the ring pull. He selected his favourite pint glass from the glass fronted cupboard above the worktop, taking his time pouring the ale. Doug took a good glug, savouring the dark ale. He would only have a few, wanting to be clear-headed in case anything happened. He set to work, chopping onions and mushroom, setting them aside on a plate as he pulled two steaks from the fridge.

The older man approved of his son's choice. *Ribeye, My favourite,* he thought as he went in search of rock salt and black pepper.

* * *

Both men watched the smoke as it poured into the sky. The whole forest was ablaze. It lit the darkening land in a warm orange glow. Jake clicked the bike into neutral, letting gravity take them closer.

"This is not by chance," Wilf said. "It's been done deliberately. They knew you were coming back."

Jake felt dread settling in his stomach. He could see as they approached that it would be impossible to even penetrate the tree line, let alone gain access to the catacombs under the forest. His thoughts went to Father Stephen, hoping that he'd either managed to escape, or the vampires had taken him with them. The bike came to the track that split the forests, Jake applying the brakes. The heat was unbearable, forcing him to turn the bike around and ride to a safer distance. He noted with dread that Amatoll was also on fire. "I'm in trouble. If the fire spreads to the doorway, I have no way of getting home tonight, if ever."

"You need to take the track to Heronveld," Wilf said. "We may be able to outrun the fire."

Jake checked his watch. "We have just over three hours until the door opens. What do we do?"

"Head there now. Forget your friend. He is either dead or someplace else. Whichever it is, you cannot help him on this night." Jake nodded, twisting the throttle, aiming the bike towards Wilf's old home.

* * *

Eddie and Karaa sat at the north edge of the Vale, looking out at the inn from the tree line. The flames were still a way to the south, giving them enough time to snare a prize.

Karaa looked at her companion, noticing for the first time how handsome he was. She was curious. "So where did you come from before this?"

"A place called Puerto Rico."

"How do you remember this? I remember nothing."

"They told me. Elias and his former kin. When I came through I was a young man. They wanted my blood, but I was too clever. I fought them off until the boy vampire bit me. I managed to escape, although I don't remember how. I don't remember being snatched from the other world, or anything about my life there."

"Who was I?" Karaa asked inquisitively.

"You came from the forest to the west. I saw you and the boy Coop. You were kin. I took you and turned you. It was for the best, Karaa. As you can see. Elias is heading there now. Any humans that dwell there will die. I managed to find you before that."

She reached across and touched his hand. His eyes were trained on the inn, trying to find someone to snatch. The contact made him smile, reaching his feral eyes. He reciprocated the touch, squeezing Karaa's hand. The contact made her smile too.

A young woman staggered out of the inn, followed by an older man. They made their way towards the vampires, giggling and swaying. Eddie and Karaa shrank back silently as they drew nearer. The woman lifted her skirts before squatting next to a tree to relieve herself.

The man stopped in front of her, unbuckling his trousers. "While you're down there, ave some of this," he said, offering himself to the woman.

"Can I finish me business first Seth? You're a mite eager 'ent ya?"

He walked past her, leaning against a tree. "I'm always eager with you Lucy. All men are."

She scoffed at his remark. "You'll be giving me a bad name, Seth Biddle. I'm not like this with all folk you know." She stood, straightening her skirts before sashaying over to him. He was old enough to be her father, reeking of ale and sweat. His face was pock-marked and flushed as he leered at her. This was not the life she had chosen for herself. She dreamed of being taken away by a handsome stranger. To live in a castle or farm to raise a family and be happy. But she knew that fairy tales were just that. At least she'd have a warm bed and a belly full of food at the end of the night. He pulled her towards him, kissing her roughly. She had picked up a few tricks over the years, using them to great effect with each customer. This one was old and smelt like dung to her. Lucy wanted to finish the job quickly so she could get back inside to peruse the rest of the revellers. Her hand went into his open trousers, grasping his hardness. She worked him back and forth, keeping the pressure intense.

"Oh! I've missed that touch Lucy. You certainly know how to make an old man 'appy," he said as she dropped to her knees.

"Well, let's see how you-" Lucy's voice died in her throat as a set of eyes appeared from the forest.

Seth's eyes opened, looking down at the top of Lucy's head. "What's up girl?" he said, his eyes following her gaze. Karaa came out of the tree line, her eyes locked on the young woman's. Lucy let go of Seth as she watched the strange creature walk towards her.

"Hola Amigo," a voice said to Seth's right. His head turned, coming face to face with Eddie. His bodily functions took over as he pissed over the Lucy's dress. She never reacted. She was smiling up at the vampire above her. Karaa offered her hand, which the young woman took readily. They stood, eye to eye before the vampire chopped her across the neck, knocking her unconscious. She fell silently to the floor as Karaa turned her attention to the old man against the tree. He was trying to get his words out, a hacking sound coming from his throat.

"He will have to do for us," Eddie said as he stood back. Karaa walked up to Seth, grabbing the front of his shirt. Her other hand grabbed his head as she pulled him towards her. In one swift movement Karaa launched him back into the tree trunk, shattering his spine and skull. She let go of him as he slid down the tree, leaving a red smear on the bark. They both instantly tasted the blood in the air, their thirst boiling to the surface. They knelt down and feasted on the dead corpse of Seth Biddle as revellers enjoyed their evening a mere few feet away. They would not give him a second thought as flames and smoke consumed the inn. An inn that had stood at the north edge of the forest since any human could remember.

The Turning

* * *

Jake and Wilf pulled up outside the former Bathurst's residence. It was unrecognisable. Only part of the front porch and side rail still stood. The rest of the structure was ash. The other buildings were largely untouched. Both men knew that it would change very soon. They climbed off the bike, stretching their limbs. Smoke was pouring into the clearing, being blown by the eastern winds.

"It's spreading quickly," Wilf said. "How long until the doorway opens?"

Jake looked at his watch, a cold dread seeping through him. "Two and a half hours. That's too long to wait. The doorway will be in the middle of the blaze by then. What do we do?"

"The only thing we can do. Get out of the forest. We can head west, towards the glades. The forest thins out there. That's as far as it can reach." Both men could now see flames in the forest. Wailing sounds carried to their ears, making the hair on their necks stand proud. "The spirits are being cooked. I've never seen a spirit cooked before, but I'm thinking we should not linger here."

"Shit!" Jake said. "I left two can of petrol next to the doorway. I need to move them before the flames reach them."

"Why? What is petrol?"

"It's like your cane spirit. It is the fuel my bike needs. If the flames get to it, it will explode. It could destroy the trees on either side of the doorway. We'd struggle to find it again, especially if the forest is ravaged by fire."

Wilf nodded. "Follow me. I know another way to the doorway that will not take long." Jake climbed back in the saddle, pursuing the older man as he disappeared into the tree line.

* * *

Elias sat at the far western edge of Amatoll. He too could smell the smoke and see the flames deeper in the forest. He had let Alison head west with the boy. Eddie and Karaa would meet her at gorge with some food, leaving Elias to carry out the next part of their plan. He knew when the doorway would open. He knew its location. The vampire could run towards it with his eyes closed. It had a power and pull to it that he didn't fully understand. Elias always thought his former master's magic kept the doorways working. That was not the case. He knew that now. Either someone else controlled them, or they were naturally occurring phenomena. It didn't matter to him. They served his purpose well. He would wait until the last moment before moving towards it. The giant wondered where Jake was, hoping he was far away, beaten back by the raging fire. He laced his hands behind his head, closing his red eyes to wait for midnight.

* * *

Alison laid Coop on the straw mattress with care. He was stirring slightly, uttering light moans from his mouth. She could see the new teeth protruding beneath his lips. They looked like hers. Curved, grey in colour. *He is ready*, she thought as she walked back to the shack doorway. She looked to the east, seeing a dark cloud hanging over the forest. The faint smell of smoke drifted over the grassy land towards the passage. Alison wondered where the two others were. They had food for the boy. She hoped they arrived before he woke. She was hungry too. *Maybe there would be some left over*, she thought, smiling in the darkness.

* * *

"There they are," Jake said as he climbed off his bike, propping against a tree. The single headlight on the front of the bike lit the forest in front of them. He picked up one of the panniers that he'd left in the forest when he'd come through the doorway.

Wilf picked up the other one. "It's quite heavy. What shall we do with them?"

"We attach them back to my bike. We can always leave them out in the glades if need be." A noise behind them made both men spin around, looking towards the east.

The Turning

"Looks like the flames are on our tail," Wilf said. "The fire's moving quickly. We must hurry or we'll never leave this place."

Jake nodded, carrying the one pannier over to his bike. Wilf followed him, laying the other on the forest floor. He left him to his work, walking several steps towards the trees that framed the doorway. He walked around them, taking a blade from his boot. He slammed it into the bark, leaving a marker in case they had to leave the forest on this night. Satisfied the blade would not move, Wilf walked towards the advancing blaze. The forest was eerily quiet. No animals could be heard, running for their lives. No birds in the trees, issuing warning cries. The forest is dead, he thought. And the fire will finish it forever.

"Wilf. Let's go," Jake said as he started his bike.

The older man walked over to him, shaking his head slowly. "All my life has been spent here. Now it will be destroyed on one night." He looked west. "If we head out to where the forest fans out, that should be safe enough." Jake nodded as Wilf climbed on behind him, holding on to his jacket. He gently twisted the throttle, propelling the bike forward at a steady pace.

They rode in silence until the forest started to thin. Jake couldn't see much except what his headlight reached. "Are we getting close?"

"Yes. Just a little bit further. Head over that way," Wilf pointed with his left hand over Jake's shoulder, making him change course slightly.

* * *

Elias heard the bike approach before he saw the light. He sat against the tree, preparing himself to move quickly if Jake spotted him. He saw him change direction, heading right towards the glade. The vampire closed his eyes to mere slits, watching as the bike passed by, a few hundred yards away. His keen vision picked out Wilf on the back of the bike. "So you did head to the coast as I thought. And now you are back, trying to head home. Well you'll not make it tonight Jake. The forest will see to that." He smiled in the darkness.

* * *

Eddie and Karaa approached the cabin that lay next to a tinkling stream. Low clouds blanketed the land, giving it an almost impenetrably dark feel. Only their keen eyes picked out the water flowing past.

Alison came to the doorway, her eyes shining bright in the night. "Did you find some food for him?"

"We did," Karaa said coolly. She did not like the other woman, feeling the same coolness emanating from her.

"Well hurry. He's waking."

Eddie walked passed Alison, the unconscious girl's head-smacking the doorway. No sound came from her mouth. She was out cold. "Enjoy," Eddie said as he deposited the girl onto the straw mattress.

Coop's eyes opened, a low keening noise coming from his mouth. His irises were yellow rimmed in red. They almost seemed to pulse and bulge as he continued a silent wail. Alison knelt down in the darkness, snapping the girl's neck. The noise was unnaturally loud in the confines, like ice being crunched underfoot. Coop turned his head, seeing the girl for the first time.

"Drink," Alison said quietly. He obeyed, crawling over to Lucy like a kitten about to suckle for the first time. He bit into her neck muscles, his wild eyes closing with pleasure as the blood flooded his mouth. The others looked on, feeling the hunger at the back of their throats. They put their need to one side, letting Coop take his first full feed. There would be more opportunities soon. Elias would see to that.

* * *

"We need to move. Look," Wilf said.

"Fuck! We've got thirty minutes until the door opens. What do we do?"

"Move further out. We cannot pass through the doorway tonight. We'd not even get close. We'd be burnt to a crisp in no time. We need to head west, towards the passage. I only hope there are no vampires out that way."

"FUCK IT!" Jake screamed. He felt helpless. He could almost taste his way home. Almost feel the doorway drawing him towards it glow.

The Turning

It was fruitless though. Jake only hoped it would open at the same time the following night. He walked over and kick-started his bike, tears pooling in his eyes.

* * *

The flames had driven him from the forest. He had walked in the darkness towards the mountain that lay to the south. Climbing the lower slopes, he found a small cave that offered some shelter. He scrambled in, throwing himself on the ground. His red rimmed eyes looked up at the ceiling, not seeing the black rock above him. He saw nothing. He felt nothing, except for the dull throb at the back of his head. It was getting worse. He lay immobile, his breathing coming under control slowly. He closed his eyes, trying to let sleep take him. After a few minutes it did take him, into a troubled sleep full of dreams. A stiff breeze blew into the cave, ruffling his dark clothing. Ruffling his dark beard.

* * *

Elias felt the doorway open. He'd moved towards the glades as the fire consumed the forest around him. It was an impenetrable wall of flames towards the east. He knew where the doorway was though. He braced himself, coiled like a spring until the last moment. He set off, his dark coat fanning out behind him. The vampire's speed increased as he weaved expertly between the trees. What little hair he had on his head was singed, his clothing starting to smoke. He couldn't feel the heat, but sensed its fury. His black coat tails caught fire as the flames closed in on him. His red eyes made out the rectangle of blackness, standing like a lone sentinel in the blazing forest. He passed through, out of Amatoll, into the Lickey Hills.

Thirty-One

Doug put the kettle on, looking at the clock on the wall for the tenth time since he'd entered the kitchen. It was just after seven in the morning. Darkness still pressed against the kitchen window as he stared out at his son's driveway. "Come on Son. Where are you?" He knew something was wrong. If Jake had made it back through the doorway he'd be home by now. Doug hoped in vain that he'd fallen asleep at a service station. He'd tried Jake's phone, being told that the number was unreachable by an automated voice. Again, he'd hoped that his son's phone had died on him. Doug was starting to clutch at straws. Movement upstairs told him that Katherine was awake. He pulled another mug from the cupboard, putting sugar and a teabag into it before filling both mugs with steaming water. He let them brew, leaning against the counter top. Hurried footsteps down the stairs were preceded by Katherine entering the kitchen. Her eyes were bleary, her hair unkempt.

"Sorry. I was up with Alicia half the night. I finally fell asleep about four." She stood stock still, dreading to ask the next question. "He didn't come home, did he?"

"Not yet love." Doug tried to look as optimistic as he could, attempting to smile. It faded when Katherine crumbled to the floor in front of him. He ran to her as she started sobbing. "Hey now. Don't cry. He'll be back. We've got to believe that."

"Then where is he?" she said, her voice cracking with emotion.

The Turning

Doug picked her up from the tiled floor, sitting her at the kitchen table. He pulled two sheets of kitchen towel from the roll, handing them to her. She dabbed her eyes and blew her nose as Doug finished making the tea. He sat down at the table opposite her, pushing the steaming mug within her reach. "Get that down ya," he said, taking a sip of his own drink.

"Thank you Doug," she said, sipping her tea. "Where is he? Where?"

"I don't know Kath. Hopefully, he's asleep in his car, exhausted from his trip. Hopefully, Father Stephen is with him, also sleeping."

"And if not. What if they are still in my world?"

"Then we wait and hope they come home safe." Tears were still falling down her cheeks as she started to get upset again. "Come on Kath. Be positive. He'll be back. We've got to believe that."

"And if not? How long do we leave it until we go looking for him?"

"You can't go looking for him. You've got Alicia to think about. I'll go."

"When?" she asked expectantly.

Doug thought about it for a moment, dreading the realisation that he would have to leave the two of them. "Two days."

He expected Katherine to explode at his suggestion. Instead she merely nodded. "Fine. Two days. Then you must go and get him."

Doug took a swig of hot tea as his stomach turned to ice. "Okay. Two days."

* * *

Way to the north, a front door opened. A dark-haired woman emerged from a house that backed onto the forest. She walked hurriedly to her black Audi, her high heels scuffing the tarmac driveway. She was in a hurry and she was angry. A loud voice from inside filtered down to the car as she fumbled for her keys. Unlocking the door, the woman dropped the key fob in the centre console.

"Beata, get here now!" the voice demanded.

She shook her head, her dark ponytail swaying behind her. "Not now Sham. I'm going to be late for work. We talk later."

A semi-naked man came to the door. He was tall and heavily muscled, his dark brow set in a frown. "No. We talk now. Or are you late for a meeting with your boyfriend?"

"I fucking told you already. Mike is my boss. Nothing more. If you can't handle that, too bad. We've got to have jobs to keep roof on our heads."

"So, why dress like a slut for work? Look at yourself. All done up like dogs' dinner."

Beata looked down at her attire. She liked the dress. She liked the dark nylons and boots too. Her work clothes made her feel important and worthwhile. It was a feeling she had never felt in her home country of Estonia. England was different. It was a land of promise. "I work in an office. This is what women wear. Get over yourself. I don't stop you going to gym in your shorts and tiny vest."

"That's different."

"Why? What makes it different?"

"Because I'm not looking for women at the gym."

Beata's eyes rolled back, her head looking to the heavens. "I cannot do this now. I have to go."

"Aren't you forgetting something?"

She looked over at him, realising he was holding her pink mobile. "Give me my phone. I'm serious."

"Why. Are there texts from your boss? Sexy text?" He tried to unlock the screen as Beata stalked towards him.

"Sham. I'm fucking serious. Stop playing these stupid games!" He retreated into the house as she walked over the front door threshold after him. Loud voices filtered from the house into the street. Some English voices, some foreign. A minute later Beata walked from the house, her pink phone in her hand. "We will finish this later," she said over her shoulder. "You need to." Her voice trailed off as she looked at where her car should be. In its place was an empty driveway. "SHAM!"

He came to the door, still pissed from the heated argument. "What?"

"My car has gone! Someone has stolen my car. Call the police!"

By the time Sham's call was finished, the crime reported, Elias was pulling onto the motorway. The fancy leather seat was racked all the way back, the height lowered to accommodate his frame. He accelerated, taking the car up over eighty miles per hour, heading south west, towards Cornwall.

Thirty-Two

"Where the hell is the doorway?" Jake said with growing frustration.

"I left a marker," Wilf said as he walked next to him. The forest floor was blanketing in grey ash. Some of the thicker trees still smoked and smouldered in the weak light of dawn. Glowing embers pulsed on the forest floor where some smaller trees had succumbed to the flames. The smell of smoke coated the two men as they headed east. The older man rounded two trees that were now blackened, beckoning Jake over. "Here. We've found it."

The younger man sighed with relief, clapping Wilf on the shoulder. "Good thinking. At least the trees survived the fire. Let's just hope the doorway did too."

"What do we do in the mean time?" Wilf asked.

Jake felt his stomach rumble. "Is there anywhere to get some breakfast round here?"

Wilf pondered Jake's question for a moment. "There is the Tacklebox Inn on the other side of the forest. Or we do some hunting. There should be animals close by."

"Hunting? Hunting what?"

"Deer. Stags. Bison. They will not be hard to find if we head west."

"I'd rather have someone serve me breakfast than having to shoot my own. Let's head for the inn."

* * *

"Fuckenell!" Wilf said as they rounded the bend. The extent of the fire was becoming more evident to the two men. "There's nothing left of the place."

Jake looked at the pile of burning timber that was once the Tacklebox Inn. The smoke blew from the inn gently across the lake next to it, giving the water a misty appearance. Two men sat in the grass, staring across the water. They were blackened by the fire, their clothing tattered.

Wilf jumped off the bike and stood in front of them. "Are you the only two left?"

"Aye," was the curt reply from one of the men. It was only then that Jake noticed blackened bodies lying in the grass. He counted a dozen or so, twisted and burnt beyond recognition. He guessed that many more perished in the wooden building.

"Did you salvage anything? Food or water?" Wilf asked.

"Over there. On the cart." Wilf and Jake looked further along the shore of the lake. A cart stood, its wheel's half submerged in water. They left the men to their thoughts, heading over to the water's edge.

"Poor folk. They are in shock. But while they are let's fill our bellies." They uncovered a hessian blanket to find enough supplies to keep them stocked for a week. Two legs of ham sat next to some odd-looking fruit and six clay jugs with corks in the stoppers. Wilf popped the cork and took a series of long glugs, the liquid drenching his beard. "That's just what I was waiting for. Here Jake, get that down ya."

The younger man took the offered jug and matched Wilf's glugs, the dark liquid running down his neck. "Bloody hell. That's strong stuff. I'm probably over the limit now."

"Over the limit?" Wilf asked confused.

"Never mind. Just something we have at home."

The older man nodded absently before pulling a leg of ham from the cart. Taking his knife from his boot he sliced two long thick slivers of dark meat, handing one to Jake. They ate in silence, looking at the ruins of what was once a way station for wanderers and traders alike. Wilf handed Jake another piece of ham, his fingers slick with pig fat.

"This is good. How much shall we eat?"

"Those poor folk have no idea what we're doing. We could take it all and they would not notice. Let's not be too free with our appetites. One leg of ham, two jugs, and a few pieces of fruit should keep us going. You could leave the men one of your crosses as a thank you."

Jake nodded as he chewed on a hunk of salted pork, making his eyes close in silent delight. "Shall we head back to the doorway once we have finished here?"

Wilf thought about the question while he ate. "We could do. Or we could do some foraging and exploring. It's a long time to sit and wait for a door to open."

"Where shall we go?"

"We could head west, towards the passage. I've never been that far. In daylight, we should be safe enough. Agreed?"

Jake nodded. "Why not. Beats sitting waiting all day. What could possibly go wrong?"

* * *

The black Audi pulled into a lay-by on the Atlantic Highway, as a steady drizzle hung over the Cornish coast. Elias switched the engine off and let his thoughts centre on his plan. He checked the display. It was almost one in the afternoon. He knew where they would be. He knew how long it would take to drive back north. The giant could foresee no issues. *I will make my move at eight. That will give me plenty of time,* he thought as he reclined his seat back as far it would go. He closed his eyes, welcoming the darkness. His mind started to wander as he drifted off to sleep. His last conscious thought was the baby. The special baby that was soon to be his.

* * *

"Can you see the entrance?" Wilf said over Jake's shoulder.

"Yes. It does not look too inviting," he said as he took in the view in front of them. The western sky was dark and low, seeming to cling to the top of the craggy peaks. As they neared they could make out a

The Turning

small stream that meandered from the gorge, out across the grasslands towards the south. A small wooden shack sat nearby, framed by a few stunted trees.

"Turn off your bike," Wilf said." Someone may hear us coming."

Jake cut the engines, coasting to a stop in the long grass. He quietly pulled his bike onto its stand as Wilf pulled a stake from his coat.

"Be quiet Jake. Who knows who or what lives around here? The sun is dropping fast too. I don't like exploring unknown places in the dark." Jake nodded, pulling his shotgun from his pack, checking it was ready. They silently walked towards the front doorway, noticing a figure lying in the grass. They stood over the prone form, their expressions grim. Wilf knelt down and turned over the body, tutting to himself as a blank pair of eyes stared back at him. The girl's neck had been snapped. Two puncture wounds were visible just under her ear. The skin was sallow and lifeless. "Vampires. They are close," he said as he looked towards the shack. They crept closer until they were standing to one side of the entrance, listening for any sounds. A blast of wind echoed through the gorge, ruffling the grass around them. It made the hairs on the back of Jake's neck stand to attention. The wind seemed to call out to him, inviting him to enter the gorge it had come from. He cast the thought from his mind, his fingers tightening around the shotgun. Wilf peeked his head around the entrance, slowly drawing in his breath.

"What is it?" Jake asked, his heart hammering in his chest.

Wilf stepped into the entrance, motioning for Jake to take a look. "The whole family. At least I think it is," he said as he tried to pick the sleeping vampires out in the dark confines.

Jake looked over the sleeping forms, his stomach tightening. "Elias is not with them." The words hung in the air for a minute as they tried to digest what this meant. "I hope I'm wrong, but my gut is telling me that Elias is not in this world."

"Fuckenell. I have to say I agree. Maybe that's why he torched Amatoll. To stop us going through the door, so he could!"

"Oh shit!" Jake said as his legs suddenly felt rubbery. "I need to get home. Elias may have…" his voice trailed off as his mind kicked into overdrive.

"How long until we can be at your home?"

"Three hours after we cross over. There will be no traffic. We must get back to the doorway. Now!"

"I agree. We must leave them sleeping. They will awake soon enough. We need to be as far away from them as possible." Another blast of wind echoed through the gorge. Eddie stirred in his sleep, turning over towards them. They slowly backed away, heading across the grass to the bike. Jake kicked it off its stand, steering the bike a full one hundred and eighty degrees until it was pointing back towards Amatoll. They headed away from the gorge, their pace quickening as a low drone came rumbling across the grass behind them. In one fluid motion, Jake jumped onto the saddle, kick-starting the bike. The engine idled for a few seconds as Wilf climbed on board.

"Hold on," Jake said as he gently twisted the throttle, propelling them towards their destination.

Thirty-Three

Katherine popped her head around the kitchen door, smiling at Doug. He was sat reading the paper, his glasses perched on the end of his nose. "Would you like some coffee Doug?"

He looked up, smiling at his daughter-in-law to be. "Why not? Did Alicia go down okay?"

"Out like a light. She will probably wake in a few hours for her late feed."

Doug looked at the clock on the wall. It had just turned eight. The sky outside the kitchen window was pitch dark, the temperature balmy for the time of the year. "I can't remember Jake and Rick's feeding times. It was that long ago."

Katherine chuckled. "Did Alison give both boys the breast?"

The question took Doug by surprise. It took a second to regain his thoughts. "Err, yes, she did. It was a different world back then. We'd only just started using disposable nappies. Formula wasn't as available as it is now either."

"I must say. Disposable nappies are a god send. Back home we either use nothing, or woven hessian. Not very comfortable for the little ones, as you can imagine."

"I guess not," Doug said as he flicked the kettle on, grabbing two mugs from the kitchen cupboard.

Katherine pulled open the fridge, reaching for the milk. "Oh. We're almost out," she said shaking the plastic container. "There should be some in the fridge in the garage."

"I'll go," Doug said as he headed for the kitchen door. An icy blast blew into the house as he made his way across the car port to the garage. *The weather's on the turn again*, he thought as he noticed the dip in temperature. The fridge was just inside the garage. He opened the door as light spilled out across the concrete floor. Doug reached into the door compartment, pulling a large plastic container out. He thought he heard Katherine's voice from the kitchen door as he closed the fridge. "Did you want anything else?" he said as he walked to the garage door. Katherine was stood at the kitchen doorway, looking to Doug's left. She was staring at something, her lips mouthing silent words. She looked to Doug like she was in a trance, gaping at something in the darkness. It was then that he noticed a red hue in his peripheral vision. He turned to the left to see what was there. Then blackness.

* * *

Jake and Wilf sat on the forest floor eating ham and drinking ale. "I need to lay off drink," Jake said. "Once we're back at my car we have a long journey ahead. The last thing we need is to be pulled over by the police, especially if I'm over the limit."

Wilf nodded, not really understanding the implications. "Let's us pray to whoever is listening that the doorway still opens."

That was one scenario that Jake did not want to consider. If there was no doorway, there was no route home. He would be stuck here, unless another doorway could be found. He pushed the thought aside, trying to be optimistic. "Hopefully we'll be home just after three. You will love Alicia. She is already quite the little princess."

Wilf smiled, although inside he was full of turmoil. "I cannot wait to see them both. I miss Katherine. She was a light in my life for a long time. I loved her like the daughter I never had. Cedric loved her too. We both knew that she would become a fine woman. Alice was different," Wilf said, fondly remembering Katherine's younger sister. "She was full of mischief. She was scatty and unorganised. I loved her, but most days I just wanted to put her across my knee." Jake smiled. "Even when she was murdered, she was up to no good. She should not have taken the path through the forest at that time. Always had her head in the clouds."

Jake remembered the story that Katherine had told him. How Alice's death had started the chain of events that led Jake from his world to hers. He would have loved to have met her, scatty as she was. He knew that Katherine missed her deeply. "Looks like we've all had our share of loss. Let's just hope that it is behind us. Let's get home and make sure," Jake said as a smoky wind blew through the remains of Amatoll.

* * *

"Ugh," Doug said as he rolled over onto his back. He was cold. His jaw was throbbing. He scrambled to his feet, looking towards the kitchen door that was left ajar, the lights on inside. *Red eyes*, he thought as he remembered the moment before the world blinked out. Leaving the milk container on the floor he stumbled across the car port, stepping into the kitchen. "Katherine." He said anxiously. "Are you there love?" No reply. As he walked into the hallway he noticed with dread that the front door was open a few inches, the wind from outside buffeting it gently. "Oh no. Please no!" Doug said as he made his way upstairs. He burst into the nursery, hoping to see Katherine and Alicia sat in the rocking chair, sharing a cuddle. Nothing. The room was empty. Tears sprang from his eyes as he stared to cry. His breathing became ragged as he checked each of the bedrooms. The house was empty. One wardrobe door had been ripped off its hinges in the master bedroom. It lay on the thick carpet, the mirrored panel reflecting the moon from outside. Doug raced downstairs skidding on the kitchen floor in his slippers. He checked the clock on the wall. "Nine thirty. Shit," he said as he looked for his car keys. Doug knew that he would be cutting it fine to get to the doorway now. But he had to try. He grabbed his keys, watch, and wallet from the window ledge before making his way to the front door. He kicked off his slippers, slipping his loafers on before grabbing his jacket from the bannister. *The kitchen door*, he thought as he headed back to the rear of the house, locking it. Securing the front door, he headed out into the cold night, fumbling for his car key. The driveway was bathed in bright light as the security light sparked into life. His already sinking heart was finally sunk as he noticed the front tyres of his car. They were flat. He checked the back tyres too, cursing when he saw the same applied to each of them. Each tyre had a ragged slash in the rubber wall. He knew who had done this. He was beaten. He had been outsmarted. *I'm so sorry Jake. I tried to protect them. But I failed,* he thought as he slumped onto the wet driveway, tears flowing down his face.

* * *

"Okay. Get ready," Jake said as the wind kicked up, sending ash swirling around the blackened trees around them.

Wilf was slapping at his behind, trying to get the remnants of the fire from his clothing. He blew out a breath as a faint blue glow appeared between the two trees in front of them. "Thank the gods for that," he said.

Jake also blew out a breath as he steered the bike towards the doorway. "Let's move." The doorway pulsed gently in the forest, its interior an impenetrable black. They crossed over, back into the Lickey Hills. "Follow me Wilf," Jake said as he pushed the bike towards the track that would lead back down to the main road. A minute later, Jake started the bike, leaning it against a tree as he made sure his pack was comfortable.

The wind was whistling through the trees, chilling Wilf to the bone. His clothing did little to keep out the January weather. A thought hit him, stopping him in his tracks. "Wait!"

Jake stopped, looking at the older man. "What?"

"Elias. What if he has Katherine and Alicia? What if he is here and wants to pass through, back to Amatoll?"

The Turning

Jake's stomach turned to stone as he looked back towards the doorway. "Fuck! How could I have not thought of that?" he said as he raced back towards the two trees. Wilf followed, struggling to keep up with the younger man. Jake saw the last few blinks of blue light before the doorway disappeared in the darkness. The route back to Amatoll sealed off.

* * *

Elias saw them appear through the doorway. He was crouched a hundred yards away. Next to him lay the woman and baby. They were under his spell. They had been since he'd bundled them into the car a few hours before. Once through the doorway he could release them from their sleep. He watched and counted as Jake and Bathurst made their way to the track. His ears picked up the noise of a bike being started. Now was the time. He picked up Katherine and the baby, holding them close. His other hand picked up the bag that he'd taken from the house. It was her bag. He knew that it contained items for the baby, opting to bring it along, just in case. His keen eyes picked out the first blink in the doorway's outline. It was getting ready to close. Elias headed towards it, holding the bag and humans tight. He saw that the two men were talking about something as he came within feet of the doorway. He felt the slight resistance as he passed between worlds. It was only for a split second, before he was through, standing in the charred remains of Amatoll. He turned as he heard hurried footsteps behind him. He would fight if needed. He would kill without hesitation. The giant vampire smiled as the doorway blinked out, closing the void between the two worlds. "You lose Jake," Elias said as he headed west towards Monks Passage. Towards their new home.

* * *

"What do you think?" Jake said.
 "I think we'd have seen him pass through."
 "You think so? I can't believe I never thought of that possibility."

"Forget it now. It's done. Let's get to your home and see how things lie."

Thirty-Four

A noise outside the front window stirred Doug from his troubled sleep. A few hours before he'd dragged himself from the driveway, stumbling through tear-soaked eyes to Jake's sofa. He'd lay there until exhaustion had mercifully taken away his pain. He'd fallen into a deep sleep, with clouded dreams. His eyes opened slightly as he heard two car doors slam. "Jake. Is that you?" he said groggily. A rattle of keys in the front door made Doug almost leap from the sofa.

"Hello." Jake said.

"Son," Doug said, crossing the lounge to embrace Jake.

"Dad," Jake said, flicking on the main lights. He noticed Doug's dishevelled appearance and blood shot eyes. "Oh no."

"I'm sorry Son. He was here. Last night. He's taken them."

Jake slumped against the wall as an older, grizzled man in strange clothing walked into the lounge. He looked at Doug, extending his hand. "Hello again, Jake's father."

Doug shook his hand. "Hello again."

Wilf walked over to the sofa and sat down heavily. He rubbed at his face before addressing the two men. "We need to finish this Jake. Once and for all. It will never end until we've done for them. All of them."

"What about Katherine and Alicia?" Jake said as his emotions spilled over. He started to cry. Doug placed a hand on his son's shoulder, pulling him willingly into his embrace. Wilf let the two men do what was needed to be done. He sat there patiently, looking around the strange room. Finally, Jake broke away from his father, wiping his red eyes. "What do we do?"

"We all go back," Doug said. "I'm not sitting here waiting for you this time."

"Sit down Dad. I need a drink," Jake said, wiping the tears from his eyes. Doug sat on the opposite sofa to Wilf as Jake headed into the kitchen. He returned a few seconds later with three bottles of San Miguel. He handed them out before sitting next to his father.

Wilf took a heavy pull on his beer, his eyebrows raising in appreciation. "Good stuff."

"What happened Dad?" Jake said as he wiped his lips.

"It was about eight last night. I was coming out of the garage with some milk. Katherine was stood at the kitchen door. She looked like she was in a trance. That was the last thing I saw. Before he hit me, I think I saw his red eyes. It was Elias, wasn't it?" Both men nodded. "I woke up on the floor in the car port an hour or so later. When I knew they were gone I grabbed my keys to go after them. He'd slashed all my tyres though. I'm so sorry Son. I let you down."

"No Dad. There was nothing else you could have done." A thought hit Jake like a thunderbolt. He looked at his father. "There is something else you need to know. Doug looked at him expectantly. "It's Mom. She's one of them too. She's a vampire. Elias must have taken her during the storm. And Father Stephen is still there somewhere, although we think he's probably dead."

Doug took the news in his stride, already emotional spent. "You've seen your Mom?"

"Yes Dad. Or what's left of her. There was a fight. I managed to escape to Shetland. The two men who tried to help me are dead, along with that Policeman, Tony Oakes."

"Huh? What was a Policeman doing there?"

"When Father Stephen went through doorway, Oakes followed him. He's leading the investigation. Or he was. He was also the one who gave me all that shit when Darren died." Doug nodded, remembering the events of last year only too well. "They were both captured. When

I got there with Mungo and Bertie, all hell broke loose. I know this is a lot to take in Dad."

"I'm getting used to it," Doug said as he took another swig. "Although what we've done to deserve all this is anyone's guess. Poor Alison. I know she was hard work over the years, but she did not deserve an ending like that." Tears welled up in his eyes as he thought of his wife. He pictured her, young and carefree. The woman he had fallen in love with decades before.

Jake nodded before continuing. "Before I got to Father Stephen and Tony I was attacked by another group of people, who live to the west. They also turned up during the fight. It was a bloodbath. How I managed to get out alive is beyond me Dad. I took my bike to get Wilf. When we came back, the forests were on fire. Elias must have done it. In hindsight, it looks like he did it to keep me from getting back home."

"He's sly as a fox," Wilf said. "We need to skewer that fox. Soon."

"Why's he doing all this?" Doug said.

"When he killed Daz, he said that I'd interfered in his work. We also killed is master and the rest of his clan. Maybe this is his revenge. Maybe he wants a new clan. He's already got quite a following. And now he has our family too. We can't let him turn them Dad. We need to fucking stop this. I've already lost one family. I can't lose another," Jake said, his voice choked with emotion.

Doug placed his hand on Jake's leg, squeezing it. "We will Son."

Jake breathed deeply, trying to remain calm. He checked his watch. "It's almost four. What do we do? I won't be able to sleep."

"We could finish these and get some breakfast on the go." Doug said.

Wilf burped loudly on the other sofa. "Breakfast sounds good. I could eat a bison. Don't fret Jake. They are alive. We will get them back. If he wanted to kill them we'd have found them dead in this very house. He must have plans for them. Plans take time. I'm sure Elias will not rush into anything."

Jake smiled at the older man from another world. Despite the dire situation, Wilf always seemed to be in control. "I hope you're right

Wilf. I really do. Okay Breakfast. We don't have bison. I think a fry-up will do."

* * *

Elias placed Katherine and Alicia gently on the straw mattress. The vampires stood in a semi-circle in the dark shack. They were all thirsty, the scent from the two humans almost unbearable. The giant vampire could sense their growing hunger as he turned towards them. "No one is to hurt them. Whoever breaks that rule will lose their head, I promise you that. Alison. This woman is your daughter-in-law. Her name is Katherine. The baby is your granddaughter. I want you to stay close to them when they wake. The baby will need her mother. We must make sure they are both cared for."

"Why?" Karaa said.

"The child has the blood of Reggan in her veins. He was my former master's brother. Jake destroyed him, but not before Reggan took a bite out of him. Jake also has Reggan's blood in his veins, although somehow he keeps it controlled. He is smart. This baby is going to be part of our family."

"And the woman?" Eddie said.

"No. Once the baby is no longer reliant on her mother you can do with her as you wish. Rip her to pieces for all I care. We can wait for years until we turn the little one. We are not governed by time like humans. But in the meantime, we need a safe place. A place where we can get food for the mother, as she is feeding the baby." Katherine stirred in her sleep, making the vampires look down at her. She pulled the infant to her breast and started snoring steadily. Elias looked at the boy. "Coop. Welcome to our family. What do you remember before you were turned?"

Coop's yellow eyes glistened in the darkness as he addressed the giant. "I don't know."

Elias nodded slowly. "We will travel west before the sun rises. The forest, Mantz, was your home." He looked at Karaa. "Yours too. I know the forest well enough. I know that it will shelter us from the sun. I

The Turning

know that it is big enough to remain hidden while we ready our family. Most of the Cravens were killed during the battle. But there will be some left. The forest falls away towards the coast the further west we travel. There are places there where we can set up a new home. Boats come and go from across the grey sea. The supply of humans should never end. But we need to make haste and be on our way."

"Why?" Eddie said as he leant against the wooden wall.

"Because when the doorway opens, Jake will return. And he will be dangerous."

"I'll stay here to welcome him. Karaa can stay with me. If he heads this way he will be mine. I've waited a long time for this."

"So be it. The two of you stay here until you've taken care of him. Once you enter the forest, keep heading west. You will find us soon enough."

"I look forward to meeting him again. This time. There will be no sport. No fun. I will tear his head from his shoulders and drain him." Eddie said, his eyes gleaming in the darkness.

* * *

The three men sat at the table, finishing their mugs of tea. Three plates sat in front of them, smeared with egg yolk, brown sauce, and the remnants of chopped tomatoes. Wilf placed his elbows on the table top, wiping a hand across his mouth. "That was hearty food Jake. I give thanks. What do we do now?"

Jake looked at the clock on the wall. "Well, it's almost six. We have all day to get ready. I think we should head north about tea time." Doug nodded. "That gives us about twelve hours to get everything we need. Not just weapons. Supplies. We need enough to last us." He looked at Wilf. We have big shops here to buy food and drink. We can stock up." He looked down at himself. "We also need to get cleaned up." He looked at Wilf. "And maybe get you some clothes. You cannot walk around Tintagel like that. Maybe a thousand years ago, but not today. Dad, would you have something at home that Wilf could wear?"

Doug thought about it for a moment, eyeing up the strange man from another world. "I think so. I'll pop home, grab a shower and be back in a bit." He gave his son a brief hug, nodded at Wilf and made his way out of the kitchen door, leaving Jake and Wilf alone.

"What's a shower?" Wilf asked.

"It's how we get cleaned up here. I have a feeling you will like it. Follow me." Wilf obliged as Jake made his way upstairs to the main bathroom. The room was square, roughly eight foot by eight foot. There were all the usual fittings that Wilf was now eyeing with curiosity. Jake smiled, trying to push the dire situation they found themselves in to one side for the time being. "Put your clothes on the floor. I will wash them for you." He pointed at the toilet. "That's the loo. Sit on it and let nature take its course. Toilet roll is there," he said pointing to the paper that was held in a chrome holder against the white tiled wall. You use that to wipe your arse when you've finished. Press that button on top to flush it all away." He walked over to the shower, pointing at the lever on the wall. "Pull that silver lever towards you. The temperature is just right. There are shampoos and shower gels on the shelf," he said pointing. You rub them in your hair and over your body. Use as much as you need. Does all that sound Okay?"

"I think so. If I get stuck I will call you." Wilf said with a degree of trepidation.

"Okay. I will be in my bathroom, doing the same as you. It's just down the landing on the right. I'm sure you will be fine. In fact, I think it will quite an experience."

* * *

The horse lay dead on its side. Father Stephen could see it was old. Its back leg was broken. He surmised that it had snapped its leg and starved to death. The Vicar rubbed his whiskers. The skin underneath was pale, almost grey in colour. His eyes red-rimmed. His shrinking stomach growled, his animal instinct taking hold of him. He knelt down next to the carcass, pressing his mouth next to the dead flesh. He bit down hard, breaking the dark brown skin that had already began to stiffen. Stephen pulled his head sideways, tearing a chunk of flesh and skin away from the dead horse. The human side of him wanted to gag as he chewed on the flesh. However, the animal in him greedily swallowed the food, returning to the wound to continue his feast. He knelt there for almost an hour, filling his belly with meat. He looked up as he heard noises coming from the charred forest. A pack of wolves emerged from the tree line, edging closer to Stephen and the dead animal. He could see that they were wary of him. They made whimpering noises as they slowly advanced on him. He stood, stopping the wolves in their tracks. He took two steps forward, scattering the pack in two. "I'm done. It's all yours," he said.

The alpha, a huge black beast bared his teeth at the Vicar in reply. *Why are they not ripping me to pieces?* He thought as he stood there in the perpetual twilight. *Can they sense evil in me?* He remembered being held down and force-fed Elias's blackened blood. Stephen could still taste the metallic tang of the thick liquid that had coated his throat. He wondered if he was now a vampire, or partially a vampire. He felt strong, his body vibrant and bristling with energy. Something in him had changed, of that he was certain. He looked about himself, feeling the pull towards the west. Ever since he'd left the cave in the side of the lone mountain, he'd felt a tug from that direction. Like an invisible strand of silk was gently coaxing him towards the mountains on the horizon. He'd obeyed the call, walking briskly through the grass lands that lay just south of the now-charred forest. The low cloud had kept the land cool and quiet as he'd walked towards his destination. Now as he stood next to the partially-eaten animal, he realised that he needed to carry on his journey. He walked slowly away from the fallen horse, keeping his red-rimmed eyes on the pack of wolves. They held their ground, their fur bristling, teeth bared. He turned away from them and headed towards the strange-looking mountains. Kenneth heard the wolves behind him, their yaps and growls carrying on the wind. They would not bother him now. They had their prize for the evening. Would he find his? Would he come across Jake and somehow find a way back home? Or was he destined to wander through this strange world for the rest of his days? Feeding off the dead beasts that littered the landscape.

* * *

Far to the west, across the misty seas, Tamatan walked along the pebbly beach towards a log cabin, framed by low trees. The sea lapped at the shore, the noise slightly calming the turmoil he felt within. Veltan came to the doorway, holding their son on her hip. Jake bore the same velvety green skin of his mother. He was growing fast. His slender green legs wrapped around his mother's waist. His arms, were wrapped around her neck as he suckled greedily from her breast.

Tamatan smiled at the sight. "I've brought us dinner," he said as he unslung three sizable fish from his shoulder strap. He placed them on a large cubed rock that sat next to a makeshift fire and spit.

"Jake is hungry," Veltan stated. "These hurt," she pointed at her turquoise breasts.

"You can bathe them after dinner, my love." He stepped forward, planting a soft kiss on her equally soft lips. She responded to him, sliding her pink tongue into his mouth. They stood, locked together as their son fed. Eventually Tamatan broke away, his breathing slightly ragged. He stroked his son's fine green hair, liking the feel of the wispy locks on his fingers. His red eyes shone with love and pride, making the rest of his face light up. His green head now sported two blunt horns that pointed to the sky. Each was covered with a fine green down. He felt more like the old Tamatan of years gone by. He was pleased to be home, but he knew it was to be short-lived. He looked at his sister. "I need to go away soon."

"Why?" she said, shocked.

"I spoke with Sica down at the harbour. Strange things are happening across the sea."

Veltan's beautiful face creased in confusion. "What things?"

"You remember the forest?" She nodded. "You remember the humans that lived there?" Again, she nodded, remembering how they had been chased through the dark expanse of trees by a tribe of crazed

The Turning

beings. Tamatan continued. "Well, Sica has just returned from there. All the humans have gone. There is talk of vampires. Folk at the harbour are scared. Scared that they may travel across the sea to our land and beyond. I need to go across and see what is happening."

Tears appeared at Veltan's eyes, rolling down her cheeks, making them shimmer. "Do not leave us Tamatan. We need you," her voice cracking with emotion.

He embraced his sister, kissing his son on his soft curls. "I will return. I promise. I just need to make sure that we are safe here. If there are vampires across the sea, they may be looking for us. I need to make sure you and Jake are safe."

Veltan nodded, handing her son to him. The infant gurgled and giggled as Tamatan nuzzled his neck. She walked down to the shore, her limbs moving with a languid grace that made Tamatan sigh. Veltan was beautiful to him. He felt his skin flush as his eyes took in her naked limbs. She loosened her skirt, letting it fall on the pebbles at her feet. She walked into the grey water until it was level with her waist. The demon turned to her brother, dropping to her knees, letting the salty water wash over her body. She felt instant relief as the salt soothed her soreness. Veltan sunk lower, until the water was at her neck. Tamatan could see her perfectly shaped body under the water. He wanted nothing more than to join her in the cool sea. *That would have to wait until later,* he thought as he cradled his son in his arms.

"When will you go?" Veltan asked.

Tamatan let out a long sigh. "Tomorrow at first light. Sica will take me across. He will then come back, keeping you stocked with what you need."

"I need you!" she exclaimed, her voice rising.

"I know. But if the vampires come, we may need to flee. And this is our home, Veltan. Look at what we have created so far."

She looked past him to their home. In the short time since they had arrived, Tamatan had constructed a small, yet perfectly-formed cabin. It kept out the sea mist, keeping Jake warm on cold nights. She liked how it looked. She liked the thatched roof and wooden window shutters. Her favourite activity was taking long walks with Tamatan and Jake into the forest behind their home. Veltan loved the weird creatures that crossed their path, asking Tamatan to explain what they were. This was her home, leaving was something she could not bear to think about. "I understand," she said in resignation. "Just promise me you will return soon."

"I promise my love," Tamatan said as he looked out across the grey sea. Something out there didn't feel right. A shiver ran down his spine as the wind suddenly kicked up, blowing foam from the breakers onto the shore. He hoped his instincts were wrong this time. He hoped the vampires were far away. Or destroyed. *Either would be just fine*, he thought as he walked his son back to the cabin that, he too, called home.

Thirty-Five

Jake killed the ignition and looked across at Wilf. He looked completely different to the wild man he'd met on a windswept rock all those months before. The Wilf sat next to him wore regular clothes. His hair was combed back, tied neatly in a ponytail, his once straggly beard combed. He looked like an old hippy or rocker, Jake thought as the sun suddenly broke through the clouds. "Right. It's probably best that you stick close to me and not say too much. This place might freak you out. To me, it's normal. To you, it will be very strange."

"What is this place called?" Wilf asked, as he looked through the windscreen.

"Tesco's," Jake said as he opened his door, climbing out into the winter sun. Wilf followed suit, walking behind Jake in Doug's shoes. They felt very comfortable, but it was taking a bit of getting used to as he awkwardly tried to keep pace with the younger man. A few minutes later Wilf was walking next to Jake, who was pushing a trolley up the first aisle of the supermarket. The older man looked at the shelves in amazement, his eyes trying to take in the thousands of strange items that filled the even stranger building. Jake in turn, was filling the trolley with various things.

"What are those?" Wilf asked.

"Baked beans. I have some camping equipment back at home. This kind of food is ideal for cooking outdoors. I'm not sure how long we will be over there. We cannot carry too much though," Jake said as his leg began to throb. *I need to get to church today*, he thought as they turned the corner into another aisle.

"Is there any ale in this place?" Wilf said, making the younger man smile.

"More than you could believe. We will take a few with us." They continued around the supermarket, gradually filling the trolley until it was almost brimming over. Jake had chosen a few nice beers for Wilf to sample, knowing it would be a world away from what he was used to. They eventually made it to the checkout near the farthest aisle. Jake started unloading the contents of his trolley onto the conveyor as the cashier was giving change to a lady, who had finished packing her shopping bags. Wilf stood there, unsure of what to do. He noticed the cashier turn and smile at him. He smiled back, noticing the intricate tattoo's that ran up her right arm. He walked past Jake who was oblivious to the exchange going on.

"Nice. Where did you get that done?" He said.

"In Truro," She said. Jake looked up, wondering what was going on. It looked to him like Wilf was chatting up the cashier. If things were not so dire, Jake would have laughed. As it was he continued to unload the trolley, letting the older man enjoy the moment.

"I've never seen one as nice as that. In my land, they are not as detailed."

"Where are you from?" the cashier said.

Alarm bells went off in Jake's head as he quickly joined the conversation. He smiled at the woman, noticing how attractive she was. She had long dark hair, olive skin, and deep brown eyes. He noted her name on her tag as he interjected. "My old friend is from The Shetland Islands. Aren't you Wilf?"

The older man nodded dumbly. "Aye. That's right," he said as he suddenly realised what Jake was doing.

Jake tried to change tack. "Are you a local girl Wendy?"

"Not really. I've been around a bit. Not in that sense mind." She blushed slightly. "I moved down here from Worcester a few years ago. Prefer it down here. It's more laid back."

Jake decided it was not good to tell her that he was also from that region. He decided to change tack again. "Can we have six bags please Wendy?" he said smiling.

"Sure. The cheap ones or the bag for life?"

"I think we can stretch to the bags for life," he said, wondering just how long that life would be.

* * *

Tamatan made his way across the shoreline towards the small harbour. The pebble beach backed onto low trees that stretched as far as the horizon. Two small deer saw him heading their way, bolting quickly into the cover of the trees as he approached. Ahead were a few small wooden buildings, built stoutly to withstand the sea's fury. Tamatan knew the harbour well from his time spent there as a youngling. The buildings were still the same as before. A store for traders to buy and sell from. An inn that served the traders and sailors. The fish monger's store was already open. A stout man was hanging large strips of whale flesh over a square pit, filled with coals and wood. Tamatan could smell the pungent aroma, making his taste buds spring to life. He would purchase a few pieces for his journey. "Hail Herman," he said as he skirted the smoking pit.

"Tamatan! What brings you here so early?"

"I'm taking a boat across the sea. To the forest on the other side."

Herman's face changed, a look of concern spreading across his ruddy features. "I've heard ill news from a few sailors. Talk of vampires and ghosts over in Mantz. Why would you be heading over there? Is your brain pickled?"

Tamatan chuckled. "Maybe. I have had contact with vampires recently. And it did not go well for them. I'm going to make sure that they are not seeking me out. And if they are, I will make sure that they do not reach these shores."

"Well good luck. I will give you some whale meat for your travels. Let us hope that no monsters start making their way to the Unseen

Lands. I would not like to leave this place, especially if I had to venture through Pagbob. Not many folk come back out of there."

Tamatan knew of what Herman meant. The forest that skirted the shoreline was vast, heading inland towards foothills and mountains beyond. It was the perpetual fog that was the danger. Many folk over the ages had become lost in the grey soupy mist, never to be seen again. He was lucky. His vision seemed to cut through the fog, which had allowed him to venture far. He remembered the river that meandered through the stunted trees. How it lead higher and higher towards a vast waterfall and high plateau beyond.

Herman cut through his thoughts. "Come back before you leave. I will give you six nice fat strips to keep you going."

"That is very kind of you. Let me go and find Sica. Hopefully he has risen from his slumbers." The stout man nodded as Tamatan headed towards the fourth and final building. It was smaller than the others, with a single word above the entrance. *Vesey*, which meant church, or place of worship. Tamatan knew that. He knew that the shaman, Kennet, would be asleep on the front pew, his belly full of rough cyder. The ringing of the harbour bell would wake him from his slumbers, telling him that a boat needed his blessing before it set off across the misty sea. The ground rose steeply ahead of him, as he passed the last building. He skipped lightly to the top of the rise as his eyes scanned the harbour, looking for signs of life. Several small boats bobbed up and down on the gentle swell of the grey sea. A horseshoe-shaped structure clung to the dark rocks, jutting out into the waters. A larger ship was moored a few hundred yards from the harbour. It looked deserted, save for the birds that flew about its rigging. *Traders from far-off lands*, he thought as he spotted Sica's boat at the far side of the harbour. His feet barely touched the slippery wooden planks as he made his way over. As he drew nearer he saw Sica appear from below decks.

He caught sight of Tamatan, waving a meaty hand. "Fine morning for a journey across the sea, my friend."

The Turning

"I hope you've plugged any leaks in this old wreck," Tamatan said as he jumped from the harbour, landing lightly on the deck.

"Never fear. She'll not be heading to the bottom of the sea for a long while yet," he said as he rubbed his palm over the smooth wooden wheel. Tamatan smiled at the sailor as he laid his bag on the deck. Sica was swarthy and powerfully built. Tamatan had seen him drag a whale from the shore, pulling it easily along the pebbles to Herman's waiting blade. He was a fine seaman. He knew the waters well and could be trusted.

"Veltan knows that you will visit. I thank you for your kindness."

"Think nothing of it friend. Are we still agreed on the plan? One moon's cycle."

"Yes. And if I'm not there after one cycle, check again on the next new moon. If I'm not there by then. Well, you know what to do."

The swarthy sailor nodded solemnly. "Aye," was all he said in reply.

"I need to pop back to Herman to secure our dinner. It should be enough to keep us fed."

"No fear. Below decks I have plenty of provisions. Ale and cyder too. The sea looks fine and calm. I see no dangers out there. If we make good time, we should be there in two days."

"So, all is well in our world. Let us not delay," he said as a wind blew from the forest, rippling the sails. "I will go wake the shaman too, while you prepare. Let's hope he doesn't catch a whiff of your cyder, or else he'll be sailing with us."

* * *

Jake and Wilf walked along the Cornish coastline as the sun made its journey towards the western horizon. The older man looked across the expanse of ocean, marvelling at its beauty. "Tis a sight to remember. I've never seen anything like this. In Shetland, you can rarely see passed the edge of the cliffs. Very seldom can you actually see anything else. I can see why you settled here Jake. I really can. We must get Katherine and Alicia back, so they too can enjoy these sunsets."

"I won't argue with that. Yes, it's great here. Katherine has really fallen in love with Cornwall. We will get her back Wilf, Alicia too. That fucking monster will not keep them for long."

Wilf nodded as nagging doubts swam through his thoughts. He hoped they were not too late. His mind could not even begin to think about any harm coming to his niece, let alone the baby. He changed tack. "When do we set off?"

Jake checked his watch. "In about an hour. The car is packed with everything we need. We should get to the doorway with a few hours to spare. Hopefully my plan with work," he said as a large seagull flew passed them. "Dad will be ready. We will pop past for him on our way home. Hopefully, he's had a few hours' sleep this afternoon. You can do the same on the journey north Wilf."

"And you? When will you sleep?"

"I'll be okay. I'm not an old man like you. I'll sleep on the other side."

"This old man still has enough energy to show you a thing or two."

Jake chuckled as they made their way back towards Tintagel from the coastal path. "Show Elias and his cronies a thing or two, not me," he said as he slapped Wilf on the shoulder.

* * *

Tamatan lay on two large sacks of grain, looking up at the perpetual mist that engulfed the boat. He could hear Sica casting his nets over the side of the boat, hoping to snare their dinner. The sea was silent. No birds flew overhead, which made Tamatan uneasy. He could almost feel an evil pulse, ripple across the waters from the huge forest beyond. The demon sat up, his red eyes shining through the grey drizzle that coated everything in sight. "What's on the menu tonight?" he asked, trying to sound jovial.

"Brazzers, hopefully. We're in shallow water here. They should be easy to catch as we pass over the sand bars. I thought you were sleeping?" Sica said as he dropped his rump on another sack of grain. He reached for a bottle of cyder, pulling the cork from its stopper with an audible pop. He took a long drink, the golden liquid dribbling down

The Turning

his neck, wetting his leather tunic. Sica wiped his mouth before handing the clay bottle to the diminutive demon. Tamatan took it readily, draining half the bottle in a series of glugs.

"Ah. That hit the spot," he said as he passed it back to the sailor.

Sica took another swig before stoppering the bottle, laying it next to the sack. "So, tell me. What do you hope to achieve over yonder?"

He considered the question for a moment before replying. "I'm not rightly sure. I'm hoping my instincts are wrong, and that I'm just an old worrier. I told you about the vampires I had come into contact with?" The other man nodded solemnly. "Well it dates back to before you were born my friend. A long time ago, Veltan was taken by a coven of vampires from another plane. Their leader, or king, was called Reggan. He was taking the long sleep. Both he and his brother had almost slain each other on the battlefield. They needed blood. Human blood, if possible. Reggan's brother, Korgan had help from his minions, who scoured this land and others to bring him sustenance. Reggan was not so lucky. His land is a barren waste, filled with mutant monsters that were of no use to him. That's where I came in. They knew of my talents. They had heard that I was a collector of human energy. So, they snatched my sister in the hope that I would do their bidding. And I did, for a long time, until the supply grew thin."

"Thin? How so?"

"Recently, I met a man called Jake. He is from a world that I visited a time ago. I scared folk, taking their energy to give to Reggan. But every time I visited I drew attention to myself. People in that world do not believe in demons and vampires as such. So, my being there, causing mayhem was drawing too much attention. So I stopped visiting, hoping instead to visit other places. However, the other places had very slim pickings. Even after I had collected a human's essence, by the time I had returned to Reggan, much of it had left me. Reggan's coven where gradually becoming frustrated with me, threatening to harm Veltan if I didn't up my game so to speak. I placated them in the knowledge that Korgan's minions were struggling too. I ventured far and wide Sica, travelling to planes that few had visited. It was purely by chance that I met two humans, who had just killed Korgan. I knew that once Reggan's clan heard of his demise, Veltan would be of no use to them. They would, of course kill her, and me when I travelled to their stronghold. I travelled with the two men and put pay to Reggan and his cohorts. That started me on the path back home. And home is where I am happiest. Korgan's vampires are still out there, roaming the lands to the east. If they get a sniff that I am hiding out in the Unseen Lands, they may come for me."

"Makes my life sound dull. But I would not trade with you, my friend. You have had enough fun and adventures to last a thousand lifetimes."

"Yes. But I have grown tired of that life. I want to raise my family and grow old in peace. Once little Jake is big enough I plan to venture through the Pagbob, to the high plateau inland. Many of my kin hail from there. Have you heard of the land of Marzalek?"

"Yes," Sica said, who'd reopened the clay bottle. He handed it to Tamatan after taking a long pull on it. "I've spoken to a few traders who had actually ventured there. Strange tales about rivers that run the wrong way. Trees that talk, and shimmering demons that live in tall palaces."

Tamatan smiled. "Yes. The tall palaces of which you speak are situated in the town of Katarzin. They do indeed shimmer, especially at night when the fireflies invade the town. It is a wonderful place. I will one day return and live out my existence there. But first I need to make sure my kin are safe."

"What happens if you never return? We've not spoken of this."

"Then you must take my family around the coast to the lagoon with the blue cliffs. Underneath the cabin, I have stashed some gold and silver coin, along with trinkets and amulets from far and wide. Take half of that as payment. Let Veltan take the rest. At the lagoon, there leads a road that skirts Pagbob. Veltan knows this road. She will take it with Jake to Marzalek. There she will be safe."

"I will tell the shaman to talk to the gods. To ask for your safe return."

"Will he do that for you?" Tamatan asked as two large black fish became caught in the nets.

"If he wants any more of my cyder he will. A man who talks to the gods. Funny how he relies so much on what is in that bottle," he said pointing at the clay jug.

Tamatan smiled. "Maybe the gods only appear after a few bottles. If we carry on drinking, they'll be joining us for supper."

* * *

Jake pulled off the motorway, indicating left as he entered the slip road. Wilf was indeed asleep on the back seat, a pillow separating his head from the door frame. Doug sat next to his son, drumming his fingers on his cords. Jake smiled at his father. "Calm down Dad. You're not normally so pent up."

"Sorry Son," Doug said gently. It's not every day that I travel to another dimension, filled with blood thirsty killers. The thought of coming face to face with what was once your mother is making my belly do somersaults."

"Let's hope it doesn't come to that Dad. But if it does, accept the fact that Mom is gone. What is in her place will kill you if she gets the chance. I know it sounds harsh Dad, but you need to divorce yourself from the fact that it's Mom."

Doug nodded absently as Jake turned onto a country lane that climbed towards the summit of the Lickey Hills. "If I do see her, do you think she will remember me?"

"No Dad," Jake said, shaking his head. When I saw her, there was no recollection from her. She just saw me as her next meal. Try to think that way. It may help." The 4x4 dipped and climbed the steep lane until they came out on a main road. Jake turned left onto the deserted road, gunning the diesel engine. Wilf farted noisily on the back seat, drawing a few chuckles from the two men. Jake turned the fan up, aiming the air towards the back of the car. "Best keep that to yourself Wilf," he said as the car began its descent down Rose Hill. Two minutes later they pulled in next to a chip shop and convenience store. The temperature was higher than average for the time of year, with clear skies above them. Jake hoped that the hills were deserted. He'd grown up around them and amongst them. He knew that it was a hive of activity for teenagers and lovers, who welcomed the privacy of the forest to indulge in their pastime of choice.

"Fingers crossed," Doug said as Jake turned left up the steep private roadway.

The car jolted, banging Wilf's head against the window. "Ugh," he mumbled as he woke from his sleep. He looked out of the window to be confronted by darkness. "Are we close?"

"We're in Amatoll already. You missed all the fun Wilf," Jake said as he steered right onto a deep rutted track.

"You're making sport with me young Jake," he said as he sat up straight, stretching his arms. If you didn't have so much fine ale in the back of your car I'd cuff you one."

"Sorry Wilf. I was just pulling your leg. We're a few hundred yards away from the doorway," he said as he turned a sharp left, propelling the car up a steep incline. "It's just up here on the right." The headlights illuminated the hillside in front of them as Jake weaved around potholes and tree roots. After a few seconds the car swung right off the pathway, into the forest. Jake killed the engine, extinguishing the headlights. The overhead light in the car fought bravely against the dark night, trying its best to light the interior. Jake opened his door, pulling the key from the ignition. "Okay then. Let's set to work."

* * *

Father Stephen had headed south away from the forest towards the grasslands. He walked steadily, making good progress towards the cliffs that now loomed over him. They seemed to touch the sky, or the sky seemed to reach down and touch them. His red-rimmed eyes scanned the massif, hoping to find a way through. It was an impenetrable wall of rock both north and south. Kenneth wondered which way to go, aware that his stomach was grumbling. He needed food too. He looked south, hoping that there was a break in the rock. His eyes could pick out nothing that offered hope. The Vicar made up his mind, heading north into the darkness. After a few minutes, he could see the edges of Amatoll to his right. The forest had panned out into a series of glades that stretched almost as far as the cliffs to his left. His eyes picked out something in the darkness. *Is that a stream?* he thought. His instincts were rewarded as he rounded a jut in the rock. He could make out a split in the gorge. He quickened his pace as his eyes could now make a cabin. He was suddenly wary. His instincts that had been on the ball a few moments before told him that danger lurked in the thick soup of night. A low hum seemed to pulse outwards from the shack, gently reverberating through him as he kept as close as he could to the rocks. It was silent, save for a few birds in the distance. Stephen edged forward until he reached the stream. The man placed his hand on the cool rock as he tried to assess the situation. The cabin was a few hundred yards in front, slightly to the right. To his left, across the fast-flowing water was a wide path that cut a runnel through the cliffs. *Ah to hell with it*, he thought as he waded into the water as stealthily as he could. He quickly fought against the current that came up over his knees, scrambling up the grassy bank on the northern side. He stood looking at the cabin, almost in a trance. The ill feeling seemed to spill out from the blackened doorway, infecting the land around it. He rubbed at his eyes as they started stinging, forcing him to one knee. "What in God's name is happening to me?" he said as he ambled clumsily to the sheer rock walls. He turned his back on the cabin, heading into the passage that led to the west. As he rounded a corner, the pain extinguished like a flame in the breeze. He sighed in relief before quickening his pace, heading westwards, towards Mantz Forest.

* * *

The three men stood next to the car, looking at their inventory.

"Do you think we will get this through the door in time?" Doug asked.

"We should do. It stays open for about two minutes. We can form a chain and pass it to each other. I will wheel the bike through last. We'll do it," Jake said. "I just need to leave the car somewhere." He checked his watch. "I have enough time. I'll probably leave it in the same place as last time. Although we may be away for a while. Let's hope no one gets suspicious."

A thought occurred to Doug, before fishing his keys out of his pocket. "Here. I've still got the garage key for Mrs Howarth who lived next door to us. Put the car in there. She will never know it's there Son."

Jake knew that behind his parents' old house was a service road. Each property had a garage at the bottom of its garden. It was a good plan. He took the keys from Doug, zipping them into his jacket pocket. "Thanks Dad. You think of everything."

"Oh. I forgot to mention. They have erected steel gates at the end of the right-of-way. There is a key on there for that too. Just make sure that you lock it when you leave. If not, someone will start prying."

"Will do. I'll be back in twenty minutes. You two stay here and crack open a beer."

Wilf's smiled in the darkness. "Best thing you have said all night young sir. I'm sure us old un's can keep each other company while you're gone."

Jake shook his head. "Just don't drink too many. We may meet someone nasty on the other side. We all need clear heads."

A minute later the car was making its way back along the hillside, leaving the two men stood in the darkness. Doug used the bottle opener to crack open two bottles of ale, handing one to the strange man from another world. They clinked bottles. "Cheers," Doug said.

"Cheers to you too," Wilf reciprocated, before taking a swig of the dark ale. He nodded his approval. "Good stuff. Your land has its perks."

"Do you have ale where you're from?" Doug asked, curious.

"Aye. But it's not as good as this. Our ale is warm, and quite thick. I have a cave under my home where I store my jugs. It keeps them slightly cooler. But I prefer this."

"Do you find all this as crazy as I do?"

Wilf thought about it, leaning against a tree to try and get comfortable. "I've never really thought about it. I'm a simple man. I've spent my whole life in a very small place. We don't travel far or see much of our world. Our lives are basic and have been very tough until recently. But at the same time, our land is filled with things that you would find unbelievable. Vampires, monsters, ghosts, and giants. So the idea that there are doorways to other worlds, isn't too much of a surprise for anyone from Heronveld."

"Heronveld? Is that your village?"

"It is. In the land of Elksberg. You'll be there very soon to see it all for yourself. It's good that you've already had your eyes opened somewhat. There shouldn't be many more sights to make you muck your britches."

"That's good to know. The thought of seeing a vampire up close is enough to do that. God knows how you and Jake have managed to stay in one piece."

"I've had that thought too. Many folk I've known have died at a vampire's hands. Or fangs. I've recently lost my niece, brother, and sister. But somehow, here I am. I'm still in one piece, just about."

"Let's hope that we are all in one piece when we get back. The thought of Katherine and Alicia being in harm's way makes me feel sick to my stomach."

"Mine too. We need to finish it though this time. Once we have them back, we cannot simply escape. We need to rid that fucking place of the lot of them. Starting with their leader, Elias. Once he's gone, the rest should be easy pickings. I know your woman is one of them Doug. I will deal with her. Do not try to take her on."

"Why?" Doug asked.

"She was your woman. Your wife. When the moment comes to finish her, you may falter."

Doug pondered that for a moment. "I suppose you're right. Thank you Wilf." He leaned against a tree, sighing heavily. "Fuck me! When did life get so complicated? Ever since Jake lost his family, things have gradually gotten more and more strange. To the point where I'm about to walk through a bleeding doorway to another world, to potentially face my wife, who now just happens to be a vampire. Jesus Christ. You couldn't make this shit up!"

"We are one and same Doug. Ever since Alice was taken, my life has taken a dark path. And now look at me. In a strange land, where steel beasts carry folk around at speeds I never dreamed of. It's enough to make my head pop. Give me my farm house on Shetland. Give me the simple life." He held up his beer. "With plenty of these to keep me going though."

* * *

The thread that pulled him towards the unknown destination seemed to be increasing in its strength. Father Stephen came out of the other side of Monks Passage, staring at the impenetrable mass of trees in front of him. In the darkness, it looked to him like a solid wall of forest was blocking his way. He made his way across the open grass, spying what looked like a collection of buildings off to his right. Ten minutes later he was stood in what was once the Cravens eastern settlement. He explored the cabins that stood at the edge of the tree line, disappointed that nothing of use could be found. He walked into the forest, bumping into tree trunks for several minutes until he reached a small clearing. He looked at the cabins, his sight adjusting to the darkness. To his red rimmed eyes, it looked like the forest had settled on top of them, such was the closeness of the trees. Kenneth walked into the main cabin, his eyes immediately picking out a large earthenware pot set on a table. He walked over and peered inside. A large spoon poked out from the contents, resting against the terracotta edge. Stephen pulled the spoon from the pot, a distinct sucking sound resonating around the cabin. "Stew," he said as he smelt the spoon. He fished the lighter out of his pocket as he spied a pair of rudimentary candles on shelves next to him. He lit them both, giving himself a fighting chance to actually see what he was about to eat. Holding the flame to the rim of the pot he could make out a blue fuzz of thick mould that coating the stew. His stomach churned, demanding food. Although the nausea rising in his throat told him to look elsewhere. His carnal cravings won out as he used the spoon to scrape the blue crust from the stew, dolloping it on the wooden table top. Satisfied that only stew remained, he sat at the table and began feasting. It was cold and greasy, making him gag with the first few mouthfuls. However once accustomed to the consistency, he began eating steadily, neither enjoying it nor loathing it. The stew was doing a job. Keeping him alive. As he finished the meal he noticed wooden torches, hung on the wall. He took the candles to them, lighting them both. The cabin was now almost cosy he thought as he rooted around for anything of use. He found two clay jugs in a trunk at the rear of the structure. He pulled the cork from the first one, his mouth instantly salivating when he smelt the heady aroma of ale inside. The Vicar attacked the contents, downing the thick bitter liquid with vigour. Stephen drained the jug, dropping it on the table with a loud clatter. He felt better. Almost human. But not quite. A large straw mattress, partly covered in animal furs lay in the corner of the room. He suddenly felt weary. His new-found strength had ebbed away, leaving the ever-ageing Vicar feeling ten years older. He fell on the mattress, pulling the furs around him. Sleep took him almost immediately. Before he succumbed, he wondered about the location of the others. *Will I find the vampires? Will Jake find me? Will I ever make it home?*

Thirty-Six

The faint blue outline gained strength before their eyes, rousing them into action. "Right. Wilf, stand on the other side of the doorway. Dad, stand here," Jake said as he handed Doug a large pack of supplies. They worked quickly, passing all the items from one forest to another. From one world to another. "Dad, grab the fuel cans," Jake said as he kicked his bike off the stand, before wheeling it towards the doorway.

The outline started blinking, making Doug start. "Come on Son. It's about to close." Jake upped the pace, urging the bike through before the void closed.

"Okay Dad. Let me through." Doug realised he was blocking his son's path, moving sideways until he was stood next to the doorway in Amatoll. His face was mere inches away from the blue hue. He reached up with his fingers, gently touching the doorway. Flickers of blue lights danced on his fingertips, making him smile. He moved his fingers up and down, causing blue sparks to cascade into the darkness around them. Before he could say anything to the others, the doorway died away, leaving only perpetual night.

"Well that went to plan," Wilf said as he stood next to the array of supplies that they had brought with them.

"It did," Jake said as he pulled two long pieces of wood from the supplies. He wrapped a tea towel around the end of each, before lighting them. He handed on to each man, "Here. Hold these while I fuel the bike."

The Turning

Doug stood there, holding the torch, looking at the strange new land he found himself in. It was deathly silent. He could see nothing but trees, or so he thought. His eyes picked out movement a few hundred yards to the east. "What's that?" he asked, his voice croaky.

"Fuckenell," Wilf breathed. "It looks like the spirits from the other place. When Elias torched the forest, they must have fled. It looks like they have come back to claim it once more."

"Jesus Christ! Am I actually seeing this?" Doug said in awe. Gooseflesh broke out over his body as one spirit floated over towards the three men, tendrils flowing behind in its wake.

"Steady Doug. They won't harm us. They have no form. No strength. They are just the remnants of poor folk," Wilf said as he swished his torch at the spirit, making it veer away from the light.

Jake finished filling the bike, screwing the cap on the fuel tank. He looked around the forest, frowning. "We could do with concealing the stuff that stays here. But I think we'll struggle. There is no greenery to cover it with. Dad. Can I have your torch please? I will take a scout about. You two stand here and keep away from the ale."

"I was just thinking about ale," Wilf said as he beat Doug to the punch, handing Jake his torch.

"You can think about it Wilf. Just don't touch it," Jake said as he headed off into the dark forest, his torch beam lighting the blackness.

* * *

Katherine lay on the forest floor, curled up like a foetus. Alicia snored gently in her mother's arms. The forest was impossibly black. The only break in the curtain of night was three sets of eyes that shone bright. Two yellow, one red. They sat on the fallen trunks of two trees that until recently were the homes of many a forest creature. Not now, though. As the vampires approached, animals cowered, taking off in every direction, fleeing from the cold radiating dread that spread through the close-knit trees. Elias looked over at the sleeping humans. "We have made good progress. Tomorrow at first light, we shall carry on towards the sea."

"How will we know when it's first light? The trees are too thick to allow daylight in." Coop said with purpose.

"The baby will tell us. She will need feeding in a few hours. The forest will come alive with her cries, until mother slakes her thirst."

"What about the humans?" Alison said. Her tone flat and monotonous.

"I'm sure they will come. They may already be on their way. They are resourceful and clever, for humans. They do not know this forest though. I do, to some extent. And we can travel much swifter than they. It would take Jake several days to get to the sea. By that time, he will be tired and weak. If he makes an appearance there, I will have him. Once and for all."

* * *

The three men made their way through the forest, each one laden down with supplies in backpacks. Wilf grumbled as the pack kept bouncing against the small of his back. He was stoic though. He would carry on until they decided to rest.

"How far west have you been Wilf?" Doug said, his own pack securely fastened around his plump mid-section.

"A way yet. The forest fans out soon into a series of glades. We are entering the land of the black unicorn."

"Unicorn!" Doug blurted.

"Aye. I've seen one of them. From a distance mind. They are not the kind of beasts to get too close too."

"Why not?" Jake said. "In our world, unicorns are meant to be friendly."

"Well the black unicorns here are not. They have evil red eyes, and a horn as long as my arm. I've heard tales from travellers and hunters over the ages that tell of men being skewered, then torn in two. Or trampled to pieces under their heavy hooves. We'd best be on our guard. If we do see one and it decides to fight, we will need your weapons Jake."

Jake nodded warily, looking in all directions as he walked along. "Let's hope they are asleep. I don't fancy being skewered." They walked on in silence, on guard in case of a sudden red-eyed charge from the darkness. Low clouds seemed to touch the tops of the scorched trees, muting the land around them. No sound could be heard, save for the sound of their feet scuffing the forest floor. Each man silently hoped they found a safe refuge as the forest pressed down upon them.

* * *

Eddie and Karaa lay on the straw mattress, limbs entwined. Both were sleeping. Eddie's lips mouthed silent words, his eyelids flickering. His companion never stirred. Her head was resting on his chest, gently rising and falling. The noise of the tinkling stream nearby filtered in through the doorway. It was a peaceful setting as the cabin was sheltered by the gorge to the west and the forest to the east. In Eddie's dreams, he was wandering through a strange town, with whitewashed walls that seemed to close in around him. The edges of his dream were fuzzy, not letting him see too much of his former life and former home. He'd recounted the same dreams countless times over the years, never unlocking the secrets of his past. His arm pulled Karaa closer to him, causing a murmur from the former chieftain. They were at peace, blissfully unaware of the three men closing in from the east.

* * *

"Wait," Wilf whispered. "Can you see the cabin? By the gorge."

The two other men nodded, Jake whispering back. "Yes. It's almost camouflaged by the rock. What are you thinking Wilf?"

I'm thinking of everything. It could be empty. It could be a nice place to set up camp. Or it could be full of monsters, lying in wait for us. We should prepare ourselves." He turned Jake around, pulling weapons and a cross out of his pack. Jake did the same to his father, handing him what he felt was needed.

"Thanks Son. I only hope the place is empty."

"So do I Dad." He turned Wilf around, foraging through his pack until he found two stakes and another cross. "How should we do this?"

Wilf looked at the pair of them, his grizzled features softer in the early onset of dawn. "We should head right, away from the opening. Then come around the walls to the doorway. That should at least keep us out of sight."

Doug nodded, the weapons feeling odd in his hands. He was not a vampire killer. He was a regular guy. A father and granddad. His idea of adventure was finding a new DIY store or walking along a new coastal path. This was beyond the realms of his understanding. "Okay. Let's do this," he said, his voice raspy and coarse.

"Follow me," Wilf said as he headed through the long grass, towards a small crop of trees near the cabin. As they drew closer, each man became aware that the crosses in their palms were becoming increasingly warm. Doug felt a cold dread settle over him, completely overwhelmed by what was about to potentially happen.

"Let's lose the packs," Jake said as he shouldered his way out of his, carefully placing it next to a tree. The two older men followed suit, stowing theirs next to Jake's. "Okay. I will lead. Wilf, you follow. Dad, you follow Wilf." They nodded as Jake set off away from the trees, heading towards the cabin that was dwarfed by the gorge beyond. Jake came to a stop as he touched the stout wooden wall of the shack. He waited a few seconds for the others to catch up. By now, the cross in his hand was almost hot. A faint glow emanated from it. The others were reacting the same way. *They are here*, Jake thought as he started edging towards the corner of the wall. He came around, on to the front wall, the doorway almost within touching distance. Looking to his left, he gave a tight smile and a nod at the two other men. He noticed that his father's skin was white and clammy, like wet putty. His eyes were wild with fear, his hands shaking. "Ready?"

"Ready," Wilf said. Doug only nodded. Jake was about to take his next step when a shriek from inside the cabin, pierced the stillness of the night. The three men fell against the wall, momentarily frozen in shock. A hiss came from inside, making Doug piss himself as he

The Turning

stood immobile. Jake took a deep breath and rounded the opening to the cabin, his cross instantly coming alive in his hand.

"PUTAS!" Eddie yelled at him as he held his cross aloft. Wilf came around the corner behind Jake, watching as the woman slid slowly up the wall like a giant bug. Her eyes glowed in the darkness. Her fangs bared. Doug finally came around the doorway, his breath catching in his throat as his mind tried to take in the scene unfolding in front of his eyes.

"Where's Katherine and Alicia?" Jake said, his voice commanding in the confines of the building.

"Far from here. You'll never find them, human. Elias will turn them very soon. Then they will be like us. Your enemies."

"You murderous beasts!" Wilf retorted. "Tell us where he has taken them!" Eddie sneered at him, making his blood boil. He looked across the cabin at Karaa, who had now slid back down the wall. Her hands were in front of her face, trying in vain to ward off the power of the cross. Wilf advanced on her, readying his stake arm. "Jake. Keep him pinned. Doug, move closer to Eddie." Doug shuffled towards Guzman as instructed as Wilf loomed over Karaa. The light spewing from the cross started to burn her flesh, making her scream in anguish.

"EDDIE!" she wailed.

Guzman looked on in horror as the older man swiped her hands away from her face with the cross. In one swift movement, Wilf buried his stake in her chest, falling on top of her with all his weight.

"NOOOOOOO!" Eddie screamed as he saw his companion attacked. Jake and Doug pinned him in the corner as Karaa uttered her last scream. Her skin started blackening as Wilf pushed the stake deeper into her chest, the cross in his hand losing its glow.

"Last chance Eddie. Where are they?" Jake said, poised to strike.

"FUCK YOU!" he screamed as he lurched forward towards the two men. The cross had slowed his movements, but he was still quicker than most men. Jake was ready though. He levelled his stake at Eddie's chest, tensing his legs, ready for impact. When it came, the force propelled Jake back through the doorway out onto the grass. Eddie's fangs swooped down at his throat, only his forearm stopping the killing stroke. Jake cried out as the weight of the vampire on top of him began to tell. The wooden stake was buried deep in his chest, missing the black heart at its centre. Eddie was not losing strength as Jake had hoped. He was bearing down, spittle from his mouth landing on the young man's cheeks. An impact from behind made Eddie curse with renewed fury. Wilf had straddled his back, driving his own stake into the vampire. The sharp wooden tip found its mark, puncturing Eddie's heart. Jake looked into his yellow eyes as they opened wide in horror and pain. They locked eyes, for what seemed like minutes as the older man began hammering the stake further in with the butt of his cross. The light went out of Guzman's eyes as he slumped sideways into the grass. He looked up at the cloudy sky as he faded away. His last thoughts of a young man, dancing in a packed club with a beautiful dark-skinned woman. She smiled at him. Her face vibrant and full of life. "Maria," he whispered, remembering the name of the young woman who he'd known back in Puerto Rico in the spring of 1951. He smiled serenely as his life force ebbed away. Sliding into the void.

"Son. Are you alright?" Doug said as he dropped to his knees next to Jake.

"I'm okay, Dad." He looked over at Wilf, who was sat in the long grass, lighting his pipe. "Thanks Wilf. You saved my life."

"Think nothing of it Jake. You've saved mine before. I'm just glad we're still breathing, and they are not."

Jake looked at Guzman's body as it started to decay, melting into the long grass. "Shame. Just think. He was born over eighty years ago, in another world. He did not choose this life. It was chosen for him. He only did what his instincts told him to do. His family probably grieved his disappearance for years after he'd vanished. And now, he lies dead in a field, in another world."

"Better him than us Son," Doug said as he sat down heavily next to Jake. He reached over, grasping his hand. "I thought you'd had it when I saw him knock you flying."

The Turning

"Me too. I would have done if it wasn't for Wilf. I missed with my stake. I'm lucky to be alive."

"What's the plan now?" Wilf said as he finally got his pipe to catch. He puffed contentedly in the darkness as Jake thought about the question.

"We either stay here for a few hours, or head through that gorge." The two other men looked towards Monks Passage, weighing up the options.

"I say we carry on," Doug said. "We're all full of adrenalin. Better to walk that off than sit on our arses in the darkness."

"I agree," said Wilf. Let's keep going while we can. Who knows how far ahead of us they are. Or what other traps are waiting for us."

"Okay. Let's grab our packs and carry on. I think we've earned a beer though. What say you Wilf?"

"Aye," said the older man, standing with the vigour of a teenager. His lips already moist with anticipation.

Thirty-Seven

Tamatan woke with a start as the boat lurched on a wave. "What is happening?" he said to no one in particular.

"Sea's picking up," said Sica. "The wind is coming from our shores. If this keeps up we will be at Mantz far quicker. You want some breakfast?"

"What is on the menu this morning, my friend?"

"The same as yesterday. You'll find what you need in the galley." Tamatan looked up, spotting Sica smiling down at him from his position at the rear of the boat. He was holding the wheel with one hand, whilst eating a flatbread filled with yellow whale flesh. Next to him say a clay jug, of what Tamatan guessed was cyder. He suddenly felt hungry. After relieving himself over the side of the boat, he headed rear, towards the small galley that hugged the right side of the vessel. The sea was indeed choppy, making his navigation from front to aft more difficult. The demon almost lost his footing before grabbing hold of one of the masts, steadying himself for a few seconds before reaching the galley. Large seagulls followed the boats swift progress across the sea, enticed by the pungent aroma that rose into the sky. Sica had already prepared two flatbreads, filled with juicy whale flesh. A clay jug sat next to the food, held in place by a small net that was fixed to the wood. He took his breakfast, noticing a large grey and white bird eyeing his food from the side of the boat. He shooed it away with his boot and sat down next to Sica, his red eyes muted as the sun threatened to break through the fog.

"Thank you captain. You certainly do provide hearty fayre," he said in between mouthfuls. "How long do you think it will take us if the wind stays true?"

"Reckon we'll be there by sundown at this rate. She almost skipping along now. Not like a normal crossing where a fart is the strongest wind out here. You may be in luck my friend. Although not sure it's good luck to be dropped off in a forest full of vampires sooner than later. You sure you want to do this?"

"I have to. Not only for myself. But for my kin. Even for you. I'd not relish the thought of these monsters calling upon you, my friend."

"I suppose you make a fair comment. I will not forsake you. I will return regularly, in hope to see your ugly face looking at me from the jetty."

"I'll be there. I may even do a spot of fishing while I wait for you. I may as well make myself useful once I'm satisfied that all is well in this world."

"You do that. The last thing I want is to sail home to tell your family that you are not coming back."

"Let's not even contemplate that Sica," Tamatan said as cold fingers danced from his head to his tailbone.

* * *

An hour after they shouldered their packs, the three men reached the eastern fringes of Mantz forest. The gorge was behind them, stretching as far as the eye could see. The three men spied a few cabins that looked like they were being slowly claimed by the trees behind them. "That's one scary-looking place," Doug said as he stopped, taking his pack off and laying it on the grass.

"You're not wrong there Dad. It looks like a brick wall, only made of wood and leaves. I've never seen trees so close together. This should be fun."

"We will need our smarts if we ever hope to leave this place," Wilf said as he sat down heavily, pulling food from his pack. "Can you feel it? Something about this place is wrong."

Jake nodded. He sat down, rubbing his leg that had suddenly started aching. *Shit. I forgot holy water*, he thought, trying to cast the thought from his mind. He needed to focus. "Let's have a quick snack then head in there. If it's as big as it looks, we could be searching for a while. Weeks maybe. We may need to have a re-think if things don't go to plan." Wilf and Doug nodded as they ate a breakfast of large sausage rolls and fruit juice. Jake followed suit, knowing that he needed to keep himself well fed for what lay ahead.

* * *

Twenty minutes later the three men were shouldering their packs once more. They quietly walked towards the first building, noticing the dark red smear on the ground, next to a makeshift spit. "I dread to think what was on the menu," Jake said as he shivered inside.

"Look at the trough in the ground," Wilf said. "It looks like that is the run off for whatever they killed. It does not bear thought as to who or what met their end in this place." They inspected the cabins, finding nothing of use or interest.

"Okay. Let's go exploring," Jake said. "Keep close."

* * *

They walked in a straight line, each man stepping between the tree trunks next to the other man. The travelled in a zigzag motion, such was the formation of the trees. The further they walked, the darker it became, until it almost felt like night time. "I've never seen trees so densely packed as this," Jake said as he brushed a low-lying branch from his path.

"It's a place where we do not want to dwell for too long," Wilf said as he looked around the forest. "I can see why folk give this place a wide steer. The Cravens would make quick work of you in here."

The Turning

"Look. Off to the left. More cabins," Doug said, noticing that the cross in his hand was warmer than a few minutes before. He held it up in front of him. "Can you feel that?"

"Yes Dad. We must be on our guard." Jake looked at the small settlement hidden in the trees. "There are about half a dozen cabins. Let's stay close. Anything comes at you, scream like mad." They headed for the largest building, barely being able to see the entrance until they were upon it. Jake pulled his torch from his pocket, shining it into the murky confines. "It looks emp-"

His words ended abruptly as he disappeared from the doorway, yanked into the darkness by a large hand. "Fuckenell!" Wilf started, his cross and stake poised ready to strike.

"SON!" Doug cried, crashing past Wilf into the cabin. The torch was in the corner, its light playing around the room. Both men saw a large figure holding Jake by the throat against the wall, choking the life out of him. "LET HIM GO!" Doug bellowed, his voice bouncing off the walls. Father Stephen looked round, meeting Doug's glare. "Father?" Doug said, suddenly quiet. "Is that you?"

Stephen relinquished the hold onf Jake, letting him slide down the wall until he sat slumped on the floor, coughing and breathless. "I think so. I'm not too sure," Stephen said as he stood there, his meaty arms hanging by his side.

"You're the shaman that helped Jake," Wilf stated. "Why is the cross reacting to you," he said holding it towards the Vicar.

"I've been infected." The words hung in the air as Stephen suddenly remembered Jake. He turned, lifting the younger man to his shaky feet. "Sorry. Are you hurt?"

"I...I think I'm okay," Jake said, clearly shaken. Stephen led him to a table in the dark room, seating him, before turning to the others. "Do you have a lighter or matches?" Doug rummaged in his jacket pocket before pulling a disposable lighter out. Stephen took it from him, lighting torches on the wall. In the brief contact, Doug felt the cold clamminess of his friend's hand. His stomach tightened, realising something bad had happened to him. He leaned against the wall as shadows danced around the cabin. The three men could now make out his features.

"Oh no!" Jake said. "What happened?"

"Elias happened. When you escaped, they took me back into the caverns. Elias fed me his blood, hoping it would make me like them. I think it has partly worked." The three men looked at his waxen complexion and red-rimmed eyes.

"Show me your teeth, shaman," Wilf said. Stephen obliged, showing them what they hoped they would see. "Hmm. It looks like they couldn't turn you fully. You look like them, but you're still a man like us."

"I don't feel like one," Stephen said. "The world feels funny. More vivid and colourful. I escaped their lair. I snapped the lock off with my hands. Something has happened to me for sure. I think I'm part vampire Jake," he said as his eyes filled with tears, spilling down his cheeks, becoming lost in his dark beard.

"Well you're not fully one. And I'm glad, because we need your help."

Stephen suddenly looked confused. "You mean, you're not here for me?"

Jake shook his head slowly. "No. Although I'm glad we found you. Elias has taken Katherine and Alicia. We think they're in this forest somewhere."

"Oh God Jake. I'm so sorry to hear that." He coughed, his chest raking something hidden inside. Jake thought he was going to be sick. Stephen hacked, the table shaking underneath his arms. He lowered his head, finally coughing up some phlegm into his mouth. He staggered to the doorway, spitting a glob of it into the forest. He came back, slumping into his seat. "Sorry about that."

"That's okay," Jake said handing him a bottle of water. He gratefully took it, swigging back half the contents in seconds.

"That's better," he said as his shoulders sagged. "So thirsty." He suddenly remembered what Jake had just relayed. "You think Katherine and Alicia are here? Why would he bring them this way?"

"Cover," Wilf said. "They torched the Vale and Amatoll. There are just withered burnt husks there now. It will take a thousand seasons for it to recover."

"I saw the fire. I made my way to the lone mountain, resting there for a while, before heading back this way. They did that?"

Jake nodded. "Yes Father. To stop us from following Elias back to Cornwall. It worked. He snatched the girls and made his way back here. There is nothing out east, but grasslands and the coast. Not exactly vampire territory. Wilf assures me that the north and south hold little appeal to anyone, let alone a group of monsters. We think they're here."

"It makes sense. Ever since I left the mountain, something has pulled me towards this place. Maybe it's them. Maybe they sense that I am like them and are calling to me on the wind. Except I am not totally like them. God it's so messed up. Why did I have to stumble into this? Why the hell did they have to take Denise from me? My dear Denise. She was a good woman. She gave her life to help others. She did not deserve to die like that. At the hands of some bastard monster!"

"I know Father," Jake said, placing his hand over the Vicar's. "I know this won't make things right, but the monster who killed Denise has been destroyed. We found them a short time ago. Him and his woman. We got them both."

"So how many left are there?"

"We think three. Elias. Mom, and a boy. Let's hope we're not too late. We need to find them and finish Elias for good. We cannot leave anything to chance this time. Either they all die, or we do I guess."

The four men let the words sink in. For a long moment, the cabin and forest beyond lay deathly quiet. A thought occurred to Stephen. "Finding them in this forest looks to be impossible. However, something made me come here. Some unknown force made me leave the refuge of that mountain, making me walk god knows how many miles to be here. If it's them doing it, then I can lead you to them."

"That's good," Doug said, a relief washing over him. "This forest is no place for the girls. Let's find them and take them home."

"Are we all in agreement?" Jake said, feeling optimistic for the first time in days.

"I'm with you. Let the shaman lead us to them." Jake noted the steely determination in Wilf's eyes. He knew the old man would gladly die, if it meant Katherine and Alicia were saved.

"Okay. Good. Let us use this cabin as a base. We can leave our packs here and travel light," Jake said, eager to be on the hunt.

Wilf interjected, taking some of the wind out of the younger man's sails. "Far be it from me to open a bag of snakes on your plans Jake, but we don't know how big this place is. I've heard that Mantz is several times the size of Amatoll. Now you've been there. You know that it would take almost a full day to walk from the glades in the west, to the eastern edge where it meets Agar. This place is bigger. And far less easy to travel in. You've seen the trees. It could take us weeks just to get to the other side. We can leave some stuff here. Things that we know will keep. However, I say we take all weapons with us, just to be safe. We also need to watch what we eat. Food will be scarce in there," he said pointing out of the door. "We don't want to starve to death in the middle of the forest. Because the first souls to find us will just find a pile of bones, picked clean by rats and bugs."

"Fair point. Let's let Father Stephen guide us. We can travel so far into the forest, maybe resting for the night, before carrying on again. I think we just need to play it by ear."

"What does that mean?" Wilf said, confused.

"We go with the flow Wilf," Doug said, patting the grizzled man on the shoulder.

"Right. Let's get busy," Jake said.

Thirty-Eight

Rick Stevenson ended the attempted call, tossing the handset onto the coffee table. He stood, taking his mug from the shiny surface in front of him. He walked through the lounge of his apartment, standing next to the floor to ceiling window that looked out over a grey Hamburg. Rick took a sip of his drink, his mind trying to figure out what was going on. He was not like his brother. Jake was impulsive, relying on gut instinct. Rick was process-driven. He relied on facts and figures before deciding on anything. His blue eyes scanned the cityscape in front of him, taking in the wonderful architecture and the natural beauty of the Lake Alster. Normally, he would drink in this Germanic sight, feeling lucky and smug that all this was his. Not today though. He'd tried contacting both his father and brother, with no response. Part of Jake was surfacing within him, as his gut was telling Rick that something was wrong. He'd rang a dozen times, leaving voicemail messages on all four lines. The younger sibling was used to things running smoothly. Ever since he'd graduated from university in England, his life had been one smooth ride. His career was smoothly ascending to the heights he'd dreamed of. He owned a penthouse apartment in one of the world's great cities. He had a group of colleagues and friends with whom he socialised on a regular basis. Added to this, he had a great girlfriend, who had recently moved from Turnhout, Belgium to live with him. Things were moving in the right direction. This latest dilemma perplexed him though. Rick knew that his brother moved around a lot, being in various places throughout the week. His new woman was mostly at home though. But his father was different. He could count on one hand the times that Doug's phone had rang out without reply. *Where the hell are they?* he thought as his phone started vibrating on the glass table. He walked over, scooping up the phone, swiping the screen with his thumb. "Hello."

"Mister Stevenson? It's Constable Thorn from Tintagel. I thought I'd give you an update."

An hour before, Rick had googled the phone number of his family's local police station. He'd relayed his concerns to the Policeman on the phone, asking him if he could check the properties for him. "Any luck?"

"Fraid not sir. I went to both properties. Your father's car is on the drive, and the house all locked up. No evidence of anything untoward. Your brother's house is also locked up, although his car is not there. I spoke to his neighbour, who was outside her house. She said that they were there a few days before. She also said that she saw Jake out walking with a man she'd never seen before. An older chap with long hair. Ring any bells?"

"None. I'm not that close with my brother. I would not know who he socialises with. I've not seen him in a while."

"Oh. I see," was the fumbled reply. "Well how do you want me to proceed? It is a little soon to class them as missing. They could have gone away for a few days. If you want some advice sir, I'd give it a week, then go from there."

"Okay." Rick said absently. "Oh, and thank you for your time."

"All in a day's work," the perky policeman replied. If you need further assistance, don't hesitate to call."

"Thank you," Rick said before ending the call. He tossed his black phone on the sofa as a key rattled in the front door.

"Hello," a female voice said.

"In here baby," Rick said as he padded into the kitchen, flicking the coffee machine on.

The Turning

"Hello you," Marlies said as she kicked off her boots in the lounge. "Any luck?"

"Nothing. The police just called me back. Both houses are empty."

She walked over to him, wrapping her arms around his shoulders. He buried his face into her dark hair, inhaling her smell. He loved her natural aroma. It was womanly and warm, with a hint of spice and shampoo. Rick pulled back, looking at her. All his possessions meant nothing without her. She added the cherry on the top of his German cake. He was totally in love with Marlies. He'd been with several women in his adult life, most of them losing his interest after a few months. Marlies was different. He'd met her at a folding carton event in Eindhoven the year before, noticing her in a crowd of men. Rick had stared at her beautiful face, a sprinkling of freckles adorning her perfect skin. He knew then that he had to introduce himself to her. It had gone from there. She challenged and pushed him more than anyone in his entire life. Even more than his parents. She was smart and worldly, something that Rick craved. Conversation. Intelligent conversation, which seemed so scant, even in the circles that he moved in. She worked as a Packaging Technologist for a folding carton company. A rising star in the ranks, who had asked to be transferred from Belgium to Cologne to be with Rick. The company obliged, reluctant to lose someone of her calibre. Rick could sit listening to her talk about print passes and fibre tare for hours. She knew how to engage him. In his opinion, she could engage anyone with her modest self-deprecating approach. He bent down, kissing her freckled lips. She returned the kiss, snaking a hand through his sandy hair. For a moment, the world was forgotten. All thoughts of missing family and hot foiling evaporated into the ether. Behind them the coffee machine began making a *plop plop* sound, prompting Rick to reluctantly break the kiss. They both opened their eyes, their vision fuzzy for a brief second. He turned and headed into the kitchen, Marlies following him silently, her socks scuffing the tiled floor. Rick busied himself with making her coffee, while sat on the counter watching him. "So, what are you going to do?"

"I'm not sure yet. The police said to give it a few more days until we press the panic button. They may have gone away for a break. It's not long since Mom died. Maybe they wanted a change of scenery. That's a logical way of looking at it, but something is telling me otherwise."

Marlies sat on the edge of the counter, her legs swaying gently, her toes wriggling inside her black socks. "I have an idea."

"I'm all ears," Rick said as he handed her a stoneware mug filled with cappuccino.

She took a sip. "Hmm. Lovely, thanks baby. Anyway. My plan. I have to go to Riga on Monday."

"Riga? What for?" Rick said disappointed.

"We've got a new client. A packaging company. They are sending out an auditor from England to how do you say? Give us the once over. Erik has met him before. It should be easy enough. We'll take him out to dinner Monday night, then a day in the Riga office on Tuesday. I'll fly back in the evening."

Rick had met Marlies' boss Erik on numerous occasions. He was more like a friend and mentor to her. Almost a second father. He knew she would be looked after. "Sounds like you'll be in your element Baby. Surrounded by sexy men in a romantic city."

She playfully punched his arm, almost spilling her coffee. "Are you serious? It's an audit and dinner. I've never met the guy, but auditors are probably not the most exciting people in the world. The conversation will probably revolve around quality management systems and ISO9001. It's hardly romantic. Anyway, you've dragged me from my plan. I will be back Tuesday night. If your family are still off the radar, why don't we fly over on Wednesday?"

"Really? You'd do that with me?"

"Of course I would baby. I love you. I'd do anything for you."

Rick walked back over to her, letting her wrap her black legging-encased thighs around his waist. "I love you too, Marlies. You're a wonderful girl," he said as he kissed the top of her head. "Let's just hope they turn up before then. If not, we will go and find them."

"I'd love a chance to go back there with you. But I'm hoping we don't need to go next week. I'd rather explore the Cotswolds with you during a nice summer break."

"Me too," he said as he hugged her. Although something in his gut told him he would be booking flights very soon.

* * *

"What time is it Dad?" Jake asked as he stopped next to a tree, his arm braced against the trunk. The forest around them was quiet. Jake could just make out daylight towards the east. To the west, an impenetrable blanket of darkness awaiting the four men.

"Five," Doug said as he unshouldered his pack for the third time since they had set out. "I'm getting tired Son. What say we camp somewhere here and continue on in the morning?"

"What does everyone think?" Jake said, aware that he too was feeling fatigued.

"I'm with you," Wilf said hoarsely.

"Me too," said Father Stephen, who sat down heavily on a fallen tree trunk, his head bowed.

"Right. That's decided then. Let's think about getting some dinner on the go," Jake said. He dropped his pack and unzipped it, pulling a selection of items as the other men got as comfortable as they could on the bracken strewn earth. Chocolate and energy bars, sausage rolls, and three lengths of black pudding. "Okay. Who wants what?"

Father Stephen's head shot up, his eyes fixing on the younger man. "Is that black pudding I can smell?"

"Uh huh. You want some?" he said, suddenly curious.

"It smells so good. Yes, please Jake, throw me one over." Jake did so, watching with interest as the Vicar ripped the one end off of the long black sausage-shaped delicacy. He bit into it, exclaiming with delight as he chewed it noisily. "Lovely," he said as it rolled around in his mouth.

"What's black pudding?" Wilf asked.

"It's pig's bl-" Jake's words died in his throat as he realised what was happening to the Vicar. "Pig's blood. Father. Have you always liked black pudding?"

"Yes," he said, half the pudding now eaten. "Why?"

"Because you said you might be part vampire."

Stephen stopped chewing, his mouth wide open. "Oh yeah. Now I come to think about it, it's odd that I could smell it so clearly. What does this mean Jake?"

"I don't know Father. I hope it just means that you've got a great sense of smell. What I'm not hoping for is that you're becoming a full vampire, who will crave our blood."

The words slowly fell to the forest floor, each man letting the implications sink in. "Shit," Doug said, his sausage roll hanging limply in his fingers.

"Then promise me something Jake?" the Vicar said, his tone flat and monotone.

"What?" Jake replied, dreading the next sentence.

"When that happens, finish me. I've got nothing back at home. Denise is gone. My faith has gone. My flock will have deserted me by now. When the time comes, kill me. Show me no mercy, because at that point I may show no mercy to you. Deal?"

Reluctantly, Jake spoke. "Deal. Let's hope it does not come to that."

"Jake. Can I try some black pudding?" Wilf said as he cracked open a bottle of ale.

The younger man tossed him one across the makeshift picnic area, Wilf catching it one handed while swigging ale. He skinned it with his knife, taking a large bite into the dark sausage. "Well I'm no vampire." He said as he chewed. "But I agree, Shaman. It tastes fuckin' great!"

* * *

The boat nudged the pontoon that ran out from the forest into the sea. It barely made a sound, such was Sica's skill, even in the dead of night. The sky was clear, the moon reflecting off the still waters that rippled gently against the shore. Tamatan had already said his farewell to the captain out at sea, telling Sica that it would be best to be quiet when they reached Mantz. There was no argument from Sica, who'd planned to turn the boat around and head back out to sea as soon as his friend's feet hit the jetty. The diminutive demon never stopped his stride, heading into the murky forest at a brisk pace. He never looked back to see his friend sail away on the silken sea. Tamatan's eyes shone bright red as he weaved and meandered through the thick forest, his footing sure. The demon skipped over rabbit holes, vaulting fallen trees with barely a whisper of sound. He could feel something. A gentle thrumming that pulsed through the forest. He knew the thrum. *Vampires*, he thought. His senses picked up another feeling that echoed through the impenetrable blackness. *Humans?* He slowed to a walking pace, eventually stopping when the feeling increased. *Are there Cravens still in the woods?* His thoughts were disturbed as a large elk passed in front of him. It stopped, eyeing him in the darkness before hurdling a fallen log, disappearing into the gloom. He sat down on the log, gathering his thoughts. *I can feel evil in this wood. It's Elias and his kin. I must not fail Veltan and Jake*, he thought as he set off again, heading eastwards through the night.

* * *

"How much further?" Alison said in the darkness.

"We still have far to go. Patience, Alison."

Katherine looked over at Elias as Alicia suckled from her, completely unaware of the peril that she faced. "Jake will come," she stated flatly.

"I'm sure he will eventually. But not just yet. I'm pretty sure he would not head towards Mantz straight away. And even if he did, Eddie and Karaa will be waiting for him at Monks Passage. We are all alone, human. You can forget about your man. Concentrate on keeping the little one healthy."

"Why? What plans do you have for us?"

Elias stared at her across the clearing. Until they had rested, he'd kept her under his spell, subduing her into a permanent drowse. He knew though that he would need to release the hold, doing so once they were well into the forest. "Why we're going to live out our days by the sea. We will have all we need. There are many sailors and travellers that will pass by, giving us all we need to survive. You will be able to hunt for food, as this forest will yield many rewards. Not just humans either."

"Hunt for food? You mean animals? How do I do that? I've never hunted in my life." What makes you think that I will be able to kill an animal?"

"You will. Trust me. You will soon be able to do many things. Things that you cannot do currently."

A cold trickle of ice ran down Katherine's spine as she drew her infant as close to her as possible. She shook her head in the darkness, tears appearing at her eyes. "What are you saying?"

"I am saying that soon you will be one of us. You both will."

* * *

"They are moving away from us," Father Stephen said as the three men sat having an improvised breakfast.

"Then we need to saddle up and get moving," Jake said as he drained his bottle.

"What is happening?" Wilf said as he appeared in the clearing, a roll of toilet paper in his hand.

"Throw that here please Wilf," Doug said. "I need to make a visit before we head off." Wilf obliged, tossing the roll across the clearing. Doug caught it two-handed before heading off in the opposite direction.

"Elias is on the move. Father Stephen can feel it. We need to get moving as soon as Dad is finished."

Wilf nodded, bending down stiffly, scooping his pack off the forest floor. "Which way shaman?"

"That way," the Vicar indicated with a point of his finger.

"Let's get this done on this day. My old heart cannot take any more worry. I need to see Katherine and the baby safe."

Jake walked over, clapping him on the shoulder. "Let's go hunting then."

* * *

Across the forest, Tamatan heard a noise filtering through the trees. "That's a child," he said. *What is a child doing in the middle of this forsaken place? Maybe some of the cannibals endured. I need to have my wits about me today,* he thought as he made his way eastwards. The demon heard the noise again a few minutes later. Far off in the darkness. He couldn't make out the distance, the trees making judging anything virtually impossible. He pressed on east at a brisk pace, his red eyes scanning the trees in front of him. He was ready for whatever appeared in the darkness. Ready to fight, ready to kill.

Thirty-Nine

The hidden sun was falling away over the western horizon as the four men eventually stopped for the day. Doug slumped to the forest floor, reaching into his pack for a drink. He took a swig, his breathing hoarse. "Does this bleeding forest ever end?" he said as the other men sat down. "This is our third day here, with no sign of Katherine, Alicia, or daylight. It's a good job I've got my watch on. At least I can keep track of the time and day."

"What day is it Dad?" Jake said as he finished another bottle of water. Water that was starting to run dry.

"Thursday. Just after six. Wilf, do you know how much farther we have to go to reach the other side of this place?"

The grizzled man, whose brow was beaded with sweat shook his head. "I'd only be guessing. I'd say at least another five days until we reach the western shore.

"Five days. We'll run out of supplies in two. We need to have a rethink soon, or else we'll starve to death out here."

They all looked at each other, noticing the tiredness they all shared. Even Jake, who was the youngest by decades, looked spent. He sported the first shoots of a beard, putting ten years on his once youthful appearance. "So, what do we do?"

"Whatever we do, we need to stay together. If we go back for supplies, we all go back. If we split up, we may never find the others."

The Turning

"One more day, then we go back to Amatoll. I know that we agreed to keep quiet in the forest, but tomorrow I think we should start calling out their names."

Wilf looked wary. "If we do that Jake, it could cause other problems. We do not know who or what is in this place. We may bring trouble our way. Some of the Cravens may still be close by. Do you really want a pack of cannibals coming at us, in their forest? We'd be cut to pieces very quickly. Then all this will be for nothing."

Jake threw his empty bottle across the clearing. It bounced off a tree, landing out of sight in the gloom. "So, what do we do? Just turn back without even a fucking whimper? They could be close by."

"Yes, they could be," Wilf said. "Or they could be far away. It's taken us three days to make it this far. If we have to make a hasty retreat, it will take us the same amount of time to reach the edges of this forest. Three days, fighting off vampires, or heathens, or beasts, in a place where you can barely see anything. I'm not saying not to do it. I'm saying that we should all be in agreement, ready for the consequences."

"Okay. Here's my proposal," Doug said. "Tomorrow. We carry on at first light. We call their names until lunchtime. If there is no response, we head back to the other forest to get more supplies."

"Sounds good to me," Jake said, a steely resolve spreading across his face.

"Aye," Wilf said, his head bowed.

"I'm with you," the Vicar said, scratching his beard.

"Then let's get an early night. Tomorrow could be a long day," Jake said as he fished the toilet roll out of his pack, heading through the trees on his own, leaving the other men to their thoughts.

* * *

"Coop, Alison. Stay here with the girl and the infant. Something is amiss."

"What's wrong?" Coop said.

"I can sense things around us. I noticed it earlier. However, it now has gotten stronger."

"In what direction," the young vampire asked, his body tense.

"At first I felt it behind us, towards the east. Now however I can feel it towards the west too. It's almost like two separate forces are closing in on us. I need you to watch them while I try to find something."

"What are you looking for?" Alison said, her tone flat, her eyes dim.

"If I remember rightly, there is something close by that could be of use, if we do have company."

"What?" Coop said.

"Our escape route," Elias said as he turned from them, heading south into the forest alone.

* * *

He sat down, resting against a fallen tree. One tree amongst millions in the vast expanse. A giant skull of an unknown beast lay next to him, picked clean by the tiny inhabitants of the forest. Other bones were scattered close by, giving Tamatan's resting place a graveyard feel. He was unfazed, concentrating his senses. He could feel something close by. Days moving through the forest had brought him to this point. He could almost smell something over the next rise. He'd heard occasional whimpers, certain now that a child dwelt somewhere in the forbidding wood. Whose child it was, he knew not. The demon just knew that he had to keep heading east, to find who the unknown person or persons were. He could feel evil close by, which confused him further. *Why would a child be so close to such evil? Unless they are travelling together. That's a possibility*, he thought as he curled up on the forest floor. Tamatan closed his eyes, letting sleep carry him away. His last thoughts before the darkness overwhelmed him were of a log cabin across the sea, and the beautiful family that waited for him.

* * *

Elias stood looking out from the cave towards the only town on the island. It was night. The island was either swathed in a perpetual fog, or under the cover of darkness for seasons at a time. He'd not visited this place since wars raged far-off lands. It was only because of need that he stood here now, looking at the rough sea as it peppered the craggy coastline. He stepped out of the cave, relieved to see the wide rocky path that led towards the town. He could make out twinkling lights that adorned hundreds of dark structures across the bay. He knew the town well enough. The giant knew he may be leaping from the frying pan. But he had little choice if his instincts were correct. He stepped back inside the cave as spray from a wave coated his back, soaking him to the skin. Elias walked steadily for a minute until a red outline appeared in front of him. His keen eyes guided him in the dark cave, his footing sure as he passed back through the doorway. He was motionless for a moment, listening to the sounds of the forest. Nothing seemed out of place. Elias was stood with the doorway behind him, looking up the steep path that led back to the others. He guessed the distance to be a mile at most. He was satisfied they could make it here if needed. The dark rocks of the cleft rose forty feet above him, giving the passage a cloying feel. The split in the land was only a few feet wide, barely able to accommodate his wide shoulders. He began walking upwards, the rocks falling away until he was back at ground level. The vampire looked back down the pathway, seeing the faint red hue a few hundred metres away. A small tree, a stunted cousin of the others around it stood opposite the path. With a swipe of his hand, the tree was cut in half, providing Elias with the marker he needed. He smiled, his red eyes burning bright in the darkness. He turned north, heading back to his kin.

* * *

Katherine lay on the forest floor, her head propped on her baby bag. Alicia was sleeping, a blessed relief under their current situation. She had never been so scared. Katherine thought all the horrors were behind her. She loved her new life. Their house, the town. It all felt so perfect. It now felt like it was becoming a distant memory as she lay in the dense forest, two vampires guarding her. The woman looked over at her once mother-in-law.

She looked back at Katherine, her feral eyes full of malice. "What?"

"Do you not remember me, Alison?"

"No. Why would I?"

"Before you were turned, we were family. Your son, Jake? Do you remember him?"

Alison blinked a few times, trying to pull something from the recesses of her mind. She shrugged. "No. Don't know Jake or anyone else. I only need to know my kin. Anyone else is an enemy. As are you."

Katherine turned away from her former mother-in-law as tears sprang from her eyes. Her body was wracked with shudders as she tried to stifle her sobs. She tried to remain in control, not wanting to wake her daughter. *Please Jake. Please find us. Before we are turned into monsters.*

* * *

"What time is it Dad?" Jake said as sat up groggily.

"Six. What I wouldn't give for a cup of tea and a bacon sandwich."

Jake's stomach growled, before he fished a sausage roll and a bottle of water from his pack. "I know Dad. That sounds like heaven. Soon. Very soon we'll be back home, enjoying life again. Where is Father Stephen?"

"He said he wanted to scout ahead. He headed west about fifteen minutes ago. I told him not to be long."

Jake looked over at Wilf, smiling as the older man snored away peacefully without a care in the world. He took a swig of water, wishing it was at least chilled. "Do you think we will have any luck today?" Jake asked, hoping for a positive answer from the one man who always made things appear better than they were.

"I hope so. I really do Son. Even if we don't, we will return until we do find them. We need to keep a bright outlook on things. It would be very easy to let our spirits drop."

Doug was about to add something when Father Stephen came bustling into the makeshift campsite. "I heard a baby's cry!"

Jake and Doug shot up from the forest floor, their expressions shocked, eager for information. "Where?" Jake said, grabbing the Vicar's arm."

"I walked for about ten minutes. I heard a whimper further on. It was a baby. I've heard enough in my time. It wasn't close by. But it was close enough to hear."

Wilf stirred from his sleep, farting loudly. "What's going on?" he asked as he saw their expressions.

"Father Stephen heard a baby in the forest."

"Fuckenell!" Wilf said, scrambling to his feet. "How far shaman?"

"Whoever it is, I'd say they're about half an hour ahead of us. And stop calling me shaman! Call me Kenneth." Stephen protested mildly.

"Fair enough, shaman," Wilf said, excitedly as he began pacing the forest.

Doug noticed the edge to the men. He knew he would have to be the calming influence, as ever. "Okay. Look. This could be great news. It could very well be them. But it may not. It may be someone, or something else. Whatever we do, let's proceed with caution. If Kenneth heard a baby cry, I'm sure we can track them down. And Kenneth said himself, something is pulling him along. Let's hope whatever it is, is close to Katherine and Alicia. Now. Let's get ready to move, before they do. And let's have everything we need ready, just in case this all goes tits up!"

Forty

They are on the move, Tamatan thought as he squatted next to a tree, doing his daily business. *They are changing course, heading south. I can almost see them.* He paused. *There are others, further away. I can feel them. Something familiar too.* "Jake!" he exclaimed as he pulled his strides up, belting them with shaky fingers. "What are you doing back here," he said aloud. *Something ill has befallen you if you've come back here.* He moved off, quiet as a leaf on the breeze, heading south eastwards, towards who knew what.

* * *

"What's wrong Elias?" Alison said as she watched the giant stiffen.

"Something is closing in. We need to move. Katherine. Don't make a sound. The moment you do, I'll take your baby and dash her brains out against the nearest tree. Do you understand me?"

Katherine nodded, clutching the infant to her breast as she fed. "I won't speak, although I cannot stop the baby making a sound."

"Just do your best. If I think you're not, she dies. Then you die. You two," he said to Coop and Alison. "Bring up the rear. Stay close." They both nodded, Coop readily, Alison dumbly. Elias moved away from the tree, walking south. He motioned with his gaunt hand for Katherine to follow, which she did, her boots scuffing the bracken that littered the forest floor. After a few hundred yards, the group entered a clearing. A single ray from the sun lit the dark wood like a lone beacon,

The Turning

bathing the trees in an ethereal glow. Elias skirted it smoothly, hoping the others would follow suit. Katherine paused for a moment, letting the sun warm her skin before Coop's cold fingers shoved her onwards. He sensed the destructive power of the sun, letting his instinct guide him around a tree, away from harm. Before Elias could react, Alison walked blindly into the clearing, the sun's rays instantly blistering her skin.

"AAAAAHH!" she shrieked, pulling her arm out of the light. It sizzled and puckered in the darkness, drawing further curses from her.

"Silence," Elias said, clamping his hand over her mouth. "We need to move. They will have heard that. Your stupidity may have cost us. Pray that it hasn't," his voice, loaded with fury, made Alison cower against a tree. She hissed quietly as he turned his back on her, hurrying south with the others in tow.

* * *

The four of them froze on the spot, gooseflesh jumping from man to man. "Fucking hell! What's that?" Jake said, his face turning white.

"Whatever it was, it's not happy. Let's go find out," Wilf said, his weapons ready in his hands.

"I can feel them close by," Kenneth said. "Follow me."

Doug followed the others, his legs like rubber, his throat like sandpaper.

* * *

Tamatan jumped behind a tree as the shriek echoed through the forest. He stood immobile, mentally counting in his native tongue of Antish-Glav. After a while he stuck his head out, scanning the dark trees around him. *Whatever that came from it was in pain*, he thought as he set off, weaving through the trees, heading south. The demon moved silently, his eyes hooded to reduce their glow, such was his caution. He knew that if there were vampires close by, they may spot him in the darkness. After a while he noticed a shaft of light towards the east. It lit the forest around it, naturally drawing him towards its welcoming glow. He caught himself after a few steps, keeping to the shadows, his eyes scanning the forest ahead for danger. Or for a baby. In truth, Tamatan, formally Spring-Heeled-Jack knew not what to expect.

* * *

Alicia began crying in her mother's arms as Katherine did her best to keep her movements as smooth as possible. Elias turned, his red eyes burning in the gloom. "Hush that baby!" he hissed.

"How do I do that?" Katherine asked defiantly. "She's a baby. She does not know what is going on. She's probably tired, and she has nappy rash. Something you failed to think of when you snatched us."

"Hold your tongue wench, or I will rip it out!" Elias spat. She didn't cower. She fronted the giant out, drawing a thin smile from his grey lips. He knew she had courage. He'd seen it before. He knew she would not die scared. *She will go out fighting*, he thought as he pulled her along roughly. For her part, Katherine tried to soothe Alicia as he moved through the trees, banging her head on a low branch that she failed to spot. Blood sprang from a gash in her hairline that made Coop and Alison wince. Elias smelt it too, issuing a command without breaking step. "Don't harm her. Or I will have your head on a stick." They hissed behind Katherine, the rebuke like a slap in the face. They obeyed their master as they followed in his wake, wondering just where he was leading them.

* * *

"Look at that," Jake said as he saw the shaft of light.

"That's a welcome sight," Doug said as he slowed his pace to a stop, enjoying the feeling of warmth on his skin.

"Father," Wilf said. "Let's put you to the test. Stand in the light. See if you are a monster, or still a shaman."

Stephen never hesitated. He walked forward, letting the sun flood over him. The other men half expected a scream, followed by sizzling flesh. Nothing happened. Stephen looked solemn though as the men looked at him. "I can feel it pulsated through my skin. It doesn't hurt,

The Turning

but it feels alien to me. I think it has answered my question. I may never be a full vampire, but I'll never be a full man either. I'm both. A half-breed."

The three men let the news sink in, their shoulders visible sagging. A solitary tear rolled down Doug's face, shimmering in the sunlight. He was about to offer reassurance when a noise from the south made them all start. It was the sound of a baby crying.

"That's Alicia!" Jake gasped as he motioned to break into a run.

Stephen stilled his departure with a strong grip on his arm. "Jake. You need to live through this. I don't. I'm done for. And I'm glad I am. Let me put myself in harm's way for you. You're young, with a life to live. I'm old, with nothing to live for. Let my last good deed be this."

Jake looked at the Vicar, a wave of recognition hitting him. "You want Elias, don't you?"

"Yes. I have a score to settle with him. Guzman killed my wife, but Elias sent him to do it. He's mine when the time comes. Now let's move. They are getting away." They set off at a jog, four abreast, navigating the narrow tree's. Even Doug, who was spent a few minutes before, was fuelled with renewed vigour. He desperately wanted to see the girls. Jake's girls. His girls. His family.

"There!" Jake said. I saw movement ahead. I'm sure of it. "KATHERINE!" he bellowed. "KATHERINE! IT'S JAKE."

"Jake! Ja-" The unseen voice was abruptly cut off as the four men picked up the pace.

"Look!" Stephen said as the men came to a natural crossroads in the forest. Ahead the ground fell away into a steep ravine that disappeared into the earth. Two things barred their entrance to the ravine. Two vampires. Fangs bared. Eyes ablaze, full of fury.

Forty-One

"Alison!" Doug said as he came to a skittering stop. His former wife stood looking at him, teeth bared, fingers curled, ready to strike.

He noticed the boy next to her. He was tall and would have looked fair if it was not for his grey skin, yellow eyes, and a black pit of a mouth. "Die!" he hissed before launching himself at Jake. The young man was ready for him, raising his cross and stake, braced for impact. The impact never came. In a blur that almost defied their eyes, Coop was smashed into a nearby tree. The four men and Alison looked on frozen as Tamatan pinned the boy to the ground, clamping his green lips over Coop's grey ones. Light spilled from Tamatan's eyes, nose, and mouth as he sucked the life-force out of the vampire. Alison made a move to help, being pinned back against a tree by Wilf's cross.

"Stay there, you evil old crow!" he commanded as she wailed and cursed them. Coop's grey skin was now black, his yellow eyes now completely sunken into his skull. Tamatan stood up, leaving the withered husk on the forest floor. Before anyone could utter a word, Alison broke, reeling down the ravine, a strangled wail ringing out across the forest.

"We've got to go after them," Jake said urgently. He looked at Tamatan. "Where did you come from?" he asked.

"We can talk later over tea and pikelets. We need to be on their heels. Because they are heading into the last place you would want them to be."

The Turning

"Where?" Wilf asked, his stomach clenching.

"The island of Tenta. A place full of murderers and monsters. A place that not even Elias is safe in."

* * *

He held the woman and child in his arms as he hurried out of the cave, a burst of sea spray engulfing him. He turned on instinct, shielding the humans from the brunt of the sea's assault. His saw the town ahead, along a rocky path that clung to the cliff. It was cold here, not like the forest he'd just left. Icy pellets of sea mist pummelled him as he made ungainly progress towards the town of Tenta, which shared its name with the inhospitable chunk of rock it lay brooding over. He could just make out the several tracks that ran in haphazard fashion from the island. They stretched out to sea, becoming lost in the night. It gave the island a bug like appearance. A nasty bug, with a poisonous bite. The landscape lay underneath a blue moon that shone down from the sky. High clouds blew across its face, reducing visibility for Elias as he hobbled along. He came off the path after a few hundred yards, almost losing his footing in a puddle. Katherine whimpered in his arms as he righted his progress, heading for cover next to the first building in the town. The sea spray lashed against the wooden structure, rattling doors and window shutters. Elias made his way around the front of the cabin, hearing shouts and curses within. Light spilled underneath the door jamb, along with an acrid stench. He looked directly up the main though fare that led across the town. *I need to lose myself,* he thought. *They will be on to me soon.* He skipped across the dirt track towards an identical cabin on the other side. The track was like a slow moving brown river of sludge, gently moving down towards the sea. A path wound its way through rickety houses, gradually climbing towards the town's summit. He followed the path, knowing of one person who could shelter him. He just needed to remember where she lived.

* * *

The four men and Tamatan stood before the doorway. They were in a single line, such was the tightness of the ravine. Mud and earth crumbled from above, peppering them as they stood looking at the red outline. "Go Jake," Tamatan said. "But be ready. We're right behind you."

Jake stepped through the doorway, feeling a slight resistance as he moved. It felt like he was in slow motion for a second before being released from the hold. He took half a dozen steps in the dark cave as the others followed. "Is that the sea?" he said, looking towards the arched entrance.

"It is. And a rough sea it is too. We must be careful. Not only of vampires, but of being swept away by a rogue wave."

"I need my torch," Jake said as he removed his pack. He knelt on the wet black rocks as he flicked the switch, the stark light making them shield their eyes. He played the torchlight around the cave, looking for danger. "Looks empty. Tamatan. Do you know where this leads?"

"Yes. Out of the cave and turn right towards the town. I will lead the way. Keep your weapons ready." They followed him, Doug taking up the rear as a wave pounded the path in front of them.

"Fuckenell," Wilf said as he clung to the wet rocks, his clothing saturated.

"We need to move quickly," the little demon said as he took off down the path towards a low-lying cluster of buildings that gently rose towards a summit, swathed in cloud.

Another wave struck the entrance, buffeting Father Stephen down the pathway, banging into Wilf and Jake. The three men went down, momentarily covered in frigid spray. Doug had seen the wave a split second before it struck, moving backwards to avoid the impact. As he stood there watching the men floundering on the rocks he felt a presence close by. Like he was being watched. He turned to his left, his eyes falling where the pathway ended just passed the cave entrance. A shape moved in the darkness, making him start. A pair of yellow eyes locked onto his, making Doug forget about his companions. The figure advanced, the light from the blue moon illuminating her face. "Alison,"

The Turning

he said, his cross and stake falling on the rocks, the clattering sound lost to the sea.

"Look at me," she hissed, her teeth protruding from under her thin lips. Doug swayed on his feet, unaware of the voices calling to him.

"DAD! RUN!" Jake bellowed from further down the path as another wave struck. The vampire was thrown into her husband, the impact of the sea dashing them into the rocks.

Doug was released from his trance as he tried to scramble to his feet. He saw his son looking at him, an expression of frozen terror on his face. Before Doug could move he felt a sharp pain on his shoulder as Alison bit down into his flesh. He tried to struggle from her grip, but was locked in cold wet vice of dead flesh and bone. Doug knelt there, an arm around his throat, holding him firmly as the vampire drained him. Slick red blood ran down from his neck, darkening his shirt as Alison worried his shoulder. Unable to move, he looked at Jake, taking in the features of his beloved son one last time. All the pain he felt, the cold that was penetrating his skin, and the noise of the sea fell away from him. He drank in Jake's features, not quite quenching his thirst. "I love you Son," Doug said smiling as another wave hit, obliterating the pathway.

* * *

Elias dropped Katherine and the baby on rough wooden planks, protested loudly under their weight. He looked around, his senses heightened. He'd made it closer the summit of the town, opting to use the cover of a large porch to take stock of his surroundings. The baby started to cry. "Shut that child up, woman!" he yelled, his usual calm persona replaced by anguish and doubt.

"She's hungry," Katherine said, undoing her top. Alicia latched on willingly, drawing a wince from her mother. "Careful sweetie," she cooed, fighting the sharp pain as little gums dug into the rubbery flesh of her nipple.

The side door of the building burst open, two men spilling out. They were both short, not much taller than Katherine. They were wiry and had a crazed look in their eyes. Ignoring Elias, they leered at the mother and daughter. "Look 'ere Frenk," one said. "We've struck lucky tonight. She's got her tits out already."

"The young un looks to 'ave claimed one for 'erself," the other said. They both looked at Elias, his face turned away from them. "You can watch if yer like, old man," Frenk said, grabbing his crotch, wringing his hardening cock with vigour.

"We'll leave a bit for ya," the other man said. "Frenk. You can fuck the babby while I roast the mother over the porch. Then we can swap over once I've blown me muck." Frenk never replied. The other man heard the thud as his body hit the planking, his head landing a hundred yards away in a dirty puddle.

Elias grabbed the other man by the throat, lifting him one-handed until he was face to face with him. "I'm afraid you and your friend are out of luck," he hissed, crushing the man's neck in his huge hand. One eye popped from its socket as the man's bowels voided, making Katherine's nose wrinkle in disgust. The giant vampire tossed the corpse into the street, the dead man skidding through mud and effluent until he came to a rest further down the hill. "Inside," Elias said almost gently. Katherine did as she was asked, grateful to be out of the rain and howling wind. The giant closed the door, blocking it with a large wooden dresser that was stacked with peculiar looking glass jars. His red eyes lingered on one for a few seconds, recognising the shape of a small human hand floating in liquid. Elias had been a vampire since time beyond memory. He had killed countless humans, vampires, demons and beasts, yet he shuddered when he saw what was floating in the pinkish liquid. He turned his eyes away, not wanting to know what grisly activity took place in this dark, putrid cabin. Katherine had made herself as comfortable as possible, settling on two bags of grain. "I would not wish that kind of treatment on anyone. I am a vampire. I feed on humans. I am not a monster. But you've seen what monsters lurk here. Haven't you?"

"Yes. I guess I should thank you for that," she said, looking up at the giant.

"Don't thank me human. I am not here to be your friend. I am here for my own interests. You and the baby. I need to find someone. I will leave now. You will stay here. I think it's safe to say that you do not want to meet any more local friends tonight?"

"No," she said as she cradled her daughter.

"Keep the door closed. Once I have found where we need to be, I will come back for you. It will not take long. Do not be foolish enough to run. You will both end up dead. And not pleasantly either. Do you really want to die, watching your daughter being sodomized by some monster?"

"I will stay here. You have my word," Katherine said, her blood running cold. Elias walked over to the far wall, opening a window shutter. He climbed out, slamming it firmly, leaving Katherine sat there, feeling alone. Feeling scared. Feeling helpless. Needing Jake.

* * *

"NOOOOOOOO," Jake screamed as water washed over them. His mouth filled with water, the force of the wave knocking him on his back, driving the air from his lungs. When he came to, his father had disappeared from sight, swept away by the sea. What was once his mother was gone too, lost to the night. "NO. DAD NO!" he sobbed as rough hands pulled him to his feet.

"We need to move Jake," Wilf said, tears in his eyes from the sea and what he'd just witnessed. "We'll die on this path. Come on." He dragged the younger man towards the town, just making it as another wave wiped the pathway clean one more. Jake collapsed on the rocks, sobbing uncontrollably.

Father Stephen lifted him easily into his arms, rocking him. "I'm so sorry Son. I cannot believe he's gone." Jake's body convulsed with a combination of pain, anger, and cold. The Vicar held him tight as Wilf looked out to sea, lost in his own thoughts.

He turned back to them, his face drawn. "We need to carry on Jake. Doug would not want us to give up now. He died a man, trying to save his kin. Honour him by saving them. There will be time for grieving later. I should fucking know. But tears can wait. They're no use to anyone now. They'll blow away on the wind, forgotten. We need to get them back to make all this worthwhile. Are you both with me?"

Jake looked up, his face streaked with tears and spittle. He nodded as his face broke once more, spilling tears over Stephen's already wet clothes. "Let's do it," he eventually said as he stood up gingerly. He rubbed at his leg. It was throbbing. His fingertips kneaded the scar tissue where another vampire had left his mark, in another land. Another world.

"I can still feel the pull of them," the Vicar said as he looked up at the town. "This whole place feels evil." He looked at Tamatan, who was stood head bowed, allowing Jake his moment.

"It is an evil den. The worst of places. The evil from the monsters that live here has polluted the buildings, polluting the very ground on which we stand. We need to be back in the forest as quick as we can. Not even I can fight off what lurks here. Lead us Father," he said as he looked at the Vicar. Stephen nodded, making his way towards the town, hugging the buildings as they neared. They followed, changing direction as he suddenly veered into different pathways, heading ever upwards. A minute later they were engulfed in mist, muting the sound of the sea around them. They leaned against the porch of a small cabin as they took stock of their surroundings. The temperature had dropped noticeably, drawing clouds of fog as they breathed.

"Where are they?" Jake asked impatiently.

"Further up the hill I think. Follow-" His voice was cut off as the sound of a baby crying filtered through the night.

"That's Alicia," Jake whispered, trying to locate the sound. They looked around as the sound came again, off to their left. Wilf hurried across the muddy street, sliding to a stop as the caught the rail of a porch that belonged to a similar cabin. Light spilled from under the doorway. It was then that he noticed a body slumped on the planks. He carefully walked over to it as the three others joined him on the porch, all of them silent. The body rolled over with a thud as Wilf flipped it with his boot. He looked back at the others.

The Turning

"The head is missing. Someone saw to this fella."

Another cry flew under the gap in the door, telling them what they needed to know. Stephen put his shoulder to the door, shoving it open wide enough to gain access. They followed him in hurriedly, coming face to face with Katherine, who was sat feeding her daughter.

"Jake!" she exclaimed, looking up at him, her face a mask of surprise.

He stumbled over, falling in front of them, grabbing at them. Tears burst from his eyes once more, his voice cracking with emotion. "Oh, thank God! Oh baby! I thought I'd lost you both!"

She returned his embrace one handed, her own tears flowing down her face. "You came for me. I knew you'd come for me Jake." She had no more words as she buried her face in the crook of his neck, sobbing uncontrollably.

"Hello Katherine," Wilf said as he knelt next to her. She looked up from Jake, seeing her uncle for the first time. His face was streaked with tears and rain. As she smiled at him he broke down, burying his face in his hands.

She released Jake, pulling him close. "I see you Uncle. Thank you for coming for me. You've no idea how I've missed you." She started crying again, the last few day's hardships boiling over into a release of tears and sobs. Alicia suckled greedily, unaware of the scene unfolding around her. She looked up at the Vicar. "Hello Father Stephen. Thank you for helping. It means so much that you are all here. Jake. Did Doug stay behind?"

Jake, who had moved to one side to allow Katherine to embrace her uncle, shook his head sadly. "Dad's gone. Mom attacked him and they were both washed out to sea. I'm, sorry babe."

Katherine crumbled into her uncle's arms, her raw emotions being flayed some more. Father Stephen and Jake let her cry as they stood looking at the blood-stained walls, adorned with skulls and weapons.

Tamatan came forward, lifting Katherine's face with his hands. "I am truly sorry for all your pain. However, we need to move. Do you know where Elias is?"

She nodded, her tears subsiding. "He said he needed to find someone's house. Someone that could help him."

Tamatan stood up, his green face pensive. His eyes worried. "We need to go. Now! He could be back any minute. We cannot risk a scene here. The locals would skin us all alive. Let's go. Before it's too late."

Father Stephen raised his meaty hands to the rest of them. "You go. I will wait here and stall him. Or kill him. Whatever happens, at least you will have a head start." Jake walked forward, about to protest. Stephen stilled his words with a hand on the shoulder. "Go Jake. You've lost enough tonight. Don't linger here, where more loss could befall you. Godspeed."

Jake embraced him fiercely, the air squeezed from his lungs as the Vicar reciprocated the hug. "If you kill him, head back through the doorway. There may still be hope for you."

"Okay. I promise I will," he lied. "Now go. Take care." Tamatan and Wilf both shook his hand, knowing what sacrifice he was about to make.

"Katherine pulled him down, kissing him on his bearded face. "Thank you Father. I look forward to seeing you again. Don't let me down." He patted her shoulder, bending down and kissing Alicia on her soft curls. They exited the cabin, leaving him to a moment of solitude. He sat down on the sacks, his mind floating back to his youth. To his life with Denise and the joy that they had shared. He closed his eyes and smiled.

* * *

A minute later they were heading back towards the cave, huddled close. Four sets of eyes on the lookout for danger. The wind had died down, the sea to their right appearing calmer. A few revellers were stumbling out of a tavern close to the shore line, near the path that led to the cave. One spotted them and shouted insults at them. "Where the fuck you going? Come back here," a large man said as he tried to cut them off.

"Take the girls back through the doorway Wilf," Jake said as he pulled his handgun from his pack.

Wilf nodded gravely, putting his arm around Katherine's shoulder. "Don't linger. Do what needs doing and be hot on our heels."

"Oi! I'm talking to you," the large man said as he went to grab Jake by the arm.

"What's the problem?" Jake said, his finger poised on the trigger.

The large man looked at Jake, then at Tamatan, his eyes widening in recognition. "MEN. OUT HERE! WE HAVE OUTLANDERS. COME QUICK." He moved towards them, a knife coming out of his tunic, glinting in the moonlight. Before he had time to cock his arm for the attack, Jake placed the muzzle of his gun to the man's chest, firing a double tap through his heart. He was propelled backwards, landing on the wet rocks. Jake looked at the other man who had hung back during the initial exchange. He was pulling something out of his coat, grinning at them wickedly. Without thinking, Jake fired two more shots into the man's midsection. Two things happened at once. Many men began charging out of the tavern, weapons in hands, ready for a fight. The second thing to happen was the shot man was engulfed in flames. He was thrown backwards towards the sea, blowing apart as the unseen weapon in his coat exploded. Jake and Tamatan were blown backwards by the concussion, rolling on the wet path that led towards the sea.

"KILL 'EM," an unseen voice hollered as more men poured out of the building. Jake scrambled to his feet, discharging his gun rapidly at the attackers. Four went down, landing in a heap in front of them. Tamatan's eyes glowed red, his hands ready for battle. Two men died on the spot as he struck them both at the same time. They hit the rocks, their necks snapped crudely, exposing bone and jets of blood.

"JAKE, HURRY," a voice said from the darkness. He looked up to see Wilf stood at the entrance to the cave, waving frantically.

A new ring leader saw Wilf, rallying a dozen men around him. "Look. More of them up there. They are trying to pass through the doorway. After them."

Jake fired at them, emptying his gun. He realised suddenly that his ammo was in his bag, making reloading impossible. "WILF, RUN," he yelled before turning to fend off an attacker. He went down, the man on top of him. Jake just managed to jam his forearm into the man's throat as he swooped, teeth bared. The attacker had one eye, set in the centre of a creased forehead. He looked to Jake like something out of a Sinbad movie. His strength was shocking as he pressed his weight down on top of him, his blackened teeth inches from Jake's throat. His free hand, still holding the gun came up, striking the man just above his single eye. The pressure on Jake's forearm lessened as the attacker howled in pain. He struck him again, shattering his nose. Thick black blood splattered over Jake's face as the man issued a string of curses. He was ready to strike again when the man's head shattered, showering the rocks and Jake in bone and brains. He shoved the man aside as Tamatan pulled him to his feet.

"They are heading for your kin. We must go after them. I will hold them off. You go Jake, get them before they make it through," Tamatan said urgently. Jake didn't need telling twice. He quickly pulled two clips out of his pack, jamming on into the gun as he took off up the path. The men ahead were almost at the entrance to the cave, yelling and hollering, buoyed by the hunt. He raised his gun, firing as the last man entered the cave, clipping his leg. He staggered before being lost from sight.

"Fuck!" Jake said as he sprinted into the entrance, gun raised. Light was pouring from the back of the cave, one man holding up a glass globe in his hand. It gave off a green phosphorescent glow that eradicated much of the darkness.

The new ring leader stood next to the doorway, a knife in his hand, which was held against Wilf's throat. He saw Jake coming towards him, drawing the blade an inch across the skin. "Halt! Come any closer and I'll stick this old cunt. He's your friend? You want him to die?" More globes were held aloft by the group of men, increasing the glare until Jake almost had to shield his eyes.

The Turning

"Katherine and Alicia made it through," Wilf said, his voiced pained.
"Kill them Jake. Don't fret about me."
"Silence you old scrote," the man said, knocking Wilf to his knees. Jake looked at him, seeing the steel in his eyes. It was the look of a man who was ready to go down fighting. He nodded at Wilf, who nodded back.
"Keep them safe Wilf. Run!" Jake said as he shot the man holding the older man between the eyes. Wilf moved with the speed of a man half his age. Jake watched as he scrambled into the blackness.
"BATIE," one of the locals screamed as they turned to face the young outlander, burning globes held aloft. Jake did the only thing he could do. He emptied his magazine into the men, shattering three globes, which set off a chain reaction. They all exploded in unison, shredding the men to mincemeat. Jake was blown half out of the cave, barely managing to cling to the path with one hand. A green cloud lit up the night, sending a plume into the air. The ground shook as Jake looked down, seeing the black sea forty feet below him. He clung there, his ears filled with the aftershocks of the explosion. A bony hand grabbed his collar, pulling him up over the ledge.
"Are you hurt?" Tamatan said as he lifted him to his feet.
"I don't think so." He reached down, feeling a gash on his shin. "A few bumps and bruises, but I'll be alright." He looked at the cave, his stomach turning to lead. "Oh no!" he said as he walked over to what was once the entrance. The cave ceiling had collapsed, cutting off their way back to Mantz. Their way back to Katherine, Wilf, and Alicia. Their way back home.

* * *

The forest erupted behind Wilf as he reached the top of the ravine. "Uncle!" Katherine shouted. "Over here." The old man was half blown across the forest towards Katherine, who was knelt behind a fallen tree. Wilf fell over the log as the shockwave rocked the forest around them. Green clouds billowed across them, a thick sulphurous smell smothering them. They lay there as the shock waves subsided, leaving the forest quiet. "What happened?" Katherine said as she checked her daughter.

"Jake told me to run. He killed the one holding me with his weapon." They stood up, walking over to the ravine. "Fuckenell!" Wilf exclaimed. "The doorway. It's buried under the forest."

"No. That cannot be Uncle. How will they get back to us?"

Wilf stood there, pondering the implications. "I don't rightly know Kath. Let's hope there is another doorway. Whatever happens, we need to go. We have a long journey ahead of us."

"Where are we going?" Katherine asked, her mind blank.

"Shetland. We need to get back to Shetland. It's safe there. If Jake can find a way back, he will find us there. Come. We need to go."

Katherine looked at the collapsed ravine, tears falling down her cheeks. "Oh Jake. Oh my love. Please find another door and get to where you belong. With us." She turned and followed her uncle towards the shaft of light that lit the forest, her head bowed.

Forty-Two

"What the hell do we do now?" Jake said as he stared at the collapsed cave. The wind was picking up, blowing spray across the path.

"That way is closed to us now Jake," Tamatan said, looking broken. He placed his hands on his thighs and stared at the floor. "I've been here before. But only through this doorway. I do not know if another doorway exists, back to where we've come from. We're on another plane here Jake. This land is not even the same as where Reggan was from. I'm at a loss."

"Well, we cannot stay here." Jake said looking towards the town. He cast his glance over the black roiling sea. "Oh Dad." He began to cry.

"We need to make haste Jake. The explosion will have roused the locals. They will be on us any minute. If they find us here, we're dead. They will skin us alive. Not even I can fight them all. You've seen the trinkets and weapons they possess. We need to leave this place now."

"Where?" Jake asked as he looked towards the town. He could see activity in the higher parts. Voices drifted on the wind to their location.

"I told you about the spits of land that lead from the island. We need to take one." He looked away from the town, turning and running up a small rise on top of the destroyed cave. Jake followed, noticing that they were on a small peninsular that jutted out to sea, away from the main portion of the island. A rocky finger of land ran away into the night, becoming lost out at sea. "We'll take that one. If we're quick, they will not have seen our escape. Come." They made their way down the other side of the peninsular, jogging at a steady pace as shouts and voices carried after them. After a few minutes they stopped, turning back to look at the island. It was almost shrouded by night, barely visible.

"Let's hope they don't follow us," Jake said, suddenly feeling weary.

"I think we are safe from them. It's the unknown out there that I'm not so sure about. I've never chartered this road. There will be danger ahead I'm sure. Let's just hold onto the hope of seeing loved ones again. Yours and mine." They carried on in silence, walking along a path twenty feet across. Jake's leg was hurting more. He couldn't see, but under the material, black veins slowly spread across his thigh. He ignored it, keeping his eyes on the road ahead. It rose and fell, the sea on each side like blackened glass. As they made their way into the night, whale calls greeted them, reverberating through the rocks under their feet. They carried on, walking blindly. Into the unknown.

* * *

Elias heard the explosion as he was stood talking to the witch who sat before him. "What was that?" he said, clearly alarmed.

"The God's are not happy. They are venting their fury," the old hag said. She sat in a large vat, filled with snakes. They wrapped themselves around her arms, slithering over her skin. Smaller ones writhed in her hair. The whole cabin's floor was a reptilian carpet, dimly lit by crude torches on the walls. Her milky white eyes were fixed on the vampire.

"Lenga. What do you mean?" Elias said as he flicked a snake off his boot.

"The green gods have erupted from the cave. The doorway is lost."

"Oh no!" Elias whispered. "I will return. I need to bring the woman and baby." He fled the building, hurrying down the alleyways and side streets until he found the cabin that had belonged to the two monstrous men. He crossed the porch, shoving the door open. He looked around the room. It was empty. "No!" He moved into the room, quickly checking it before he'd head down to the water's edge.

"You're too late," a voice said in the dim room. Elias span around, coming face to face with Father Stephen. "You lose Elias. Jake has them. They are out of your reach."

Elias glowered in the darkness, his eyes twin pools of red fury. "We'll see about that shaman. I will find them and finish them all. No more games. No more plans. Death to them all. But you first."

"I was hoping you'd say that," the vicar said as he brought his hands from around his back. In one he held a cross that was glowing a faint white hue. In the other he held on of Jake's wooden stakes. Fear crossed Elias's face. An uncertainty that he rarely felt. The Vicar almost matched him in height and was much heavier. It was not just his size though, the vampire could feel the evil seeping out of him, through his black clothing. Stephen advanced slowly, his cross aimed at the giant's chest.

Elias feinted left, letting Stephen commit himself to the attack. The Vicar did so, momentarily out-foxed by the vampire. Before he could counter, Elias took him down to the floor, smashing his fist into Stephen's chest.

"AAAAAAAGH," the Vicar hollered as the fist crashed through flesh and bone, obliterating the dying black heart in his chest.

"You die, shaman," Elias said, smiling down at him.

"Join me," Stephen said as he buried the stake into the vampire's sternum with the last of his strength. Elias's eyes opened wide in shock as the crude tip buried itself deep in his cold white flesh. Stephen shoved him off, rolling on top of him, letting his bulk settle on top of him. The stake sank further, piercing the vampire's heart, ending his millennia's spent in different worlds. Stephen died on top of him, smiling as he welcomed the end. His last thought was of his beautiful Denise, whom he hoped was waiting for him on the other side.

Epilogue

The black saloon pulled up outside the house. January was heading into February, as a western wind blew across the Cornish coast. Rick climbed out of the car, the wind ruffling his sandy hair. Marlies climbed out the other side, closing the door as she too was buffeted by the cold wind. She pulled her long brown coat tight, tying the sash around the waist as she walked up the driveway holding her boyfriend's hand. They rang the bell, standing there for a minute as a light rain started to fall. Frustrated, Rick walked around the side of the house, walking up the driveway towards the car port and garage. He looked through the window, seeing an empty kitchen. No signs of life could be seen. He placed his hands to the window, peering in. It looked orderly. Nothing seemed out of place in his brother's house. He walked back towards the front door, where Marlies had rang the bell for a second time. She pointed to the pile of unopened mail in the porch.

"Where the hell are they?" he said, starting to feel panic setting in. Before pulling up at Jake's, Rick and Marlies had visited his father's house. A growing unease settling over them as they noticed the slashed tyres on Doug's Micra. They had let themselves in with Rick's key, checking the house over. Everything seemed as it should, except something in the garage that caused them concern. They had found a piece of wood, wickedly sharpened at one end. It reminded them of something seen in 1960's horror movies. They had left it on the counter top, before locking up the house, heading to Jake's.

"Maybe we should call in at the police station and let them know they're still not home." She wrapped her gloved hand around his, pulling him close.

"Hello," a voice said behind them. They turned, seeing a young woman stood on the pavement, chewing her thumb. She was dressed in baggy jeans, trainers, and a hooded top. Her unruly black hair was being blown about by the increasing winds. Her glasses were spattered with rain drops. "Are you looking for Jake?"

"Yes we are. I'm his brother Rick. This is my girlfriend, Marlies. Are you a friend of Jake's?"

Kerry stood, kicking the fence post with alternating feet. She looked uncomfortable as they approached, her brain frantically working out what to say. "Yes, I am a friend of Jake and Katherine's, although I've not seen them for a few weeks. Are they not home?"

"No," Rick said offering his hand. Kerry took it nervously, briefly shaking it before doing the same with Marlies. She warmed to the woman more, liking her freckled nose, which almost matched her own. "I've been calling them for almost two weeks now. I live in Hamburg. Germany. I was getting concerned so I thought I'd visit. It looks like they're missing. Did they say anything to you the last time you saw them? Anything unusual or did they seem concerned about something?"

"Shit," Kerry said, twirling her hair impulsively. "I probably shouldn't tell you what I'm about to tell you. You'll think I'm crazy."

"Please. Tell us," Marlies implored, taking Kerry's hand in hers.

"I need to pop home first. There is a tea shop, just off the high street, opposite the public car park. I will meet you there in twenty minutes."

"Okay. Thank you," Rick said. "We really appreciate this."

"Just one thing." She said, getting their attention. "Have an open mind as to what I am about to tell you."

Shetland

The sun bathed the craggy peninsular in warm spring light. Katherine sat on the stoop on Wilf's farmhouse, feeding Alicia. She looked across the grass covered ground, seeing the villagers going about their daily routine. Animals were being led around on leashes by children as men chopped fire wood. It was a carefree scene that would ordinarily have warmed her heart. Not anymore though. Her heart was heavy, leaden down with the loss of Jake. Wilf walked out of the front doorway, handing her a steaming mug of tea.

"Get that down you Kath," Wilf said, gently folding his ageing frame into the wooden chair next to hers.

"Thank you Uncle. Just what I need," she said as she took a sip of the sweet brew. She looked across at him, a tight smile on her lips. "What are your plans for today?"

"We have two lambs that are ready to birth. I will head over to Pat's stable to check once I've drank this. What about you? What are your plans?"

Katherine took another swig of her tea, placing it on the table next to her. She lifted Alicia from her breast, gently winding her. The baby, burped loudly, drawing a smile from her great uncle. Katherine stood, placing her in a wooden pen that Wilf had made especially for his great niece. The sides were cladded, giving protection from the wind. Alicia lay there as her mother covered her over with furs. By the time Katherine had sat back down, taking another swig of tea, the baby was

The Turning

drifting off to sleep. "I'm going to continue to plot my search Uncle. He's been gone almost a moon's cycle. I have to believe that he is somewhere out there, trying to get back home."

"I agree Kath. But the where's and the how's are lost on me. We've no idea where that hell hole was in relation to where we are now. Jake could be anywhere. There must be doorways scattered around this land, leading to who knows where. Maybe one day he will find his way here. But for now, you have to concentrate on your child. Don't go running off on some fancy escapade, never to be seen again. I'm too old for looking after her on my own. And I'm definitely too old to be running through strange lands, fighting monsters and murderers. Our place is here. Let Jake find you. I've never met a man as resourceful as him. He's got the cunning of a fox and the heart of a black badger. He'll never give up love. If he's out there, he will be trying to find us. Hold that tight to your heart. But hold your kin tighter. Because they need you. Jake doesn't. I only hope that he and Tamatan are still together. That gives them a much better lick at getting home."

"I know you are right Uncle. Really, I do. I will try a few things though. Zeebu and Zeeba have told me about doorways along the northern coasts. When the time is right I will leave Alicia here and take a trip up there. I only hope my old uncle will come with me." She leaned across and squeezed his knee.

"Well. If you put it like that. I suppose this old wreck can take one more monster hunt."

Katherine hugged him, her emotions spilling over into sobs. Her skin used to the salty cascades of tears since she'd lost Jake. "Thank you Uncle. Father would be so proud of how you look after me."

Now Wilf started crying, squeezing his niece with all his strength. "Stop it girl. This old man cannot take all these tears."

She broke away, looking at his red-rimmed eyes and smiled. She kissed both cheeks and his forehead, placing her head on his. "He's coming home. He's out there. Searching for me. It's only right and proper that I search for him too, wherever he may be."

They sat together, holding hands. Staring out across Shetland, towards the sea beyond. Hoping.

THE END?

Not yet.......

Dear reader,

We hope you enjoyed reading *Unknown*. Please take a moment to leave a review, even if it's a short one. Your opinion is important to us.

Discover more books by Phil Price at https://www.nextchapter.pub/authors/phil-price-horror-author-united-kingdom

Want to know when one of our books is free or discounted for Kindle? Join the newsletter at http://eepurl.com/bqqB3H

Best regards,

Phil Price and the Next Chapter Team

Story continues in:

The Witch and The Watcher by Phil Price

To read the first chapter for free, head to:
https://www.nextchapter.pub/books/the-witch-and-the-watcher

Books by the Author

Unknown (The Forsaken Series Book 1)
The Turning (The Forsaken Series Book 2)
The Witch And The Watcher (The Forsaken Series Book 3)

Printed in Great Britain
by Amazon